THE VOYAGES OF JOHN PAUL JONES COME ALIVE!

"If you enjoyed C.S. FORESTER'S Horatio Hornblower series you'll love HENRY LUNT."   *-H₂O Magazine*

"In addition to a great adventure story, I really liked Tom's writing style, it was reminiscent of Rudyard Kipling's 'Captains Courageous'."
          -Mike Brady, Copley Cable TV - Los Angeles

"Tom McNamara is the Tom Clancy of a bygone era."
          -Jack Baldwin, WMVU Radio (NH)

"Tom McNamara is a man of many par~·· ~·· ~ ·⁴·⌐
foremost business consultants in the worl
a U.S. Presidential Commendation for H
darn good sailor in his own right. His E
novels are extraordinary good entertainm
          -Sir ,
          "Dean of Australian

June '95

Tom,

Enjoy the
adventure

Tom McHam

HENRY LUNT & The SPYMASTER

Tom McNamara

NUVENTURES
PUBLISHING
La Jolla, California 92038-2489

HENRY LUNT & THE SPYMASTER

Library of Congress Catalog Card Number 90-061642
ISBN 0-9625632-5-0 $10.95

NUVENTURES® and its logo are registered trademarks
of NUVENTURES® Consultants, Inc.

NUVENTURES® Publishing is a division
of NUVENTURES® Consultants, Inc.
SAN 200-3805

In Memory,

Larry D. Brown

GREAT ADVENTURES
BY TOM McNAMARA

"Henry Lunt & The Ranger"

"Henry Lunt & The Spymaster"

"Henry Lunt At Flamborough Head"

"Skull & Cross Bones"

Tom McNamara

has also co-authored the critically acclaimed non-fiction:

"AMERICA'S CHANGING WORKFORCE -
About You, Your Job & Your Changing Work Environment."

Prologue

The roll of drums ceased abruptly as the bailiff began to read aloud from his scroll.

"By order of his Britannic Majesty, George the Third, lawful King of England, Scotland, Ireland, Canada, India, the various uncharted lands of the Pacific and Southern Seas and..." the speaker's voice sharpened to emphasize the next few words, "...the American Colonies. You, George Aitken, alias John the Painter, have been sentenced this day and this hour to forfeit your life for acts of high treason."

The drums rolled again and the bailiff looked briefly up into the prisoner's face to view the reaction of terror he had so often before observed in the doomed. But Aitken, now resolute after his prolonged ordeal of many months, only stiffened his back an instant. His hands and arms were bound tightly behind him, and the hangman's noose already fitted around his neck. To the extent his constraints permitted, Aitken bent his head forward to study the gaping square of ugly blackness crafted into the gallows floor, just inches before his toes.

As he stared downward, Aitken's mind raced so that his entire life seemed now to swirl somewhere in that dark void. He saw himself as an infant sitting amid the purple Scottish heather with his mother softly caressing his hair. Behind them, the Cairngorm range still crested with snow at its highest points. His mother was whispering fondly to him ....

'You have been found guilty of the murder of three of the King's officers, and of the foul attempt to burn the Royal dockyards at Portsmouth, of the actual burning of the Royal naval storehouses at Bristol, Depford, and ...'

The soft maternal scene before Aitken's eyes suddenly transformed to white hot flame. The fire seemed to emanate upwards rapidly from the depths of the gaping blackness. He now envisioned the entire fleet at Portsmouth amid a massive conflagration. He saw himself circling the dockyards, torch in hand, setting everything he could ablaze. Then, just as suddenly, there was blackness again.

Despite his constraints, Aitken began to take tiny, imperceptible steps which moved him most of a quarter circle to his left to bring him face to face with the bailiff who now shouted the King's written word directly into his face instead of his left ear.

'For aforesaid acts of treason, murder, and arson you shall be hung this hour by the neck until dead, and your lifeless body taken forthwith to the bone house at Portsmouth for later use in scientific experiments by the Royal College of Surgeons for the

2

betterment of human ..."

Aitken's heart pounded furiously, his fists jerked violently, straining against their hemp bonds. His blood seemed to burn. He sought to twist free, and failing that, he then abruptly lashed out his right boot aiming for his tormentor's groin, as best he could, despite the tight constraints of the hangman's noose.

Aitken saw the bailiff groan, stumble backwards, and lose his footing altogether and then topple off the side of the platform. The crowd screamed in shocked reaction. But the moment was ever so brief. Swiftly, a steel butt of musket smashed into Aitken's ribs pitching him sideways into the deep square of darkness. Aitken gasped for breath as his whole body tumbled in free fall for what seemed a great long time until there was no more distance to fall and his head jerked violently to one side as he arrived into the blackest bowel of the pit with a thud. In reaction to the abrupt, unaccustomed burden, the bones of his neck and spine elongated unbearably and then snapped. A thunderbolt of sudden light and intense pain suffused his entire body. Crimson red flowed over the pervasive blackness of the pit. He could not breathe as he swung twisting helplessly in total darkness with no capacity to gasp the precious air of life. The red continued to fill in over the blackness and then slowly passed into a bright light as he now swung more gently in a field of heather. The boy had grown into a man and now stood up beside his mother amidst the purple flowers. Both of them stood together gazing at the Scottish highlands and the white fleecy clouds that moved so swiftly above them.

*　　*　　*　　*　　*

After witnessing the death certificate, two well dressed gentlemen walked slowly back towards their mahogany carriage, whispering. Their tricorner hats tipped sideways to come together. Their tiny puffs of breath, visible in the frosty Portsmouth morning air, hinted of their muted conversation.

"He never revealed his contacts to the end? Where or how he gained access?"

"Never, to the last!" William Eden, Under Secretary of the Foreign Office shook his head in frustration. "He only taunted us by screaming that he was number three hundred and six and then sang stupid, cryptic songs about fire and burning. We were obligated to listen to them all in the hope that his madness would deliver us a clue. But nothing discernible ever came of it."

"Good Lord, you mean the Americans have over three hundred operatives? Where does Franklin find the time?"

"I sincerely doubt that it is Franklin directing the anarchists. It's not the style of that old Quaker fart to send people out to burn and pillage. It's turn the other cheek with his kind, you know." Eden cleared his throat and continued, "Franklin's hoping desperately that somehow by fraternizing with the Parisian philosophers and what remains of the French Encyclopedists, you know Voltaire and that crowd, that he will somehow turn all the courts of Europe to the American side." As they entered the carriage, the two men chuckled together over that diplomatic improbability.

Inside, Eden continued more soberly, "No, I believe that Franklin genuinely dislikes espionage and all its trappings. Wishing to remain aloof and instead maintain his facade as the champion of a highly moral cause, I believe that what he has done has been to substitute someone else,....someone very clever, into the game, ...a Spymaster for want of a better term!"

"Like you?" the other man blurted out, hoping to please Eden, but then realized that he had instead committed a kind of veiled insult by virtue of an improper comparison between the efforts of the Crown and that of the colonial rabble. He could sense Eden bristle under his normally smooth veneer.

"Sorry," the other man apologized quickly.

Eden's scowl softened as he nodded his polite acceptance of the mistake and then settled into meditation amidst the pounding of horses' hooves and the clattering of carriage wheels along the hard dirt road leading back to London.

After a quarter hour, Eden began to think aloud. "I can think of a dozen or so incidents in just the past half year. They are now too numerous to be pure chance. This American Spymaster is obviously a dangerous and resourceful fellow. I doubt if he has over three hundred zealous anarchists in his service. I suspect that he may have even instructed Aitken the Painter to reveal a high code number to make us believe there are many more of them than there are, and thus make us suspicious of everyone amongst us, even our friends. The man, Aitken, was clearly mentally deranged. He was not the planner of all of this, only the instrument... and a half witted one at best.'

The mid morning sun warmed the carriage and Eden removed his great coat, placing it on the chair opposite and settled into his seat as the coach continued clattering along. 'With this foul attempt on our dockyards and the murders, Franklin has clearly appointed a fellow who will do anything to undermine our purpose.'

'Don't we have spies in place who can find him out and eliminate him?' questioned the other.

'Oh that we do, that we do,' smiled William Eden to himself.

1
Triumph

Driven by a brisk evening westerly and a following sea, the Continental Corvette Ranger and her two prizes roared past the most westerly tip of Ile d'Quessant and into view of a swift French schooner on station along the chain of small islands which guarded the roads into the harbour at Brest. High above Ranger's foremast the special reconnaissance signal of three white and two red lantern lights announced to the French fleet that an ally was approaching. Within a quarter hour another schooner and then a frigate, La Belle Poule, beat towards the unfamiliar flotilla who they initially perceived as fortunate American merchants who had broken through the building English blockade.

A brilliant flash of red and white light roared outward from La Belle Poule's hull as she fired a single warning shot from one of her twenty-fours. The moonlight caught the plume of white foam erupting a quarter mile ahead of Ranger as a warning for the strange flotilla to reduce sail and stand inspection prior to being permitted to come within possible cannon shot of the French fleet at anchorage far within the harbour at Brest. Obediently, Ranger's Captain sent men aloft in the moonlit darkness to furl all royals and topgallants, leaving only the topsails and lower course sails in full bloom.

The wrecked hull of the vessel in tow behind Ranger also rapidly slowed to a crawl. Her two jury rigged sails were attached to what remained of the main and mizzen. Half a league behind the two vessels was the stout hull of an obvious merchant, also obeying the command to reduce sail. Out across the Atlantic, no where in sight on this clear evening, were the sails of the English Men of War on station to inspect traffic coming to and from French ports. Since late April the hugh mountains of sail associated with first raters of the English channel fleet could so often be seen patrolling as near as five leagues west and southwest from the outer islands of Brest harbour. Fortuitously for the returning American flotilla, they were on a nonconvergent course that evening.

One of the French schooners tacked again so that her course would bring her across Ranger's bow. Her duty officer hailed Ranger in French. Perplexed, every man on board looked to the quarterdeck where Captain Jones stood as the sole officer on deck, bareheaded, but dressed in his bright blue and red trimmed coat, his curly hair blowing freely in the breeze. In perfect French, he responded proudly through his speaking trumpet.

"This is the Continental Ship of War, Ranger. Under tow is H.M.S. Drake, our prisoner. To our stern is an English merchant vessel, also our prize."

"An armed English ship, a man of war?" came the questioning French voice over his speaking trumpet as the two vessels passed out of hailing range. The French schooner continued another two cables on her course, her officers and men leaning out over their gunnels staring incredulously at the blackened hull of H.M.S. Drake and of the stumps that represented what remained of her masts and rigging. Commands were given and the vessel tacked and then fell off to run with Ranger. Across the outer harbour, La Belle Poule and the second French schooner had also adopted a course to merge with Ranger further along the roads.

As La Belle Poule adopted a parallel course and drew within hailing distance, she began to shout similar inquiries again of their name and of the prizes, confirming again that the hull in tow was what remained of an English fighting ship. Satisfied, her Captain ordered "follow me" in French and set greater sail to ensure she was the lead vessel to announce the news to the French fleet. The two schooners returned to their duty stations.

By morning light, Ranger had entered past the guns of the Brest battery and was shown a location in which to anchor beneath the guns of an enormous vessel nearly three hundred feet in length whose markings bore the inscription, Bretagne. As the hours of Friday morning progressed, a carnival atmosphere developed as news of the American victory spread through the French fleet. Naval officers arrived in longboats from nearly thirty other vessels and boarded Ranger and her prize to see, with their own astonished and envious eyes, that a small American corvette of eighteen guns had fought and captured an English sloop of war of twenty-two guns.

As the party of congratulating French captains and senior lieutenants continued to swell aboard Ranger's quarterdeck, a joyous officer's party erupted. Many of the visiting French officers had the foresight to come equipped with bottles of wine. Despite his pleasure at the French enthusiasm, Captain Jones was deeply concerned about the condition of his crew and the prisoners who were quartered below deck on both the Ranger and the Drake. Each time that a new longboat arrived, he saluted his new visitors and then immediately requested of them food enough to spare for his hungry crew. But always, he was diverted to retell bits and pieces about his engagement with the Drake for the latest arrivals of French officers.

Suddenly a senior Captain tapped his shoulder and whispered into his ear in broken English, 'Pardon, Captain Jones, Admiral Comte d'Orvilliers is coming aboard.'

Jones eyes flashed toward the larboard rail and he began to call out commands.

'Full Marine compliment, Lt. Wallings...' mid sentence he corrected himself and felt renewed remorse for the officer who had lost his life in the midst of the engagement with the Drake. 'Sergeant Miers, bring to quarters every able bodied seaman except those on immediate guard duty with the prisoners."

Jones and the French officers now stood attentive to the larboard rail where a set of hands were just appearing on the guide ropes which led up from the Jacob's ladder. An enormously plumed, white tricorner hat began to appear and then the smiling patrician face of Admiral d'Orvilliers. A junior officer squatted to give him a hand as every man on deck was called to attention by the Fleet adjutant. The Admiral shrugged off the assistance and proceeded to climb up onto the deck in an awkward movement in which he had to throw one uniformed knee and then another up onto the deck, and then rise unsteadily to his feet.

As d'Orvilliers tugged his uniform into place, he sniffed the air. He said aloud in French for all of his officers to hear, "I smell gunpowder, not the white smoke of training, endless training which the sailor must endure in times of peace. I smell action in the winds of change that this proud American ship, the Ranger, has brought us. I sense that this is but a harbinger of great battles at sea to bring France to final glory against our ancient enemy,..." he pointed westward towards the open sea, "...who now patrols our coast, without right, as if she owns it."

The diminutive frame of Captain Jones stood proud and erect as he listened to the Admiral's eloquent pronouncement from the gundeck. Then after a brief pause, Jones took his tricorner by the right wing and doffed it in a polite bow to d'Orvilliers.

In the distance, a marine drummer beat a brief tatoo.

The Admiral returned the salute by touching the right wing of his cap briefly and then strode up the two steps to the Ranger's quarterdeck smiling at Jones as he extended his hand, his face radiant. They shook hands, the tall patrician Admiral, who represented the tenth generation of his family to go to sea in the service of his King and the Scot who had fought and charmed his way upwards into Colonial command despite his humble beginnings as a cabin boy.

Unaware of their host's humble background, the French Officer corps all assumed that the American Captain, because of his outward confidence and gentlemanly manner amongst them, had somehow acquired a similar breeding in that distant land called America, where there must certainly exist a similar highborn class empowered by destiny with rank and privilege for the course of their natural lives.

Ordinary seaman, Jonathan Harken, standing immediately behind Jones, began to offer the Admiral a glass of wine, but his gesture was intercepted by a French Lieutenant who nodded a polite acceptance and personally handed the wine glass to his Admiral.

'Ah, Merci,' replied d'Orvilliers. Sipping the wine briefly, he turned about staring upwards approvingly at the rigging of the Ranger. 'The wine is a French Bordeaux. A very fine one. May I ask how you acquired it?'

'T'was cargo on one of our prizes,' said Jones.

'How many prizes have you taken in this brief

voyage of a month?' asked the Admiral.

'We have taken some eight merchants and of course, H.M.S. Drake,' responded Jones.

'Where are your other officers?' inquired the Admiral.

'One is in temporary command of the Drake, another is in command of the merchant prize. One other Lieutenant is missing, my second in command is in detention below, and my Lieutenant of marines was killed in the action with H.M.S. Drake.'

'One of your officers in detention?' the Admiral raised his eye brow for an explanation.

'Sir, before we discuss the specifics of this cruise, which will take some time, I have nearly three hundred men aboard these three vessels. They are hungry. All of the men, prisoners and crew alike, have had only half rations for the past three days.'

'How did this happen, certainly on such a short cruise you had adequate provisions?'

'We captured so many ships and had so many prisoners, sir, that we ran out of provisions.' The officers gathered about the American Captain chuckled in unison as they listened to Jones describe in French how he was compelled to man the Ranger with fewer and fewer men as the voyage progressed because as he had been obliged to send some of his own men back with each prize being returned to a French port. Finally, after the capture of the Drake, it became evident that the cruise of the Ranger must end because they were undermanned, and burdened with a huge number of captured prisoners, all underfed.

The Admiral interrupted Jones, "You have a remarkable story to tell us all. And I invite you and what remains of your officers and ... a key mate or two," he looked around at the faces of his own officers to command their approval, "to join us for dinner aboard my flag ship this evening. But first, let us suspend the story telling for the time being. What provisions do you need from your friends this afternoon, Captain Jones?"

Jones looked forward towards the marines and other sailors assembled at attention on the gun deck, and made sure that they heard his reply, which he shouted crisply in English so that every American ear on the one hundred and ten foot deck could not fail to hear him. "What do we want, the Admiral asks me. I say for my men: fresh red meat, potatoes and butter, fruit, sweet water, some good French baguettes, and perhaps a very excessive ration of rum for my men to celebrate." There was a roar of approval from the crew who had stood inspection now for several hours for the parade of French naval officers.

Jones lowered his voice, and turned to the Admiral, "Also, Sir, the loan of perhaps two of your surgeons and medical supplies for the many English prisoners who are wounded. I fear several may not live the night if adequate care and fresh dressings are not made available. I also need urgently to send a dispatch about our arrival to Dr. Franklin at Passy."

D'Orvilliers drew closer, "You say you have British

14

sailors and soldiers prisoner aboard this ship in a French harbour?" His eyebrow was raised in disapproval.

"Yes, Sir, a hundred and twenty three British seamen and another sixty five merchantmen. I have not released these prisoners because I did not know whether France would be formally at war with England by the time I returned. I felt that we could use them to arrange for a possible prisoner exchange. There are several hundred American seamen in English gaols. During this cruise we did rescue a handful of American sailors, but the English have never consented to an exchange..."

Admiral d'Orvilliers turned away from Jones and proceeded to pace the quarterdeck, hands behind his back, occasionally stopping to speak with some of his senior French Captains. Jones stood more or less at attention while the Admiral conferred with his advisors for several minutes in diplomatic tones. In the midst of the unpleasant silence, as the Ranger's Captain and crew were unsure what was going to happen, there came the sound of a muted struggle from behind the doors leading to the Ranger's great cabin. Then came the hiss of a gunpowder flash and a pistol discharge. Immediately, several of the French officers drew their swords and crowded round their Admiral. Jones pulled a pistol from his belt and started for the door.   The door burst open and a remarkably beautiful woman stepped onto the quarterdeck, pushing a young sailor before her. In the woman's hands were two pistols, one still smoking. She wore what had once been a white evening gown with low decolletage. As she flung back her long chestnut hair she had the attention of every man on deck and she knew it.

In French, the lady began to speak, 'I am a subject of Louis XVI and I demand to be taken immediately to Versailles, to the offices of the Minister Vergennes. I will not be detained by Captain Jones any longer.'

'Madame Chatelain,' said the Admiral, stepping out from among his ring of French Captains, 'What are you doing on this American vessel?'

Jones stared at her defiantly and then spoke first, 'The lady was found in Belfast, in the midst of our enemies. I requested that she stay in the cabin until I could advise Ambassador Franklin of the situation. It is one of some complexity.'

'Captain Jones, I request that you release Madame Chatelain to my recognizance.' The Admiral strode over to the lady and took hold of each pistol barrel and extracted the small arms from her grip. 'No one is hurt?' he gestured inside.

Marie shook her head and smiled, 'I only needed to create some commotion so that you would know I was aboard.'

The Admiral took her hand and bowing his head, kissed it gently. 'You can spend the evening as a guest aboard my flag ship, and tell me of your situation. We will see that the finest dressmaker in Brest is

16

aboard within the hour.'

She smiled, looking across the water at the enormous vessel which bore the name, Bretagne, on its stern. She had returned safely home.

For a few more moments, Admiral d'Orvilliers whispered to his staff and then strode across the quarterdeck to stand before the Ranger's Captain.

'Captain Jones, I think you will understand that there is much inexplicable in this cruise of yours. You hold a lady of the French court in detention and, by your own admission, one of your own officers. However, of most immediate concern to me is that you have many British prisoners on board and France is not yet at war with England. The matter of the proper disposal of British military prisoners in a French port is a diplomatic decision, not a military one. The minister, Vergennes, must be advised. I think you understand that I have the greatest admiration for your capture of H.M.S. Drake and the eight merchant vessels,' he gestured over his shoulder at the burnt hull of a ship lying alongside, 'but I must request that every man on this vessel remain aboard until I can ascertain what Versailles wishes me to do. I'm sure you can appreciate that improper actions on my part could plunge France on a course that might be inappropriate.'

Jones countered, 'Sir, it could be weeks or months before these matters are decided, I have men to feed...'

'And this is a French harbour, Captain Jones.

I will see to the feeding of your crew and captives within the hour. But you are not permitted to let anyone leave either the Ranger or its prizes. Am I understood?"

"Yes, Admiral, but I must inform Ambassador Franklin of our return."

"I will see to it that anything you wish is delivered to Ambassador Franklin, unopened," he stressed, "by diplomatic courier. It is a journey of only 12 hours to Versailles by rider. Passy is nearby."

"Then I am a prisoner," said Jones, his face red.

"No, Captain Jones, you, your crew, and prizes are in what I hope is a temporary state of quarantine," d'Orvilliers winked at him. "At your earliest convenience, however, I would request you send me a written report about your cruise. Particularly explaining the items we have just discussed. It could help immensely for me to have such a document to get this matter resolved in the most expeditious manner possible."

From the taffrail Jones glared downward as Marie Chatelain descended from the Jacob's ladder into the longboat which would take her to the Bretagne for the evening. The Admiral joined her and placed his cloak over her white naked shoulders. Everyone was most attentive to her comfort. In a matter of minutes, the beautiful lady spy of King Louis had done what the entire British fleet had been unable to accomplish in an entire month's time...with a well timed pistol shot, she had taken away his triumph and had placed

John Paul Jones in irons.

* * * * *

Lunt dismounted from the saddle of the third successive horse he had stolen from outside a tavern in the past four days. The mare was lame, but she had reached the outskirts of Wexford in the extreme southeastern tip of Ireland. Lunt carried news of betrayal within the American Ambassador's offices. Lunt was unsure how much of the information he carried was accurate, or how much was simply the ravings of a severely wounded man. Notwithstanding, he must get the information to Ambassador Franklin before it was too late.

All of Ireland now buzzed with news of the daring raid, over a week before, by an American Colonial warship on Belfast harbour and of the capture of the sloop of War, H.M.S. Drake. Throughout the island country, posted handbills warned that American insurgents or sympathizers could be anywhere and that the French and the Americans might soon try to attack British strongholds anywhere in the British Isles. Early that morning, Lunt had stopped to read a handbill he had found nailed to the side of a tavern along the road over the Slieve Bloom Mountains through Roscrea.

Because of his Yankee accent, Lunt dared not speak a word in Ireland and simply ignored anyone who had spoken or waved to him during his bruising

ride of nearly two hundred miles. So far, by traveling
fast and avoiding villages and stealing his food from
farmyards, he had managed to avoid human contact.
Although the owners of the stolen horses had certainly
sent pursuers out, thus far, Lunt had managed to elude
them. All Lunt wanted to accomplish for the remaining
hours of this day was to reach the harbour at Wexford
and spot a vessel that he could commandeer later.
Then he hoped fervently to find a quiet, hidden place
in which he could sleep until the middle of the night,
and then, God willing, find a westerly wind that would
carry him the three hundred miles across open water
to France.

Lunt, seeing a graveyard and church at the top
of one hill, walked slowly upwards. His two pistols
and sword were hidden in the canvas bag he carried.
His boots were severely chafed by three long days
of rubbing against the stirrups. The afternoon sky
was bright and fresh and the clouds swam earnestly
by. The landscape was as green as he had ever seen
it. A family in mourning was gathered about one burial
site, while a parson read aloud from a prayer book.
The obvious widow and her children were dressed
in black. Lunt stayed to the far side avoiding the small
party and wondering what service the British government would give his own remains if he were caught.

After cresting the hill, he wandered down into
the town of Wexford to buy a loaf of bread, if he could
manage it without speaking. As he walked along the
harbour, he surveyed the available craft. The harbour

was enormous, nearly seven or eight miles in length and protected on its western exposure by a long spit of land that almost closed the harbour off from the Irish Sea. At the narrow mouth was the expected stone fortification guarding the channel entrance.

Nearing the mouth of Wexford harbour, a Royal Navy sloop was beating its way upwind toward the harbour's entrance. O'Mally had told Lunt that Wexford had been the traditional site of Irish smuggling to and from the continent, and so the harbour was usually guarded by many Royal Navy revenue cutters. However, a great many more fishing boats also dotted the harbour. All Lunt had to do was to steal one and sail it out under cover of darkness, avoiding detection.

Lunt looked up towards the sun, which was beginning to cloud over. There was the hint of an approaching storm.

The street along the harbour front contained many shops; a bakery, a candle shop, a boot smith and tailor shop combined, and a chandlery. Lunt stood outside the chandlery for a quarter hour glancing into the worn, multi-pane window, whose wooden divisions had been recently recaulked. He thought of his father's shop in Newburyport and wondered how his wife and young child were surviving the war at home.

It had been nearly a year since he traveled home and so much had happened. First he had taken passage aboard the privateer Dalton and had been captured at sea, spent an unbearable period as a prisoner in the freezing eternal darkness of the British

Man of War, Reasonable, where a third of the prisoners had died from the squalid conditions. Then he had been imprisoned at Plymouth for four months through the deepest part of the winter of '77 and '78. In the spring he had been transferred to Wales for road work. But the local authorities had never procured any equipment, only prisoners without shovels or mortar with which to do their work. The prisoners had languished there playing chess for endless weeks until one night, quite unexpectedly, Captain Jones had rescued the dozen of them, bringing them down the cliffs into a dark wild ride at sea, eventually boarding the Ranger.

Aboard the Ranger, Lunt remembered that Jones had been deeply concerned that there were saboteurs aboard and not without sufficient reason. Lunt now carried with him the names of the two British spies who had shipped out on the voyage of the Ranger.

"Can we show ye some'in of interest?"

The proprietor of the chandlery had come outside his shop and interrupted Lunt's thoughts. Lunt looked blankly at the ruddy little man, started to speak and then remembered that to do so was to call immediate attention to himself. He shook his head, turned, and walked off down the street. After he had passed a few more store fronts, he glanced back to find that the ruddy little man was still looking his way. He walked on faster and got to the end of the street where a carriage was parked. He turned the corner as if to go up the cobblestone street and instead pressed himself backwards up against the mortar wall of the building. He realized that he was very, very tired. He was allowing himself to look suspicious for nothing.

He breathed slowly, deeply and deliberately. He had made Wexford harbour, there were certainly a number of twenty to thirty foot vessels about that he could steal and sail out during the night. But it was only mid afternoon now. He must have sleep. He must.

Towards the top of the hill, Lunt saw the steeple of an Anglican church on a parallel street. If he could get there, he could perhaps find a sanctuary. Before moving up the hill, he decided to glance back along the harbour street one more time. He peeked around the corner and saw the chandlery proprietor walking in his direction but looking down. Lunt felt the man did not see him, but he decided to hurry up the hill before the man reached the corner. He ran as swiftly as his legs could carry him, his sailor's canvas bag swinging wildly in his right hand. He reached a small windowless warehouse building and dove down the dirt alley beside it. He must get safely back to France with the information he possessed. He must.

*   *   *   *   *

Under the horn lantern, Jones examined the French manifest detailing the supplies and noting that they were a loan from the French Naval Stores to the American Office of Diplomatic Affairs to be repaid within one month's time at a price of 2,000 Louis d'or. Jones had no choice but to sign the document. However, until the debt was repaid in full, he knew that he and his small squadron would be detained by the French fleet.

"Excuse me, Sir. I've made the corrections to the letter you requested. It is ready for your signature," explained his secretary, Gooch.

Jones nodded, and then asked the French Lieutenant, who had handed him the manifest, to wait outside on the quarterdeck for the diplomatic message he wished to send onto Ambassador Franklin informing him of the return of the Ranger expedition and of the financial predicament he had been obliged to accept. His men needed to be paid, he needed to be able to purchase fresh supplies rather than be in the debt of the French navy. He needed to have court martial proceedings started against his second in command, Lieutenant Simpson, for several incidents of direct disobedience during the cruise, and finally he needed the Ambassador's suggestions for the proper disposition of the prisoners of war, and advising that this could become a diplomatic issue.

Jones took the letter he had dictated to Gooch and asked his secretary to go outside and physically verify that the stores they had just received matched the manifest he had been asked to sign. After Gooch closed the door to the great cabin, Jones opened a drawer of his desk with a small key, and took out a twenty year old copy of Poor Richard's Almanac. He opened the worn book to a specific page and wrote the following on a piece of foolscap.

DRAKE CAPTURED, BUT NOT NEW CANNON WHICH DOES SEEM TO HAVE PRACTICAL ADVANTAGE. THE FRENCH WERE AWARE OF ITS EXISTENCE. WE INADVERTENTLY MAY HAVE FOILED THEIR ATTEMPT TO GET THE WEAPON. POSSIBLE ILL FEELINGS COULD RESULT. ONCE FRENCH ARE COMMITTED, ADVISE WE WORK OPENLY WITH THEM ON FUTURE ENDEAVORS.

Using one page of the Almanac as a guide, Jones substituted a number for each letter of his message until he reached a situation where the fourth letter of a word was either a vowel or had a double consonant occurring as one of the fourth letters. At that point each numeric code for a letter shifted one letter earlier, beginning with the next letter. He thus shifted the coding in the midst of the words: cannon, have, advantage, were, have, their, attempt, result, once, committed, advise, future, and endeavors, until the numeric code for the letter 'N' became the same as that of 'A' at the beginning of the message. Using a quill and ink, Jones then signed his name beneath the regular diplomatic correspondence he had dictated to his secretary, Gooch. He then withdrew a special vial and small featherless quill from behind a drawer of his writing desk. Jones wrote the numeric code with invisible ink on the bottom of the parchment.

Jones folded the parchment to one eighth its normal size and turning down one corner, he sealed the document with hot wax onto which he pressed his personal stamp. He called for the marine guard at the door of the great cabin to give the signed manifest and the diplomatic package to the French officer who awaited them. Next, he ordered Gooch to have the purser issue double rations of food to the crew and prisoners...and eight measures of West Indian rum to each crew member not on duty that evening. It would be a late evening aboard the Ranger.

Much later, Jones collected together the remnants of the four bottles of wine which had been uncorked to host the French naval officers. He went to the shutters of the great cabin and flung them open violently.

'Are you all right, Sir?' came the voice of his marine guard posted outside the great cabin.

'Yes, Corporal, thank you.'

Jones extended one of his legs out onto the sill of his window and then the other. He emptied the remains of one bottle of bordeaux into a glass and leaned back to stare out at the many ships bobbing in the gentle wavelets of Brest harbour. Forward on the Ranger, a much deserved party had begun and the men were singing sea shanties and laughing together. Less than two cables away lay the enormous 300 foot Bretagne, bobbing parallel in the current next

26

to Ranger. Jones gazed at her enormity and wondered if he would ever get command of a vessel of that size, or even close to it. For the French, Bretagne was a perfect ship capable of controlling a classic line of battle in the European tradition. But Jones had never fought a battle like that, no American officer had. America simply didn't have that size of ship.

Jones leaned out and looked down the harbour at the sixty four gun, Iphigenie. Now there was the size of ship he'd like to command. Her lines showed her to be swift, her hull broad but still maneuverable. But if she were his, he'd restep the fore masts and main masts back five to ten feet, something like he'd done with the Ranger. It had made her bow ride higher, and swiftness was tantamount to victory in most sea battles. Jones made a silent prayer that this expedition, just concluded, would eventually bring him a ship larger than the small one hundred and ten foot, 18 gun Ranger he presently commanded.

As he sipped his wine, Jones began to reconstruct portions of the cruise just past. How he had sent Lieutenant Lunt and O'Mally to scout out the disposition of the Drake and any other ships in Belfast harbour, and in the meantime had proceeded himself with the raid on Whitehaven harbour on the English shore of the Irish sea. Two evenings later he was to return to rendezvous with Lunt and O'Mally at Carrickfergus, half way into Belfast harbour.

Jones recalled that it had been the Irishman, David Smith, the Ranger's purser, who had been originally designated to go with Lunt into Belfast. What a disaster that would have been. O'Mally, luckily, had pleaded with Jones to be sent with Lunt instead, and at the last minute Lunt had also insisted that O'Mally be his companion. Jones had promised to let Smith go on their next expedition, which proved to be the next night's landing at Whitehaven.

They had not been ashore at Whitehaven a few minutes when David Smith slipped from their presence and began running about the town pounding on doors and warning the citizenry that an American raid was in progress. All of the grenade wicks had also been dampened so that the fire bombs Jones had planned for all the ships in the harbour did not function. On the return to Ranger that evening Jones had convinced himself that it must have also been Smith who had loosened the capstan craw to deliberately drag the anchor during their first attempt to capture H.M.S. Drake in the darkness of Belfast harbour a week before the eventual battle. Also the similar malfunction when Jones and Sergeant Miers had gone ashore in Wales to rescue Lunt and the others from their prison. The Ranger had mistakenly drifted off her anchorage, thus almost abandoning them on the return from the landing to rescue the American prisoners of war.

At the time, Jones had thought that, with David Smith having shown his true colors, all the strange incidents aboard the Ranger would cease. But within a day there had been an attempted mutiny just prior to the final engagement with the Drake. Only Lunt's dramatic escape with O'Mally and the French spy, Marie Chatelain, had stopped the incident, along with Jones' promise of amnesty for all aboard so that the crew would focus on the coming engagement with the Drake.

But even in the days following, when they were being pursued by the British fleet, there was constant trouble and several more incidents.   Lieutenant Simpson, given command of the captured Drake claimed that he did not receive several signals, and indeed Jones found that once the back glass plate of the two ship's horn lanterns had been greased so as to mask their visibility from the stern. And then during the final leg of their escape, when they were passing by the mouth of the river Shannon, the most dangerous area along the west coast of Ireland where they might hazard a chance encounter with Royal Navy vessels, someone had tossed an oil lantern on a pile of work canvas at the forecastle, causing a fire which deeply charred the foremast before it was extinguished. Ironically, the incident had led to the capture of a well stocked British merchantman, who had mistakenly steered towards Ranger thinking she was the lighthouse beacon at the entrance to the River Shannon.

Jones pitched the first empty bottle of wine out into the harbour watching it splash with a brief show of white foam. He tipped the small contents of the second bottle and part of the third until he had filled a second glass of wine. He shifted his gaze again toward the Bretagne. At the stem of the vessel he could see lamp light from within the Admiral's enormous great cabin. He almost believed that he could see the hourglass figure of Marie Chatelain walking amidst her French countrymen. There was no telling what she was saying about him to Admiral d'Orvilliers and the other officers. There must be many questions about the Ranger. They would have her viewpoint before his own. Every detail of the recent engagement would be seen through her eyes as a friendly neutral observer, one of their own countrymen obviously in Belfast on her own mission for the powerful French Minister, Vergennes.

Lunt had surprised everyone, when he had returned from Belfast to the Ranger with not only O'Mally, but also Marie Chatelain. Apparently, the French had been in clandestine pursuit of the same small cannon which the American Spymaster had ordered Jones to seize from aboard the Drake. That part of the mission had failed as the dying British Lieutenant of the Drake had managed to successfully push the cannon into the water before the Americans could secure his vessel. Immediately following the engagement, in the confusion after the battle, Madam Chatelain had tried to sneak aboard the Drake and steal the plans from the British Captain's quarters.

Jones shook his head. He had made the mistake of leaving the British boatswain, Mr. Snead, ashore with the severely wounded. He had deeply respected that man who'd had the presence of mind to enter his dying Captain's quarters and destroy all the engineering plans for the gun before the Americans or Marie Chatelain could capture them. Suddenly, a thought struck Jones and he quickly swallowed the remainder of his glass of wine and went to his writing desk to make a note for the morning. During his quarantine, there might just be a way to identify any remaining British spies aboard his ship.

He returned a few minutes later and resumed his reminiscences. Lunt had been an extremely faithful and valiant officer. On behalf of Jones, he had personally challenged the Royal Navy to come out and engage the Ranger, but in doing so he had upset the cover of Marie Chatelain. Somehow he had escaped an impossible incident at an Inn and, with the Redcoats in full pursuit, had evaded them and brought Jones the Drake for good measure. Somehow in the midst of it all, during that escape, the beautiful, but deceitful lady spy, in her forties had fallen in love with the young Lieutenant Lunt in his mid twenties.

Another mistake. Why had he let Lunt take O'Mally off the Ranger to bring him to his home as they passed the islands at the entrance to Galway Bay? Jones balled his hand into a fist and slammed it into his right leg. He poured his third glass of wine, but decided against throwing the last bottle of wine into the harbour. He sat it beside his foot for the orderly to secure in the morning.

Just why did he allow Lunt to leave the Ranger? His shipmate, O'Mally had broken his back and lost a leg during a crucial portion of the engagement with H.M.S. Drake. He seemed to be dying and several times had requested to see Jones, but the one time that Jones had spent with him he had drifted off into delirious talk of Banshees and that he wanted to have his body put into the ocean so that it would drift into Galway Bay driven before the wind. But Lunt had managed to visit O'Mally several times and came to Jones' cabin requesting that he be allowed to leave the gallant seaman with his mother, just 'half a day's sail away in a small boat.'

Because the morning that the Ranger had arrived opposite Galway Bay coincided with the third time that they had lost sight of Lieutenant Simpson commanding the captured Drake, fate had decreed that Jones would have to backtrack for at least two days along his course to find the Drake. So reluctantly Jones had acquiesced to Lunt's request on the promise that Lunt would continue to serve with Jones once the voyage of the Ranger was completed.

Jones remembered Marie's anger, at his letting Lunt sail with the wounded O'Mally into the Isle of Inishmore in just a small skiff, and her ferocity when Lunt did not appear at the designated location the following evening. She had made such a display of pounding against his chest in front of the entire crew that he'd had her confined under guard to Lieutenant Simpson's vacant quarters beside the great cabin, until after the cruise was over. Apparently she had picked the lock and secured the pistols from Lieutenant Hall's adjacent cabin. The latter had been placed in command of the captured British merchant prize during the final few days of the voyage. Knowing just the right moment to make a scene, she had shattered his victory party and now he and his crew were quarantined.

Tomorrow, after Marie Chatelain departed, he'd work on softening up the French Admiral. He'd start by requesting permission to come aboard Bretagne and present the Admiral with H.M.S. Drake's battle flag, complete with four grapeshot punctures. Then, if Jones could secure permission to go ashore himself, why not simply sell one of the merchant prizes? That way he could present the Admiral with his two thousand Louis d'or sooner than anticipated. There was an American Naval agent at Brest.

Jones missed Lunt. Rescuing him from prison in Wales had been a triumph, but losing his shipmate of many voyages so soon afterwards had been a tragedy. Lunt and O'Mally had both served with him when he was still Lieutenant Jones. Together they had raided the British gunpowder stores in the Bahamas and had served in his first command aboard the Alfred. A rare breed of loyal and true friends. O'Mally was surely dead by now, and Lunt was missing. He poured his fourth glass of wine and held it up to the harbour lights of Brest.

'Rest well, Sean O'Mally, me bucko, and Henry Lunt, wherever you are, Godspeed.'

Henry Lunt & The Spymaster

2
Passy

The Prime Minister rapped his clay pipe against the brass ash tray sternly and with such ferocity that it startled many in the room who were talking in small groups of two's and three's. Bright May sunbeams streamed through the high window pane that held in its reflection a picture perfect rose garden.

'Gentlemen, gentlemen, you can catch up with gossip another time. We are here to see that Britain's naval and intelligence strategies are for this season in accord with Tory objectives.'

Lord North looked around the room and was met by a dozen staring sets of eyes, all attentive to his words. He gestured for them to take their seats. 'Lord Sandwich, what is the condition of our fleet?'

'Ready, your lordship.'

'How ready? Could I have every rater on the water within 72 hours? Are we strong enough to stand off the French and Spanish fleets combined? Are the accusations of our loyal opposition unfounded?'

'Well, eh,' postulated Lord Sandwich ready to give his prepared analysis.

But Lord North interrupted him, 'This morning's rumor has it that if the French sail it may,... it may be a run directly from Brest to Plymouth. A blockade of our fleet and a landing party to be put ashore to burn everything in the harbour.'

'Yes, and another has them landing at Grimsby, another at Hastings,' interjected Lord George Germain. 'Rumors are cheap. What we need is reliable information.'

All of the heads in the room turned towards William Eden of the Foreign office.

'Gentlemen, Britain has its ears tuned to the American Commissioners. There is not a item that they contemplate of which we are not aware. Our undersecretary in charge of France, Paul Wentworth, is in Paris at this very moment doing everything he can to pry open a schism. According to our sources the Americans are on very shaky footing with the French until their Congress approves the Alliance their King has signed. From an intelligence standpoint, if we are ever going to do anything, I recommend we do it now. If we can succeed in breaking up that alliance before it gets underway, gentlemen, we will have squashed the American rebellion.'

'Mr. Eden, you have my leave to try anything which is reasonable but, barring an unexpected success, we have to treat the evolution of matters as if we are going to be at war with France at any moment.' As he puffed on his pipe, Lord North thumped the knuckle of his index finger down onto the mahogany table for emphasis, 'Gentlemen, remember that our priorities now have shifted. When we learned that Franklin had convinced Vergennes and the French King to sign an alliance with the Americans, then it was no longer a matter of merely putting down a rebellion three thousand miles away. It has become a real possibility that we are now about to be engaged in a world war. We have interests in the West Indies, India and other parts of the world to protect and now, also, we must prepare for the very real possibility of an invasion attempt on England herself.'

Lord North exhaled a measured volume of smoke and continued, 'I am aware that Mr. Eden's agents have succeeded very well in keeping tabs on the American Commissioners, but the French are the only power who can do us genuine harm. They are the only ones who have the naval force to defeat us at sea.'

'Then it will be the first objective of our Red Fleet to continue to build our blockade of the French.' stated Sandwich for the Admiralty.

'Who will lead your blockade of Brest?' interjected North.

The First Lord of the Admiralty folded his hands in contemplation, and then spoke up, 'Well, yes, as to who should lead the Channel fleet in a blockade of France, it should be Hugh Palliser, one of our own.'

'Wasn't he in charge of that Jones fiasco, just past? He allowed that American pirate to escape with one of His Majesty's ships.' North shook his head sternly, 'No, I think it suitable that we place another in charge. How about Keppel?"

"Augustus Keppel!" Sandwich spat out an invective, "Why the man's a traitor! He's refused to fight against the Americans. He's a Whig through and through, related to Rockingham and Fox. You can't mean it,"

Someone else offered, "How about Rodney?"

"Another Whig, he's just been released from his gambling debts in Paris. Fill everyone in on the story behind that, Mr. Eden," requested Germain.

Eden cleared his throat, "For the past year Rodney's gambling note was held by a French bank, with an odd counter lien on it. As things started to deteriorate with the Frenchies, I tried earnestly to have Paul Wentworth repay it, but his efforts were blocked. Then, quite fortuitously, a Frenchman, Marchal Duc de Biron stepped up and paid the debt at the beginning of this month. He is apparently one of Rodney's personal friends, who did not want him to languish in a French prison should hostilities break out. "

"I don't feel I want a gambler, especially Rodney, in charge of the channel fleet," stated Sandwich emphatically.

His remark caused several at the table to smirk inwardly thinking of Lord Sandwich's personal gambling bordello, a former abbey, on the west end of London affectionately called, The Castle. Most high placed Tories had frequented the establishment more than occasionally. One of London's more sensational journals had recently dubbed the company within its walls as "The Order of Medmenham Monks."

"We are back to Keppel," stated Lord North

"A Whig in charge of the defence of England?" Lord Germain shook his head.

"That's precisely why we should put Keppel in charge of the French blockade. One of our loyal opposition's best darlings," said Lord North.

They stared at the Prime Minister in disbelief.

But he continued, "Shouldn't it be fitting that His Majesty's Government and her Admiralty demonstrate the objectivity to call upon the best that our nation can bring forth, regardless of political considerations."

There was a long moment of silence.

"Oh, I say, so if there is a failing, a difficulty, it will be a Whig at fault, not a Tory," offered Lord George Germain.

"Here, here!" sounded the parliamentarians at the table.

"You've said it, not I," said North grinning with his lips pursed together. "The whole arrangement will run just a brief period anyway. I've recalled Viscount Howe from New York. He should be ready to take command of England's defence by the end of the summer."

"But if Keppel destroys the French fleet in the meantime, then he will be a hero. It will be embarrassing to this Admiralty," protested Sandwich.

"But it will bring us peace this summer in Parliament, perhaps a little welcome respite from the verbal assaults on the preparedness of our navy by Burke and Fox. Oh, assign Palliser, Harland, and a few choice others as van Admirals in that fleet," conceded North, "If there is success on the water, then we'll see to it that by the time the news is out that the voting public will perceive the victory as a Tory one. After all, who had the wisdom to appoint Keppel in the first place."

"Here, here," resounded around the table.

North continued, "Lord Sandwich and I have also deemed it advisable to give the French a quick little jab in the eye to punish them for meddling in our affairs. With Howe's orders to return home, we have also sent instructions to dispatch some of the New York fleet to the French West Indies to await Rear Admiral Barrington's dispatches from Plymouth. Once the outbreak of hostilities is formalized, their ultimate objective, gentlemen, will be to immediately take the French colony of St. Lucia in the West Indies."

Whistles of surprise and smiles of approval went around the table. "That may teach the frogs to keep their hands off our colonies," someone commented.

North held up his hand, "But of course, we can't do anything until we are quite certain that we are at war with France." The Prime Minister turned his attention back to William Eden, "Well, Mr. Secretary, what is the situation?"

"Gentlemen, as I said earlier, it is still up in the air. I receive weekly dispatches from Paul Wentworth, our man in Paris. Franklin is still anxiously awaiting word of the formal ratification of the French treaty by the American Congress. It has been five months now since King Louis signed his commitment to that secret treaty."

"Some secret, we knew about it three days after it had been signed," interjected someone at the far end of the table.

"Could it be that the American Congress will not accept French help?" put forth Lord Germain.

"It's more like the American Congress resembles our Parliament," observed Lord North. Then he added for clarification, "Can't agree on anything, but to disagree."

There was laughter.

"While there is still time," interjected Lord George, "perhaps we should try a more proactive approach with the American Commissioners in Paris." He had the attention of his Tory counterparts, "We have just dispatched the Carlisle commission to Philadelphia with authority to concede to the American Congress anything reasonable, save independence, including full representation for the American Colonies in the Parliament. A like gesture might well help slow down Franklin, Lee, and Adams. They might be less energetic about engaging in activities with the French, as they consider the personal advantages of courting the goodwill of the Crown."

"Refresh my memory, who is Adams?" queried North.

"He is a solicitor from Massachusetts Bay. Has

just taken Dean's place. In '72 he successfully defended our troops during that shooting incident and the subsequent trial in Boston,' Germain informed them.

'Ah, yes. Then we may have a more sympathetic ear than we've had in the past.'

'We may,' agreed Secretary Eden.

'Then, let's try it. Any activity which weakens their resolve is money in the bank,' said North. 'We still have our operatives in place, within the Commission? So that we can test their reaction?'

Eden nodded.

North changed the subject, 'What about this gun, the one the Americans were trying to capture aboard H.M.S. Drake?'

Lord Sandwich responded, 'It is called the carronade. It was part of a research grant to the Carron company, up in Scotland. It was intended to see if they could improve the range of naval cannon by using a lighter piece and some special engineering.'

'Does it function?' inquired North.

'It may,' said Sandwich. 'We truly don't know. We haven't had it tested adequately. The Colonials were there before we got it to fire in a formal test.'

'Did the Americans get the weapon?' asked North, concerned.

'It doesn't seem so. According to survivors, Captain Hardy and his Lieutenant managed to drop the weapon into the water, before the Drake was captured. Both of them lost their lives in the action,' reported Sandwich.

"How do we know for certain that the Americans did not capture the plans to the weapon?" questioned North. "There must certainly have been engineering plans in the company of the weapon. If the action was as fast and furious as everyone says, how do we know for certain that Jones and his pirates did not get hold of this information?"

Lord Sandwich looked up, "A seaman, the boatswain, said he tore every record into pieces including the drawings. He was one of those put ashore in charge of the wounded on a little island outside Belfast."

"How considerate of Captain Jones, that he just, by happenstance, leaves behind a source of information that our secret weapon is safe and sound." Lord North shook his head doubtfully.

"Do we have the information to duplicate the weapon?" asked Lord George Germain.

"Not precisely, but we do have two earlier prototypes of the cannon still in Stromeferry," reported Sandwich.

"If it was important enough for the Americans and the French to be after it, then it's important enough for us to safeguard. Get that weapon and everything associated with it down to Greenwich. Do the testing on the Thames in sight of the tower, if you have to. Protect it until we know what we have. If it performs satisfactorily, I want it aboard our ships."

The First Lord of the Admiralty nodded his

affirmation.

North continued, "The question is, how did the Americans know about this weapon? How did the Pirate Jones even know enough about our activities to try and attempt a capture of something like this from aboard the Drake?"

North looked to William Eden.

"We do not know," confessed Eden. "The only logical explanation is that Franklin has someone in London feeding him information. He, after all, spent nearly a decade here in London representing several of the colonies, right up to the outbreak of hostilities. I suppose he had built up certain loyalties over the years."

North contemplated aloud, "This is as important as any other consideration, to identify Franklin's spy network and smash it. We must assume that if we have spies, then the Americans must have them as well. Mr. Eden, I would think that the place to begin is among the landing party from the Ranger, they are all certainly involved. Capturing one or two of them and putting the screws to them is certainly a starting point. Can we identify them?"

"Yes," nodded Eden, "I have someone who can do that. A regular army major by the name of Pitkan who was in service at Belfast. He was also a close friend of the unfortunate Captain Burden. Major Pitkan met all the American and French participants on shore during the Drake incident. On his own initiative he had already discovered that Captain Burden's mistress was a French spy. He was just about to unwrap her cover, but events moved too fast for him to do so. A bonus is that the Major is fluent in French. He was a prisoner of the French for four years during the last war in North America.'

'Sounds ideal,' remarked Lord Germain.

'How are we coming with obtaining the numbers and conditions of ships in the Brest and Toulon fleets?' pressed Sandwich to Eden, 'I can't properly put our channel fleet to sea until we know what the size of the French force is that we will be up against. I must know it, particularly those at Brest under d'Orvilliers.'

'I have just obtained a list for you by vessel name and by number of guns. I say just, the listing was compiled only three days ago.' Eden reached into his breast pocket and unfolded a paper, 'Including Bretagne, and the behemoth, Ville de Paris of 120 guns, there are presently some 20 first through third raters now at the harbour of Brest. But they are continuously moved. My operatives will update this list in their weekly reports.'

Sandwich took the listing and examined it closely. 'Very well, I'll have the Admiralty board study this tomorrow. We'll send Keppel fairly matched for the Frenchies, gun for gun.'

'And give him written orders not to engage until war is formally declared. And certainly not to engage until he has a like number of ships and guns,' said North. 'If he is defeated because we failed to supply him adequately, then we'll have to answer for it. Do make sure that he does not go in harm's way undermanned.'

North continued, 'A little more news. I was at St. James this morning, and the King has graciously consented to help with the war effort by attending every Royal Navy ship christening hence forth.'

'That should help get the press and public more enthused about the war effort,' said someone down the table.

North continued, 'Also we are working at getting Lord Stormont back into France, not reinstated as an official Ambassador, but as a liaison, in case the French want to communicate with us. Does anyone else at the table have news?'

Sandwich spoke up, 'We have just instituted a new system of Signals by Night for our ships. It will make the job of conducting the blockade of France much more efficient. Also, because the responsibilities of our war ships are now going to be world wide, I would like to recommend that this body consider reinstating the practice of commissioning privateers using formal letters of marque. I have here a list of ten ships whose captains would willingly convert their merchant vessels for this endeavor. I remind you that the Americans have been using privateers since the outbreak of hostilities and we have lost hundreds of merchantmen. I think it is high time we gave them and their frog friends a taste of English piracy.'

'Here, here!' resounded around the table.

The conversation continued for another two

hours before the assemblage of high Tory appointees to the Admiralty and Foreign office took their leave. Lord North asked his servant for a service of tea and quietly stepped into his rose garden. There was a chill in the air, but he seemed immune, his mind replayed over and over something that he had said quite spontaneously earlier in the meeting, 'We are now about to be engaged in a world war.'

It gave his blood a certain rush of power and pleasure to think that he should be in charge of so titanic an endeavor.

*　　*　　*　　*　　*

Lunt reached the gates of Passy an hour or so after midnight. The man who had driven him the last few miles did not speak a word of English, but he had recognized in Henry's speech only the name, 'Franklin.' The Frenchman had first put his hand to his chest and imitated a heart fluttering while he had continued to speak in the jabbering, breakneck, incomprehensible speech that Lunt had recognized to be French. Then the man had pointed to him and asked, 'Amer-y-cane?'

Lunt had nodded and the man had thrown his arms about him. Immediately the man led him to his carriage and drove him almost all evening through the streets of Paris and along the Seine. Eventually they arrived at a small village in the countryside, and then in front of a mansion with a hugh wrought iron gate. The man pointed to the building and said, "*Voila!*"

Lunt then reached into his canvas bag and began to extract an English shilling, but the man held up his hand and shook his head. Then he unexpectedly seized Lunt and kissed him first on the right cheek and then the left. Lunt stood perplexed, not knowing what response he should make. Thankfully, the man simply smiled and jumped back into his carriage and drove away leaving Lunt in front of the gate, alone.

The massive wrought iron gate was locked. A vast open courtyard and elaborate gardens stood between the gate and the main building. In the moonlight, the leaves of great dark vines rustled in the light breezes of evening. Two oil lanterns lit the interior courtyards sparsely. There seemed to be another building or group of buildings off to the right, an even greater distance from the gate. The entire complex was surrounded by a great stone wall, twice the height of a man. The gate was the only obvious entrance. Inside the grounds of the chateau, Lunt heard the whinny of a horse and then quiet.

It was the middle of the night, and Lunt contemplated whether or not he should shout out. There must be servants who would hear him and let him in. But it was imperative that he talk only to Franklin first, no one else. If he should be so obnoxious as to wake everyone up, he might not be permitted to see the Ambassador, or would be required to deal

48

first with secretaries, perhaps for days. With the information he possessed, he must act prudently.

Lunt yawned and stretched from fatigue. It was warm that evening. He decided to simply put his canvas bag on the ground in front of the massive gate. He pulled his worn leather vest about his chest and laid his head against the bag. He was soon asleep and did not hear the open carriage which arrived in front of the gate some time later.

"Monsieur Franklin, you must have another volunteer. Who will it be this time, a Russian Czar, or a Baron from Liechtenstein?"

There was laughter. The great man descended from the small carriage and bent over the sleeper saying happily in French, "It must be a countryman of mine. A Frenchman would have a warm bed and a woman, and a Baron or Czar would never sleep in the street."

There was laughter again. Lunt felt himself firmly, but gently being tugged by the arm. He sat bolt upright in the darkness, startled by the laughter about him, and by the carriage lanterns which blinded his vision. There was a man bending over him. He tried to get to his feet, when the man spoke to him in French.

Lunt shook his head to signify he did not understand. "I am an officer in the Continental Navy. I am here to see Dr. Franklin."

The man shifted his stance, standing aside to let the full carriage light illuminate Lunt's face. Lunt repeated his words but the man ignored him entirely, instead saying something to his companions in French. Then there was the crack of a whip and the carriage simply drove off. The man went to the gate and produced a long stout key from his coat and turned it with both hands. Somewhere, deep within the wrought iron, a tumbler creaked across resistant metal and then snapped. The massive arched gate sprung forward a few inches and then rested. The old man set both hands against it and shoved. The hinge creaked a stentorian protest as it swung open in reaction to his weight.

The man stood holding open the gate and motioned for Lunt to enter. He closed the gate and then locked it again. He gestured for Lunt to accompany him. They walked along a long thoroughfare of crushed stone for a few minutes in silence, until the man spoke up in English, "You are from the Spy?"

Lunt stopped and looked at the man warily. What kind of a question was this to ask a stranger? The man turned to face him. By virtue of the yellow light from the courtyard oil lanterns Lunt could see that he wore spectacles. His long hair hung about his shoulders, without benefit of a pigtail. On the man's head was a simple round beaver fur cap. The man's coat and breeches were either totally black, or very dark.

"I am Benjamin Franklin. What is your name and what ship are you last from?"

Lunt paused, not entirely sure of what to say. He responded carefully, "I am Henry Lunt, sir. I have just come ashore three days ago at St. Pol de Leon. I am a lieutenant in the Colonial Navy, I must speak to you in private.'

'You are from the ship, the Spy. You have a dispatch for me?

'No, sir, a message.'

'Then tell me, lad, what is it?'

Lunt looked around, he had no certainty that this was Franklin. It was dark. O'Mally had warned him that he was to trust his message with no one but Franklin.

'Sir, Mr. Ambassador, can we go inside?'

'What is inside your canvas bag?'

'Two pistols, a sword, a greatcoat, and some bread and cheese,' reported Lunt.

'I suppose if you were here to kill me, you'd have done it by now,' muttered Franklin. 'Follow me.'

They walked together in silence, both the old man and the young man, each in his own thoughts looking for a way to verify the identity of the other. A path veered off to the right and the old man took it and eventually arrived in front of a smaller, dark stone edifice of two stories. The wick of what had once been a fully lighted oil lantern still held a gentle flame. The old man removed another key from his pocket and squinted at it in the meager light. Finding the right edge, he inserted the key and the door swung open. He stood aside for Lunt to enter, but as Lunt proceeded he noticed that the man had taken hold of his canvas bag.

'I'd like to ask you to leave your bag outside. It will be safe, I assure you. You see, I am a Quaker. I will not have guns or swords in my home.'

Lunt stood at the threshold a long moment and then decided to put the bag behind a bush at the side of the door. He followed the old man inside, putting his trust in the man's words. He glimpsed a sign of relief in the old man's face. A lone candle had been set out some time ago and had almost burned down to its base. As the old man picked up the saucer and moved across the room ahead of him, Lunt noticed for the first time that the man limped badly, favoring his left leg.

'I get a touch of the gout in the dampness. This old body has not much more distance to travel.'

Lunt followed the candle light, respectfully, a few steps behind the older gentleman. As they ascended a flight of stairs, Lunt became aware that the first floor room was enormous, the meager light of the flickering candle just touched only one wall close to the main stairway. An elegant tapestry hung from the ceiling of the second floor into which they were ascending.

Franklin paused at the top of the stairs.

'Careful' he warned. Spread on the second floor were at least a hundred papers all seemingly sorted in some particular fashion. Lunt carefully stepped around and over the papers, careful not to disturb any of them.

'Voltaire's last manuscript. He's just passed on,

you know."

Lunt nodded. He had heard of the name, Voltaire, but he couldn't immediately recall who the man was. He remained non-committal.

Lunt followed the man down a long corridor, and into a dark room. The man lifted the edge of a lantern glass, lit it and then two others. As the room became more and more bathed in light, Lunt became more and more awed by the room's opulence. Delicate crystal sparkled everywhere, spaced between enormous landscaped paintings, some of them as much as ten feet across. All were hung on wall covering that seemed to be of gilded gold. The furniture was carved in dark woods with marble inlays on every surface. Lunt just stared.

"It's a bit too elegant for the mind to comprehend, isn't it?" remarked the old man. "When Ambassador Adams arrived here last month he spent the first day gaping and then the remainder of the week lecturing me about the hardships that our soldiers are enduring and that I should sell all of this and send the money or the arms they might buy immediately to Philadelphia. But I cannot. You see, none of this is mine. Please sit down, eh, Lieutenant Lunt?"

"Yes, sir."

"Before you think ill of me, let me explain about our benefactors. All of this Hotel de Valentinois property belongs to Monsieur Jacques Donatien Leray de Chaumont and his Madame. They are a shipping family and close friends of the Minister Vergennes.

They are obviously wealthy beyond all our comprehension, unless of course you have first seen Versailles."

"Versailles, the palace?"

"Yes, the palace of the Sun King. But first let me return to Leray de Chaumont. In addition to being a great commercial success, he is also a minister of supply for the French Government. He believes that a show of wealth and power is necessary to gain acceptance among those that I must influence in the French court. I have found that he is right. But I am a humble Quaker and I do not believe in such trappings. Thus, I dress in my own simple manner and live here in the middle of great opulence. A dichotomy, isn't it?" he mused shaking his head. "What is it you have to tell me in secret?"

Lunt noticed for the first time a desk in the corner of the room and behind it was the flag of the United States, the one he had first seen unfurled during the engagement with the Drake. Then, he spotted a desk beneath the flag, complete with feather quill and ink. Lunt strode over to it and wrote a series of numbers he had memorized onto a paper. He passed the paper to the old man.

The man adjusted his spectacles, and stared at the numbers, "An old man's memory needs refreshing." The old man pushed himself up from his chair and walked over to a bookcase, picking out a book which Lunt recognized. For a few minutes the old man compared an open page of the book with the sheet of paper onto which Lunt had written his message. He placed the book back in its place on the shelf and then turned back to face Lunt.

"Where is Mr. O'Mally, now?"

Lunt stared for a long moment. He didn't know just how to ask the next question, but he had to protect everyone.

"Sir, please forgive me, but I must ask this indulgence of you. Can you prove for me that you are truly Ambassador Franklin? I have met no one tonight who I know, who knows you. I'm sorry."

The old man shook his head. He got up again and limped across the room, somewhat with exaggeration to indicate his disturbance. Then he squatted in front of an elegant gold trimmed dresser. He partially tugged open a lower drawer and gestured for Lunt to look inside.

Lunt went to the drawer and knelt down. Inside, stacked neatly, was a collection of coins, medallions, silhouettes, ladies broaches, rings, and other paraphernalia all with various poses and likeness of one man. Some of the silhouettes bore the name, FRANKLIN, beneath them. Others bore only the likeness.

Lunt withdrew one of the gold coins and held it up facing the old man. Obligingly taking a humorous stance, the Ambassador turned his head sideways, his eyebrow raised rakishly.

"I've been hiding these from Ambassador Adams. Each of the manufacturers usually sends me one, I presume because they tacitly wish my approval. I certainly did not mint them. What can I do? The women pin them onto their bosoms. The sight of them would gall Mr. Adams into a terrible temper. Please keep it a secret. I must get along with him, for all of our sakes.'

'I'm sorry, Mr. Ambassador. I had to ask, a lot of people's lives could be forfeited if I gave information to the wrong people.'

'Just how much do you know?'

'I know everything, sir, everything, and I regretfully carry information that you may not know. You have a British spy in this mission.'

Perhaps it was a contraction of wood flooring in the coolness of night, of old wood fitted too close together in the floors of the venerable building, perhaps it was a whisper of a wind seeping through an ancient fissure, perhaps it was something else that creaked out in the darkness, downstairs. The Ambassador put his finger to his lips and leaned close to Lunt, 'The walls here may have ears. There are over two hundred servants, from milkmaids to barbers to cooks, residing on the premises of Hotel de Valentinois and here at le Petit Hotel. Our own embassy staff represents about two dozen more. And, of course, the main hotel may house fifty or sixty guests on any given day. In addition, seven of the hotel's servants live at the back of the first floor of this building, le Petit Hotel. Tomorrow is Tuesday, and I wish you would come with me to Versailles. We will talk on the way while we are alone in my carriage.'

*   *   *   *   *

Four miles away and three hours earlier, a lone horse and rider pounded up a Paris street until they reached the building near the third street lamp from the corner. The rider tied his horse at the side of the three story house and proceeded, without hesitation, up the outside wooden frame staircase. When he arrived at the third floor rear door, he knocked in a clear and distinct pattern. From inside came a return signal. The man outside gave a new sequence of knocks and the door was opened. He looked into the eyes of an occupant who stood in his night gown, his sandy hair was tousled.

"Who are you?" demanded Paul Wentworth.

"Mr. Wentworth, I am Major Pitkan in His Majesty's Service," said the sinewy, almost totally bald man in his mid-fifties. "I have been sent here to help you to catch a spy."

Henry Lunt & The Spymaster

3
𝔙𝔢𝔯𝔰𝔞𝔦𝔩𝔩𝔢𝔰

Lunt awoke very early as sunbeams penetrated
through his eastern facing window, striking his face.
The Ambassador had hastily given him a small room
with a built-in window bed. Ordinarily, the room was
utilized as the linen closet for le Petit Hotel. Lunt had
been too tired to even take off his greatly worn boots.
He now tried painfully to extract them, but stopped
when he felt the heel of his boot loosening. He would
get help later. For now he would get up and check
outside for his canvas bag. There was a bit of bread
and cheese inside.

Lunt descended the stairs, again admiring the
large pastoral murals which adorned the walls. The
main salon below was huge, on the far side several
doors were closed, near the rear of the massive room
an archway opened into the rear of the building. Lunt
surmised it must house the kitchen.

The furniture in the vast salon was cheerfully
decorated in various silks of intricate design and color.
Various settees and plushly adorned sofas seemed
to be arranged together in groups around ornate center
tables of calamander veneer. High marble busts of
several Greek Gods were cleverly used to demarcate

portions of the salon so as to provide privacy for four or five simultaneous meetings. Although spotlessly maintained, the room had the appearance that it was used a great deal.

At the far end of the room were several burr walnut writing bureaus with a high polished veneer backing. They were placed back to back creating the semblance of a private work space for several staff members. Suddenly, out amidst the furniture, Lunt thought he saw a stir of movement. He turned away, took a step and then turned back around swiftly. There was a giggle and another rush of movement.

Lunt moved swiftly through the salon furniture and saw that his prey was a very small boy who had scooted under a large divan. Lunt dropped to the floor and peered beneath the sofa. He looked directly into the smiling face and wide innocent eyes of a boy of perhaps nine or ten. The boy was holding a small black knight in one hand and a mounted white charger in the other. He had obviously been jousting with the two figures.

'I'm not supposed to play with Dr. Bancroft's chess pieces, but I haven't hurt them, really. You won't tell my father, promise?'

Henry smiled, and extended his hand in a gesture to examine one of the pieces. After a little hesitation, the boy handed him the white piece, mounted on a charger.

'It's like a real knight, some of the others are castles, with turrets and everything. Want to see them?

Lunt nodded and followed the boy as he extricated himself from beneath the divan and then ran enthusiastically across the room, repositioning a foot stool so that he would be tall enough to open the swinging door of a large walnut secretaire cabinet with bone inlays. Lunt followed behind and peered into the cavity. Inside was truly the most magnificent chess set he had ever seen. All of the painted pieces were intricately carved medieval Kings, Queens, Knights, Castles and foot soldier pawns. Lunt looked wistfully at the board and remembered that just a very long month ago he had been a prisoner of war in Wales, playing chess with patches of cloth cut out from strips of wool blankets. His board then was constructed from stone scratches he and the other prisoners had made in the prison floor.

Lunt placed the white chargers on the second tile from the corner and gestured for the boy to return the other piece he had taken. The boy gasped when a voice spoke out sharply shattering the morning quiet.

'John Quincy, you have been told repeatedly...'

'Yes, father, I was just showing them to...'

Henry winked at the boy and turned to meet John Quincy's father.

'I am Lieutenant Lunt, sir. I came in late last night with Dr. Franklin. At my request, the boy was showing me the chess pieces. I enjoy the game a great deal.'

'I'm pleased to meet you, Lieutenant. I am Ambassador Adams.'

Lunt stood erect, not daring to extend his hand first.

"You are, I presume, from the Spy?" Adams asked enthusiastically. His round face became instantly more reserved when he heard Lunt's reply.

"No, sir, I have most recently served on the Ranger."

Adams face continued to sour, "You're not the Lieutenant that Captain Jones is trying to court martial..."

Adams speech was interrupted by a calm, resonant voice from above on the staircase. "Ah, early to rise makes a man healthy, wealthy, and wise."

Adams and Lunt turned from their conversation to look up the stairway at a smiling Dr. Franklin, who continued, "Of course, I did manage to leave out the first part of that adage, since neither Lieutenant Lunt, nor I were particularly early to bed. Forgive me for interrupting you both, but I did not wish to miss any portion of Lieutenant Lunt's harrowing adventures this morning. I enjoy hearing about the exploits of our men in arms. Ah, I see that Madame Le Roux is up preparing a bountiful breakfast in the kitchen. I can smell her muffins." Franklin ambled past them, limping slightly, shouting in French. The only word that Lunt recognized was "*pasterie.*"

Adams motioned for Lunt to follow Franklin to breakfast. The boy, John Quincy, grabbed Lunt's hand and skipped beside him, leading him.

As they ate, they were joined at the breakfast

table by several others on the staff, including a Nathaniel Hubbard, and a Mr. Jeremiah Hanson. A breakfast of large brown, hard boiled eggs, cheese, ham, and warm croissants was passed around the table. Initially the conversation centered upon the progress of young John Quincy's French lessons. Madame Le Roux and another helper, a shy young girl of fifteen, remained near the table to attend to their needs.

Lunt was not asked anything about his reason for being there until after breakfast was completed, and then, upon Dr. Franklin's urging, he began to tell of his rescue from a Welsh prison by Captain Jones, of his subsequent involvement in the capture of H.M.S. Drake.

Halfway through the story Lunt could see that he was losing the attention of Mr. Adams, who looked politely down at his hands. However, Franklin and the boy, John Quincy, and the others at the table were eager listeners.

After Lunt finished, Adams patted his mouth with a cloth napkin and looked up at him with deliberateness, "An incredible story, most incredible. Tell us again how you happened to leave the Ranger, the second time."

"It was on account of a seaman..." Lunt looked to Franklin who gave him a nearly imperceptible movement of the head from side to the side, "...an Irishman, who was severely wounded in the battle. At my urging, Captain Jones let me bring him ashore.

We happened by chance to be passing only a few miles from his home.'

'Most unusual that Captain Jones should halt a ship being pursued by the enemy, and to subsequently endanger that ship, and the lives of all aboard it just to get one man off,' observed Adams.

'No, sir, it was not that way. Captain Jones had to turn around to retrace his route in order to find the prize ship, H.M.S. Drake, again. Lt. Simpson had not kept up with us. We were then halfway down the west coast of Ireland. I did not return to the rendezvous in time. I missed the Ranger. It was not Captain Jones at fault, but myself.'

After several of the staff had excused themselves from the breakfast table, Adams inquired discretely, 'Are you aware of any friction between Captain Jones and Lieutenant Simpson?'

'Yes, sir, I was, but both of them treated me fairly while I was aboard the Ranger,' stated Lunt, feeling like he was being cross examined at a trial.

'Are you aware that Captain Jones has brought court martial proceedings against Lieutenant Simpson?'

'Only when you mentioned it earlier in the salon,' replied Lunt. who then adopted the sober expression of Adams.

Adams continued. 'Well, it's a fiasco. Certainly not the kind of display that the Continental Navy should be putting forth in front of the French Navy, and most especially while we are eagerly awaiting a courier message which is supposed to be delivered by the sloop, Spy, indicating that the Congress has finally ratified the treaty that King Louis signed over four months ago. Until we get official word of its ratification, everything is on hold here, and any embarrassing incidents like this play right into the hands of our enemies."

Adams looked Lunt sternly in the eye, "I must ask you about one other item, Mr. Lunt. How did you obtain the title of Lieutenant?"

"John, really!" Franklin interjected.

Ambassador Adams held up his hand for Franklin not to interrupt. His stern round face and eyes examined Lunt's visage as he responded. "Captain Jones promoted me immediately after the rescue from Wales. I had previously served with him, both in the Caribbean and on both sides of the Atlantic."

Adams reflected openly, "Possibly what Captain Jones was trying to do was to get another ally in the officer corps who would stand with him against Lt. Simpson."

Lunt balled up his table napkin in his fist and stood halfway up responding forcefully, "No, sir, that is not true. While I was aboard the Ranger, I was never ever asked to take a position against Lt. Simpson. If you knew Captain Jones as I do, you would know that he fears no one and is quite capable of acting alone when he believes he is in the right..."

"Gentleman, we are on the same side, are we not?" interjected Franklin. "Please."

Both Mr. Hubbard and Mr. Hanson quietly

excused themselves and left the table. Adams watched them depart and swallowed hard, shifting in his seat to face Lunt, "Your father is Matthew Lunt?"

"Yes, Sir," said Henry, softly, not knowing what to expect.

"I have a letter for you, from your Father. I brought it over with me last month, along with those of many other Massachusetts sailors. Unfortunately, they are all stored at the offices of the former Ambassador, Silas Deane. I am going there now. Tonight, I will bring that letter back and any others that may have come for you during your internment.

"Mr. Deane left a tangled mess of paperwork when he departed for America last month. One of the reasons that we cannot get Captain Jones out of his current predicament and get him some money to feed his crew and the British prisoners is that our third Ambassador, Arthur Lee, will not sign anything until I get the paperwork of Mr. Deane back in order. Apparently a lot of debts were incurred for war supplies already shipped to the United States, but there are few coherent records. It is an ugly task, which sours my disposition. I'm sorry, Mr. Lunt."

Lunt nodded, and rose in his seat as the Ambassador got up to leave. Adams walked away, until Franklin called after him, "John, then you will not accompany me to Versailles today?"

"No, Benjamin. Really, I have been there with you every Tuesday for four weeks, I do not speak their language. I am ever fearful of making the wrong gesture as I stand there for hours as people speak a torrent of words about me that I do not understand."

"You need to try and speak their language, John. They understand that you are not fluent, but they want to talk to you, to try and understand the country that they are going to go to war for."

Adams responded, "I cannot waste time being just an ineffective observer. If I do not resolve these issues with the merchants of Nantes, Brest, and Paris, then American liberty may be lost because the French merchants will be angry that we have not settled their accounts. There will be riots. It has already begun. We honestly owe a good many people money. It is my unfortunate lot to have to straighten out a mess left by another man. But if I succeed in doing so, supply shipments to American can begin again in earnest.

"One other item," continued Adams, bending over the table towards Lunt, "I serve on the marine committee of the Continental Congress. Up to the time I left less than two months ago, your name, Mr. Lunt, has never been put on the waiting list for promotion to Lieutenant."

Both Franklin and Lunt started to speak up, but Adams held up his hand, "We all know that Captain Jones is very unorthodox, and I can understand his possible need for an additional officer on the Ranger during a time of eminent battle, but absolutely no papers have ever been passed on to me. You will thus refrain, Mr. Lunt, from using the title of Lieutenant until I have had an opportunity to speak to Captain Jones about his motives for this promotion. I know that I may seem unduly harsh to a young man who has apparently served his country in good stead, but many hundreds of others have served faithfully as well, and have been waiting patiently in line for their promotions for a very long time. Each case has to be treated according to its merits. There are established procedures which must be followed.'

'Surely, John, you can overlook...,' said Franklin.

Adams abruptly turned away and left the dining room. His young son trailed after him with shoulders slouched.

Henry felt like he had just been shot.

*   *   *   *   *

After an hour, there was a knock on Lunt's door. 'Come in.'

'Mr Adams has departed. My secretary, Dr. Bancroft, left for Brest very early this morning to try to do something to help out the crew of the Ranger. Arthur Lee doesn't like me. The gardener just trimmed my prize roses too short. The draft from a window left open by the chambermaid has scattered Voltaire's manuscript all over the upstairs hallway. My shoes are too tight, one of the buckles is loose. It may rain today...'

Lunt looked up to the warm smile of Dr. Franklin.

'Henry, I wish you would accompany me to

Versailles or else I am going to feel bad all day. Besides, you have something important to tell me.'

Lunt nodded.

'Here are some dress clothes and a gentleman's wig, which I have just secured from Monsieur de Chaumont's household. You said you have a sword in your canvas bag. Bring it. There is a gentlemen's leather sash with the clothing. It might interest you to know that at Versailles, it is required that all gentlemen wear a sword, except of course, certain unorthodox Quaker ambassadors. I will be downstairs at the carriage in a quarter hour. I cannot be late for my weekly audience with the King.'

*   *   *   *   *

The small two seater rig had drummed along for a full five minutes before Franklin asked him, 'How is O'Mally? Will he live?'

'I don't know, sir. His leg was amputated below the knee. His back was all twisted and burned from the cannon that he fell upon during the battle with the Drake. Once I landed in Ireland with O'Mally I found I had a choice between either keeping my rendezvous with the Ranger at the designated hour or bringing my friend all the way home directly to his mother. I had to do what my heart told me. I have sailed with Sean O'Mally on three ships. I couldn't just leave him on a nearly deserted island with a few fishermen that I did not know.

"Later, when we were at his mother's cottage, when his delirium cleared, he began to tell me about the espionage, about Poor Richards Almanac and the code it bore for each vital member of the revolution here in Europe. O'Mally told me he was your keeper of codes, assigning page numbers for particular people to communicate without endangering each other. And that he was, by your authority, the only other person, besides yourself, who knew which page numbers of Poor Richards Almanac were assigned to each person."

Franklin kept his eye on the road ahead. "O'Mally performed vital tasks that had to be done for our cause. These were tasks that I personally dislike participating in because of my spiritual beliefs. But Sean O'Mally performed them admirably. From the outset he began to go far beyond his original charter and to organize certain clandestine activities."

Franklin reminisced, "I first met O'Mally seven or eight years ago in London, while I still represented the interests of several of the American colonies. One night I was in a tavern meeting with some merchants, and I happened to stay too long. Some ruffians tried to assault me as I left the tavern and Sean O'Mally saved my very life. A few years later he had gotten into some difficulties with the English authorities because of his United Irishmen connections. There was a warrant out for his apprehension. It would have meant his certain death to be captured. So I returned the favor and arranged passage for him to come to Massachusetts Bay under an assumed name."

'It was aboard my father's ship,' said Lunt.

Franklin nodded, 'A little over a year ago, I came to France in my present capacity. I happened upon O'Mally in Nantes and asked him to accompany me to the Hotel de Hamburg, my first residence on rue de l'Universite in Paris. I needed someone to take on the much needed work of espionage. Under my predecessor, Silas Deane, there just seemed to be none. The British Ambassador, Lord Stormont and his cronies did everything from loosen the axles on my carriage to spreading the most preposterous lies imaginable through the court of Versailles. But I endured.

'O'Mally had contacts in England, mostly working class people, but people in key positions who could be trained to observe a great deal. The beauty of what he invented with Poor Richards Almanac was a system of communication where no one knew the other. It was thus impossible for a person on the outskirts of our cause to give away a confidence. The unfortunate arsonist, George Aitken was O'Mally's. No matter what they did to him before they hung him, he did not know anything but the page number of the man he took directions from. He had met O'Mally once casually at rue de l'Universite, but never knew he was our organizer of spies.

'One of O'Mally's pages is an Irish woman who cleans Admiralty House in the evenings. The English aristocracy never perform manual labor themselves, that is one of their great vulnerabilities. Their servants often despise them.'

Lunt nodded, 'Hence we discovered that the Royal Navy had a new cannon and where they were working on it.'

Franklin leaned closer to him, 'It was not two months ago that I ordered O'Mally not to go on that voyage with the Ranger. It was too dangerous. He knew too much. But he went regardless. I do not know why, except perhaps his obsession with stealing the British gun.'

Franklin paused, 'Who does he believe the British spies are within my delegation? And is it Passy or possibly those among Mr Lee's service? We have separate offices you know.'

Lunt drew a breath, 'O'Mally said to watch out for Silas Deane and at least one other spy in your office. Because of his injury, O'Mally has not been able to get back to his contact for clarification. But past information from this contact has been very reliable.'

As the carriage passed from a forest road to a large sunlit wheat field, Franklin deliberated only a short while, 'No. I don't believe all of this. Entirely on his own, Mr. Deane did too much for the American cause early in his tenure. He sent ship after ship to America filled with munitions, gunpowder, uniforms, right up through last fall. I do believe that Mr. Deane made a lot of impossible promises that he couldn't keep, and from which Mr. Adams suffers today, but I do not believe that he conspired with the British.

Did O'Mally indicate why he suspected Deane?"

Lunt answered, "O'Mally, himself, had been watching Deane's office in Paris all during February. One night he saw someone go behind the office and then come out only a few moments later. O'Mally sensed a message had been dropped. He searched and found a note shoved under the window sash from the outside. The sender apparently thought he had a secure drop and so the message was not coded. Incidentally, the first one at the office that morning was Silas Deane, himself. O'Mally suspects that he was possibly there to retrieve the message before any one else arrived."

"Go on!" said Franklin.

"From the note, O'Mally was able to determine that two crew members on the Ranger had been planted. Their names were David Freeman and Hezekiah Ford. O'Mally hastily went to Nantes where Captain Jones was within a day of departing on his voyage. O'Mally got a look at the crew listing, but no such crew members were shown as actually having been enlisted to sail with the Ranger. O'Mally suspected that two members of the crew had assumed false identities. He did not want to tell Captain Jones or there might be a witch hunt among Lt. Simpson's men from Portsmouth. He was fearful that Jones might confuse loyalty for Simpson, the original Captain of the Ranger, with actual espionage. So on the night before the Ranger was due to depart, O'Mally signed on. He told me to tell you that he had no choice at that point but to disobey your orders.'

'And O'Mally was right, two of Jones' crew were spies,' concluded Franklin. 'Fascinating, go on.'

'O'Mally also wanted to get the carronade very badly, but he did not have the information yet as to its location. He knew the Ranger would be up into the British Isles. He dispatched one of his agents to London to eventually deliver information about the weapon's whereabouts to a farmhouse in Wales. Through a recent escapee from the Plymouth prison, O'Mally also knew that there were American naval prisoners on a work project near that Welsh farmhouse. By selecting the farmhouse as the rendezvous point for the Ranger there were two advantages. First, he gave his agents a couple of more weeks to pinpoint the location of the carronade research and second, to rescue some American seamen. Before the Ranger departed, he sent Jones a coded message to eventually go to that location in Wales. He knew that by that time Captain Jones might need more crew. It was a perfect plan. As he was aboard ship, at any time he could use his own copy of the Almanac to reveal his true identity to Jones as the Spymaster.'

Lunt continued, 'The plan was operating smoothly until I was selected, I should say, I was volunteered by Captain Jones to go into Belfast, and David Smith, who we now know was really David Freeman, a British spy, was so eager to get off the Ranger, that he volunteered to go with me. It was then that O'Mally knew he had to leave the ship. If I were to go into

Belfast alone, he could lose both me and the opportunity to capture the Carronade. He had no proof, only suspicion, that David Smith might be the spy so he decided to chance leaving him untouched, not knowing that Captain Jones was planning to go storming into Whitehaven to burn the harbour the following evening and would take Smith with him as part of that expedition.'

'So, the Freeman-Smith chap was the traitor who went about Whitehaven during Captain Jones' landing and yelled and pounded on people's doors to alert them to the American raid on their harbour?' asked Franklin.

'Yes, and he was probably the one who let the anchor line loose twice almost destroying the mission, either he or Hezekiah Ford, whomever he may turn out to be. You said the crew of the Ranger is still at Brest.'

Franklin sighed, 'Yes, virtually quarantined. No one is permitted to leave the Ranger. Of course, by this time Dr. Bancroft, my secretary, may have already found some solution to all of the Ranger's difficulties. Although I feel that it is unlikely that we will ever be able to find out who Hezekiah Ford is, nevertheless, from Versailles, I will post a courier directly to Captain Jones to alert him about Hezekiah Ford before the quarantined crew is allowed to leave the Ranger.

'Now,' continued Franklin, 'Tell me, why did O'Mally want to leave the Ranger after he was wounded?'

Lunt replied, "I asked him that many times in our days together at Galway. In order to amputate his leg, they got him roaring drunk. He was delirious for days and in terrible pain. In his delirium, he believed that he had seen a Banshee while he was in Ireland with me and that it was fated that he was going to die. He was not especially lucid when I first took him off the Ranger. It was only later that he proceeded to tell me all of this in fits and starts. He said that he was just plain tired and selfish, and was afraid if he tried to tell Captain Jones all of this story, that he would be taken back to France, never to see Ireland again. He wanted to be with his mother, if he was going to die."

As they began to pass through a small village, a young French peasant girl recognized Franklin and began to shout for others to come and see the great man. People came outside their shops and began to scream, *Le grand Franklin.* Franklin smiled at them and waved his hand. In front of one house, a woman rushed inside and reappeared with a placard bearing Franklin's silhouette.

Franklin asked Lunt to slow down the open carriage so that he could converse in French with the people who ran alongside. Eventually the crowd of people began to fall behind and the two of them were alone again. Lunt, in that moment began to truly appreciate the great popularity which Franklin had achieved among the French people. He felt very humble to sit beside the great man.

There was silence for a few long minutes as the carriage trotted along. Finally, Franklin commented, 'I suppose that it could be someone in Silas Deane's office that the message was left for, there are still several of his old clerks working there. I must say I was surprised to find that Ambassador Deane's paperwork was as much in disarray as Mr. Adams and Mr. Lee have reported. Had I known this, I would never have let Mr. Deane return to America, when Mr. Adams came to relieve him just last month.'

Franklin continued, 'Perhaps someone has thrown some false information into Mr. Deane's papers. You know, destroyed the real bills of laden, and substituted false paperwork with the names of merchants that either don't exist or are British sympathizers. Their purpose being to dry up our resources by satisfying bogus accounts. That would be not unlike what Lord Stormont's cronies did to me when I first arrived in Paris. I'll talk it over with Mr. Adams, we'll compare some papers I have in my office with what is showing up in his search. We might be able to detect a pattern in this. Now you have also stated that I have a British spy at Passy?'

'Yes, one of O'Mally's other operatives cleans an office building at Whitehall. There was a dispatch in French, which the sweeper could not read. He had only a moment to glance through the papers, but the cover note was from Lord Stormont, himself, in English. It said that enclosed was the weekly report from their agent at Passy. That's the only information O'Mally had. But he wanted me to tell you to be careful.'

'Oh, dear!' said Franklin.

There silence for a few minutes, then Franklin spoke after a period of obvious reflection, 'You know, young man, you personally could be in very great danger.'

'Sir?' responded Lunt, surprised.

'From what you have told me, you are certainty one person which the British sympathizers at Versailles may be able to identify as having gone into Belfast. They know that you were trying to get their secret cannon. It may be that they could come to believe that you are the Spymaster. I would not be surprised to find that the British soon have a marker out on you. Please be very careful, stay close to me today at Versailles.'

'Why wouldn't they also harm you, sir, the American Ambassador? I was surprised to learn that you often travel unescorted to Versailles and other places. Isn't it dangerous for you? Don't you believe you should always have an armed escort?'

'If you had the opportunity, would you really kill George III, supposing you could?'

Lunt thought for a moment, 'No, I might like to kidnap him for a week or two and teach him a lesson, but no, I wouldn't simply kill him.'

'Why?' inquired Franklin.

'The British people would be furious if we killed their King. Everyone now sympathetic to our cause in the Parliament would immediately turn against us. It would become a rallying cry throughout Britain.

Lord North's Tories would capitalize on the situation. America might surely lose the war.'

'And if they killed Franklin?' asked Franklin.

'It would put all of French sympathy on our side. The British would certainly have a united enemy against them.'

'So you see it as I do, though Mr. Adams does not agree. There is at least some protection for me in being famous. But if the British suspect that you either know something that you shouldn't or have information which would be valuable to them, then it is not inconceivable that they could try and capture you, young man.'

'I shall be attentive, sir,' replied Lunt.

* * * * *

They traveled through a forest and then out into an open meadow atop a small hill. Before him, Lunt beheld the grandest complex of buildings and grounds he had ever seen. A high, massive, arched wrought iron gate and fence with a marble base stretched out for several hundred feet to either side of the entrance. Extending outward a great distance on either side from the gate structure was a solid marble wall which eventually connected to the side of a building. Beyond the gate Lunt could see massive inner and outer courtyards. The courtyards were bounded by a symmetrical series of long stone buildings, each about four stories high, with windows protruding on the highest floor through a mansard roof. A myriad of gardens and reflecting pools were dispersed among the inner and outer yards. A series of connecting thoroughfares transported hundreds of people in carriages and on foot strolling among the various points of interest. Here and there fountains and statues commanded the attention of a crowd of people.

Franklin pointed towards the scene before them. "There are twenty thousand people who live in and around Versailles. It is a city in itself. Everyone of importance in France must either be here or have a representative here. Because there are so many people, they must be fed and clothed, so in places the Palace has the appearance of a bazaar. You can buy anything you can imagine in Versailles," warned Franklin. "All gentlemen, and the word is used very loosely as that can also mean gangs of fifteen year old boys, are all roaming around the palace with swords at the ready. They are anxious to engage in a duel to prove their manhood. The duels are so commonplace here that there is no particular urgency for the authorities to stop them. Ambassadors and dignitaries are spared, because we receive an armed escort to and from the salons of the Government. But the outer, less traveled corridors and walkways are to be avoided, Henry. I will attempt to get you into the salon of the Foreign Minister, the Comte de Vergennes, before I meet with the King. There are several people I wish you to meet there."

"Whatever you think best, sir," said Lunt matter

of factly as he continued to stare in astonishment at the facade built by the Sun King, the current King's grandfather.

Six mounted riders approached, their horses in a lope. Their uniforms were sparkling white with luxuriant gold trim and a sash of gold supporting their swords. Franklin ordered Lunt to pull the horses to a halt.

"Bonjour, Ambassador Franklin - may we escort you to the east gate?"

Franklin said something in French that drew a smile from the officer, who then waved his hand with two fingers extended. It took nearly a quarter hour, at a fast moving pace, for the entourage to arrive at the east portal. During that time they traveled through immense gardens of every color of flowering plant imaginable. Here and there exquisite fountains sustained the feeling of opulence and majesty.

When they finally arrived at the portal, Franklin descended to shake hands with a small throng of well wishers chanting, *Viva, Franklin.* The guards opened the entrance gate to the inner courtyard and Franklin and his party entered. Just inside the inner gate's entrance was a small group of Franciscans with hooded robes who also waved to Franklin. Within the walls of the inner gate, only two escorting riders remained with them, as Lunt drove the carriage across a huge parade ground until he could proceed no further because of the many merchant carts lined up this way and that.

Together, Franklin and Lunt proceeded on foot towards one of the many building entrances. But after only a few steps a small dark man with a wide smile stepped in front of their path. Lunt heard him greet the Ambassador by name, but the remainder of their conversation in French was difficult for him to understand. The Ambassador clearly said "No!" a couple of times and attempted to walk past the man, who clung to the front of his black coat. The man dogged the Ambassador for a few more steps, pointing to Franklin's leg and speaking rapidly at him until Lunt felt obliged to grab the man by the scruff of the neck and firmly push him off.

"Thank you," said Franklin, "Every time he wishes me to take his sedan into the palace. This time he was insistent because he had spotted from my step that I have the gout."

"Is it a long way, sir? Perhaps you should?" said Lunt.

"I do no think it suits my image. Can you imagine me in this plain black cloth being carried about the palace like a sultan in an elaborately gilded seat by four African gentlemen with red fezzes. It would be a sight. No, I think I will find it within me to walk. Besides, this is your first time at Versailles. I will enjoy the expressions on your face as you view the palace for the first time," said Franklin.

Lunt followed the Ambassador by approximately two paces and passed through the portal, on either side of which were French gate guards who stood at attention. Behind one guard, a young man lay prostrate in the sun, his face covered with a cloth, his trunk bloody.

Franklin motioned for Lunt to walk beside him, "Behold the work of the duelists."

Lunt nodded.

Inside the main hall of the building, Lunt found himself walking through a kind of bazaar, with every conceivable type of merchandise on sale; melons, apples, fish, cloth, plateware. Lunt never imagined that a royal palace would be populated by the variety of people he observed. There were ornately dressed Noblesse with powdered wigs, beautiful ladies, more Franciscans, entertainers, and many merchants in colorful jackets. The bazaar continued for the equivalent of several city blocks. Once Franklin stopped to look at an enormous clock, on its face was a map of the entire world. Small cylinders indicated the month.

"What contraptions will they think of next?" observed Franklin. "Surely anyone capable of affording a clock such as this would know what month it was." One of the merchants then recognized Franklin and began calling out his name. An artist, who had been painting a sketch of a gentleman, knocked over his easel as he hurried towards the Ambassador pleading to do his portrait. Franklin put his hand firmly up and continued along smiling to everyone, making short comments in French, always trying to move forward through the crush of people. Lunt caught sight of a cobbler's booth which had on display dozens of different shoes and boots. If he had time later, perhaps, he could try on some of the man's wares.

Franklin was beginning to be crushed by the well wishers, and so Lunt stepped forward again to clear a path. The pressing crowd ignored him until he began to shout out in English, "Please, make way for the Ambassador."

The New England accent startled the crowd. Franklin picked up on the crowd's instant anger and explained in French, "American Marine, my escort. Please excuse me, I have an audience with His Majesty. You are all very charming, but I cannot be late. I will return later in the day."

The crowd parted, including some Franciscans who apparently had entered the portal door at the same time as Lunt and Franklin. Lunt realized again that it was potentially dangerous for Dr. Franklin to be passing among so many people without protection. He tried his best to shield the Ambassador until they reached a corridor that was less crowded.

"Sir, you should have more protection when your come to public places such as this."

"Yes, Mr. Adams has said so. But as I have told you, I don't believe that Lord Stormont would do anything to harm me physically. It would do enormous damage to their cause. Besides who would they have to negotiate with when all of the killing and savagery is done with? I think they would prefer it to be myself. They know I understand them."

There was a few moments of silence and then Franklin spoke again, "I couldn't help notice that you were looking at those shoes longingly."

"Yes, Mr. Ambassador, I have had these French boots with the narrow tips since Captain Jones rescued me. They are most uncomfortable, and now very worn," responded Lunt.

"You will pay too much here. At Passy I know a country cobbler. If we let him measure your foot, within a few days he will fashion you a most satisfactory replacement. When we get back to Passy this evening I can loan you a pair like this for a few days."

Lunt glanced down at the Ambassadors' black shoes with dull silver buckles, high heels and rather chubby square toes. They looked comfortable, but not a fashion normally worn by a young man.

As they strode together down a long corridor, Lunt turned around and could see a few people walking along in their direction, including the group of Franciscans. He observed one of the priests give a passerby a blessing. Ahead a few youths were standing in the corridor talking excitedly, their hands all playing with their sword hilts. Beautiful tapestries with splendid pastoral and occasional battle scenes adorned the walls.

"We will go first to the primary salon of the Comte de Vergennes," informed Franklin. "You are no doubt hungry?"

Henry nodded.

"There is a wonderful selection of foods at this

salon. I am very partial to the pasterie with raspberry filling. Should you observe some of them and I am busy greeting people, I would be very grateful if you could retrieve a couple, which I could eat later."

Lunt nodded with a smile.

Franklin continued, "The system of salons is uniquely French. We are invited to the Comte de Vergennes salon prior to our audience with the King. As we stroll about the room many persons in his staff and his guests will attempt to engage us in conversations. Some of these people may have been invited solely to influence or to meet just us this day." The Ambassador raised an instructive finger, "In each of these preliminary conversations, these people will try and find out what it is we are going to say to the King today, or what our opinions are about certain issues. Then they will communicate this to the Comte or his associates. It is all done in a very pleasant, festive atmosphere, while we stroll around and look at the latest art acquisitions or enjoy a musician playing the harp, but we must be continually mindful of what is said."

"You forget, sir, I speak no French, I cannot possibly disclose anything. They would not understand me."

"No, Henry, you are mistaken. The French have a unique attitude regarding their language. It is almost a national ploy that they cannot speak English, but most of the nobility have been to England many times during the past decade of peace. They usually speak and understand some English, but will not let on that they do. Almost to the point of absurdity they will not divulge their little secret. But by their pretended ignorance, they can sometimes learn a great deal about your sincerity and what you think of them. Mr. Arthur Lee, our co-Ambassador, has a very disagreeable habit of talking to himself under his breath, in English. He has made a lot of enemies here because of this mannerism.

"In your case, Henry, I expect they will be very tolerant. I have sent word that a young Lieutenant from the Ranger will accompany me today."

"But, sir, Mr. Adams said..."

"Today, young man, you accompany the only Ambassador that has proven he can deal with the French court. Today, I need you here because you will serve as a certain distraction since we have not yet heard from Congress. I could not get Captain Jones here, because of some difficulty he is having with the French fleet. You will function in his stead. Naturally, omit from your conversation any of the matters we discussed while coming here. If you simply tell of the capture of H.M.S. Drake, just as you did at breakfast, it will be the sensation of the French court this day."

Now, immediately before them was a door guarded by a group of six soldiers in brilliant plumage with large pikes in their grasp. They were dressed in uniforms of a century before, from the days of the Sun King and his musketeers. Milling about in front of the door itself was a collection of well dressed merchants and other influence peddlers, all trying to get past the guards. Several beautiful, heavily painted young ladies also flirted with the guards. A handsome cavalier with a large feathered hat and a charming smile saw Ambassador Franklin approaching. He bowed to acknowledge Franklin, his broad hat, fashionable in another time, was doffed with a flourish. They exchanged pleasantries in French and after a minute or so Franklin said in English.

"Lieutenant Lunt, may I present Captain Gerard of the King's Musketeers."

Lunt saluted. Smiling, the handsome Captain touched his hat.

"They are ready for us now," whispered Franklin.

As the Ambassador and Lunt entered the salon, they immediately found themselves walking beneath the crossed pikes of nearly thirty musketeers. Lunt could hear someone with a booming voice announcing Ambassador Franklin and to his surprise he heard his own name announced in connection with the Ranger. As soon as they entered the large anteroom over a hundred people crowded round the Ambassador, all eagerly wishing to exchange pleasantries with him. As Lunt watched, Franklin seemed to transform into an actor, gesturing here and there and embracing people as if he knew them all intimately. His plain black suit with contrasting white shirt and stockings looked conspicuously unstylish amid the powdered wigs and vivid costumes of purple, canary yellow, and emerald. Many of the men's faces were elaborately made up, their eyebrows seemingly painted on. On two occasions one of these painted men came over to Lunt and hugged him and enthusiastically shook his hand. Lunt did his best to be polite, but felt extremely awkward.

Lunt began to survey the room beyond the immediate throng of people who were surrounding the Ambassador. On the far side of the room were scrumptious tables of food, with meat carvers waiting to serve anyone who asked. Red wine was being served by waiters in pinkish costumes and very abbreviated powdered wigs. At the extreme opposite end of the room Lunt observed several groups of more refined people who seemed to huddle together in small groups. He scrutinized them one by one until he saw her.

Their eyes found each other across two hundred feet of room. She had been standing with two older men and then suddenly left them both in mid conversation and proceeded to walk hurriedly across the room towards Lunt. Her own hair was set in an exquisite twirl of two pie shaped mounds, one atop the other, her decolletage revealed her amble bosom, pressing tight against the gold and silver bare shouldered dress. She picked up her full gold skirts so that she could move faster. Lunt just stood there staring until she was before him. Her arms immediately surrounded his plain brown suit. She hugged him genuinely as Lunt stood stiff, very aware of the press of her body.

"Henry, I really did not know you would be here, until I heard the announcement," she whispered to him. Her hand lightly touching the nape of his neck. Henry tingled all over. He hugged her back gently.

"I was so angry at Captain Jones for not waiting for you."

"I had to get my friend home. It was my decision. It was not the Captain's fault."

"How is your friend?"

"I believe he'll live. I left him in the charge of his mother and then escaped south to Wexford where I found a boat I could sail here."

"You sailed back all by yourself from Wexford?"

Henry nodded.

Marie looked down at her feet. "I remember sailing with you in Belfast harbour. It's always exciting to sail with you, Henry."

Their eyes met briefly and there was electricity which would have made Franklin's kite crackle without being sent aloft. There was a pervasive silence around the room, and Lunt and Marie looked up to find themselves the focal point of the salon's occupants. Marie quickly took his hand and spun him around. "There is someone I want you to meet." She started to tug him towards the far end of the Salon.

Lunt resisted, "I am here to accompany Ambassador Franklin. I cannot just leave him."

Marie looked over towards Franklin who was still surrounded by well wishers. "He is occupied. This will take only a few moments. We will not have to leave the room. Please, the situation is embarrassing for me now, everyone is looking at us. I have to have had some purpose in rushing over to meet you. I was so relieved to see you, well, I could not control myself."

Obediently, Henry followed her.

Marie spoke in French urgently to one of the men that she had been standing with when Lunt arrived. Within a few moments a small man with closely curled hair came out of an inner salon. He bowed slightly to Henry and then extended his hand with a smile.

"I am the Comte de Vergennes. I have heard much about you from Madame Chatelain. You were very brave. It was unfortunate that our espionage efforts were not coordinated. Had they been, we might now both have the benefit of the gun. I understand that Captain Jones did not capture it when he seized the English ship."

Lunt was very aware that the gentleman was nearly the most important person in France. The man had shrewdly let his sentence drop off so that Lunt was compelled to give some sort of answer. Quickly, Lunt glanced over his shoulder towards Ambassador Franklin, who was still surrounded by well wishers. Lunt stammered a moment and then, looking directly into Vergennes eyes, replied, "Sir, I have been in Paris only one evening. I have no authority to discuss such matters."

Vergennes' face was devoid of emotion, studying

him. Lunt felt compelled to say something further, "I don't wish to be rude to our friends. I just cannot..."

"It is the answer I expected of you, Lieutenant Lunt. I will discuss the matter with Monsieur Franklin. Oh, they are signalling us now." Vergennes motioned for one of his companions to get Ambassador Franklin away from his admirers.

"Pardon us, Lieutenant, but it is time for the Ambassador and I to see the King." Vergennes nodded a goodbye and then stepped away.

Franklin and Lunt exchanged a brief glance at each other as the Ambassador was whisked through an exit over which hung a large tapestry. Lunt was left standing alone with Marie.

"Well, you engineered that situation well. I see nothing has changed since Belfast. Do you still carry knives in your bustle?" quipped Lunt.

Marie looked up into his eyes, "Honestly, Henry, I had no idea Vergennes was going to try and pry information from you about the gun. I was as embarrassed as you. I don't think he actually expected a reply from you. He was just testing your mettle." She changed the subject, "Are you aware of the difficulties of the Ranger?"

"I have heard of some of them," replied Lunt. "But, I have not been back aboard."

"So, you had responsibilities other than to get back to your Captain Jones immediately." Marie smiled at him. "Are you the Spymaster after all, Lieutenant Lunt?" There was a twinkle in her eye.

Henry's cheeks turned scarlet. Irritated, he looked about the room for an excuse to leave her presence.

Marie lay her hand on his arm, 'Perhaps you are hungry after such a long journey to get here. The salon's food is always superb.' She slipped her hand round his arm and led him towards a counter where a carver trimmed bits of meat from a lamb on a vertical spit. Marie kept on, 'Of course, he doesn't carve meat as well as you, but would you care for a little anyway?'

Marie nodded for Lunt to take a plate from a waiter. Suddenly there was an interruption as an announcement was made. There was a great deal of applause and several musicians entered the salon in a row following each other in a sort of parade. Somewhere a drum rolled. There were both string and horned instruments many of which Lunt had never seen before. All of the orchestra wore highly powdered blue white wigs. There was another announcement and the orchestra began to play. Lunt stepped back as some of the participants formed two rows to dance. For a few moments Marie and Henry stood awkwardly in silence admiring the splendor of the costumes and the quality of the music.

A gentleman with a painted face approached Marie and bowed to her. They exchanged pleasantries and Marie held out her hand to Lunt, 'We must dance now, I have declined the Marquis on the pretext that we were about to begin.'

'I cannot dance, not that,' Lunt protested.

"If you do not, America may lose a valuable friend in the French court," whispered Marie. Just in front of them, the Frenchman had curtsied politely to allow the couple to take the floor in his presence. Lunt had no choice. He could feel the hint of perspiration forming on his forehead. He drew a deep breath and then proceeded onto the floor led by Marie.

She smiled and laughed at his inexperience. "Would you prefer this were a sword fight?" Marie squeezed his hand.

"Almost," murmured Lunt, dead serious, now more conscious than ever of his tight toed boots. Perhaps he would take Dr. Franklin up on his offer and try the buckles for a few days.

"Just follow me," she whispered as they began to parade following other couples around the floor in a great circle that extended under all the glistening chandeliers. They made two passes around the floor and there was gaiety in the air. For awhile, Lunt began to relax, until Marie whispered, "In a moment, we will split into two rows. Men to the left, ladies to the right. Just mimic what the other men do."

Lunt's heart began to pound again.

The time came and Henry found himself in the center of a line of noblemen facing the ladies several feet away. The music was dominated now by violins. Lunt was very aware that he was dancing with the most beautiful lady in the great hall. Her figure and face were perfection. He saw other men to the left and right of him stealing glances at her. Lunt moved awkwardly through a series of steps which involved curtsies, quick swapping of partners, and delicate pauses. The music seemed to help him place his steps. He looked at her admiringly.

The files of dancers came together again and Lunt closed with Marie and again they began a promenade around the salon. She squeezed his hand and he squeezed back. Suddenly, a worried messenger appeared at their side jabbering something to Marie in rapid French. Lunt recognized only the word, *Pardon.* Soon they had extracted themselves from the floor and moved to the rim of the great parade of dancers.

Marie spoke with the messenger a few more sentences before she turned to him. "Henry, you will wait for me here, please, my duties require me to be in the other salon immediately." Without waiting for his response, she followed the messenger at a brisk pace through the entryway into the inner salon.

Lunt was alone. For a few moments, he watched the other dancers and then turned towards the pastry table to search for the raspberry tart that Dr. Franklin had mentioned he craved. But he was unable to determine which of the many pastries was the one he wanted. He decided to reach for one, when suddenly he heard a French, "No."

A red breeched waiter bustled by him indignantly with a set of silver tongs, apparently Lunt was not supposed to select the food himself. The waiter made an elaborate gesture and then handed Lunt the portion of pastry he seemed to have been reaching for. Lunt smiled as he accepted the piece. The filling was tart to the taste and yellow in color. He said, "Raspberry," but the waiter just shrugged his shoulders, bowed and proceeded to serve another.

For nearly a half hour Lunt wandered about the salon, unable to speak meaningfully to anyone. He was conscious that he was conspicuously dull in his drab, dark brown suit amidst all the bright colored silks and feathers. Occasionally someone would come up to him and attempt to engage him in conversation, but Lunt was only able to smile and bow politely. Several times he went back to the pastry table to see if anyone had selected a dessert with a red center. All of the time Lunt was made very aware of the extreme disadvantage he faced being totally ignorant of the French language. He sympathized with Ambassador Adams' descriptions of that morning.

"Lieutenant Lunt."

Henry wheeled about to face the handsome musketeer, Captain Gerard, whom he had met upon arriving with Franklin. The man bowed and handed him a petite white envelope. Lunt opened it to read the plainly scrawled hand written note...

Lieutenant Lunt,

Please meet me immediately in the Stone Gallery on the ground floor, southern wing. Come discreetly.

Franklin

The Ambassador must have exited the King's chambers via another door other than going through the Vergennes salon. Where exactly was this Stone Gallery? He had to be discreet.

The Captain stood in front of him, studying Lunt's perplexed face.

"May I be of any assistance?"

"Where did you get this?" questioned Lunt.

"A boy passed it to one of my men a quarter of an hour ago. I was indisposed,...uh.. the toilet." He coughed into his gloved hand. "So they did not know who Lieutenant Lunt was. Is the message important? I apologize that it was given to you so late."

Lunt almost asked the Captain for more precise directions, but then remembered the warning, discreet. He excused himself, saying, "I must take leave of you now, thank you for this message." Lunt moved towards the door out of the salon.

"You are sure I cannot give you some directions?" offered the Musketeer.

Lunt turned and shook his head, "No, thank you," and then rushed out into the corridor. It was full of people passing this way and that, just as it had been when he had entered with the Ambassador. Lunt decided to look outside to see which direction the sun faced. He found a window. It was afternoon. He identified the west and then the south. In that direction, he hurried down a corridor he had not traveled with Franklin.

He practiced the pronunciation of the word

"gallerie," in his mind, but he did not know how to say "stone" in French. Far along the corridor to the south, Lunt saw a Franciscan in his brown hooded robe. He started to approach the priest, but the man, seeing him coming, began to walk away briskly. Were the Franciscans the Catholic clergy who took a vow of silence? Perhaps that was why the man had turned away. Lunt settled for stopping a lone fruit vendor with a push cart loaded with small red apples. Lunt tried, "Gallerie?" and then, "Stone?"

The man first insisted on selling an apple to him. Lunt reached into his pocket and took out an English coin. He said, "Gallerie," again.

"Oui," the vendor nodded that he understood. But the words, "rock," and "stone," had no meaning to him. Finally Lunt rapped his knuckles on the floor and then a marble statue nearby. Finally the man caught his meaning, screaming out, "Gallerie de Pierre." The man gave him directions in the form of a series of exaggerated hand gestures. After the third repeat, Lunt understood fully.

Lunt took a flight of stairs to a basement floor and then continued along through spacious hallways, occasionally passing groups of people arguing or discussing events. At one intersection there was a group of priests from an order which wore black robes without hoods. Their belts were lengths of white rope. A few moon faced nuns stood to one side. All were gazing up at a rich tapestry of Christ speaking before the multitude. Lunt had never seen such a work of art. He wanted very much to stop and admire it but he had to obey Franklin's message to come quickly.

He got to the T intersection which the green grocer had described and started to turn right into a dark corridor at which a hand lettered sign in French bore the word, *'Ferme,'* Lunt was unsure what it meant. He turned to a young couple walking hand and hand coming the opposite direction along the T. Lunt gestured toward the vacant leg of the T and called out his best pronunciation of the words, 'Gallerie de Pierre?'

The young couple giggled, snuggling together, and then one of them looked up at Lunt saying, 'Oui' and resumed their intimate whispering. The great hallway became progressively darker. The floors were of white and black marble diamonds inlaid. At intervals of every fifty feet along the corridor, there was one of a series of oval stone arches. The crest of each oval arch was fully fifteen or more feet high. On the walls of the corridor, between the arches, there was formed a similar archway design. Under each of these was a magnificent piece of art, either a tapestry, a painting, or a statue.

At the extreme far end of the hallway, at a distance of a couple of hundred yards, Lunt could just make out a great door. The light from a tall casement window provided only a sparse light.

The sound of Lunt's boots echoed along the corridor as he walked towards the massive dark door at the far end of the present corridor. Occasionally, he glanced backwards, not at all comfortable that Franklin would have him come to this location. Lunt stopped and positioned himself beneath the available diffuse light from one of the few high windows and again examined Franklin's note. There must be a purpose.

4
The Stone Gallery

The twin, fifteen foot high, winged doors to the Stone Gallery were fitted into one of the high arched portals which had reoccurred along the corridor at intervals of every fifty feet or so throughout the lower floor of the palace. Lunt noted that the two doors seemed to be slightly ajar. He tried to peek through the gap without touching them. There seemed to be a source of faint light emanating from within, but no sound or movement was discernable.

Lunt tugged at the ornate door knocker and half of the massive arch began to open slightly towards him. He tugged harder, and acquired a finger hold on the far edge of the door. The hinges moaned from the ponderous weight which was pivoting upon them. Lunt glanced once more back over his shoulder down the long arched corridor. There seemed to be no one in the hall immediately behind him, excepting four or five brown hooded Franciscans who had gathered together near the T several hundred yards back. Lunt could not determine whether they were heading away, or towards him, but they did not seem to be hurrying in any particular direction. They appeared to be studying one of the many religious works of art which adorned the walls.

Lunt grunted as he pried the ponderous arched door further. He wedged his boot into the gap. Inside, in the far distance, perhaps several hundred feet into the gallery he saw a haze of diffused light emanating from one of the far archway segments. From his vantage point, Lunt could not immediately identify the source of this gentle light.

For a long moment, Lunt continued to stare into the darkness until his eyes adjusted to the much reduced light. After some concentration he was able to distinguish the same intricate floor pattern of white and black squares that had persisted throughout the long corridor through which he had just passed. However what was different within the gallery was that at the bases of each of the stone arches there seemed to be a series of human sized figures perched on stubbly columned pedestals. Lunt strained to see what they were, but it was too dark. He pulled the door open further and sucked in his chest so that he could slip between the arched doors and into the Stone Gallery.

For a long moment Lunt stood with his back to the arched oak doorway. He considered calling out for Dr. Franklin, but decided that anyone who was already in the room with him would have seen him open the doors. He glanced to his right and left. On each side of the first archway pattern the faint light bounced off the dull polished metal of ornamental men in armor who stood a timeless guard duty on their short marble pedestals. Both figures stood facing each other across an expanse of perhaps sixty feet of checkered marble flooring. One held mace and chain. The other a battle axe.

Lunt stared ahead. From one side of the haze lit segment ahead, he could identify a solitary, flickering candle flame. It seemed to be set on a small table, and beneath it there was something stark white. He left the security of the arched door at his back and proceeded across the cold marble floor. The hard inflexible leather of his boots resonated with each cautious step. He looked to his right and left, and felt more secure when he rested his hand upon the hilt of his sword. Halfway across the first segment he made a guess in his mind at why he had been summoned to this place.

It must be Marie. She had been summoned away from his company, but had wanted to be alone with him. Perhaps she had deliberately made him leave his duty to Ambassador Franklin so that he would come to her without anyone observing them. Lunt was not ready to cope with the passion he had felt earlier for this deceitful woman as they danced amidst the music of the salon. There was the remorse and guilt he knew he would feel later if he betrayed Sarah and his own infant child far away at home in Newburyport. The thought that Marie Chatelain might have contrived so deliberate a dark encounter as this so infuriated Lunt that he almost turned and left the place. But now that he was nearer the flickering flame, he could see that under it lay a white envelope.

Two stone statues guarded the entrance into the second arched chamber. One seemed to be Perseus clutching the head of Medusa, the other some heroic figure that Lunt did not recognize. He walked forward, deeper into the gallery.

*　　*　　*　　*　　*

Franklin and Vergennes reentered the main salon. They were smiling over the King's disclosure that Marie Antoinette was now so close to bearing a child that her continual haranguing of Louis for having signed the Alliance with the United States was losing its place to her maternal preoccupations. There was also the news of the Ranger's success which greatly pleased the King. He had been interested in meeting the young Lieutenant from the Ranger, but at another time, after the British prisoner issue had been resolved.

Shortly after the two had taken a toast of wine together, Marie Chatelain entered their company hoping to receive an introduction to the great man. While in waiting she heard Franklin say, 'Where is Lieutenant Lunt?' Looking about, he said casually in French, 'He was supposed to have secured my favorite pasterie. Oh, well, I'll just have to get my own, it was an unfair amount of time to expect him to guard it. Difficulty is, I can never identify which ones have the raspberry center until after I have bitten into them. I thought somehow that Lieutenant Lunt might have discovered an easier way."

Marie stepped forward, a little concerned, "Monsieur Ambassador, did you not send a message to the Lieutenant Lunt in a small white envelope? Captain Gerard said Lunt received a small white envelope, and immediately departed the salon a quarter of an hour ago, in great haste. He would not tell the Captain where he was going."

"I did not send Lieutenant Lunt any message," said a worried Franklin. "I think we should endeavor to find out where he has gone. I can think of no reason why he would have left the salon."

Marie excused herself, and rushed to secure the help of Captain Gerard to begin a search.

*   *   *   *   *

The walls of the second chamber beneath the vaulted arches contained dark tapestries whose subject Lunt could not discern in the meager light. But their dankness filled the vault with a musky odor that reminded Lunt of a crypt.

Another set of stone figures on pedestals guarded the entrance to the vaulted arches of the third chamber. The marble figure to the left appeared to be Michael, the Archangel with raised sword. Beyond the figure was the small table with the flickering lone candle and the small white envelope. For the first time Lunt had the perspective wherein he could see well enough into the segment to identify the source of the haze of light. Instead of an enormous tapestry on each wall, the wall decoration for that segment was a hugh mirrored pattern, composed of hundreds of individual mirrored squares cut and set so as to completely fill the arched wall pattern on both sides. The mirror segments each reflected and re-reflected thousands of times the image of the tiny burning candle and the stark white envelope which lay beneath it. Someone had deliberately set up this illusion to confound him.

Across the patterned white and black floor, a considerable distance into the next chamber, Lunt could just see a dark figure move on the outskirts of the haze. Lunt pretended not to notice the movement and went directly to the table. His own face was now reflected eerily back and forth among the hundreds of mirrored panels. A thought entered his mind, was Dr. Franklin trying to demonstrate some uncanny experiment in light to him? He did not know the man very well. Famous men are sometimes eccentric. Was this why he had been called to this location?

It was obvious that whomever was in the room with him would reveal himself after Lunt opened the envelope. Lunt elected to play the game.

He picked up the small white envelope slowly. It was unmarked on the outside. Bending the envelope slightly, he inserted his index finger behind the wax seal and broke it. He extracted a small white card tightly packed within. There was only a figure drawn on it.

As he studied the card, there came a metallic click from the far end of the gallery in the direction from which he had first entered. Lunt glanced in that direction, but saw nothing. Perhaps the suction of a corridor breeze had closed the twin arched doors more firmly shut.

Lunt remained silent and looked again at the figure drawn on the card. It was the symbol that the Spymaster used on some of his messages. Lunt remembered that Marie knew the significance of the symbol. In Belfast she had taunted him with that knowledge. She had told him that their American espionage was far too unsophisticated and that O'Mally and he would fare better in the company of a more experienced spy. How many others also knew this symbol?

A voice reached him from the edge of the fog of light. "I am pleased that you have made it safely back to France. I trust that YOU have succeeded in getting me the drawings for the carronade, Lieutenant Lunt."

It was the very same question that the Foreign Minister Vergennes had asked him in the salon, less than an hour ago. It had been the very question that Lunt had declined to answer without consultation with Franklin. Why would Vergennes or his minions put Lunt through such a mysterious meeting right here in Versailles, just to receive the same response. Was there something sinister about their French allies that he did not realize? Or was this another faction of the French court? Lunt had heard that the Queen, Marie Antoinette, was not in favor of the American alliance.

But none of this troubled Lunt as much as the characteristics of the voice posing the question. That voice, it was so familiar.

Lunt almost gave a non committal answer to the question, as he had in the salon, but some instinct bid him remain silent. Until this moment he had not felt especially threatened, only terribly confused. Now from behind, he sensed a slight displacement of air. The candle beside him flickered in response. Just as he started to look behind him, the familiar voice spoke again.

"Please, Lieutenant, a great many people risked their very lives to get our cause this weapon. Have we succeeded?"

Now Lunt was conscious of more sounds behind him. Was this a test of him by Franklin or was there some sinister purpose? Were the French trying to find out for sure if Captain Jones had indeed captured the weapon or not? Was this one of Marie's tricks?

Lunt could see the figure now, it was fifty or sixty feet away circling closer to him at the rim of the haze of light. Because he was in bright light looking out into darkness, Lunt could see little distinctly beyond the well of light. He had a brief impulse to snuff out the candle beside him. If he darkened the room, he might never identify the perpetrator of this meeting. No, the right thing was to try and lure the man towards him. He could always get back to the candle if there was real danger.

Lunt forced himself to speak.

"Why should I answer you?"

As he spoke, he decided to close slowly towards the figure, just as the familiar voice answered him.

"Because I am the Spymaster," said the voice.

That was enough. Lunt decided to catch the Imposter.

"Please, Lieutenant, remain by the candle," warned his tormenter.

"Sir, I do not know what trickery you attempt, but you are not the Spymaster."

"Because you are he, Lieutenant Lunt?" roared back the Imposter.

Lunt had to know who this was. The voice had a harsh midlands English accent. Lunt now decided to try and catch the man. As soon as he proceeded to quicken his pace towards the figure, Lunt saw a swirl of robes and heard the unmistakable grate of sword on sheath. He had a glimpse of the man's nose and jaw beneath the covered hood of a Franciscan robe, but not long enough to recognize him. Lunt pulled his own stubby naval sword from its sheath as he ran.

"Capture him," screamed the Imposter.

From behind Lunt suddenly heard a torrent of shouts in French and the pounding of many boots rapidly running towards him over the hard marble floor. Lunt halted his dash towards the Imposter and looked back over his shoulder for an instant. Four hooded Franciscans were charging into the hazy fog of re-reflected candle light. The dark brethren were all carrying something between them that stretched nearly the full distance across the entire sixty foot width of the Stone Gallery. It swayed violently in front of them as they ran. It was thirty feet back for Lunt to retreat to the candle and the four hooded Franciscans were almost that distance from him now. Lunt reversed course and darted headlong back towards the candle, the only discernable source of illumination in the room. He had to snuff it out. The hooded friars advancing along the gallery floor were now closer to the candle than Lunt. The figure closest to the candle held a rapier in his free hand and the end of the net in the other. From behind, Lunt heard the Imposter shouting orders in French.

110

The hooded man at the end of the net stepped in front of the candle to protect it and awaited Lunt's charge. The blade of his rapier was several inches longer than Lunt's short stubby naval sword, but did not have its greater weight. Lunt raised his sword overhead and screamed as he charged at the man trying to startle him.

"Eeeeyyyy ..Aaaah."

The man flinched backwards and placed his blade over his head to parry off Lunt's coming overhead blow. From behind, Lunt could sense that the Imposter was now pursuing him. If Lunt could just push that net man backwards, and drive him into the candle, it would be difficult for his attackers to find him in the darkness. It was his only hope to avoid being encircled by the net. Instead of coming directly downwards in the expected strike of his blade into the man's prepared rapier, Lunt altered his stoke and whirled the weapon in a great arch to the right and then towards the front again. The tip of his blade cut through the air below the defensive plane of the rapier, biting through the cloth hood and into the flesh of the man's cheek. The man howled in pain, dropping the end of the net to clutch his face. He still blocked the candle. Lunt drew his sword back from the first strike and thrust outward in a short powerful jab which buried his sword into the man's abdomen. The intensity of the man's screams heightened as they echoed back through the darkened crypt of the gallery. The image of the deadly duel played back in macabre giant shadows upon the arched walls and ceilings of the Stone Gallery.

Lunt's second strike had skewered the first assailant. The man's body fell backwards pulling Lunt's sword arm with it. Lunt tumbled forward catapulting over the man but losing his grip on his sword which was now buried several inches into his foe's stomach. Lunt landed on his side, looking up towards the Imposter who was now only a few feet away, the razor edge of a gleaming sabre poised threateningly for a drive downwards on him.

The flickering candle and the table were only five feet away. Lunt swirled atop the collapsed end of the net and threw his body towards the table kicking out with his feet. The Imposter changed course trying to get between Lunt and the candle. Just as he made contact with the table leg, Lunt felt the deep bite of a blade cut into his right boot. Despite the pain, he pushed outward, kicking both the Imposter's leg and the table in the same movement. His last image before total darkness fell over the room was of that of the robed Imposter tumbling into the table, fitfully trying to catch the falling candle.

Lunt knew he had to leave the place where he lay, but he was weaponless. The screams of the impaled man were coming from only a few feet away. He crawled on hands and knees towards the sound of the man's writhing body. He located the protruding sword. Lunt rose to his feet, despite the pain from his right foot, and took firm hold of the hilt of his

112

sword. The dying man was screaming something in French. Lunt put his foot on the man's chest and pulled upwards. There was a faint suck of air. Beneath him Lunt could feel the net being tugged with him on it. Behind him there was the swoosh of a blade in the air. The Imposter was coming in his direction again, whirling his sabre blindly in the darkness before him as he went.

Lunt stepped back and instinctively put his sword before his face. Poised there in the darkness, he felt a warm trickle of his victim's blood flow down his sword and onto his hand. Out of the black nothingness before him, suddenly his sword was displaced violently to the left by the smashing sweep of the Imposter's blade. Sparks flew in the darkness, and in that faint light, Lunt saw only the briefest of glimpses of his adversary's face. He saw hatred in black gleaming pupils and flaring nostrils, and then there was total darkness again. Each man brought his weapon to the ready and then slashed out into darkness. Empty air was displaced violently.

Instead of remaining in position, Lunt started moving back towards the direction of the great arched doorway. Survival meant getting out of the gallery. As he moved Lunt felt warm blood sloshing around within his boot.

In rapid French, Lunt heard the midlands accent of the Imposter scream out something and within a few steps came the unmistakable hiss of fine powder that served as a prelude to a pistol discharge. The weapon had been fired upwards by one of the hooded net carriers. The brief illumination showed Lunt and his adversaries where they all were. Lunt could see that the net carriers had circled backwards in the direction of the arched doorway and that he would have plunged directly into them had he continued his course. Behind him the Imposter saw Lunt clearly and charged towards him. Lunt turned to face him as the light faded again to total blackness.

Lunt thrust out from low to high hoping to hit his assailant. He heard the blade swoosh to his left. Suddenly, the great arched doorway opened at the far end of the gallery sending a rapid, ever widening shaft of light along the checkered floor. Through the gap poured musketeers in large floppy hats with drawn swords. In their company was a woman. Distracted only an instant, Lunt turned to face the Imposter who charged directly at him.

Lunt blocked the first powerful thrust of the Imposter's sabre with his short sword, but in a second exchange of strokes the hooded figure altered the course of his sword suddenly. Lunt parried, and then swerved his own blade in a direct low arc striking his assailant in the thigh. He heard a shriek of pain from beneath the dark hood, but before Lunt could return his blade to the front of his own body in a defensive mode, the Imposter's own unchecked thrust hit Lunt high in the left side. The point of the sabre drove deeply into the flesh and bone of his upper chest, knocking the wind out of him. About him there was

114

much screaming as collectively the other assailants dropped their hold on the giant net and ran wildly for their lives towards the opposite end of the dark gallery.

As Lunt sank to his knees under the impact of the blow. His assailant drove the blade deeper to finish him. He cried out, trying to bring his sword tip up towards the man's face. A pistol fired from somewhere down near the opened archway and the Imposter shrieked, tumbling backwards, extracting the point of his sable involuntarily. Lunt continued to tumbled backwards and collapsed onto the floor.

The Imposter regained his footing and was about to make one more run to finish him, when Lunt rolled on the ground towards the opened archway. He saw the Imposter pause, clutching his arm, deciding whether or not to go after Lunt again. Then the Imposter also turned and fled towards the darker extremities of the gallery and away from the arched doorway.

Lunt struggled to get to his feet, but the pain in his chest was all pervading. As he rose feebly, everything began to grow dark. His sword fell clattering across the marble floor. As he spun out of control back to the floor, he heard another report of pistol from the direction of the arched doorway and somewhere near him another assailant screamed out and crashed to the floor.

Just as he lost consciousness, Lunt heard the thuds of running feet and the clash of swords somewhere beyond him. Voices screamed in high pitched French. He tried to lift up his head to see, but then there was only blackness as his face fell into a widening pool of his own blood.

5
𝔇𝔦𝔰𝔠𝔬𝔯𝔡

At Franklin's insistence, the regular Thursday evening meeting of the three American co-ambassadors had been moved to the home of the Comtess d'Houdetot, a confidant of Rousseau, whose pro-American salon had supported the themes of the American revolution since its inception. In extreme privacy, Franklin reported summarily about the assault at Versailles, leaving out his suspicions about motivation. Then reported that he had just learned that there had been spies aboard the Ranger who had almost caused the entire mission to be a failure.

In his high pitched, wheezing voice, Arthur Lee interjected, "You see Franklin, I warned you." He pointed his finger and then pounded the table and began to make wheezing sounds of exasperation that had accompanied his presence all during the meeting. "I've told you for the longest time that there are English spies everywhere. That you must clean everyone out, and start anew."

Adams cleared his throat and persisted with moving the conversation ahead despite Lee's histrionics. "What shall we do about getting the Ranger supplied? All those men have to be given food, clothing and medical treatment, including the English prisoners. What is Captain Jones to do?"

Franklin replied, "I sent Dr. Bancroft down to Brest earlier this week to try and help out. I'm sure he's done something for Jones and the crew by now, but there is a limit as to what he can do without money. The other problem is the French. Until we hear from Congress that they have ratified the treaty, everything is frozen."

"As it should be," interjected Lee. "Frozen here too! I won't give my signature to anything. That is final." Arthur Lee swept his open palm across his high forehead, and examined the sweat he had accumulated from his brow in the humid air.

"If that is the way you wish it, Arthur, then that is the way you shall have it. You do wish then to have it on your conscious that several hundred men, mostly our own sailors, will now starve aboard our own ship? Men that have gone into the enemy's home waters and actually landed in England carrying our flag. Men that have dared the impossible and have actually fought and captured an English ship, and now have brought it back for everyone on the continent of Europe to see." Franklin raised his voice in even more of a chastising tone, "You would now let them starve! Surely you will lend your signature to release sufficient monies to just feed them, if nothing else."

"No, I shall not lend my signature to anything until Mr. Adams cleans up Mr. Deane's papers. Nothing, until we hear of ratification from the Congress. And that is final."

"Then good day to you, sir. I shall have a letter

to that effect drafted to Captain Jones with the signature of all three Ambassadors. It shall be a document of shame, but Mr. Adams and I shall sign it, and send it over to you in the morning for your signature before it goes on to Captain Jones. I know that you shall sleep well this evening with your bottle of port, because I now know that you have no conscience for the suffering you cause brave men.'

Lee started to speak, but Franklin put up his hand, 'Please, away, Ambassador Lee, I dare not have you in my presence a moment longer for fear of what else I shall say tonight, and that I should be caused to regret at a later time.'

As he departed, Arthur Lee slammed the door in a fit of temper. Soon they heard his carriage depart the grounds of the d'Houdetot chateau. Adams offered sympathetically, 'You have had a great deal to endure from this relationship. I pity you.'

'Do not. I imagine that President Hancock and the Congress feel that they need a balance here. He has Lee here to represent the Southern colonies.'

'And I to represent the North,' quipped Adams.

Franklin smiled, and looked over the top of his spectacles. 'No, John, I do not feel that way towards you. You are doing a splendid job assembling our financial papers. You now know that Mr. Lee is completely incapable of accomplishing that task. That is why he has used his signature and his seniority here to push that task off on you. How much longer will it take?'

"Weeks, many weeks," sighed Adams. "What are we to do with the Ranger and her crew?"

"I confess that is not quite as desperate as I have portrayed to Mr. Lee," admitted Franklin. "I just wished to get Arthur's signature to release funds in general. I felt I could appeal to his patriotism. Apparently he is steadfast. When I first received news of the situation in Captain Jones' letter, I asked Madame de Chaumont for a recommendation. She has met Captain Jones before and is much enchanted with him. So I appealed to her regard for our dashing Captain. Her husband, you appreciate, has many contacts in shipping. At any rate she has arranged to have a Nantes merchant, by the name of Monsieur Bersolle, purchase one of Captain Jones' merchant prize ships. This will give our intrepid Captain sufficient funds to give at least partial payments to his crew, buy supplies, and even pay back the loan of 2,000 Louis d'or he took from the French Navy. Monsieur Bersolle will also extend additional credit to Captain Jones if needed."

"Good," Adams nodded, "but what else have you not told me?"

"The following is of the greatest secrecy. It is the reason that I took the unusual precaution of having tonight's meeting somewhere else other than le Petit Hotel. However, I have had a change of heart in the last half hour as to how much information I was willing to share with Arthur Lee."

Adams nodded, and reminded him, "I am one

of the original Sons of Liberty. I assure you of my discretion.'

Franklin continued, 'Lunt also brought back an allegation that we may have a British spy in our delegation, and also an accusation that Silas Deane, over the past half year, may also have acted as a spy. Although I don't necessarily believe the latter, it certainly deserves our attention.'

For the next two hours Franklin briefed Adams for the first time about the existence of the Spymaster, the system of codes they had been utilizing, the network of informers which O'Mally had set up in England, and the manner in which they had first identified the existence of a new English cannon, and how the principal objective of the Ranger's voyage had been to take both the Drake and the new weapon intact. Well into their conversation, Adams asked how it was possible for O'Mally to have communicated his information back and forth from England so swiftly.

Franklin explained,'John, do you recall visiting Madame Brillon's villa one evening? It was, I believe, the second evening after you arrived at Passy.'

Adams thought a long moment and then nodded.

'Do you remember that the beautiful madam had a rather strange hobby?' continued Franklin.

'Eh,' stammered Adams, 'Oh yes, the pigeons. You said that you were conducting experiments with the feather coloring of successive generations of pigeons and that Madame Brillon was funding the experiments for a paper to be given at the French Academy of Science.*

Poor Mr. Adams. I am afraid I did mislead you. However, at the time I did not know you as well as I do now. I have regrettably had the legacy of one distinguished Ambassador from Virginia who is one of the most malicious men I have ever had the displeasure of serving with anywhere, and then Mr. Deane, who has just left us for America with his papers in disarray, and who is most lately accused of being a British spy. In this company I have been keeping as co-ambassadors, Mr. Adams, I hope you understand why I was a trifle guarded in the information I shared. I hope you now realize that I hold you in the highest regard.

Adams expressed his appreciation for the statement and sat back to listen further, his jowls resting on his starched collar.

O'Mally's greatest legacy was very likely those pigeons. They were no experiment at all. They are quite the finished product. They are, in fact, carrier pigeons, dear Mr. Adams. Each has a home coop somewhere in Britain. There are still many in England, most likely the better part of a hundred, that would willingly fly right back immediately to Madame Brillon's if they were released this very night. The problem is, until we hear from Mr. O'Mally or someone he designates, I do not know where in England they are kept.

Adams stated, *I had always heard that carrier

pigeons were generally timid about flying over water, especially as treacherous an expanse as the English Channel." Adams leaned forward, in anticipation of hearing more. After some weeks of disappointment, he had just, this evening, only begun to appreciate all that Franklin had been accomplishing right under his nose. He had been so disappointed in Franklin when he had first arrived, going constantly to parties at the various salons every evening, getting up late and living in luxury at Passy. But now it seemed that Franklin had pursuits under the surface, and that he actually was on top of many situations. Much of his behavior had apparently been a sham, a ruse to fool the English.

"No, John, certain species are very reliable for great distances. Did you know that when Julius Caesar was sent to conquer England, then a worthless, remote Island, that he brought with him 500 pigeons, and that each day he released one pigeon so that word of his exploits would be carried back to his friends in the Roman Senate each day. Meanwhile, news from greater generals like Pompey would sometimes take months to reach Rome. In this way the daily exploits of an obscure Roman general, seemingly exiled to a remote corner of the Roman Empire, soon began to capture the imagination of the most powerful nation in the world. The rest is history."

Franklin continued, "John, thanks to O'Mally, what we possess in this espionage game is very rapid communication and to my best belief the English do not know it, or have it themselves. Even if O'Mally never returns, this is something we can use to our advantage. On the last day that O'Mally spent with Lunt, he promised that he would attempt to find us a replacement in England as soon as he was strong enough to attempt it."

"In case he is not able to accomplish that, do we know all of O'Mally's contacts? Who they are?" questioned Adams.

Franklin shifted in his chair and pulled a petite notebook with a horned cover from his vest pocket. He handed it to Adams, who opened it. "Why, it is just a series of numbers, separated by commas," Adams observed, "...in lines. A code?"

Franklin nodded, "O'Mally always updated it for me, when he added a new number. Every leader of the revolution on this side of the Atlantic has a number. So too, all of O'Mally's operatives, and even a few discreet members of the Parliament among the royal opposition. Because a man has a number, it does not necessarily mean that he knows about it. For example, Ambassador Deane had a number, Dr. Bancroft, my secretary has a number, and Ambassador Lee has a number. None of the latter know they have a number. On the other hand, Captain Jones has a number and receives messages regularly from the Spymaster. I think he assumes they are from me. The system obviously works well and most importantly it has not been detected by the British."

"You mentioned a book they all have to utilize

in order to decode it," asked Adams, "...which book is it? The Bible?"

"No," Franklin looked over the top of the spectacles at his co-ambassador, and cleared his throat a little embarrassed at the coming disclosure, "Poor Richards Almanac, 1756 printing. The edition most commonly found in England."

Adams raised an eyebrow, but continued to listen to the philosopher-scientist-ambassador as he produced a copy of the Almanac from a drawer of the desk at which he had been sitting.

"If something should befall me, and it is now within the realm of possibility that the British may attempt it, I feel you will need to understand how to read the code. Listen closely." Franklin held the Almanac open to a selected page, "Using both page nineteen of the Almanac and the first line in the horned notebook you can identify the first operative, in this case myself. My name is spelt out on that line of the notebook in numbers, by referring to the last letter of each word from the bottom up on page 19 of Poor Richard. We selected this page because it is the first that contains nearly all 26 of the letters as a last letter of at least one word on that page. This is also the manner in which each operative is assigned his own page number. John, you are only the fourth person to ever know the code. I am telling you because we are unsure if O'Mally is alive or dead and I need a backup in case a misfortune befalls me as it has Lieutenant Lunt."

Adams interrupted Franklin's description, "I did caution you against going everywhere without military escort. Don't you think it's time we had some protection at Passy? If you don't possess personal fear, I admire you for it, but at least think of young John Quincy and the other children."

"Yes, yes, but that is another matter," said Franklin, "Please let me continue, the horn shell notebook has a series of numbers on each line. From page 19 of the Almanac you can identify the name of the person by counting the number of words backwards up the page from the bottom. The last letters of those words spell out first the name and then the page number assigned based on the corresponding letter of the alphabet. For example, a last letter of 'E' is the digit '5' and so forth."

"How many of these notebooks are there?" inquired Adams.

"Two, O'Mally had one with him. Lunt brought it back with him, so now I have both. I keep one always on my person. The other is now hidden at Madame Brillon's, at the bottom of a bin of pigeon feed. Our individual operatives do not know about the horned notebook that is controlled by the Spymaster. They only know that they decode messages using say page number 102, and they are told which page number to report to. Naturally, when they send the messages they sometimes try to use additional decoys. Here," Franklin pulled from his pocket the recent message from Captain Jones and pointed to the bottom of the page, "Invisible ink, Jones sent a message to me that he did not want the French courier to see. One that reported that they did not get the Carronade with the Drake."

Franklin went on to explain the intricate coding and decoding of a page to send and receive messages. He used the Jones message as an example. When he finished, he concluded his lesson by saying, "It is simple to utilize, and it leaves anyone caught unable to identify the entire espionage network."

"You said earlier that affairs were falling apart. Is that because you have lost O'Mally?" inquired Adams.

"O'Mally had many activities in the fire. A great many. One unfortunate consequence has been that Admiral Rodney has slipped through our fingers."

"Rodney?" said Adams, "That name is not immediately familiar to me."

"He is very likely England's most competent Admiral. But fortunately for us he has been under debtor's arrest here in Paris for the past year." Franklin took a sip of his wine and then continued, "Rodney is a Whig, not a Tory, thank heavens. About a year ago, O'Mally used some funds raised for us by Madame d'Houdetot to buy the Admiral's gambling notes. The man is penniless, save sufficient amounts earned by writing a column for a Whig journal. But the amount was only sufficient to pay for his lodging, which according to O'Mally was very meager. The man is a compulsive gambler, and I'm told a heavy drinker, but he has one asset all of the other members of the Admiralty lack."

"Yes, go on?" Adams said.

"Experience, actual experience in naval war. The French fear him. Ask Admiral d'Orvilliers. At any rate, I was aware of the situation through O'Mally's weekly briefings, but I did not know that a well meaning French nobleman, a personal friend of Rodney, would buy back the note from the bank out of sheer benevolence in order to get his friend out of France before a formal war was declared. I just assumed that O'Mally had the entire note secured."

"Where is Rodney now?" asked Adams.

"He is no fool. He was on the way out of Paris weeks ago. I assume he is back in England already. For the moment he is no threat, as I have said, he is a Whig and no one is invited to Lord Sandwich's Bordello who is of that persuasion. Besides, about a year ago, Rodney, in one of his Whig papers stated that he would never fight against the American colonies as their cause was just. But, oh, let the French be involved, and he would go to war instantly to protect England. Let me emphasize to you the difference between Rodney and, say, Admiral Howe. The latter has just sat in New York harbour with his Fleet for two years now. In that time, Rodney would have been into every back water of the entire American coast pursuing Washington's army and its supply routes everywhere. He is a gambler by instinct. He would not take the safe course."

"You speak as if you know Rodney, personally."

"Yes, I do, as a matter of fact, quite well. Remember, I did spend over a decade representing our interests in London. Before the Boston Tea party there was no better friend to us. Augustus Keppel, too, both men of integrity. Were they in charge of the American war, I fear it would be over by now. Let us hope that Sandwich's bordello cronies stay in charge. This is why I warned Captain Jones about not harming any British civilians during any raid on English soil. As a consequence, much of the British press has treated him as sort of a folk hero. Do you know they are singing songs about him in the London taverns? He has become another Robin of Locksley."

"You have mentioned a bordello several times."

"Yes, Lord Sandwich's Castle. It is mentioned in some of the English papers on occasion. Lord Sandwich has a mistress, a singer by the name of Martha Ray. She resides on the west end of London in what looks literally like a small castle right on the Thames in Pimlico. Anyone of consequence in the Tory establishment has visited there at one time or another. It is rumored that King George himself has been there many times. In disguise, of course."

"The Satyrs. Can you imagine the secrets that must be discussed there?" Adams squirmed in his chair. "If we could..."

"Sean O'Mally has been inside. He has sung there, but Madame Ray is very cautious. Last year, Mr. O'Mally was let in to sing and then escorted out.

It was too early in the evening to learn much. What O'Mally has been trying to do for the better part of a year is to get an agent in there. But he has been unable to find someone who would risk their very life. Not just once, but a person who would be willing to reside there, to be a ....well, there is no better word for it, ...a whore to the Tory Admiralty. But one who is in fact a spy for us.'

'O'Mally tried to turn someone who was already in place and came close to tipping his hand. He was almost caught. I must confess I have extreme distaste for this sort of thing, but having served in this position now for well over a year, I understand now why governments must maintain their spies, simply because their enemies or potential enemies do. But I personally do not wish to be involved, and I would advise that you too, as Co-Ambassador, John, remain aloof of this type of activity. There are men, like O'Mally who have a penchant for this sort of endeavor. We need them, but we cannot taint the image of our just cause by being associated with their deeds too closely. All this is an unsavory and somewhat deceitful fact of life.'

Adams nodded his acquiescence, and then changed the subject. 'How is Lunt? I realized you did not want to discuss the matter in detail in the presence of Ambassador Lee.'

Franklin sighed and shook his head, 'I remained at Versailles all last night. As you know the young man took two wounds. He was wounded in the foot from a sabre slash. That wound is not life threatening."

Franklin sighed and knitted his brows, concerned. "But for the other wound, the King's physician believes Lunt's chest wound may have penetrated through to the chambers of his heart. There is a puncture in his chest just about where the heart is on the left side. It may have punctured the organ, it may have only grazed it, or it may have missed altogether. We simply do not know."

"What are his chances?"

"I'd say that Henry Lunt has the finest medical help of our time."

"I'm interested to know if there is anything, which in the presence of Mr. Lee, that you may have neglected to tell me about the Lunt incident. I'm particularly curious, how the assault was interrupted in time?" asked Adams.

"Ironically, it was Madame Chatelain, the spy who Lunt and O'Mally rescued in Belfast. She was in audience at Comte de Vergennes' salon. She had been dancing awhile with Lunt, but was called away suddenly, and upon her return could not find him. She discovered from Captain Gerard of the King's Musketeers that Lunt had received a message. She asked me why I would have required that he depart so soon, and when we determined that it was not my message, the chase was on. Shortly after we had all departed the salon, Madame Chatelain and Captain Gerard came across a greengrocer who Lunt had asked for directions to the Stone Gallery."

'It was a very long run, I simply couldn't keep up. Along the way we saw that the scoundrels had set signs out in French that the corridor leading to the Stone Gallery was closed. This ostensibly was to keep anyone from wandering upon the scene. On their way, the Musketeers and Madame Chatelain heard a pistol discharged and ran very swiftly to the door of the Stone Gallery, and upon opening it, found Lieutenant Lunt still dueling with his assailants disguised as Franciscan monks. There were five assailants in all. Lunt had killed one man, had wounded another, and was apparently eluding them and their net in the darkness by rolling upon the floor. There was blood everywhere.

'From the entrance Madame Chatelain shot two of the assailants. The man Lunt had been dueling with was wounded at that point, but escaped, the other man she shot died instantly. The King's Musketeers managed to catch up with another of the assassins and killed him when he would not surrender. Incidentally, Madame Chatelain made both pistol shots from a distance of several hundred feet. Everyone in the court is talking about her marksmanship. Unfortunately, two of the assailants escaped.'

'Why was this attempted, do you know?'

'Lunt regained consciousness for a few moments after I reached him. He whispered that the British believed he was the Spymaster and that they did not know if Jones had the Carronade or not. Apparently they were trying to kidnap him by capturing him with a net in the Gallery. The Musketeers found a funeral carriage outside the garden door to the Stone Gallery. The chamber is most often used for state funerals, so none of the guards outside thought it was unusual to see such a vehicle near the garden entrance to the gallery. Apparently they were going to bind and gag Lunt and take him off the grounds of Versailles in that vehicle, inside a casket."

"Why could they not apprehend the other two men, especially in the palace?"

"They were dressed as Franciscans, and apparently there is a college of Franciscans visiting Versailles this week. There are hundreds and hundreds of them everywhere. Once they lost sight of us, the villains simply shed their robes. They could be anyone. Within fifteen minutes, the search parties found the discarded robes in one of the Queen's chapels. One had blood on it."

Franklin continued, "At any rate, the King's physician recommended that Lunt lie in total quiet for the next few weeks. It is possible that if he makes no sudden movements the wound might heal over completely. All night the physician has been draining the stale blood and humus from the wound by use of a reed. Starting today he will have someone in constant attendance applying moderate pressure on the wound. At least there is hope. Lieutenant Lunt's fate is in the hands of God."

There was a long pause of silence and then Adams spoke up, "Incidentally, I have located some forty letters belonging to Lunt. The two I carried over personally last month, and another thirty-eight in Ambassador Deane's office. Some of them are nearly a year old. Deane, incidentally, had in his office hundreds and hundreds of letters, presumably written by our prisoners' families. Have we not been able to even get mail to our men held in English gaols?" asked Adams.

"No, the English have not been especially sympathetic, and we fear there could be reprisals after the war because of the written information within those letters. Deane and I, and even Lee had agreed that the letters should remain here, until there is a formal prisoner arrangement between the combatant nations. Leave Lunt's letters in my office, I will to it see that they are sent to his bedside at Versailles. If he regains consciousness, they should comfort him greatly. Well, I believe it is time to call it an evening."

Adams nodded, rose from his chair, patted his co-Ambassador on the shoulder and ambled across the room. "I am going to spend a few hours with John Quincy in the morning. I can't neglect his studies. Oh, did you pass out the invitations to our Independence Day party?"

Franklin looked up, "I personally gave one to every Ambassador to the court of Louis the XVI."

"By the way, where is Lunt staying in Versailles?"

"Why, didn't I tell you? No, so much has happened in the past two days. It has been a whirlwind. When the King heard of the incident, he was insistent that both Lunt and I spend the evening at his personal family quarters. Because of this tragedy, I have spent more time with the King in the past day, than I would have if I had met with him regularly every Tuesday for the next year. I even gave the King an invitation to come to the Independence Day celebration. I don't suppose that he will come, but he seemed very pleased. Oh, one secret is out, the King does speak English, not perfectly, but quite well. He translated for me for his physician, as to what they were going to do for Lunt. Of course, the King would never dishonor his own court by speaking English there, so you will still have to learn French, Mr. Adams.'

Adams clicked his fingers good naturedly and made preparations to return to Passy.

*   *   *   *   *

In his quarters, John Adams could not sleep. Several times during the night, he looked in on his son who was sleeping soundly. At one point he opened the upper drawer of his bureau to check the prime and condition of the two small pistols he kept there. He knew that in case of danger, he would never be able to get to them in time, but having them was comforting. They must have protection, he decided emphatically, despite Franklin's apparent nonchalance. Carrying a candle, Adams marched out in his night gown to his usual desk at the back of the great salon of le Petit Hotel. He took a quill, dipped it in his ink well and wrote a brief note.

Captain Jones,

I know that you will have heard of the unfortunate incident with Henry Lunt by now. Because of this outrageous attack I now feel strongly that those in the embassy must have the personal protection of our own military. As you are the most senior American officer now serving in France, I entreat you to immediately do what ever is within your resources to see to the personal safety of those within this mission at Passy.

Sincerely,

John Adams

Adams started to fold the letter, but then had an additional thought, which he added to the bottom.

Postscript. Incidently, you have never sent me any correspondence regarding Henry Lunt's commission. I would recommend that you do so at your earliest convenience. I believe that this member of the Marine Committee of the Continental Congress would be favorably disposed at this time.

136

6
Confrontations

"Who gave you the authority to conduct this assassination?" demanded Lord Stormont from his seat across the table. "Do you have any idea how extraordinarily tenuous England's relationship is with France? Can you fathom that I have spent weeks and weeks trying to rebuild sufficient trust so as to reinstate our embassy here? And now you do this."

Major Pitkan, dressed in civilian attire, stood at ramrod straight attention, a few wisps of gray hair fell in solitary strands at the sides and back of an otherwise completely bald head. His scalp and face glistened from both the sultry Parisian atmosphere and his proximity to the warm white candle burning on the table immediately before him. His heart still beat furiously in the aftermath of the incident of a few days ago. His left arm, supported by a black cloth sling, still throbbed from the removal of the pistol ball. Yet, his brain stayed inwardly calm and clear throughout the ordeal of the Ambassador's invective.

Paul Wentworth sat in the corner of his small salon. He had privately concluded that Lord Stormont had found a scapegoat upon whom he could lay blame in his explanations to the King and Prime Minister about why he had been unable to regain the favor of Louis XVI. Wentworth had seen Stormont do this before, he was trying out his argument against someone who didn't have sufficient rank to defend himself. Stormont would only stop if the Major made a counter defense that was strong enough to indicate that Stormont's argument was flawed. With the Major's military training, the man was not likely to answer back to a superior, and it seemed that the Ambassador was going to hone his argument through until the Major, himself, had even accepted the premise that through this one careless incident, he had single handedly caused England to fail to regain her diplomatic recognition at Versailles.

As the haranguing continued, Paul Wentworth remained a quiet observer. The rich smoke of his pipe rose in intermittent columns to the ceiling where, after cooling, it became diffused throughout the room to further taint the atmosphere.

'On what authority, Major, did you conduct this assault? I demand to know.'

Pitkan glared defiantly over the hot candle flame and across the table towards his country's former Ambassador to France. 'Mr. Eden of the Foreign Office, Sir,' Pitkan raised his voice, 'sent me to report to Mr. Wentworth.' Pitkan, wise in his years, now added for effect, 'And I was told, Sir, that Mr. Eden's orders came directly from Lord North. These orders were, Sir, to identify and smash the American Spymaster and his ring. And I have done so, as ordered, Sir.'

In reaction to the defiant tone of the Major's voice, Lord Stormont slammed his fist down violently onto the stout mahogany table. The candle flickered violently in reaction. "You fail to understand, Major. I don't care if you did kill the man. My complaint is that you chose to do this at the Royal Palace. Don't you have any common sense? For the past several weeks I have been attempting to arrange for King Louis and King George to meet together privately so as to avoid a war that would drain England's resources at a critical time. And, just as I'm making progress, then, suddenly you come onto the scene and unravel everything I've been striving to accomplish by carrying on a brutal assassination not more than five minutes walk from the King's chambers? What the hell is the matter with you?"

"Sir, I am a soldier. I do not set policy. I follow orders," barked out Major Pitkan in a deep angry voice. "We suspected that the man, Lunt, might have knowledge or possession of the secret to a new naval cannon. That is why I was sent here to Paris to specifically identify him and to stop him, immediately! When your spy arrived a few nights ago, and I learned that Lieutenant Lunt would be visiting Versailles the very next day, I believed it to be my duty to either capture or eliminate him immediately, and to accomplish this before he could pass anything onto the French. And, Sir, I do not believe that this incident can be traced to us. It will likely be blamed on the many duelists who lurk about the palace."

Lord Stormont seemed not to listen, and elected to continue his relentless accusations from the other side of the candle flame for several more minutes, wherein Pitkan calmly placed his right hand on the hilt of his sword and withdrew his sabre as the former Ambassador was in mid sentence. The grating sound of a sword being extracted from its sheath caused the verbal assault to cease abruptly. Pitkan raised his sabre up high into the air and then brought it down swiftly to cleave the annoying, thin white 'I' of the hot, burning candle neatly into a 'Y,' ten inches deep at the throat. A portion of wick remained burning from either end.

Wentworth, not knowing what Pitkan might do next, swiftly threw his arm over the top of his soft sofa as a precaution. His hand closed upon the handle of one of many small pistols tucked away around his apartment. He sat watching, silently, as he held the small pistol firmly, but out of sight, to be used only if violence prevailed.

Major Pitkan's action caused Lord Stormont to lose his composure. The gleaming point of the sword came to rest only a few inches from the end of his nose. Stormont gaped at the two flickers of flame and then cautiously got out of his seat and then moved backwards to the security of a far corner of the room. Major Pitkan then swiftly returned his sword to its sheath and again stood ramrod straight staring blankly ahead. For several minutes, tension hung as thick as smoke in the humid air.

When it was apparent that nothing else was going to transpire, Wentworth took the opportunity to speak up for the first time in a half hour, "Major Pitkan, can I ask you to take a walk for an hour or so?"

Pitkan nodded, took a deep breath, and calmly strutted across the room in the general direction of Lord Stormont, who withdrew to one side so as to place a chair between himself and the Major. Ignoring him entirely, Pitkan strode into another room, was gone for a little over a minute, and then returned carrying a cape and a tall hat, of contemporary fashion. Still staring forward, he walked across the room and out the door, without saying a word to anyone.

There was silence for a few moments as both remaining men kept their tongues while Pitkan's steps could be heard descending the wooden stairs and then eventually fading along the cobblestone street in front of the row house.

Disregarding any pretense at etiquette, Stormont first removed a doily from a nearby butler's table and wiped his profusely sweating forehead. "I thought the man was going to kill me. From what wretched jungle did Mister Eden recruit him? May I have a drink, Paul, please."

Wentworth nodded and gestured towards his bar. "Major Pitkan has had a difficult life. During the Seven Years War, he was a prisoner of the French for several years. That is why he is so proficient in their language. One particular you don't realize about the Major is that the mission to get Lunt was a very personal one for him.'

'Paul, that man frightens me. How does he come to know the identity of our spy at Passy? He could ruin everything. He is a loose cannon.'

'That was quite the accident. Pitkan had arrived here only a few hours when our operative came directly up here in the middle of the night, instead of leaving his usual message for me at Tuilleries gardens. For weeks his messages have been demanding more money. I hadn't answered him so he took the most unusual step of coming here to confront me,' explained Wentworth.

'As the man burst in, Major Pitkan had the presence of mind to quickly hide in the butler's pantry, and just stood there listening until the recent arrival of a Lt. Lunt from the Ranger was mentioned in passing. Because I knew that Major Pitkan was listening, I got our operative to tell what he knew about Lunt. It was mentioned that both Lunt and Dr. Franklin would be departing for Versailles together the very next morning. I had absolutely no idea that Major Pitkan would move so swiftly to accomplish his mission. He simply left here before dawn without waking me and took this action on his own initiative.'

'Yes, he certainly possesses unusual ardor for this assignment,' observed a more composed Lord Stormont as he glanced again at the severed candle. One bitter end had finally extinguished itself from lack of wick. Stormont took a swig of brandy.

Wentworth continued to sit calmly in his sofa,

smoking his pipe as he explained more about the Major. "You may have heard that a Captain Burden of H.M.S. Drake was killed during the capture of his vessel by the Continental ship, Ranger. The unfortunate Captain was our Major's best friend. They had served together during the Seven Years War. Apparently, just prior to the Ranger incident, Major Pitkan had discovered that a current mistress of the late Captain Burden was not the lady she was pretending to be. Major Pitkan suspected petty larceny, but he had no idea that the unfortunate Captain's mistress was a spy. Apparently, he was just on the verge of unmasking her subterfuge when Lieutenant Lunt showed up at a retirement dinner for Captain Burden in the disguise of a meat carver. After dinner, Lunt personally challenged H.M.S. Drake to a naval duel just outside of Belfast Lough on behalf of his Captain Jones. Lunt then proceeded to escape with the lady and another man."

"Extraordinary tale," said Stormont, not truly believing what he was hearing.

"That's not all of it," continued Wentworth. "During Lunt's escape from Belfast, he killed the Sergeant Major of Pitkan's regiment in a sword fight."

"I see. So Major Pitkan had two fallen comrades to avenge...is that supposed to be his excuse for acting like a lunatic?" Stormont went to the window to glance outside to ensure the Major was not lurking outside on the street. "It does not excuse his behavior. He should be ordered back to London and then run out of the service. Immediately! Imagine brandishing a sword about like that, while he is being reprimanded.'

There was still a slight tremble in his voice. Lord Stormont went to the small bar in Wentworth's salon and poured himself another brandy.

'Yes,' Wentworth admitted, 'but until I was sent Major Pitkan, I had absolutely no one here who was capable of identifying Lunt. And the Foreign Office is convinced that Lunt was the American Spymaster we have been trying to uncover for the past year.'

'But now that Lunt is dead, certainly Major Pitkan's usefulness here is over. I say send Pitkan back to London. We can't have brutal, irrational people connected with our mission in Paris.' Stormont took a sip from his brandy. 'You are certain that there was no evidence to trace of this incident to us?'

'I am confident that all the men that Major Pitkan engaged were common Parisian thieves from the east bank. They were hired expressly to help capture Lunt at Versailles. Two of them were either killed or captured, but none of them had any idea who Pitkan was representing. They were simply told they would be paid handsomely if they were successful in kidnapping Lunt. Since Major Pitkan escaped the incident successfully, there should be no way to trace anyone to us. Just keep denying any knowledge of the incident. As long as Lunt was killed, the French Royals will not know who the ring leader was. They may suspect, but just keep denying it.'

'We are certain that this Lunt is dead?' asked

Stormont.

'You are going to Versailles tomorrow, Mr. Ambassador. This is something we need to know for certain. Major Pitkan says that he stabbed Lunt full in the chest. But he was himself shot before he could verify that the wound was mortal.'

'I will listen tomorrow, but in the meantime you must get Major Pitkan away from here. If he is ever identified with us, it will be as disastrous as the Spanish King's confessor being discovered as one of our spies a few months back.'

Wentworth nodded gravely, 'I know of a place far away from Paris where I can send the Major for a time. It will do him some good, perhaps give him some finesse, and better judgement.'

'No, I think you had better get this man out of France. Behaving like this he will inevitably make some grievous error,' said Stormont.

'I can't do that. Not just yet. There is more to this than I have told you.' Wentworth continued as Lord Stormont got up and poured himself another Brandy. 'Mister Ambassador, have you ever seen a very beautiful woman with red hair at Versailles?'

'What a question?' snapped Stormont. 'Every beautiful woman in France finds herself at Versailles, at least for a time. A great many woman have red hair, if you can peek under their wigs. Why do you ask?'

'When Major Pitkan was wounded during the attempt on Lunt, did you know that he was shot by

145

a woman?"

Stormont listened with interest as Wentworth continued.

"That woman was the very lady who was Captain Burden's mistress in Belfast, not two months ago. We must identify who she is, and for that reason I may need Major Pitkan later, Mister Ambassador. Apparently the Americans and the French have been working together for quite some time and we have missed it. Can you perhaps find out who she is, Mister Ambassador?"

Lord Stormont sat on the edge of his chair, twirling his third brandy. "I will do what I can, but you must at least get Major Pitkan out of Paris immediately."

Wentworth nodded his agreement.

Lord Stormont began to get up to leave, but then paused, "How is the pamphleteering program proceeding?"

"Last week our red fleet seized a Virginia tobacco ship, the Augustus. Our agents are selling her at this very moment. Shortly we will have pamphlets prepared which will contain evidence that the Americans and Doctor Franklin, in particular, knowingly diverted that ship to the Lowlands and sold the tobacco for their own personal gain, rather than using the cargo to satisfy just debts here in France. The pamphlets will demand that current French merchant credit be satisfied first before more goods are shipped to America on credit. We will be ready to launch this program and bring matters to a boil as soon as we get approval from Whitehall.·

·You'll concentrate on the merchants of Brest and Nantes in particular. That is where much of the saltpeter is being shipped from.·

·Yes, Mister Ambassador, we'll get Brest and Nantes in particular. And hopefully you will succeed in finding out for certain if Lieutenant Lunt is dead and who the beautiful red headed spy is who shot Major Pitkan at Versailles.·

·Yes, Paul, I will endeavor to do my best,· assured Stormont as he gathered up his belongings, again going to the window to see if his carriage was still outside and if Major Pitkan was about. Satisfied that the way was clear, he started for the door.

*   *   *   *   *

Captain Jones dismounted his horse on a commercial street in the southeast of Brest. It was the same street, where several blocks away, there was a tavern frequented by the men of the Ranger. An agreement had been struck with the French Navy, that his crew be allowed to leave the vessel a dozen at a time to row Jones ashore in a longboat in order to retrieve supplies. All of the crew had returned on schedule after the first evening. Jones had resolved to continue to do this until he had obtained the result he wanted.

The boy, Andre, met Jones at the same prescribed time and place as the evening before. They spoke quietly together in French for a few minutes and then Jones walked to the deserted coach house around the corner and sat in the darkness. From his waistband he drew one of his three pistols and momentarily checked the tightness of the screw which held the piece of flint in place on the cock. He then put the pistol on the flat stone fence and leaned back inconspicuously against a shadowy tree. The last overnight coach for Paris had departed an hour ago and the area should remain relatively deserted the remainder of the evening. Perhaps he was wrong, perhaps he was right. Time would tell. But he could think of no other way to do this.

Andre entered the tavern. It was even more raucous than the evening before. The Yankees were recognizable immediately from the sound of their out of place English and their deep laughter, far noisier than any of the French sailors which regularly frequented this tavern.

One of the serving wenches was flirting with them in broken English, "Oh, you sailors have been too long at sea. I will not come a little closer. To choose this old hag, you must be truly desperate or blind."

The Americans laughed. The tavern maid, a very stout women of nearly fifty put her hand on her hips and wiggled off after setting down the flagons of ale. The men whistled. One stood up and make an obscene gesture, the others tipped their mugs.

'Damn, 'tis a joy to be off the Ranger, if only for a few hours. Where'd you think the Capt'n disappeared to?' said one.

'Likely has a room filled with women somewhere,' offered another.

'The Frenchies don't want us ashore a'tal, but Capt'n talked 'em into it. Says he's taking a chance with us. We gotta stay here.'

'Maybe it would be better if he just gave us our rightful share.' The men around the table nodded.

'What would ye guess will be our share of the booty, Peter?'

'Got to be three hundred pounds each, what with all those ships we took.'

'You'll never see it all,' remarked Colwell Haggart. 'We'd be better off if the Ranger had never sailed.'

'Stow it, you complainer!' warned Kennedy, 'Captain got us all fed like he promised. Sold the merchant ship, says he'll have some money from that to pay us part share in a fortnight.'

'Par...don, mariners.' It was the French accent of the tavern maid back again.

Sandy haired young Kennedy stood up, 'Yes, ye sweet thing!' He put his arm around her massive shoulder and kissed her on the ear using his tongue.

'Gotta be disparate, Jimbo.'

'I am, I am.'

They all roared with laugher, while the maid stood there twirling a towel with which she good naturedly took a smack at Kennedy and then in her poor English asked. "Is one of ye rowdies named Ford at this table, Mr. Hezekiah Ford?"

"T'aint nobody here a Mister," yelled one of the sailors. The others laughed. "Who wants to know?"

"There's a lad at the door with a message for an American sailor by the name of Ford. That's all."

"T'aint no one by that name here. T'aint no one on the Ranger by that name a'tal," offered Kennedy. He and the others returned to their speculation about the amount of prize money.

One of the men glanced furtively across the tavern at the young lad by the door. The maid sauntered over to the boy shaking her head. They talked for a few minutes and then the boy departed.

"Let me out for a piss," said one of the men.

"Remember what the Capt'n said, gotta stay here in the tavern," reminded Kennedy with a laugh.

The man puffed up his mouth to appear as if he were going to burst from excess urine. The rest of the crew pushed away to allow the man past them and out alone into the street to relieve himself.

"Wait,...boy, wait!"

The boy, Andre, turned in the street and waited for the sailor who was now running to catch up with him.

"You have a message for a man named Ford?"

"Oui,...but only for Mr. Hezekiah Ford," said the lad. "Are you Mr. Ford?"

The man looked nervously back over his shoulder and seeing that no one had followed him out, he responded to the boy by asking a question, "Who gives ye this message? Name him."

"He had no name, t'was an Englishman by his speech. He was tall and well groomed. Had a high hat, real genteel like. He didn't give his name."

The questioner looked back again towards the door to the tavern. This might be the opportunity to get away from the Ranger and collect his pay. He rubbed a torn end of his jerkin across his mouth, which was still wet with ale. "What's the message?"

"Are you Mr. Ford?" asked Andre.

The man cursed under his breath. "Stupid bastard, not supposed to use my name," he muttered under his breath. "Yes, what's the message?"

"Here," Andre handed the man a folded slip of paper. Ford opened it. There were words on it. Why did they write to him. He could not read. Something was wrong. He looked up to find that Andre was walking away from him.

"Can you read English, boy? Wait, what doth it say?" The boy reluctantly returned to his side.

Contradictions and doubts troubled him as he struggled against the influence of several flagons of ale. Didn't they realize he couldn't read? They were never supposed to use his real name. But if this were a real message the whole mad voyage would be over.

The English would pay him. But if he left the Ranger now, he might lose his share of their prize money. But if he didn't answer this and the British thought that Hezekiah Ford was dead, killed aboard the Ranger during the battle, he might never get the money the English had promised him. He had to take the chance. Besides, Captain Jones had gone off somewhere on his horse, seemingly in a great hurry. He probably wouldn't be back for hours. It might be weeks before he could get off the Ranger again. He had to reestablish contact, but he would be cautious. He reached down to his boot and for reassurance located his knife handle with his right hand.

Then, he straightened his large frame and handed the message back to the boy. "Read it, now."

The boy held the message up to the faint light of a street lamp and reported, "Monsieur, it says 'Meet me at the Paris coach house immediately.' There is a signature, but I do not recognize it. It is unreadable."

He snatched back the paper and squinted at it under the oil lantern. The words were not recognizable to him. "Where is this coach house, boy?"

The boy pointed as he answered. Ford needed to go down past the warehouses for three streets, until the next oil lamp and then turn left. The coach house would be across the street from there. He would see the coaches. Ford made a grab for the boy to drag him along, but the boy evaded him. "I must go home to supper, Mr. Ford."

In the clumsiness of his ale soaked reasoning,

the man weighed the possibilities of a trap, and decided to go down the street slowly. Better yet, he would take the next street over and come to the coach house from the other side. He would be real cautious. It would be all right.

He walked across the street along towards a victualer shop that was just closing up. There were a few harlots on the street. He talked to one of them a few minutes, looking around as he did. They would be his alibi, if this was a trap. He thought that if he still needed to return to the Ranger after talking with the English, he might just stop off here on the way back. He'd hit up his contact for a little money and spend it with the ladies as his cover. No one could blame a poor sailor for that. Couple of days extra duty as punishment, be worth it.

He got to the second cobblestone street and stopped to straighten out his soiled breeches and carefully look around. The street ahead was a solid front of closed warehouses. A few people could be heard on the next street over. He crossed the street and walked on, carefully choosing his steps. He saw coaches ahead, their horses detached and put into a stable. There was a blacksmith barn. There was no sign of anyone. An oil lantern burned dimly at the end of the street.

He peered around the corner into a yard. It was filled with empty coaches. He stood and listened. There was only the neighing sound of horses off in the distance somewhere. There seemed to be no one about. Not even a guard for all these coaches. Strange, very quiet. He started to retreat, then thought of calling out, decided against it, and proceeded forward. He peered into one of the first coaches he found. There was no one inside. The waiting area was lit inside. He started to enter.

There came a creak behind him. As he started to turn, a familiar Scottish accent greeted him from under a tree adjacent to the waiting room, "So Mr. Colwell Haggart 'tis really Mr. Hezekiah Ford, British spy. You certainly caused my crew and ship a lot of misery, mister."

His hand on the waiting room door, Ford's entire body began to tremble with terror. He felt his hair stand up. His brain fumbled for words, to say something, to say anything that was believable. "Sorry, Captain, I didn't stay in the t'vern, Capt'n, sorry. I was looking for a woman. It's been a long ...."

Ford, who hadn't yet fully turned towards Jones, was hit across the forehead, suddenly and violently, by the walnut butt of a .50 calibre Kentucky pistol. He toppled over face down into the dirt, seeing stars and blinding red pain. He lay paralyzed there for only a few seconds before he was kicked violently in his side. He felt one of his ribs crack. He sensed blood was streaming from his forehead.

"On your knees, Mr. Hezekiah Ford, or you'll never take yer face off the ground again. Up now and answer me truthfully or it be the end of yer life."

Struggling to obey the deadly command, Ford

put one hand under him and then the other. All hope of deceiving the Captain was useless. Jones had found out everything, somehow. All Ford could think of was to tell anything or say anything to live through this. He started crying. Jones reached down and grabbed his ear ripping it with a violent twist, pulling him upwards. The pain was excruciating, he could feel blood flow down his neck as he succeeded in getting to his knees.

"There'll be no blubbering in front of me, you cringing coward." Jones kicked him again. "Open yer mouth," ordered Jones, pushing the barrel of the cocked horse pistol onto Ford lips. "Open, now," commanded Jones. His intense blue eyes, caught in the lantern light from the waiting room, glared hatred at Ford.

Attracted by the commotion, several people, out to take a refreshing walk in the sultry atmosphere had stopped at the sight of an American officer beating a sailor in the street. One observer was the best friend of the owners of a Brest weekly journal. The latter encouraged another onlooker to run off in search of the gendarmes.

Ford obediently opened his mouth, and Jones jammed the pistol barrel forward catching his tongue against the roof of his mouth. Ford coughed, but stayed up on his knees, trembling, his head contorted backwards from the thrust of the pistol.

"I'll send the back of yer head flying into the stable across this street, if you do not answer every question I ask. Blink to say yes. Your name is Hezekiah Ford, and you are a British spy."

Blink.

"You several times tried to incite mutiny on my ship, the Ranger."

Blink.

"Is Lieutenant Simpson a British spy?"

The fear in Ford's brain had shaken off all effects of the flagons of ale he had consumed. He thought quickly. Would it serve his purpose to indict Simpson too? To spread the guilt?

Jones sensed the man was thinking. He put the question to Ford again in another way and pressed forward with the pistol barrel.

"Is Lieutenant Simpson simply a fool, who you tricked into attempting mutiny?" Jones looked up momentarily sensing observers had gathered around them.

Ford responded. Blink.

In French, Jones called out his identity to the dozen or so civilians who had been attracted to the incident. He informed them that he had just caught a member of his crew who was a British spy. He then continuing his questioning of Ford in English.

"Did you wet the powder of my grenades on the evening that we were going to raid the British harbour at Whitehaven?"

There was a slight shaking of Ford's head from side to side.

"Was it the man called David Smith?"

Blink.

"Did you slip the anchor in Wales, the night we rescued Lunt and the other American prisoners, almost leaving both the entire rescue party and the freed American prisoners stranded in Wales?"

Ford's brain raced, should he admit to it, or blame it on Smith? He couldn't remember whether Smith was in the landing party. A mistake or a lie and Captain Jones would kill him. He would confess to anything, it was all over.

Blink.

"Did you have anything to do with the murder of Lieutenant Lunt?"

Ford's eyes widened. He was surprised by the accusation. He shook his head to the extent he could.

"I have one question left, if you lie I will know it and I shall end your wretched life this instant. Do you agree to disclose all the persons from whom you took orders to go on this mission as a British spy? And anything else you have as to signals, codes, whatever? I know a great deal already, your answer had better be truthful."

Blink.

Jones slowly withdrew the pistol from Ford's quivering mouth. Ford started to collapse to the ground when Jones ordered. "On your hands and knees. Give not a thought to the blade in your boot, or it'll be the end of ye."

There was silence as Ford struggled to get his breath.

"Speak."

"All right, t'was Mr. Stephen Sayre."

"And where can I find this Mr. Sayre?"

"He is in Ambassador Deane's office. He is Mr. Deane's secretary."

"Ambassador Deane has left for America," stated Jones, realizing that Ford had been upon the Ranger since February. He would not know that Deane had left France.

"And was Mr. Deane connected with this treason?" asked Jones.

Ford shook his head, "I don't know. The only person I have ever dealt with was Mr. Sayre. I am not a traitor, I am an English subject from Nova Scotia. I have told you everything I know."

"How much were you paid for your patriotism?"

"Five hundred quid, that's all."

Jones turned around to speak in French to two gendarmes who had just run up to the scene.

Hezekiah Ford collapsed and lost consciousness.

7
Marie

Pain, throbbing pain, was his first conscious thought in four days. There was a pressure on his chest over his heart. He drifted back into nothingness for what was seconds or perhaps hours, then he was awake. There was a continual sharp pain in his chest, and a terrible hunger. He opened his left eye. There was a person with their hands on his chest, gently, but firmly. He could not tell if it was a man or a woman. The face was middle aged with deep crows feet about the eyes. The hair was outlined by a white cap. He moaned.

They made eye contact, and the face smiled and turned its head to call out in rapid French, 'Madame Chatelain, your friend is awake, come.'

Lunt heard a procession of quick steps across a hard floor. Marie soon leaned over into his field of vision. She held her hand up for him not to move.

'Listen to me, Henry, the point of the sabre either penetrated or scraped your heart. Your nurses are under orders from the King's doctor to keep pressure on your chest in a certain way for a few more days. You must remain still and quiet. It is very important for you not to move so that your body can have a chance to repair the wound.'

Lunt started to say something.

"No, even speech is too much exertion for you." Marie put a finger on his lips for him to remain quiet. "Henry, Dr. Franklin has found some forty letters from your family. They are from your wife and father. With your permission I can open them and read them to you."

Lunt closed his eyes and gave the slightest of nods. He was drifting off. He heard her voice as in a cloud. She was saying that there would be some warm chicken broth coming. Her voice was trying so obviously hard to be soothing, but her eyes told her fear.

"But first Henry, we have an important decision to make, before we open these letters, should I read the earliest ones first or last? Do you want to know of what is most recent first or to enjoy the progression of events which they tell?" Marie looked at him, he looked so tired, his face was white.

She bent over him a few inches above his face and gently kissed his lips. His eyes opened. "Poor Henry, you have women from both sides of the Atlantic trying to get your attention. Shall I read you her earliest letter?"

Henry nodded.

"The first one is dated Christmas day, 1777. The envelope is addressed to the care of Silas Deane, American Ambassador, for the mariner Henry Lunt, prisoner of war taken on the Brig Dalton, Christmas Day, 1776." Marie stopped her narrative, "You have written her since you were rescued?"

160

Lunt nodded feebly.

"Once again, Henry, you wish me to break the seal of this letter?" She said in a light tone, "I will know all about the great American Spymaster."

Henry smiled weakly and waited for Marie to continue.

Marie noticed that the stroke of the writer's hand was very firm, but definitely feminine. The letter began:

"*My dearest Henry,*

Our child is now almost a year old. Today we had Christmas dinner at your father's house. You and your brother, Ezra, were much of our conversation, but I think you already know that he is safe.

Your father brought in a wonderful Christmas tree. Little Henry is showing signs of being able to walk. He picked himself up by the bough of the Christmas tree and clung on shaking it so violently out of his joy of standing up that your father had to catch the tree before it toppled over.

For Christmas, we gave each other things that we each had made during the autumn. I made your father a leather vest just like the one I gave you when you first left to..."

The word was crossed out, probably Henry's wife had wanted to avoid all mention of the war should this letter fall into British hands. Marie looked to the top of the letter again there was a number 24 in the upper right hand corner. Had she numbered all of her letters so that Henry would know how many she had written, and how many he had missed?

The chicken broth came and she gave him three large spoonfuls. She turned to put the bowl down and then turned back to find that Henry was fast asleep, but grimacing from pain.

Once again in her life, Marie had monumental decisions to make with very little time to do it. She must make them now. There was one way clearly to make that decision. She read the remainder of the letter, and the last paragraph several times.

> *"Henry, you are the love of my life. Your son and I will wait patiently for you to return. Never, never doubt it. Not for a moment. Even if, God forbid, you should suffer some wound or disfigurement, I want you back, the man inside.*
>
> *Sweet dreams, my love,*
>
> *Sarah*

A tear came to Marie's eye. She left the bed and went to the window standing there for a few moments looking upon the approaching daylight. She looked at Henry. He was fast asleep. She picked up the basket of letters, searching for the most recent one from his wife. It was posted early March of 1778, just about the time Henry was rescued by the crew of the Ranger. She muttered 'forgive me Henry' in her own language and gently broke the waxen seal of the private correspondence. Instead of being addressed through Ambassador Deane, it was simply a note to be hand carried by Mr. John Adams, Ambassador to France.

Inside, the tone of the letter was much the same. Marie observed that the number on the upper right hand corner was now 161. She read the letter, again very short, containing only family things, nothing at all about the war at home. The closing was also similar expressing her love for Henry. In a few weeks Sarah would have Henry's own letter reporting that he had been rescued by the Ranger.

Marie folded the letter and sighed. It was impossible from the start. She had now passed her fortieth birthday, and Henry was in his mid twenties. He had a wife and a child, something that 'le belle sterile' could never give him. It was never to be. She had been the consort of this King only a few years ago, because there had been no danger of her bearing him children. And now the Queen, Marie Antoinette, was finally with child. The Queen had changed her permissive behavior. All of her own sexual antics of the past, her orgies in the country were to be swept under the rug. The Queen had been furious to see Marie at Court again. It would only be a matter of days before the Queen forced Lunt and her out of the King's private chambers. Her fury might come to affect Henry's very recovery, if he were forced to be moved from this bed prematurely and thus lose the direct attention of the King's physician.

Yes, she could depart to her Chateau until Henry had recovered or the worst had befallen him. She could lure him there. She could steal his letters right now and lure him there to get them. She could corrupt his flesh. She had felt his reaction, sensed his passion for her when they had danced together among the Ambassadors. It was enough to know that she could have him, at least for a time. But she knew that after a brief time he would be off again on his ship and she would be isolated from the court and from the intrigue she craved.

Minister Vergennes had offered her an interesting assignment. They had found a cover in the disguise of the widow of a British colonial bureaucrat returning from service in India. The woman, a Madame Sheila Armstrong, had been herself affected by the plague and had died along with many of the crew aboard a Dutch merchantman. The vessel was now under quarantine in the port of Lisbon, the bodies had been taken away and burned. The Dutch Captain had sold all the lady's papers to an agent of the French embassy. It was perfect. Madame Sheila Armstrong had been twenty years in the Indian subcontinent.

Few in England would know her, but she was entitled to a fat pension from the British government and the ability to mingle in certain circles.

Unlike the situation in Belfast, it would take months and months to trace her, if anyone even tried. But the window of opportunity was closing. Vergennes had urged her to accept the challenge and to use this cover and her beauty to get into a strategic situation before the war formally broke out between England and France. The challenge thrilled her. She shivered and returned from the window.

Marie walked out into the hall connecting the all of the King's chambers and asked the servant for a quill and pen. As soon as she had it, she sat at the writing table and wrote Henry a short, four paragraphed letter in English, and then two brief notes in French. She put all three inside one wrapping, spread hot wax on the seam and pressed her personal stamp from her purse. Within a quarter hour she was gone from the King's chambers.

*   *   *   *   *

A few mornings later, a carriage roared through the gate and onto the grounds of Hotel de Valentinois at Passy. Its conspicuous noise, as it clattered along the quarter mile of entrance road, awoke many of the Hotel's residents from their sleep in the early dawn hours. The carriage turned at high speed in front of the great hotel and circled around the small reflecting pool to stop with deliberateness in front of le Petit Hotel.

Nine green uniformed soldiers with white cross straps and short white and green caps rushed out. Each soldier carried a musket with a gleaming bayonet in place.

'Form ready for inspection.'

'Attention!' cried the Sergeant.

Captain Jones exited the carriage in his finest dress uniform, dark blue with striking red lapels, his gold epaulets reflecting in the growing sunlight. A silken neck cloth with ruffles adorned his chest. His face was clear and proud, his brownish red hair drawn back into a cue.

'Gentlemen,' he spoke loudly and without deference to anyone's sleep as he stood addressing the squad. 'I charge the United States Marines with the responsibility of defending this embassy and our ambassadors and staffs within to the death. I expect each of you to be observant, but courteous to all who pass through these doors. I charge each of you with the responsibility to only assume your station with your uniforms in their best condition possible, and to always have your arms in a condition ready for instant use....'

A crowd of people, primarily in their night clothes had assembled in front of the main Hotel and were walking towards le Petit Hotel. They had never seen American soldiers, let alone marines. The French did not use marines, simply ordinary army soldiers, to fight on their ships...

The first one out of the American Embassy door was ten year old John Quincy. It was John Paul Jones and the Marines, better than any dream he could have conjured up in an entire year. He bounced up and down with enthusiasm until his father found him and held his hand for fear that his son would topple off the stairs.

Ambassador Franklin followed, his brow arched in anger. "John, did you authorize this?" he whispered over Adam's shoulder.

"Yes, sir, I have a son to think of. I am tired of spending each night worrying if we are going to have a grenade thrown through the window. It is affecting my work by day. If you, yourself, do not wish the protection, then I wish it alone as co-ambassador."

A dozen of the embassy staff had joined the Ambassadors on the steps of le Petit Hotel as the Marines raised an American flag to mark the beginning of the day. Among the staff was a British spy, who watched the proceedings with increasing timidity. He had heard what had happened to Hezekiah Ford. It had been in the newspapers. Feigning a stomach flu, he retreated to his room and remained there the entire morning, afraid that he could not hide his fear in public. Beneath his pillow was a cocked pistol. He waited for the dreaded knock on his door in total terror.

Across the garden on a westward facing balcony Madame de Chaumont looked out at the scene standing there in the shadows in her negligee. Her husband, one of the richest men in France, benefactor to the Americans, and owner of Hotel de Valentinois and a hundred merchant ships, slept soundly in their bed behind her. But the man of her dreams was the handsome American Captain, calling orders to his men below.

The meeting at Passy between Jones and Ambassadors Franklin and Adams was brief. The Captain explained the circumstances of how he had uncovered the spy, Hezekiah Ford, who had confessed that he had been recruited by Stephen Sayre, a British spy, then working in the office of Ambassador Deane. Both Ambassadors knew Sayre and informed Jones that they would take the matter under advisement.

Then John Adams first thanked Jones for complying with his request for protection so swiftly, but then opened a second subject, "Captain Jones, since the unfortunate Mr. Ford has vindicated Lt. Simpson of any complicity, are you now going to drop your charges against him? It is a matter of considerable embarrassment to our Navy."

"Is the naval department going to authorize my command of another ship? One of sufficient size that it might do serious damage to the Royal Navy."

"I'll not bargain with you, sir. I know that Lieutenant Simpson did not follow your orders to the letter, but he did fight bravely in the engagement with the Drake, did he not?"

"Yes, sir. But you..."

Adams held up his hand, 'I think, Captain Jones, that you should return to duty aboard the Ranger. Ambassador Franklin and I will take up the matter of the spy, Sayre. And for goodness sake, Captain, should you identify any more spies among your crew, please do not beat them into insensibility in a public street. The incident made the papers in Brest. If it hadn't been for the assassination attempt on Lt. Lunt, the incident would now be the scandal of Versailles. In the future, simply put any suspects under arrest, and let us know. We are quite capable of handling the situation. Ambassador Franklin and I will look forward to your presence at the Independence day party here on July 4th. Good day, Captain Jones.'

Ambassador Franklin walked the Captain to his carriage, putting his hand on his shoulder in a fatherly fashion. 'John, please go cautiously with Mr. Adams. He is on the marine committee, he admires you greatly, but he is your superior. Think about the things he has said. The matter of a court martial for Lieutenant Simpson, no matter how much he has angered you, is just not what we need now while we are stalling, awaiting the news from Congress of their signing of the French Alliance. Until such time, we are in a form of limbo. Do not embarrass us, John. Our enemies will use every situation that they can, true or imagined, to discredit us. Take the high road in all matters. Again, think about the prudence of Mr. Adams' advice.'

Captain Jones saluted and entered his carriage. Franklin continued talking through the carriage window,

"Lieutenant Lunt came to consciousness for a brief time yesterday morning, but he is still in the King's chambers. When I see him, I will tell him of your good wishes for a speedy recovery. But under no circumstances are you, personally, to go to Versailles. Mr. Adams and I are delaying a tribute to your capture of the Drake until a time when it is more opportune. This is not the diplomatic moment. Please be patient and return now to Brest and prepare the Ranger for another voyage."

When Franklin returned into le Petit Hotel, he mused to a quiet and reflective Mr. Adams over breakfast, "If our brave little Captain is really the great man he thinks of himself, he will soon heed the wisdom of your advice. Until that moment, I think we'll let him sit awhile, Mr. Adams."

*   *   *   *   *

The spy left le Petit Hotel, past the marine sentry, and eventually walked down the road towards the Tuilleries Garden. As usual, in the early evening the whores were plentiful in the park as they stood on the public benches along the promenade lifting their skirts to show any well dressed gentleman their offerings. After he stopped in front of one of the benches, ostensibly to banter with a red headed woman too old to be really making a lively living at her trade, the spy casually looked this way and that to see that he had not been followed. He said goodbye to her and continued a couple of hundred yards further along and then suddenly changed direction going into a dense grove of trees off the pathway. He took the small pouch from his cap and tossed it violently into a hollow tree. He then moved several hundred feet further along, pausing to relieve himself, partly as an alibi and partly because the tension was affecting his bladder. The spy then continued his course through the trees coming out on another public pathway.

Later in his apartment, Paul Wentworth decoded the message to read: 'Lieutenant Lunt lives, but is still gravely wounded at Versailles. Captain Jones made a brief visit this week bringing a permanent marine guard to be now on station at the embassy. However, both Ambassadors seemed displeased with him over something. Their conversation was held in the utmost privacy in Franklin's office so that the staff could not hear a thing. Since last week there seem to be no new initiatives. Everyone is awaiting the Congress' return of ratification of the French treaty. The entire tone of le Petit Hotel is very guarded. AM I SAFE? Are you certain that neither Mr. Ford nor Mr. Sayre knew my identity? I insist on a reply by Saturday at the Greengrocer, or I will simply walk out of le Petit Hotel forever. No amount of money, and particularly the small amount you pay me, is worth the constant terror that I must now daily endure. If he catches me, I know Captain Jones will do much the same to me as he did to the unfortunate Mr. Ford.'

*   *   *   *   *

Lunt awoke suddenly. His bed chamber was bathed in candle light. There was a rather ordinary man in his room, wearing chamber clothes. The man wore thick spectacles and was observing him intently. The nurse was no longer pressing on his chest.

The man smiled down at him. 'Ah, I see you are awake, Lieutenant Lunt. Are you in pain?'

Henry nodded. The young man was very cultured in his speech, but the French accent on his English was unmistakable. The man appeared to be about his own age.

'But it is better to be here among the living, and in pain, no, than not to be here at all?'

'I would rather just get up and take a walk,' responded Lunt with a small smile.

The man held up his hand, 'Please, that of all things you must not do for at least another week. We are unsure of the healing of the wound to your chest. Your bandages are changed four times a day. Everything that has touched you is sterile since you came to this bed. Please do not get up and ruin the good Doctor's work. He runs between you and the Queen by the hour.'

Before Henry could speak, the man asked him a question, 'Where do you live in America? Tell me what it is like so that I can pretend to see it.'

172

'I am from a place called Newburyport. It's a small village, by the sea, where the Merrimack River joins the sea, about a day's ride north of Boston. A long day's ride.'

'Ah, Boston, where the Indians threw the Tea into the water. Does the harbour still taste of tea?'

Henry smiled, 'On a warm summer afternoon, you can take your cup to the waters edge and taste just a bit yet.'

They both laughed together, until Lunt coughed.

'Too much talk for tonight, please be still. The nurse will be with you in a few moments. There are letters here from your family, and I believe Madame Chatelain has left you a note. They are all in the basket for you. The nurse you have now is Irish. She can read the letters as you wish. I will return again soon. I am very interested to hear more of America.'

The young man, about Henry's age, departed without saying his name, but instinctively Henry knew it was Louis, the King.

Over the next few days, Henry had the Irish nurse read all of his letters starting from the earliest on. There was little except family news. Everyone was healthy. The letters made him wish and dream that he was with his family, in bed with sweet Sarah or out on Water Street in Newburyport, walking with his son in hand, or just sitting atop the climbing tree on Plumb Island talking with his father. After each letter, he dreamed of these things. The images were very vivid. He longed to go home, to be out of this place as beautiful as the palace was.

The Irish nurse said, "There is one letter left in the basket which you haven't opened. The one from Madame Chatelain. Perhaps you are ready to read it now? I can simply open it and let you read it for yourself. I believe that you are strong enough to hold the letter, in your right hand."

The woman was very wise, she had been present through the reading of all of his letters, and through them she had learned much about the man she cared for. She was also wise in the intrigues of the Chateau Versailles and the intrigues that had driven Madame Chatelain to depart from the King's chambers so swiftly.

"I'll read the letter tomorrow. Leave it on the stand for me to see when I wake up. I am tired now."

Later, when Henry awoke he opened the seal clumsily with his thumb, and found that there were three notes inside. Two were very brief and in French. He read the letter in English first.

> "*My darling Henry,*
>
> *Like you I have a country and a duty to perform for that country, and so I have had to leave the palace. I suspect I shall be gone a long time. But I leave for you some advice and some help.*
>
> *I have read some of your letters, more than I should have. Forgive me, I understand now that your heart lies across the ocean and*

why. Truly I envy you. If I were you I would return home to your family and do whatever fighting you must from that side of the great ocean.

But sometimes what we want is not ours to have. I therefore leave for you two pieces of help should your duties require you to remain in France. The first letter is an introduction to the Count de Batz-Castelmore. He is the master of a school with no name which is famous across all of Europe. Only its graduates have a name for it, l'Ecole des Espions, or the school of spies. Should you present this letter to the Count, I doubt if you will ever again lose a duel in the Stone Gallery.

The second letter is an invitation at any time to my chateau which lies in the mountains north of Joigny near a tiny, but tranquil place called Dixmont. My estranged husband maintains it for me with a small staff for the duration of my life. I am rarely there. I offer you its tranquility and beauty at any time, without obligation. Simply present the enclosed letter to the staff. Both the school and the chateau are very close to each other.

To the dreams which cannot be,

Marie

*   *   *   *   *

The weeks of June of 1778 were among the hottest ever recorded in mainland Europe. The stench of the city of Paris even drifted as far away as Versailles. People everywhere wore the briefest of clothing, out of necessity. In the palace, the Queen was miserable with the heat in her final month of labor and that meant that hundreds of servants were equally miserable. Louis, the King, found solace in his new found friend from America.

On Lunt's first walk around the perimeter of his bed, Louis was present. "Soon you will be a free man, I envy you."

"Your Majesty envies me, and you are the King?"

"Ah, yes, I am the King, but also a prisoner. You are free to do the ordinary things of life; to sit under a tree; to choose what place to go to next; to go here and there across the sea. Do you have any idea of what a King's life is like? Let me tell you just a little.

"First, when I wake up, I am not allowed to get up. So I must sneak about in a plain suit in the early hours of the morning. This is the only time that I am free, for as the hour approaches eleven thirty, every day of my life, I must go back to bed, for the Ceremony of the Lever. Since the time of my great grandfather each of the Ministers comes to the King's bed chamber and hands him one article of apparel. One his shoes, another his shirt, and so forth. It, I suppose, is a tradition which cements the fact that I still trust each man. When I was a child it was not so bad, but I am now a grown man." The King put up his finger for emphasis, "You think to yourself, I know, why does the King not simply declare that there will be no more Ceremony of the Lever. Ah, I have tried to do this. But there is no way out of it. If I declare it is to be no more, then I hurt many people and their feelings. Not to speak of the many hundreds of people who help the ministers prepare for the ceremony each day. They would be out of work, and many of them have worked for the King's family for generations. So, alas, in front of my ministers, the King dresses for the day. And from then on, until nightfall I am on a schedule set by others. Some members of the court are even present when I go to bed at night."

Lunt started to say something to the effect that he, the King, could change all that despite the wishes of his subjects, but felt that the time was improper. He really knew too little about the situation. Instead, in French, he signified his understanding."

"Je comprendre, Votre Majeste."

Louis the XVI smiled. "Ah, you are learning our language. I am very pleased. What is it that you wish to happen to you when you leave here, when the doctor says you are recovered? Tell me."

"Since I received the letters from my wife and family, the greatest thing I wish for is to return home. At least for a little while."

"How long has it been since you were home?"

"Almost two years."

"And we have talked over the past weeks about all those places in Massachusetts and New England. You have sailed all those waters? You know the harbors, the currents, and so forth?"

"As good as any man you might find."

"There is a situation, a possible need for such talent with Admiral d'Orvilliers. Please do not speak to anyone else about it, but I will see what I can do. But first there is the Independence Day celebration at le Petit Hotel."

"You mean you are really coming? Ambassador Franklin will be delighted."

Louis held up his hand. "It must be a secret, Henry, truly a secret. For if I say I am coming, then all of Versailles will come and the grounds of the Hotel de Valentinois will be overrun. There may be ten thousand, no, twenty thousand people. It would be a stampede. No, let us say, between friends, that I have scheduled a hunt for that day. July the fourth, is it not?"

Henry nodded, smiling.

8
July 4th

Lunt returned to le Petit Hotel during the fourth week of June. His assignment was to convalesce. He was given a downstairs bedroom off the main salon with a full bed. There was a small reception for him at which sweet cakes and tea were served. As Lunt was excused to lie on one of the sofas, Franklin and Adams introduced him to the nearly twenty members of their ambassadorial staff consisting of everything from secretaries, linguists, messengers, valets, cooks, and housemaids. In addition there were the staff's families, the marine guards, and a dozen or so servants from the main hotel who lived in the rear of le Petit Hotel, behind the kitchen.

Lunt had met both Nathaniel Hubbard and Jeremiah Hanson before on the morning of that fateful day when he had departed with Franklin for Versailles. Hubbard was a tall man in his thirties with a deep scar on his right cheek. Hubbard's duties consisted of scheduling individual meetings for the two Ambassadors and events such as the Fourth of July party to come the following week. The planned embassy protocol was that anyone desirous of meeting with either Dr. Franklin or Mr. Adams was first supposed to be scheduled by Mr. Hubbard. However, the reality of the day to day routine was that often visitors were able to frustrate Mr. Hubbard's assignment and see the Ambassadors without an appointment.

Instead of lying alone in his room most of the day, Lunt elected to spend a great deal of his time reading in one of the great salon's many settees. Ever conscious of the reasons which had originally brought him to Ambassador Franklin, Lunt observed closely the workings of the ambassadorial staff. In that first week only one visitor came to see Mr. Adams, a ship's master from Massachusetts who had succeeded in breaking through the ever increasing British blockade. But well over a hundred individuals or groups of persons came that same week to see Dr. Franklin.

Among the daily parade of visitors, Lunt found that he could categorize them into three distinct types. There was first and foremost a parade of persons dressed usually in a flamboyant variety of military regalia, who claimed vast military experience in some European conflict, and who sought to receive important command appointments in General Washington's army.

One evening as they were all seated for supper, Mr. Adams, in a rare touch of humor stated that if Franklin could keep the rate of military volunteers flowing at such a fever pitch, it might be possible for the Continental Army to field the first ever army composed entirely of general officers. There was a chuckle down the long table, and then Franklin remarked that they had better all be on the look out for at least one private so that the generals would have someone to give orders to. The ensuing laughter was deep and hard.

In his duties, Mr. Hubbard found it especially difficult to intercept these military applicants once they had identified the now famous Franklin profile and happened to observe him in the main salon.

The second most common type of visitor was someone either from the French merchant class or nobility who were willing to help the struggles of the infant nation with a bequest of goods for the war. When Mr. Hubbard was able to identify these individuals or groups, they were given priority and usually escorted immediately up into Franklin's office where they might spend from fifteen minutes to several hours with the great man.

The third type of visitor were those who were just passing by and wished simply to shake Franklin's hand for a moment. Hubbard often kept these individuals waiting several hours until there were enough of them to make Mr. Franklin's time worthwhile. Despite his gout, Franklin obligingly stepped downstairs several times a day and spent a quarter of an hour with each group of well wishers. Weather permitting, this type of reception was ordinarily held outdoors in the garden opposite the entrance to le Petit Hotel so as to cause the least amount of disruption to the many letters being produced each day in the main salon.

Lunt observed that no matter what their motive for visiting, each person was given a cordial reception and listened to politely. Despite whatever Franklin's personal predisposition might be about the merits of a particular visitation, Franklin always displayed charm and grace towards each of his guests. After each visitation, Franklin would usually need to dictate some letter or correspondence concerning it, and an archival copy, usually a first draft with corrections, was retained in the embassy files. Often the visitors were not conversant in either French or English and Lunt soon discovered that another reason for such a large ambassadorial staff was that many of the staff, as a second skill, were conversant in a variety of European languages including French, Russian, German, Dutch, Danish, Spanish, German, and Polish.

Perhaps from the stress of serving as appointment secretary, Mr. Hubbard showed signs of a penchant for alcohol in his complexion. and did not quarter at le Petit Hotel. He thus perhaps deliberately evaded the vast parade of people who also wandered by at irregular hours. Rarely was an embassy meal consumed without the arrival of some unexpected visitor who had to be invited to sit at the table during a dinner in progress.

Hubbard spoke fluent French and stood with Franklin's French speaking visitors during their visitations. Hubbard also often translated Franklin's dictated letters into perfect French. On the very first day that Lunt returned from Versailles, Hubbard went to his desk in the main salon and loaned Henry a rare book which discussed French grammar in English.

Thereafter, whenever the two came into contact, Lunt and he exchanged at least a few words in French. Lunt studied the book intensely during the entire time he spent at le Petit Hotel. By the end of a week he had memorized a couple of hundred words, and practiced their proper pronunciation constantly with Hubbard, and with the cook, Madame Le Roux, and many others of the Hotel de Valentinois staff.

Another senior member of the ambassadorial staff residing at the embassy was Mr. Jeremiah Hanson, whom Lunt had also met at breakfast the morning he had departed for Versailles. Hanson was in his fifties and had a midlands accent, and perpetually smoked a pipe from dawn to dusk. He had once been a watch maker in London. He had lost his business when his wife had left him.

Several years before, Franklin had invited Hanson by letter to join him in Paris after Franklin had been obliged to flee London because of a warrant for treason issued by Lord North. Lunt found out that initially Hanson had worked for a time in the office of Ambassador Deane. But for the present Mr. Hanson seemed to be performing a lot of courier duties to various locations in Paris and the seaports. Hanson, a meticulously detailed man in his manner of organization, was appropriately in charge of the organization of the bulging embassy's files which contained one hand written copy of each letter sent to and from the Embassy. Mr. Hanson was also in charge of a group of two clerks who issued visas, and other legal documents.

Franklin's most senior member of his immediate staff, however, was another English expatriate named Dr. Edward Bancroft, who owned property in New Hampshire, and who Franklin had first met during his tenure as colonial agent in London. Bancroft was a medical doctor and a notoriously good chess player. Residing at le Petit Hotel, Dr. Bancroft acted as Franklin's personal secretary and took dictation from the Ambassador at any hour of the day that correspondence needed to be sent to someone. Frequently Bancroft would also go on long errands for Dr. Franklin.

Upon their introduction on the first day, the good natured, slightly built man had said, 'Lieutenant, may I call you Henry?...the King's doctor has sent me a note that he would advise that we continue to change bandages on that wound at least twice a day while this infernal heat persists. I am given to understand that you like to play chess. Perhaps we could make one of these daily changes while Doctor Franklin sleeps during the late afternoon, and afterwards we might enjoy a chess game.'

It became their custom over the course of the next few weeks, that in the later afternoon, Dr. Bancroft and Lunt routinely went to a small stone table in the garden directly in front of the Hotel and played until either it became too dark, or until the mosquitos became unbearable. As they played, Lunt found he could observe various members of the staff leaving the grounds of the Hotel Valentinois at the end of the day.

Nearly every evening about seven, Ambassador Franklin, in his black Quaker suit with stunning starched white cravat, also departed the embassy to attend an affair at one of the so-called, 'American salons,' or at a nearby casino which was run by members of the nobility friendly to the fashionable American cause. Usually his hosts dispatched a carriage to pick up Franklin at le Petit Hotel and then returned him safely, often in the wee hours of the morning.

From the initial moves of his first game with Bancroft, Lunt knew that he had encountered a master chess tactician. Not only did Bancroft's openings properly seek to control the center four squares of the board, but also his development of intermediate pieces like the Bishops and Knights was flawless. Where an average player might generally succeed in getting two, or at best three, of his intermediate pieces in strategic positions before the board became clogged with a morass of pawns, Bancroft was unusually skilled at maneuvering nearly all his pieces into position.

Early in a typical game Bancroft would offer Lunt frustrations and as Lunt took a move to address each local problem, Bancroft would use the lapse in Lunt's forward game to maneuver an additional piece into position. By that time Bancroft was in control of the middle, and, inevitably, the end game.

During their play, Bancroft asked Lunt many questions about how he came to be in the Colonial

Navy. Over the course of several evenings, Lunt told Bancroft of his upbringing in Newburyport, of his family, his wife and child, and of his service with the Colonial Navy. Owning property in New Hampshire, himself, Bancroft was familiar with the northern Massachusetts coast, and had a decade before even spent several evenings in Lunt's pleasant little seaport community.

'Where did you get the opportunity to play so much chess?' inquired Bancroft.

'My father taught me the game, though not in any formal way. However, when I was a prisoner, I found that playing it was a way to distract the others in my cell from their plight. We used scratches in the stone floor for the board, and parts of a tattered blanket for pieces. A far cry from these beauties,' observed Lunt, taking up a castle from his side of the board to observe it closely. 'Where did you obtain them?'

'I didn't realize you had been a prisoner of the English? When?'

'From Christmas day of 1776 to March of 1778, when Captain Jones and the Ranger rescued us.'

'Oh dear,' paused Bancroft, 'you have had it rough, and now you're wounded...but let me tell you about these pieces by way of telling you about my own sordid past before I became Dr. Franklin's secretary in London. I once was retained to be the only medical doctor for a large plantation in Surinam, on the northeast coast of South America. There were large sugar and tobacco interests there and a staff of several hundred Europeans.'

Bancroft held up one of the pieces, 'I observed that the natives had an extraordinary talent for carving wood to make their idols. The thought occurred to me that perhaps I could get them to carve me the chess set of a lifetime. So, I took some illustrations I had in a book of Shakespeare's plays and got them to carve Hamlet's castle, then the King and Queen of Denmark. I took a background figure from the merchant of Venice to show them a Bishop.'

'And the knight?'

'My wife had a medal with St. George on it. You know, fighting the dragons, that's why the horse is up on its back hooves, rather dramatic,' he observed.

Lunt thought a moment, 'I did not know you had a wife. Why is she not here at the Ambassador's residence?'

Bancroft did not answer for a while, pausing to concentrate on the chess board in front of him. Finally he spoke up, 'As Dr. Franklin is aware, my wife resides in London. He has met her. I'm afraid we are a bit estranged. I hope one day that we shall be together again.'

'I'm sorry,' said Lunt, not wishing to inquire into the man's obvious personal despair.

A few minutes later Bancroft said, 'You know, I'm not the only member of the staff with a wife in England. Jeremiah Hanson also has a wife there. When we first came over we did not anticipate that this conflict would ever really endure for more than a few months. As Englishmen, we did not expect to find ourselves in a cause allied with the French, and working against England."

"Then, why do you continue to serve this embassy?" probed Lunt, "You may own property in New Hampshire, but you are not an American."

"I think you have hit upon a most interesting point, Henry," replied Bancroft, not looking up, but continuing to study the chess board, puffing on his pipe, reflectively. "I have been assisting Dr. Franklin in all manner of scientific as well as political endeavors for the better part of a decade. When I was down because of events in my personal life, he helped me greatly. He lifted me up with his spirit. He is truly a man without malice. Yet, over the past couple of years of exile, he has had to endure a great many stressful relationships with the other co-ambassadors, their agents, and the continually vacillating Congress and not to forget, of course, the efforts of Lord Stormont and the British."

Bancroft sighed, "I guess you could say that I am here chiefly out of continued loyalty to Dr. Franklin, over and above any other consideration. And now, of course, because of the depth of my involvement I would certainly be hanged should I suddenly surface in England and again attempt to pursue my livelihood as a medical doctor. I have it on good authority that my name has been expunged from the list of the Royal College of Surgeons. Remember that it is in my own hand that so many of the good Doctor's thoughts have been preserved on paper, both in the political realm as well as the scientific. I presume that the Tories would like nothing better than to hang me, as well, for any small part I might have played in this rebellion. So I cannot easily go home to my wife and attempt a reconciliation until this is over. I have written her many times. That is all I can do for now. That, and trust to God and Dr. Franklin's judgement that we have all chosen to pursue the right course. But, I remind you that in continuing to serve here I join the ranks of a great many Englishmen who feel that this Colonial cause is just.'

'Up to only three years ago, we all considered ourselves Englishmen, even those of us living in America,' Lunt informed him.

Bancroft puffed one more time on his pipe and then announced, 'Checkmate.'

*   *   *   *   *

On that most important morning, the sun rose over the grounds of the Hotel Valentinois and its smaller adjacent building, le Petit Hotel. Since long before dawn, there had been workers busily preparing decorations. Madame de Chaumont had been working at a fever pitch for several days. She had brought thirty of her personal servants into the effort in addition to the regular hotel staff. A few days before she had asked Ambassador Franklin what she could do. He had correctly guessed that it would be hot, very hot. He requested if his hostess could perhaps supply melons so that the people who came would be refreshed and if she could secure several large tubs so that any children of the guests could bathe and splash in water to keep cool.

On the big day, everyone was pressed into service, from the noblesse to the common gardener to the Ambassador of Spain, who came very early to avoid traveling from Versailles in the heat of the day. All cheerfully worked together to get into the American spirit.

And the magnificent cake, the cake was the centerpiece of it all. The four stone ovens of the Hotel Valentinois ran constantly for two days to produce forty enormous sheet cakes that went into the creation of the 'Le Grand Cake.' The sheet cakes had been placed on the top of doors, that had been taken off their hinges from the hotels, lain flat, and then elevated onto wooden horses. The large flat cakes had been joined together with sweet frosting on the top to form one huge cake flag, five by eight sheets in dimension. The frosting had been applied in the cool before dawn. It was red with white stripes with a field of blue in the upper left corner upon which thirteen ornamental white stars had been placed. The flag cake had been set out under the shade of a large oak tree to the side of le Petit Hotel.

By mid morning two huge horse drawn carts arrived from Paris carrying kegs of ale from a brewery.

A troupe from the theatres had come to entertain with festive songs for the day, and to dance and to juggle everything from apples to swords. About mid morning, Captain Jones arrived from Brest with a coach filled with fourteen more marines in full green and white uniforms, each button and each bayonet glittering in the sun. On their uniforms, they each wore a small blue button with a tiny copper medallion hanging from beneath, on each was inscribed simply the word, Liberty. A half hour later, Admiral d'Orvilliers and his officers arrived in two more enormous coaches with their brilliant white uniforms, red sashes and feather plumage. The party was on.

And of course the spies watched. There were several of them, who for the most part did not know of each other's co-conspiracy. They hurried about, ostensibly busy, but inwardly angry and jealous because every important foreign ambassador to France was present. How would Lord Stormont and Paul Wentworth react to this?

At ten minutes before noon, the crowning moment came just as Ambassador Franklin was about to mount a special stage constructed for the occasion. The crowd hushed suddenly, when from across the meadow in the direction of the tiny village of Passy there came the stentorian bellow of a great stag horn. After it, growing in intensity by the moment, came the thunder of hundreds of horses' hooves. Everyone knew that the horn that sounded was the famous one used at Versailles to signify the King's return from a successful hunt of an enormous stag, one of truly magnificent proportions. Every Frenchman scurried across the grounds of Hotel Valentinois and towards the main gate to view the arrival of their King.

The royal hunting party was dressed in blood red suits, with various series of attendant riders, dressed in black or purple. Behind the party rode some sixty lancers in full regalia, their silver helmets glittering in the bright morning sun. The crowds swept apart as the King and his fellow huntsmen entered. Somehow, someone had mercifully corralled and restrained the hundreds of dalmatians which normally comprised part of the spectacle of the King's stag hunt.

From the high platform, the faces of Franklin, Adams, and Lee beamed in delight. Franklin descended the stairs of the platform as best he could, but once accomplishing that, he walked to the side of the King's horse. He bowed, with his co-Ambassadors just behind, emulating his gestures. He spoke in French. "Your Majesty, you do us an enormous honor to have your presence at our humble festivities."

"Nonsense, we were on a hunt, the stag came this direction. He must have known instinctively where there was going to be a truly great party." For the first time ever, in public, the King had spoken in English. The Americans all understood him and they laughed at his witticism. Following that, for just a moment there was an awkward silence. No one knew what to do or to say next.

Captain Jones seized the moment, stepping

forward from the grounds beneath the front of the platform. "Would Your Majesty care to hear our marines play Yankee Doodle?"

The King nodded. Captain Jones called out and there came instantly the deafening volley of sixteen muskets firing in perfect unison into the air. Many of the horses of the hunt bolted in a split second of terror, but quickly were calmed by their riders as the green and white uniformed marines began to march directly forward into the front of the crowd of spectators; two drummers, four fifes, and sixteen high stepping, musket twirling marines in three rows took an abrupt right face upon order by Captain Jones and strode, with smoking barrels, dramatically across the front of the crowd.

Captain Jones, himself, seized an American flag from its location in front of the platform and ran to march at the head of his marines. As they marched, he urged the guests, by hand gestures, to fall in line behind the forming parade and led a course back down the thoroughfare towards the main gate. When the company reached the main gate, Jones ordered an abrupt left across the lawn and then another to turn back to pick up more participants. The horses of the King's lancers fell in behind.

By the time the impromptu parade was ready to pass by the platform a third time, the King, his ministers, and the three co-ambassadors had all ascended the platform. In the front of the parade, the handsome Captain with glittering gold epaulets on a crisp blue uniform with blood red lapels, called out in French, his hand extended, "Will Madame de Chaumont, as deliciously beautiful as the cake she has prepared for us all...will she lead the parade for us?"

From the platform, the Leray de Chaumont, one of the powerful shipping magnates in the world, turned briefly from his conversation, raised an eyebrow, looked at Jones and then nodded his consent to his wife. Then he turned back to his conversation with others of the noblesse, who had not yet been swept up in the mounting enthusiasm of the spontaneous parade and the flood of music and song which filled the air. Jones and Madame de Chaumont, her face beaming in delight, marched at the head of the formation waving in gestures for all to join in. After several more tours of the great lawn, Jones brought the entire troop to a halt in front of the stage decorated with red, white, and blue bunting that fluttered vigorously in the wind.

"Does... does your Majesty have anything to say?" shouted Franklin, his face sweating in the heat.

The King shouted back so that as many as possible might hear his response, "I have only come to party with my American friends, may this unity we demonstrate today forge a great bond between our two nations."

There was a spontaneous, "Here! here!" shouted in several languages and then much applause.

Franklin raised his arms and announced, "Your

Majesty, Monsieur Ambassadors, Lords and Ladies of this Kingdom, Ladies and Gentlemen, this is truly a unique American celebration on your soil, and so I offer to you the benefit an old American tradition for celebrations such as these. The tradition is for all our guests to be as comfortable as possible on such a terribly hot day. And in order to achieve comfort on this particular day, I invite everyone, even our military, to take off their jackets as I am doing now.' Franklin set the example.

Below, in front of the crowd, Captain Jones removed his tricorner hat, and then his dress blue and red trimmed coat. He beckoned his marines to follow his example. Beside him, Madame de Chaumont stole an admiring glance at her escort's broad shoulders and slim waist, earned in a life time of arduous work aboard naval vessels. He turned his smiling face to her and winked roguishly as Franklin began to speak again.

'There is another American tradition...'

Someone in the crowd, already in his cups, shouted out in French, 'Next, Le Grand Doctor would have us take off our britches.'

There was raucous laughter amongst most of the guests, soon to be joined in everywhere as the English speakers had the remark translated to them.

'No,' shouted Franklin smiling broadly, 'For the ladies' sake, I dare not do that! But we Americans do always roll up our sleeves when we work hard and when we play hard.'

Franklin rolled up the sleeves of his once starched white dress shirt, now laden with perspiration. "And now before it all melts from the heat," he gestured with his hand, "I invite good King Louis to help me cut the Liberty Cake."

The King smiled, and with his dress red coat tossed away to a servant, he attempted to roll up his sleeves which were too tightly tailored to his arm and not designed to open, and so after a moment of struggle, he had to resign himself to only rolling up his sleeves only one lap and tucking it neatly in place. Not to let the temporary frustration of his tailored dress get the better of him, he said smiling to those within earshot, "I like this American party."

Everyone laughed. Beer, singing of French and American songs, and many jugglers' performances followed. Several times during the festivities, various Ambassadors from other nations approached the King about matters of state, He gestured as if he was shooing away a fly, saying, "Tomorrow, tomorrow."

After a half hour of observing the festivities and even in joining in songs with the crowd, the King approached Franklin with deliberateness and whispered, "Mr. Ambassador, I would very much like to see the office of the great Doctor Franklin. The man who discovered the electricity in the heavens, and who now electrifies my kingdom. I would like to see where he works and thinks."

Franklin bowed and motioned for the King to enter le Petit Hotel. The King, along with the Foreign Minister

Vergennes and Admiral d'Orvilliers, toured the grand salon downstairs for a few minutes admiring the portraits loaned to the mission by Leray de Chaumont.

Franklin pointed to the tables in the salon. He stretched the truth a bit by saying, "Often, each of the co-ambassadors conducts a separate meeting at the same time among these clusters of tables. The salon can be a very busy place."

The King smiled and turned to face Arthur Lee, "... and even you, Mr. Lee, you conduct your meetings here, working hand in hand with the other Ambassadors?"

Lee swallowed hard. Franklin and Adams raised their eyebrows and then looked at the ground in embarrassment. With that single line, the King had let them know that he knew a great deal about their problems working together.

They stood ashamed for another moment, until the King broke the tension, the mood of festival could be heard everywhere from outside, "...and your office Doctor Franklin, it is here or upstairs?"

"Upstairs, Your Majesty." Franklin gestured with a sweep of his hand out for the King to precede them up the stairway. Vergennes, and the Admiral followed, looking unusually informal in their shirt sleeves. The three Ambassadors trailed close behind. Most of the principal staff lingered for a few moments at the foot of the stairs, unsure of what to do, but seeing that no one paid attention to them, they soon followed the party upstairs to Franklin's office.

197

When the King entered the room, he walked about examining paintings for a moment, and then asked Franklin, "May I be seated, Doctor Franklin?"

"Certainly, Your Majesty."

The King took his seat in an upright chair and began speaking immediately in English, "You know that it is a matter of great embarrassment that your Congress has not yet ratified my treaty. I know with certainty that your Congress received that treaty on the tenth day of March, and, gentlemen, this is now July. The passage across the Atlantic is sometimes as short as two weeks, at the worst a month. I would have presumed that your Congress would have acted upon such generosity within a matter of days, not so many months. Gentlemen, I may have risked a kingdom for a treaty which is not yet ratified. Admiral d'Orvilliers' fleet will depart in two mornings time when Gabriel bares her breasts."

Vergennes and d'Orvilliers looked nervously at each other, each in turn glanced backwards at the dozen members of the ambassadorial staff who lingered by the door. Vergennes attempted to interrupt the King, but was waved off by his sovereign.

Adams caught the gesture and coughed loudly so as to actually interrupt the King. Bancroft was the man he knew the best. Clearly, the staff had innocently followed them upstairs into the office thinking it was part of a tour, not expecting a hastily conceived diplomatic meeting. Adams spoke up before the King could start again, "Dr. Bancroft, I have some premium

198

madeira wine downstairs in the cupboard above my desk, will you escort everyone down to enjoy it?"

Bancroft nodded his agreement and his concern to Adams that too much had been said already. He ushered everyone out.

Unnoticed by anyone, inside or outside the room, the spy lingered behind the staff who were most enthusiastic about getting down the stairs briskly in anticipation of being the first to enjoy some of the Adams' wine. The spy listened at the closed door for a few more precious moments. As a ruse, if caught near the door, he quickly dropped a cuff link onto the floor and stooped as if to pick it up. He could say he had gone back for it. He squatted for as long as he dared, his head and left ear pressed as near as possible to an infinitely tiny crack near the hinge of the door.

The King was still talking, 'Admiral d'Estaing and the Mediterranean fleet has already broken free of Gibraltar and is at this moment racing across the Atlantic. I have it on good authority that the English Admiral Parker, with 13 ships of the line, left England nearly three days ago in pursuit. The English Admiral Keppel has come out of retirement to lead a blockade of our Atlantic ports. Gentlemen, I could not at this moment prevent a war if I wanted to. But your Congress' inaction has left me very, very vulnerable. If Frenchmen die for nothing, I will be considered a fool, and France's influence in Europe will diminish. This pro-american act of mine is not very popular among the other Bourbon Kings. Perhaps Catherine of Russia will soon send her armies west because they perceive an advantage in all of this, or perhaps my Queen's relatives in Austria might challenge us, and hope to steal just a little piece of France.'

Franklin spoke up, 'Your Majesty, I am astounded as well that we have not heard. I approved the treaty and Mr. Adams, who is a sitting member of the Congress, thought it was most generous and could not understand why his colleagues would not have ratified it instantly.'

Adams nodded to the King for verification.

'In the treaty, Your Majesty,' Franklin continued, 'You have given us everything that we could have ever wanted, with the simple proviso that the United States will not make a separate peace with England other than that which France also accepts. It was most generous. I have sent three separate dispatches now to President Hancock, urging that they send the ratification onto us, post haste. Mr. Adams and I co-signed the third dispatch.'

Arthur Lee's eyes widened in surprise, realizing that he had been omitted from the circuit, but had the good sense not to open his mouth about it during the meeting.

'I believe that is all I have to say, gentlemen.' The King got up and prepared to leave the room. Then he turned, 'Admiral d'Orvilliers' has orders to test the resolve of Viscount Keppel's blockade of my kingdom. If we find that it is only so much smoke, then under the cover of that smoke we plan to deliver some cannon and salt peter that we have promised via a portion of his fleet. That partial fleet will need to be piloted into a friendly New England port, one which is no longer occupied by his Britannic Majesty's forces, say Boston or Newport.'

Admiral d'Orvilliers nodded his agreement. Pleased by his prince's grasp of events, Vergennes smiled to himself. After so many years of being a shy recluse, the American incident had sparked a sense of purpose in his Monarch. Perhaps in time, this young man might develop into an even greater leader than his grandfather, the Sun King.

The King continued, 'I spoke to Lieutenant Lunt a few minutes ago. He seems now to be quite ambulatory. The Admiral and I think he could be an excellent pilot to bring our ships safely into unfamiliar New England waters.'

'Yes, quite so, an excellent choice,' replied Adams, 'I believe the lad deserves a tour at home after all he has endured. He has no current ship assignment.'

'Very good.' The King nodded to Admiral d'Orvilliers, making it obvious that they had both discussed the assignment earlier.

*   *   *   *   *

The revelry of the second Independence Day's festivities continued until the last guest left the compound after night fall. Henry Lunt had gathered all of his things into two canvas bags, and went about le Petit Hotel saying his goodbyes that evening. The carriages with the French Admiral d'Orvilliers and Captain Jones were going to depart at dawn for the long journey back to Brest.

Lunt hugged and then shook hands with Dr. Franklin. Next was Mr. Adams, whom Arthur Lee was admonishing for some supposed impropriety. After several minutes of standing by politely, Lunt finally interrupted them, "Mr. Adams, it has been a pleasure," and then Lunt turned to Ambassador Lee and likewise shook his hand.

About to leave their presence, Adams detained Lunt for a moment, "Henry, I want to tell you that shortly after the incident at Versailles, I had an opportunity to chat with Captain Jones about your performance on the Ranger. I have subsequently written President Hancock my recommendation that your name be included on the next Lieutenant's roster. No doubt the formal appointment will reach you forthwith. As Chairman of the Marine Committee, I would ask that you immediately adopt that temporary rank for the purposes of your mission with the French fleet, Lieutenant Lunt."

"Thank you, sir," Lunt saluted him enthusiastically and then thrust out his right hand which Ambassador Adams shook firmly, smiling briefly, before he turned his ear again to hear Arthur Lee's fierce vitriolic comments.

Lunt sought out young John Quincy in his bed, and then the cook, Madame Le Roux, and Jeremiah Hanson. Nathaniel Hubbard had already departed le Petit Hotel for the evening and Lunt returned his French grammar book by his desk and thanked him in a note for its use and the gift of a translation notebook.

The odor of stale ale lingered everywhere, so Lunt went outside le Petit Hotel for a breath of fresh air. After a few moments of walking about admiring for the last time the grounds of the Hotel Valentinois, Lunt saw a figure he recognized coming in through the gate. He waited along the promenade.

'I took a long walk, it felt very good. Perhaps it is a good time to continue our latest game, Henry,' said Dr. Bancroft.

'I'm afraid we cannot. It must be a game left unfinished for a considerable time,' said Lunt.

'How so?'

'I have been ordered to go on an assignment at dawn. It may be some time before we can resume our game. For me it is truly unfortunate that we could not finish the match as I believe I had an opportunity to at least challenge you this time,' stated Lunt.

'How so? You certainly must have a moment to discuss strategy briefly, please show me,' said the Doctor.

Inside, Lunt walked first to the board, where they

had placed it yesterday, out of harm's way, before all the frenzy of the festivity preparations had disrupted the embassy.

"Your queen bishop will be lost in two moves, my knight will jeopardize both your rook and bishop simultaneously by moving here." Lunt put his finger to a square in the seventh file.

Bancroft smiled and gently shook his head, "No, Henry, that is what I wanted you to think. To accomplish that you must first move this pawn, and getting you to do that was the linchpin of my strategy. While you wasted the next move developing a knight cross, I had you in the position of an irreversible discovered check, one which will force your queen to be sacrificed to momentarily save your king. However, once without the queen, defeat is inevitable."

Bancroft looked directly into Henry's eyes. "This is how I have defeated you nearly every time, Henry, the discovered check. I lure you to a target that I have selected. You move a seemingly innocent piece while getting there and it is fatal."

Their eyes met with unusual intensity. They stared at each other eyeball to eyeball, their hands tightly clasped in a handshake. "You are truly a master chess player, Dr. Bancroft."

Bancroft enjoyed the flattery for a moment, and then looked away, "I have been playing this game for many years, Henry. In time you will notice things that you could not see in your youth."

Bancroft had suddenly changed the intensity of

his demeanor and patted Lunt's shoulder, whispering "Godspeed, Henry, be careful, and get home safely to that family of yours."

*   *   *   *

Paul Wentworth had retired early, but was awakened shortly thereafter by an urgent series of knocks at his back door. He arose in his night shirt, his feet hitting the hard floor with a start. He paused a moment, while the noise continued, and took a small pistol from his coat, which was draped across a nearby chair.

"Yes?" he asked.

"It is I, open please before I am seen. It is urgent," said the messenger.

"Here," a slip of paper was passed to him through the crack he had allowed the door to open, having blocked its opening any further with his foot. The dark figure was quickly off into the early morning darkness.

The message was not even coded. It read simply, *"D'Orvilliers fleet will sail in two mornings time, when Gabriel bares her breasts."*

Wentworth went to his kitchen table and stared at the message. It was the third report he had received in two weeks. But this was by far the most reliable and detailed of all. The other reports were from spies at the harbour with indirect information concerning the loading of unusual amounts of apples and cabbages aboard. Another report had mentioned the requisition of large amounts of extra canvas, as might be used in an Atlantic crossing. Now there was solid information that the time had come.

Wentworth went quickly to another apartment in the building and knocked on the door. A lean, bald headed man in his late fifties opened the door to allow him to enter. Wentworth whispered to him, 'Major Pitkan, the French fleet sails. I need for you to set out the signal lanterns at St. Malo. Can you leave within the hour?'

The Major nodded.

*   *   *   *   *

During the middle of the night, there was also a knock on Lunt's door. He rose from his bed thinking at first that it was the pre-dawn wake up by the marine guard. It was the marine guard, but about another matter.

'Sir, I'm sorry, we don't know what to do about something. I dared not disturb Captain Jones.'

'Yes?'

'Madame de Chaumont is outside, sir, with her carriage. She demands to see Captain Jones. Said that she would come inside and get him up herself

unless I do her the courtesy. She says she wants to
take him for a ride, sir." The marine guard whispered,
"She has a glass of wine in her hand, sir. She is a bit
in her cups and, sir, she is in her nightgown."

Lunt had served with John Paul for three years
now and had been used to his amorous adventures,
but certainly he would not risk an affair with the
woman whose husband gave the Americans their very
embassy. Lunt drew a deep breath, "I'll take care of
this, corporal."

Lunt pulled his breeches on, and knocked on
his Captain's door. He was surprised to receive an
instant, cheery response. "Come in."

Inside, Captain Jones was naked to the waist,
pulling on a shirt. He went to the mirror to stare at
himself, brushing his hair briefly.

"Sir, Madame de Chaumont wishes to take you
for a carriage ride. I can...."

Jones interrupted, "Ah, the things I must do to
serve my country. I presume that Leray has departed
on his business?"

"Sir!" Lunt objected emphatically.

"No 'sir' in that manner to me, Lieutenant. Listen
to me," he put up his index finger as a warning, "I am
a deserving Captain who needs a tall, stout ship and
the lady's husband has a hundred. I ultimately only
wish to serve our cause and to smash the British.
I've come this far from nothing, by seizing opportuni-
ties at my own initiative, and now it's time that John
Paul Jones took charge of his own destiny. This

political wrangling over the Ranger could take years. There is a war out there and I mean to be in it and in command of my own ship, and by God I'll soon have it. If you return to Europe in time, I'll be proud to have you aboard as one of my officers. Until then, Lieutenant Lunt,...' Jones strode up to him almost nose to nose, 'I give you your last order, the same one I will give my marines outside. Not a breath, not a whisper of this incident to anyone. Do you understand?'

'Yes sir,' said Lunt snapping to attention.

Jones' demeanor changed from sternness to one of charm in an instant. 'Good! Then, get a good night's sleep, Henry. I'll be back in the morning in time to take the carriage ride with you to Brest. There will be time then both to sleep, and to reminisce.'

Jones slapped Lunt on the shoulder, threw a black civilian cape over his white shirt which was open nearly to the waist, winked at Lunt, and left his Lieutenant standing alone in the doorway.

9
Ushant

Lieutenant Lunt stood atop the quarterdeck of the Bretagne. To his lee lay the great English fleet of thirty ships of the line, their fore and aft sails taut in harmony as they beat in a perfect line formation towards the northwest, attempting to come within cannon shot of the French line of ships. Lunt judged they were still ten miles distant. Despite the fact that the French fleet had been two and a half weeks at sea, the charts in the great command cabin of Admiral d'Orvilliers indicated that they were still less than a hundred miles from France, and tomorrow would surely bring a colossal battle.

Jones and Lunt had come aboard the Bretagne together and had shared dinner in the great cabin with all of the French officers on the evening before the departure of the French fleet. Over the course of the two days after they had left Passy by coach, Jones and Lunt had spent much of their time together reminiscing about each of the three previous Colonial Navy ships on which they had served together; the Alfred, the Providence, and the Ranger.

Just as they were about to part, Jones had said, 'Remember what I told you in ernest a few nights ago,'

Lunt nodded, as Jones cast his eyes up across the gigantic main mast, his scottish accent putting the letter 'r' more than occasionally where it did not belong, '...I shall command a gr...reat ship, one which will defeat the British. By the living God I shall make that my destiny.' Jones turned his determined eyes directly into Lunt's, 'If you're back in Europe in time, I'll be proud to have yer with me. In the meantime, be sure to say hello to Sarah for me.'

Lunt nodded and they shook hands a final time. He watched Jones' longboat lowered away on davits to take him back to the Ranger.

A brief quarter hour later, Lunt, his eyes filled with tearful remembrances saluted Captain Jones silently across the few hundred yards of water between the two vessels. Somehow, Jones had caught the gesture. Lunt saw him smile, and return his salute before going below to discuss turning the command of the Ranger over to Thomas Simpson.

From his first moment aboard the Bretagne, Admiral d'Orvilliers indicated that Lieutenant Lunt was to be allowed all courtesies due the senior American officer serving with the French fleet. As a consequence Lieutenant Lunt would be permitted to attend all strategy meetings held in the great cabin.

Lunt soon came to learn that Admiral d'Orvilliers had received a lengthy set of written orders which were very vague in respect to the circumstances under which he might engage the British fleet. Aboard the fleet of thirty-two ships, d'Orvilliers had a little over three thousand land soldiers which he was to eventually concentrate into four or five ships. If it seemed that the British blockade was without resolve to fight, the French Admiral, at his discretion, might elect to send this portion of his fleet to America as part of a first land contingent to help General Washington's forces. The plan was to land in a secure American port, Boston or Newport. With Lunt's knowledge of New England waters, he would serve as pilot for that portion of the fleet. And if there were time, d'Orvilliers was also to send word to Brest for a French merchant supply fleet, already loaded, to join them. The five or six men of war to detach from d'Orvilliers main fleet would be their escort.

However, d'Orvilliers had also received orders that his fleet was not to be split in such a manner until he received word at sea that the American Congress had formally accepted the King's treaty. And so for several weeks of July the French fleet had sailed back and forth in the Bay of Biscay, their destiny in the hands of others.

*   *   *   *   *

It was three evenings after their enormously successful Fourth of July party. The Ambassadors were still reveling with enthusiasm at the stupendous success of the event. It had now become the custom on certain evenings for Franklin and Adams to gather upstairs in the senior Ambassador's office and to share a bottle of wine together. The boy, John Quincy, was near the windows playing with a set of tiny wooden soldiers which one of the King's ministers had given him. The young boy was talking to himself animatedly, busily pretending he was general of one army and then the other. Between the opposing forces the young boy had folded a rag to emulate a small hill that one of the imaginary armies was trying to capture before the other.

Downstairs, Dr. Bancroft and Jeremiah Hanson shared a pot of tea over a game of chess. Because of an unusual rush of thank you notes that needed to be written in French, Nathaniel Hubbard sat in a far corner of the salon working late into the night. Madame Le Roux and one of her assistants kneaded bread for the morning's baguettes at the long kitchen table. Unknown to most of the mission's occupants, someone had left a candle burning in the window of the room that had formerly been occupied by Lieutenant Lunt.

Outside, on the hilltop of Passy, riding along the main road, a lean rider paused at the corner of the property that belonged to the Hotel Valentinois. Looking towards the smaller building on the property, he reached into his saddle bag to secure the item that Paul Wentworth had prepared.

The rider turned his horse up the small cow path which led in from the road along the outside perimeter of the stone fence. A considerable distance along the trail the rider was able to identify the burning candle in a lower window. The ambassadors were in and upstairs. He would not have to wait, he would give them a surprise. Franklin's office windows were on the second floor, just alongside the fence. The very middle window would be best. The rider used his sleeve to wipe the sweat from his forehead. He looked about, the American marine guard would likely be stationed in the front of the building. They would not see or hear him until the missile was launched. This would be easy, simply heave it a matter of thirty feet into the window and then be off in a gallop back the same way and then cut across the wheat field of an adjacent chateau and then back along the Seine towards Paris.

The glass erupted inward, shattering splinters all over the room, many of the fragments falling on or near young John Quincy. Far more agile than his corpulent frame would suggest, Ambassador John Adams dropped his glass of wine and threw himself off the couch towards his son. The projectile was still twirling on the floor. Adams seized his terrified son, and rolled with him behind Franklin's desk, shielding the boy's body with his own.

Franklin put his arms up in front of his face. He

was an old man, he could never get out of the chair in time. He braced himself for pain. Was this how it was going to end? Outside, one and then a second musket fired off into the night at the galloping hooves. There was a very long moment of silence.

Franklin lowered one arm. The projectile lay silent. He could hear his staff rushing up the stairs to his floor. The item seemed to be a bundle of papers wrapped in twine. Franklin pulled himself out of his chair, and hobbled towards the missile.

Bancroft entered first and then the others, "What is it, Mr. Ambassador?" The boy was crying. He was bleeding from one of the glass splinters, which had lodged in his cheek.

Having unrolled the twine, Franklin found himself with six or seven distinct pieces of paper, all hand written in a thin, but neat hand. "It's all right, John. You can get up now. It is just a message, a very long one."

A gust of wind from outside blew the curtains into a torrent of activity. One of the off duty marines came crashing upstairs into the room to find out if everyone was all right.

Within an hour, the shards of glass had been swept up, and a temporary barrier put up against the open window. Oblivious to the activity, Franklin still scrutinized the message carefully.

"What do you make of it?" said Adams, after the room had been cleared, and his son's minor wound attended to.

Franklin put down the papers. "A simple out and out attempt at bribery, the writer claims to be Charles de Weis——, I can't read the rest of the name. I believe the message might even be in Lord Stormont's hand."

Adams' face tightened with rage as he read one of the several pages of the message. "Does he really believe we would meet him at Notre Dame, so that he could carry what terms we might suggest directly to King George?"

Franklin jested, "But John, if we do this, the letter says I could become titled. Imagine me, at my age, returning to Philadelphia as the Earl of the Schuylkill," said Franklin.

"Ah, but I might become the Viscount of Quincy," laughed Adams.

"Tomorrow is Tuesday, the Ambassadors' day at court, why don't you come with me, John, meet some people and get a trifle more practice in French?"

"Yes, I think that is an excellent idea. I think we have the British truly worried now, or they wouldn't have attempted such a shallow ploy."

"And tomorrow too, while this event is still fresh, I think we should pass this entire affair over to Vergennes. We clearly seem to have no espionage effort of our own any longer," said Franklin.

"No pigeons have come?"

"No pigeons," confirmed Franklin.

*   *   *   *   *

On the first day out from Brest the French Fleet had encountered the British frigate, H.M.S. Lively. At d'Orvilliers' orders, a small French escort cutter of ten guns was dispatched to ask the British Captain to come aboard his vessel. His purpose had been to ascertain whether or not the English fleet was desirous of war, or if there had been some declaration of war. And if this was the reason that the English were attempting to blockade a French port. In no mood for talk, the Captain of the English vessel had fired upon the cutter and the Iphigenie, a larger French frigate which had been standing by in case of difficulties.

Lunt saw the flashes of flame and the cloud of white smoke grow in size across the ocean haze. He soon learned that the French Admiral was a thoughtful tactician. Admiral d'Orvilliers utilized a flag signalling system, wherein he could send messages to any specific ship in his entire fleet from atop the Bretagne's mizzen or the main masts. Each ship in the French fleet had a special flag which designated that the orders under that flag were for that ship alone. Lookouts were kept constantly on duty aboard every one of the French ships to ascertain if the masts of the flag ship currently bore a signal for them. The flag of the small cutter and of Iphigenie were displayed with a signal which Lunt presumed meant to engage

H.M.S. Lively.

The remainder of the French fleet were soon out of the safety of Brest harbour on a windward tact, which presumably meant they were pursuing another course. This lasted a full twenty minutes and then another signal was hoisted and the fleet tacked back a full three miles windward of the engagement. Within the hour, H.M.S. Lively struck her colors with some thirty ships of the line surrounding her. Her Captain had fallen for d'Orvilliers' trap and had risked staying too long in an attempt to engage with the cutter and Iphigenie.

That evening at dinner in the great cabin, d'Orvilliers stood up and proposed a toast. He held his glass up high, *'Vingt-neuf y restent!'*

Lunt translated it easily aloud, but was unsure of its meaning, 'Twenty nine remain.'

Captain Gautier to his left responded, 'Ah, your French is coming along very well, Lieutenant Lunt. The intelligence the Admiral received was that Viscount Keppel had thirty ships of the line in his fleet when he departed Portsmouth, and now only twenty-nine remain for us to eliminate.'

During the brief skirmish with Lively, Lunt first observed the unique tactical board which informed Admiral d'Orvilliers of his fleet's position at any time. When unfolded, the board was approximately 10 feet square. Painted onto the board was a grid of black lines, each supposed to represent a scale of approximately 1 nautical mile. The black grid lines divided the table into a matrix of ten by ten squares representing a sea surface of approximately 100 square miles. It was explained to Lunt that in special situations the scale of the board could be changed.

Under normal conditions the stark white board was set down on the floor of the great cabin, where several junior officers set up and updated the board during a battle or an exercise. They received their information from a team of spotters in the fighting tops of the mizzen. When ships were still difficult to see from that vantage point, spotters were sent as high as the cross trees.

Based on the known height of the rigging of each ship in their own fleet and the estimated height of certain classes of enemy sips, the distances from the flag ship to the ship in question were estimated by the spotters comparing mast heights on the horizon with specially prepared cards. These cards depicted the known height above water of the masts of first raters, second raters, etc. based upon their distance from an observer of one mile, two miles, etc. Everything shown on the tactical board below was always relative to the flag ship, Bretagne, whose own model never left the center of the grid. Other ships might move on or off the grid, but the flag ship was always positioned at its center.

On the tactical board, flat, quarter inch high deck

shaped blocks of wood represented each French and British ship. Each of the French ship models also had their individual ship's insignia permanently painted onto one block for easy identification. When the observers aloft discovered an enemy ship's name and estimated number of guns, this information was also quickly chalked onto the flat, top surface of one of the unmarked blocks.

On the tactical board, the bow of the model representing Bretagne always pointed towards the actual bow of the flag ship. However, when the Bretagne changed heading, two colored wooden arrows also changed the direction in which they were pointing. The red arrow always pointed towards magnetic north, the blue in the direction from which the true wind was coming.

The entire display could be viewed from the quarter deck by way of a special hatch cover, which opened by sliding into a reserve space beneath the deck. There was a crude horseshoe shaped bench around the resulting opening into which the Admiral and his staff would peer and discuss their strategy before issuing commands. In a major fleet maneuver it took approximately ten alert men both aloft and in the great cabin to keep the display board current.

Many times during the initial two weeks, Admiral d'Orvilliers did not require that the tactical board be maintained. Then, on the 15th day of their voyage up and down the Bay of Biscay, when they were nearing the ragged rocky island called Ushant, the lookouts aloft spotted the English Fleet. The first command of Admiral d'Orvilliers was for both fore and rear van Admirals to beat to windward to seize the weather gauge. His second order was to setup and maintain the tactical board.

That evening, during a hurried supper, Admiral d'Orvilliers again reminded his officers, 'I am not under orders to engage the enemy. I have received no word that we are yet at war with England, despite the fact that we have captured H.M.S. Lively which fired upon our vessels first. I will attempt to stay windward and out of reach of their guns, but should they succeed in closing with us, I will, of course, defend our fleet.'

As the next day pressed on, two French ships of the line were unable to maintain as strong a beat to windward and eventually angled off from the main line of the fleet. They were for a time in danger of falling off too far leeward into the pursuing English fleet. Their captains were signaled to tact onto a southerly run so that they would not fall into a situation of being out numbered some twenty-nine to two. By the end of the day, it was apparent that the two French stragglers had eluded their pursuers, who began to rejoin the rear van of the British battle line.

As Lunt stood at twilight by the taffrail, he saw Admiral d'Orvilliers leave his command center and also move to the rail for a last real glimpse of the British Fleet. Lunt moved to his side.

'Sir, is there some duty I can perform, if there is a battle tomorrow? Some detachment I can supervise?"

The Admiral turned to him with a smile, "No, Lieutenant Lunt, I cannot put you in charge of a single French soldier or sailor. You might cause an unintentional disaster, because you do not yet know our language instinctively." The Admiral looked at him, "For example, if you found yourself suddenly put in charge of one of the thirty-four pounders on the weather deck and wanted the sailors to discharge it, what would you command?"

"Why, fire, or *feu* in French," replied Lunt.

"Ah, in your language the word fire has two meanings, but in French there are instead two distinct words. What you have said is to give you a flame. We have another word to discharge a cannon, it is the verb, *tirer*. There are hundreds of other situations for possible confusion. It will be best, Lieutenant, that tomorrow, if there is a battle, for you to stay in my proximity should I need to communicate with the British via a speaking trumpet. That you can do more intuitively than any other officer serving aboard this ship. But of course, if you do see a situation in which you can provide assistance personally, without involving the command of French soldiers or sailors, then we would welcome your assistance."

The Admiral drew a breath as the last rays of the sinking sun ended abruptly from the west. "For example, if we grapple with another ship, every man will have to lend assistance. But if this becomes only a long range action, the prudent thing for you to do is to squat low and enjoy the spectacle of an unfriendly meeting between the two mightiest navies in the world."

The Admiral turned away as if to end the conversation, but then remembering something, he turned and faced Lunt again, whispering, "Lieutenant Lunt, may I ask you something especially sensitive, something which should only be discussed with those that we trust?"

Lunt was perplexed by the phraseology, but replied, "I am discreet, sir."

"You were for a time billeted at Passy with Dr. Franklin and Mr. Adams?"

"Yes, sir, but only a few weeks."

"Did you ever have the impression that there were things you could not understand going on? Did you observe anything out of the ordinary?"

Lunt looked puzzled, "Sir, why do you ask?"

"Your discretion?"

Lunt nodded and the Admiral sighed, looking out to sea, his hands folded over the taffrail, he continued talking in a very low tone, "It is not truly possible for a large fleet like ours to prepare for departure from a port like Brest without observers from shore being easily able to detect the movement of personnel and supplies on board. The English have their spies at our ports as we have ours at theirs. Thus, we only attempt to disguise the exact moment of departure."

"Of course, sir."

"When we captured H.M.S. Lively, as is our custom,

our Captain and his officers drank a few bottles of wine with the British officers. In doing this, we deliberately segregated them by rank, and one of their junior Lieutenants got a bit into his cups. Separated from his senior officers he began to brag that they knew the exact hour of our departure, while we had tried so hard to make any observer from shore believe that it would be another week or more before our fleet departed."

"Then you believe that the British knew your plans."

"Yes, and I believe I was present at the very moment the information was leaked," observed d'Orvilliers. "And this is where I need the discretion you have demonstrated to us before. The information I relate can tarnish the reputation of my Prince and myself."

Lunt nodded.

"During Franklin's 4th of July festivities, the King, Minister Vergennes, and I went up into Dr. Franklin's office. Louis was so very, very enthusiastic, and had bit too much of your American beer." d'Orvilliers raised his eyebrow, "Well, he happened to mention the exact time that our fleet would depart. It was from then, only two days later. As he spoke, both Vergennes and I turned to observe that eight or ten of Dr. Franklin's personal staff were still in the office. Mr. Adams was quick to get them out, but I now know the damage was already done."

D'Orvilliers mused, "It's ironic, several times I

thought of changing the departure time. But that would have meant sending many messages back to Paris, and having to make explanations, which might embarrass Louis. All because I thought there might be a slight danger. There was no certainty. Up to the time of our encountering the British Lieutenant, Loose Lips, I had every reason to believe that anyone in the personal staff of a man as shrewd as Franklin must be beyond reproach."

"And so you think that there is a spy at Passy," stated Lunt.

"I know there is. It is a certainty."

"Sir, do you know who exactly was in the room, at the time that the departure was mentioned?" questioned Lunt, now very concerned.

"No, if I had to pick them out of a crowd today, I could not. They were just staff that I nodded to. I certainly did not know their names."

"Sir, forgive me, but how can you be certain that it was that very incident?"

"This is how I am certain, Lieutenant, just before Mr. Adams cleared the room, the King mentioned specifically that I would sail in two mornings' time, when Gabriel bared her breasts."

Lunt smiled, but still looked puzzled.

The Admiral continued, "We Frenchmen are romantic. Any Frenchman acquainted with the harbour at Brest knows that a few miles out along the roads are two rocks that protrude above a shoal, Gabriel's breasts. They are covered only during high tides. If

I were to sail just as she bared her breasts, it would be right after the high tide was beginning to ebb, an expected maneuver for a fleet of men of war working their way to windward. However, since our captured British Lieutenant Loose Lips from H.M.S. Lively used the exact phrase, *when Gabriel bares her breasts*, that is how I am certain that it was at that moment that the King's conversation was overhead. I believe that the spy may not have known the exact meaning of that term, and, not wanting to transmit confusing information, he passed on that exact phraseology. You Americans have a spy in your midst. I am certain of it.'

Lunt and the Admiral discussed Captain Jones' capture of Hezekiah Ford and of the latter's indictment of Stephen Sayre, the former Ambassador Dean's secretary. Lunt explained that Minister Vergennes had placed Sayre under observation for weeks and that he now worked in the offices of Ambassador Lee, who refused to believe Jones' charges. Lunt ended his story with the sentence, 'Regrettably, Ambassador Lee has taken the side of Sayre, saying that any man who would beat a man in a public street was a ruffian, not a gentleman, and shouldn't be given the responsibility of command.'

'And Mr. Sayre was at the Independence Day celebration?' asked d'Orvilliers.

'No, sir, Captain Jones has sworn that if he ever sets eyes on Sayre again that he will kill him instantly. You know that Captain Jones is a man who means what he says," stated Lunt convincingly.

The Admiral nodded his agreement. "It is a bit unfortunate that Jones handled the incident so openly. The French papers were not kind to him for beating Mr. Ford, or whatever his name was, in the streets without a trial."

Lunt nodded, looking down.

"You know another thing which Lieutenant Loose Lips told us, that you especially should know."

Lunt looked into the Admiral's eyes.

"The British believe that Captain Jones is aboard the Bretagne. They have promised instant promotion to the man who kills or captures John Paul Jones. I know this because when Lieutenant Loose Lips came aboard Bretagne for his wine, he caught sight of you in your American uniform. He asked if you were Captain Jones. The mere asking of the question told us a lot, that Captain Jones had been observed coming aboard Bretagne the night before our departure. If there is a battle tomorrow, and we come close to the British ships, you should be most careful. Sharpshooters looking for an instant promotion will be looking for a deep blue uniform."

The Admiral continued to put the pieces together, "Have I heard correctly that Mr. Adams was dispatched to Paris, partly because the Congress had not received any of Dr. Franklin's correspondence for an entire year?"

Lunt nodded as d'Orvilliers continued, "And in my opinion far too many of the supplies which French merchants have shipped have been captured by the British at sea. The British have been getting especially good intelligence. These are just more of the reasons that I say to you with a certainty that there is a spy in Doctor Franklin's office."

The Admiral was about to say something else, but was asked a question by one of his staff and Lunt had no further contact with him that evening. Everyone slept fitfully.

For three more days the French line of ships successfully beat to windward well ahead of the British line. The tactical board provided a concise summary of the panorama unfolding on the horizon before them.

At dawn, on the fourth day after sighting the British fleet, Lunt scrambled to the quarterdeck to see how the ships had repositioned themselves. The center of the British fleet, with Admiral Keppel's H.M.S. Victory, was six or seven miles leeward of Bretagne on the same tack as the French fleet. However, the forward van of the British fleet commanded by Harland was stretched far ahead, but in a ragged formation.

Apparently, during the night, the British Admiral had given command for individual ships to beat to windward in preference to maintaining a strict line of battle. Henry went to the center of the quarter deck and looked down at the tactical board. The rear van of the battle line to the leeward of H.M.S. Formidable was placed off the board at the extreme right rear of the square. Walking back to the lee rail Lunt looked to the stern, his hand shading his eyes, squinting toward the morning sun. Twelve to fifteen miles distant lay the rear of the English fleet, well away from their appointed line. For awhile, the British fleet could be engaged at only two-thirds strength.

As morning progressed, the dreadnaughts of their age, reassembled in picture perfect columns to parade across the deep blue of the harsh North Atlantic under a dark mantle of cloud. Majestically, with only a hundred yards separating the bowsprit of one colossus from the stern of its predecessor, the parade continued, utilizing a tight tack of fore and aft rigging straining under a maximum load of sail. The decks of both fleets heeling to the lee at an awesome pitch.

By mid morning the winds had shifted and the procession changed tact as the entire French fleet, beginning with St. Esprit as the lead vessel, moved through the wind onto the starboard tact. Like a floating snake, one after another of the French fleet followed in emulation of its predecessor. It was getting to be time for Bretagne, at the center of the fleet, to follow the forward van into its new course. Commands were screamed through speaking trumpets in high pitched French and repeated all across the yards, as hundreds of men scurried high in the air and on the deck to stand ready to loosen restraints on the hundreds of lines that clung to belaying pins along the weather rails.

The French helmsman began to turn the great wheel to port to accomplish the turn and to have the Bretagne follow the others onto the new starboard tact. Everything in Henry's line of sight shifted dramatically and his perspective of the English fleet shifted to the stern. Some of their ships now began to tact as well, but in less uniform precision. Overhead, great gaffs and booms soared rapidly over the Bretagne's deck driven by the enormous shifting pressure of the wind. The tautness of every fore and aft sail eased for a moment, luffed, and then resumed their proper shape as sheets were tightened on the leeward rail.

Far ahead on the foredeck, there was a sudden and shrill scream followed by the unmistakable thud of a human body striking the deck. An unfortunate seaman had missed his footing with the awesome shift in the vessel's pitch and had plunged to his death on the holystone deck below. Officers and seamen quickly hurried to his assistance, and soon a lone runner brought word to the stairs of the quarterdeck, facing up at the Admiral and shaking his head. Lunt saw the Admiral bow his head for a moment and make the Catholic sign of the cross.

As the Iphigenie began to pivot immediately behind the Bretagne to follow in her wake, Lunt observed that beyond her more of the British fleet were beginning to tack. As each behemoth of the French line in turn accomplished her tact, Lunt observed that the wind had become lighter, and that the vessels moved more slowly than they had before. The shift in the French line had been accomplished, but the British line appeared a little closer.

"Croissant, Lieutenant, just from the oven?"

Lunt turned to see the smiling face of Captain Gautier, who had adopted him as a companion since the first day of the voyage. Lunt nodded and took from the straw basket before him what was to be his only food of the day.

"This is what every naval enthusiast dreams of, is it not?"

Lunt turned to look into the Frenchman's eyes which seemed oddly filled with pleasure. The man was literally smiling, "To be part of an enormous expedition in which you battle against a worthy opponent. To be part of a force in which the lives of thousands of men ultimately will fight for the very fate of their nation. I am here, Henry, because I want to be. It is magnificent."

Lunt remained silent and took a noncommittal bite of his croissant, and stared away remembering all too vividly the carnage of past naval engagements in which he had participated.

Captain Gautier sauntered off after taking a large bite of the roll in his hand. He went to another officer and shared his enthusiasm and his basket of rolls. Lunt looked towards the sea and studied the positions which were evolving. The forward and center vans of the English fleet had now also completed their own tacks and were in some semblance of a battle line. To accomplish this, H.M.S. Victory and some of the closer members of the British fleet had reduced some of their sail to allow the lost remnants of their vans to assume their rightful positions in a line of battle. H.M.S. Formidable and the rear van were still hopelessly out of the fray.

Lunt picked up a spy glass and studied the lost third of the British fleet. Several of the vessels were displaying downwind sails and were heading to a position to intercept the French if d'Orvilliers chose to give the command to fall off before the wind. Clearly, the British rear van would be out of the action for a good while.

Lunt moved to view the tactical board. The Admiral and his aides were peering into the hatch, having an intense debate. Lunt noticed immediately that the green arrow indicating the wind had shifted from the southwest to directly westward. One French officer, so heated in his enthusiasm, had actually jumped down into the hatch and was now standing on the board, and pointing with his sword to indicate what would happen if the French fleet persisted following the more northerly wind shift on this starboard tact. On the new course, the forward van of the French fleet might just pass windward of the British, but the French rear van might pass perilously close to being cut off by the leading elements of the British line which had also just tacked towards the south. Lunt heard several times the French pronunciation of the letter, 'T'.

Henry remembered back to one evening aboard the Alfred, when then Lieutenant John Paul Jones had suddenly cleared the entire mess table of dishes and had ordered that every spoon be immediately brought up from the galley as he laid out theoretical lines of a mock spoon ship battle and had challenged Lunt and the other junior officers to imagine that they were in charge of an enemy command and what they would do if the winds shifted. Again and again that night, Jones had driven home the point that one must not let a ship of the line have its 'T' crossed allowing the enemy to rake shot across the entire length of the deck. The bow and stern of a ship of the line carried comparatively little armament. The captain of such a ship must always keep his broadsides pointed towards the enemy. This was why the theory of maintaining a battle line had persisted for hundreds of years.

Another of d'Orvilliers advisors, less animated than the first, recommended falling off and making a run southeastward for the third of the disconnected rear van of the British fleet. The officer in the pit wasted no time in putting a quill pen on the board to represent how the British might move in response and split the French fleet in two. Lunt understood sufficient French to see that the proposal was discarded.

Calmly, the Admiral stood up onto the horseshoe shaped bench. His sea worn face peered out over the starboard rail at the British fleet now only three miles distant. He drew a deep breath and gave the order to follow the wind. But then, he gave separate orders for the rear van of his fleet to maintain their present course for another ten minutes and then harden to the wind and thus get back into the French battle line.

Lunt rushed to the starboard rail of the quarter deck and observed, as far ahead the entire line of the French fleet shifted firmly a full point to windward. The English line would be passing just to the east of them on a port tact, each vessel within trying to beat as tightly to the wind as their design would permit. Not all of the enemy were in a perfect line, some of them would be closer to the French, some farther away. Half a mile ahead the St. Espirit was closing not more than four hundred yards distant from H.M.S. Monarch and Shrewsbury. Lunt saw enormous bursts of sheer flame spurt out, then gigantic funnels of pure white clouds rushed out over the water from the hulls of the lead opposing vessels. A moment later, there was a thundering roar and crackle. It was deafening.

Someone tapped him on the shoulder. It was a seaman with a basket. Lunt could not hear what he said. The man pointed into the basket where small balls of a translucent substance lay, 'Cire.'

Lunt was unsure of his meaning. The sailor picked up one of the balls and motioned to put it into his ear. Lunt understood and took two of the balls which now he recognized to the touch as beeswax. He stuffed them in his ears. Already the thunder of approaching cannon fire became more and more omnipresent. On the weather deck, during an uproll from the waves, Lunt observed a considerable number of the French cannon being elevated by withdrawing their quoins. The muzzles of the heaviest were being stuffed with larbridge, or two iron balls connected by a stout piece of chain which were designed to be shot up into the enemy's rigging to help render the enemy vessel immobile and an easy targets for the succeeding passes of fire.

Looking ahead up the line, the action of opposing lines was closing to only three hundred yards distance. Behind the most recently engaged vessels, the entire screen was obscured by mountains of smoke and eye stinging cordite. Here and there, burst forth huge spikes of flame, thrusting out over the water, lighting the white smoke eerily, and then a split second later came their roar, which occasionally caused a sailor on the deck of Bretagne to lose his footing from the sheer concussion of air and sound. Lunt could no longer hear anything above the roar of battle. There were now only six French vessels to go before the lead English vessel would come opposite the Bretagne. Lunt saw gun captains on the weather deck go to their pots to seize their slow matches in anticipation of their receiving the French equivalent of the command to fire.

Just then, H.M.S. Monarch seemed to shudder from the impact of a French broadside. There was the crackle of wood and her upper foremast tumbled to the lee, sweeping great sheets of white canvas and miles of rigging with her. Yet, she continued on her course, still firing. Her capability to maintain a beam reach to the wind had to have been deteriorated, yet her forward momentum persisted for awhile, seemingly held there by sheer determination of will. However, by the time she was within two ship lengths of the French flagship she had fallen away with the wind considerably.

Suddenly, out of the clouds of cannon smoke, H.M.S. Shrewsbury bore onward towards them. Her broadside crackled sharply towards the huge Ville de Paris, the third ship ahead of Bretagne. The burst of flame was flung directly out and angled downwards. The British were aiming at the water line. An instant later, Lunt heard a secondary explosion, whomever Shrewsbury had hit, their magazine must have erupted. The men on Bretagne's main cross trees were giving urgent hand signals to indicate some message for the Admiral's attention. Lunt saw d'Orvilliers look upwards and then give a message to the Captain beside him. Flags on the mizzen were drawn out to give a particular message, Lunt presumed for one ship to fall off from the line.

Gun captains on the three decks of Bretagne were now within seconds of firing. There had been a few water spouts shot at their hull from H.M.S Monarch, but Bretagne had let her pass. It was obvious that the Admiral wanted the first broadside of his flag ship to be at H.M.S. Shrewsbury, which was almost abreast of their position, perhaps a hundred and fifty yards distant. Lunt saw d'Orvilliers pull his sword from its sheath. For a long, long moment there was only a background of roaring battle moving ahead and then the Admiral dropped his sword. Within a split second there emanated, from deep within the bowels of the third deck of guns through the second deck and up onto the weather deck, a primeval quake followed by a momentous thunderclap and then a blinding flash of intense light and fire. The air in front of them was literally seared with the intensity of the fire. Lunt felt his face burn from the heat. The fiber of every plank of wood on the deck trembled and the entire great vessel shook to its core. On the visible deck surface the white wooden carriages and blackened barrels of the naval guns roared back toward the centerline of the deck, spewing bright white mountains of gray white smoke before them. The whole vessel seemed to rock as a blast of deafening sound shook out over the water slapping at the air around them with such violence that the very air they breathed was pushed back. For a split second it was impossible to take in any air, there was none. It had all been blown forwards. Losing his footing, Lunt was thrown to the deck, as were hundreds of others.

It took long moments for the billows of smoke across the expanse of still water to clear, for there was no longer any wind, it had been simply blown away. Only the sheer momentum of the Shrewsbury still carried her forward. Lunt could see she had taken a terrific pounding, rigging was tumbling everywhere, and great billows of black smoke and flame seemed to consume her aft quarter.

Lunt decided then and there, that if ever given the choice, he would never elect to be on the lead vessel in a naval line of battle, and thus be the one to collect the first fire from every passing enemy ship of the line. Lunt would learn a day later that the first van Admiral, aboard the lead French vessel, the St. Espirit, had come to the same conclusion and had quitted his deck to run below into the partial safety of his own cabin, where despite the admonishments of his junior officers, he steadfastly refused to come up again until the last ship of the British line had passed, an action for which he was later court martialed.

As Lunt looked towards the stern, Shrewsbury was listing badly to the lee. They passed the next British vessel in the line as forty-three starboard gun crews on three gun decks scrambled to reload. The crews of twelve each began to service the great thirty - four pounders as dripping wet sheep's hair sponges were thrust down the barrel at the end of long poles to cool the over heated guns and dampen any surface sparks. Next iron worms were thrust down the barrel to ream out any unexploded powder and remaining sparks which might cause a dangerous premature discharge of new fresh power. More sponge work, and then, drying towels were inserted and then yanked out again. Bags of dry power were stuffed in and smashed into place with ramrods so that they broke open, packed tight within their barrels. Next, wads of old canvas, then cannon balls were held in place by more tightly packed canvas.

Just as most cannon balls began to roll down the barrel, the Bretagne received her first full enemy broadside. It hit her deep. Some of the enemy cannon balls hit the water and drove towering spouts of water over the height of the freeboard. Lunt was drenched by the splash from one of them, his tongue instinctively licked the salt from his lips. There was a shudder far below in the bowels of the hull and Lunt heard the call of, *Allons aux pompes!* relayed in screams many times from somewhere below.

On the weather deck all was unscathed, and the smoke cleared to reveal another British ship of the line looming just ahead. The Bretagne's gun crews, seemingly oblivious to whatever had happened below, were lined up to stroke out another broadside upon command. The Captain gave the command and again there was fire, smoke, sound, heat, and fury before them. Eyes and lungs singed in the acrid atmosphere of blinding white cordite that was all pervasive and terrifying.

Lunt saw that on the windward side they were coming close to two French vessels who had fallen off from the line ahead and were obviously in distress. Out of the mist ahead it seemed that a short line of three British vessels were attempting to maneuver on a course two points higher and breech the French at the gap caused by the wounded Frenchmen. They had succeeded in pushing closer through the wall of continental fire than any of the British vessels before them. Lunt guessed their lead vessel to be a distance of less than two hundred yards, a long musket shot. There were commands from the second level and a stream of French soldiers in white uniforms were soon climbing up the ratlines on both sides of the vessel, they carried their muskets slung over their backs, their bayonets still in their belts. The Admiral gave a command to Bretagne to fall off a half point so they could broadside the onrushing enemy sooner in the low wind. The command to discharge the cannons was given again and the fury of the concussion shook several of the white uniformed soldiers from their perches to fall to their deaths either onto the deck or into the sea below.

Busily the gun crews of Bretagne scurried about on the deck, absorbed in their task of reloading their deadly guns. One of the French vessels ahead had lost her bowsprit, but it was hanging on by a few cables slowing their course through the water. Men stood atop the knightsheads chopping away furiously to release the drag. Very close to windward of her, one of the three British ships which had altered course cleared its way through the haze of smoke sufficiently for the men aloft to identify that it was Viscount Keppel's flagship, H.M.S. Victory, of 84 guns.

Ahead of Bretagne were the French ships, Fortune of 74 guns and Victoire of 84. Both successfully raked H.M.S. Victory's rigging and freeboard with stupendous broadsides. Each time, Victory shook upon impact and, from her rigging, men toppled to their extinction onto the decks below. Still she kept coming relentlessly. It was obvious that she had saved her next broadside for Bretagne and her 86 guns, whatever the consequence to her own condition. The men of Bretagne struggled to reload their guns in time to be the first to fire before the two great flagships came abreast.

A stupendous barrage of fire vaulted out from H.M.S. Victory. Everywhere its concussions shuddered the Bretagne as rails, decks, freeboard, and masts exploded from the impact of great iron balls. A million splinters were launched into the air stunning the atmosphere with piercing tiny whistles. One ball hit the main mast at its base, not severing it, but altering its angle to the rhumb line of the vessel. Everywhere men howled and pieces of men lay on the blood red butcher block of a deck. Lunt, seeing the volley about to be fired, had dropped to the deck and put his hands over his head. His back and legs had collected only a half dozen minor splinter fragments. He looked behind him where the Admiral was sitting calmly with his staff, his only concession to the effects of battle raging about him had been to pull off his wig and use it to cover his mouth to avoid breathing in the acrid smoke directly. His shock of white hair stood disheveled as he continued intently to study the strategy board and issued orders to be transmitted up and down the line by flag. All save one of his advisors had been spared injury from the last volley. The unfortunate senior Lieutenant lay stunned, his head supported against the base of the mizzen, blood flowing freely between his fingers from a neck wound. Several seamen were coming to his assistance.

Below, Lunt could see that several of the major guns on Bretagne's weather deck had been hit and thrown asunder. Near the waist of the vessel, a huge crater had been chewed out of the freeboard by a massive concentration of fire. From the edge of the crater, one could see men at every level struggling to get their pieces to bear. On the weather deck, one of the thirty-fours had snapped its breeching rope and was in danger of falling down the great gap now rent in the side of the flagship. Only two men were struggling with lines amidst the carnage to prevent the great iron behemoth from sliding further away. Should its great weight cascade downwards, it could land with sufficient momentum to breach the hull.

Lunt vaulted over the thin rails which separated the quarterdeck from the weather deck and ran, hurtling over twisted lines and men, to help the struggle to save the cannon from falling into the void. Meanwhile, the French command to fire was relayed among the still active gun crews and the Bretagne shuttered again as she delivered a return broadside towards H.M.S. Victory, the concussion from which tossed Lunt to the ground amid a pool of blood and the remains of a man's trunk. He forced his stomach to remain calm and crawled forward until he found the bitter end of a fallen bunt line and chopped it free with an axe which lay idle beneath a fallen spar. Lunt went into the crevice and quickly secured a bowline knot about the barrel of the disheveled piece. He tossed the bitter end of the line across the gap to one sailor who stared astonished at the sight of an officer performing a seaman's task.

Another line was secured to the cannon's wheel. It was obvious that the piece would be inoperative for the duration of the battle. Many of Bretagne's guns were now firing independently struggling to keep up a steady rain of death at their mortal enemy. From a deck below, two or three guns discharged simultaneously, their thick white smoke oozed up through the vent. Lunt looked down the length of the weather deck. Four guns down, the gun crew was inactive. There were men lying on the ground mostly dead, or unconscious, but the gun carriage looked secure. Lunt gestured at the three men on the other side of the gap to meet him at that gun further along. At the gun, one man, who Lunt later learned was named Pierre, bravely put his face into the muzzle of the great gun. Coming up, he gave a thumbs up sign. Apparently the gun had been already loaded, when the crew had been swept away en masse by the impact of the first broadside from H.M.S. Victory.

Lunt ran to an iron kettle in the center of the ship and secured a slow match. He returned to the gun, briefly analyzing the trajectory of the weapon. He was not familiar with firing thirty-four pounders but he knew it was too high. One of the hastily comprised crew found a quoin and was wedging it beneath the barrel

242

on the downroll to pivot the muzzle down. Suddenly there was a whiz through the air just past the end of Lunt's hawk nose and one of their gun crew fell over clutching his knee cap. Overhead, Lunt heard the crackle of more musket fire. The soldiers in white on the ratlines above them were returning the fire that British marines were spewing onto the deck. Lunt remembered d'Orvilliers warning about his blue uniform, but H.M.S. Victory was passing directly abreast of them, only seventy yards distant. He had no time to discard his uniform jacket.

Lunt stepped to the side of the likely recoil of the gun, blew on the slow match to raise a spark, and then stretched the linestock which bore it across to the touch hole. There was a faint whiz of fine powder and the gun exploded with blinding fury belching a bright orange flame out before them some fifteen feet. Then there was the ensuing torrent of white smoke and stinging gases which turned faces away involuntarily. Lunt never saw where his shot impacted or what damage was done to the Victory from that shot, or even knew what kind of shot had been loaded into the muzzle. The makeshift gun crew was too busy reloading.

Victory was moving slowly past, if they hurried it was possible to fire one more round at the British flag ship. Lunt saw a cannon ball, but at this short range grape would be better, more damaging to her crew. He looked around quickly, but the finely made grape canisters of the colonial service were nowhere to be seen. Then, lying against the base of the main mast, he saw what he wanted, buckets of stray nails and jagged metal pieces. The impromptu crew had cleaned out the muzzle and were ramroding the powder base into the gun when Lunt returned with the bucket of metal shreds. The man named Pierre laughed rakishly and jabbered excitedly as they tipped the gun muzzle upwards to receive the charge, as another broadside from Victory shattered into the stem of Bretagne.

After the loose shot was loaded, one of Lunt's gun crew ripped off his tattered shirt and stuffed it into the muzzle, while several men manhandled the ramrod. Lunt retrieved his slow match and touched off the cannon. He strained to watch this time as across the narrow expanse of water a swath of deadly metal bees buried themselves into the enemy's mizzen, taffrail, and quarterdeck. They loaded and fired again six more times until the last English man of war had passed. There was a cheer up and down the decks and a French chant arose spontaneously, but Lunt could not discern it, and merely mouthed the words as his impromptu crew sang vigorously. Thereafter, he returned to the quarter deck to see if the Admiral needed him to translate anything to the British.

The Admiral and his remaining advisors were still intent. Lunt looked over their shoulders into the hatchway. Some of the British ships had already tacked back through the eye of the wind, in pursuit.

The rear elements of the French van were engaged occasionally in long distance gunnery. Several of the advisors wanted to fall off and engage again, but d'Orvilliers shook his head, pointing out that several of his fleet were incapable of sustaining another round of broadsides. He intended to give orders for his fleet to tack again in queue and to maintain the weather gauge until the extent of their damage was ascertained.

The Bretagne, herself, was listing badly, but was still more mobile than several forward van ships she had passed. The Admiral gave individual orders for two ships to tact with the fleet and then continue to fall off in a run towards the east and into the safety of Brest. The remainder of the French fleet headed further out to sea, while the British fleet took several hours to regroup and, as the afternoon wore on, that seemed merciful amidst an atmosphere of all pervasive screams of agony emanating from the surgeon's block below. As twilight came the French still held the weather gage with the British, again, miles behind in pursuit. Lunt took off his uniform jacket and washed the blood of other men off its facing by plunging it into one of the buckets of fresh seawater which the crew were using to wash the gore from the decks. It was better to be damp, this warm July evening, than to have to bear the immediate smell of rotting petrifaction.

At sunset, d'Orvilliers was having a vigorous discussion with his advisors and even the Captain of the Bretagne was pointing toward the rear portion of the flotilla. There was some occasional sound of gun fire as the lead English ships were trying with long range gunnery to pick off stragglers on the tail end of the French line. But as soon as darkness fell, there was silence.

At the stern of each of the French vessels there was a single light which served as a guide for the ship immediately astern. It was the darkest of nights as a low cloud cover obliterated all but the strongest of nocturnal light from piercing the cloud mantle and reaching the ocean's surface. The Admiral sent signals fore and aft along the line, with a speaking trumpet, for all ships to stay in close configuration and that orders would soon be awaiting them.

The Admiral moved his staff below. The great cabin windows were covered with blankets and the senior officers discovered that the surgeons, for lack of space had moved several of the amputees into the corners of the great cabin. A lantern was lit quickly, and someone handed it to Lunt, who took it and held it high so that the Admiral's staff could study the final configurations of the two fleets at dusk.

The Admiral and his advisors discussed, debated, and even, at points, screamed at each other for over an hour studying the situation and deciding what to do next. Somewhere during that hour, a bosun had knocked on the cabin door with a report which the French officers immediately understood. Their faces were grave. Lunt quizzed one officer who was leaning on the tactical board before them. The officer told

Lunt that the bosun had reported that every pump on the ship had been in service now for three hours straight and that absolutely no progress had been made against the rising water level in Bretagne's hold. If the French flagship was to remain in open water for very much longer, she would sink.

Ignoring this, d'Orvilliers pointed to various ships on the tactical board and asked their condition, as far as the spotters knew. Within ten minutes of his request, there came word from outside that only five of the original ships were in top condition, and that four others in addition to Bretagne were not seaworthy. The remaining eighteen ships of the line had received some damage, not totally repairable at sea. The loss of life was as much as a quarter on some vessels. After contemplation, d'Orvilliers sent a signal along the line of speaking trumpets that every half hour certain ships should shoot off three rocket flares each to windward. The Admiral and his advisors went above deck. Lunt remained in the great cabin for several moments studying the fleet alignments, his horn lantern in his hand. The wind was still westerly, but light. The French were on a larboard tact, and the English were believed to be split between two tacks, but at least five miles behind.

Above on the deck, Lunt would learn later that the field officers had debated whether or not they had concluded their duty. Admiral d'Orvilliers had restated that his orders were clear that he was not supposed to attack the British unless provoked. He had done precisely that. There was no doubt that the English fleet was as severely crippled as were they. This would mean, that until they repaired themselves, which would certainly take the duration of the summer months, that the English blockade was effectively neutralized. Shipping to and from French ports and America could continue unhindered, excepting for the English privateers. And any British convoy coming up from the Indian subcontinent home to England would now be in peril. The Admiral therefore concluded that any further loss of life would be unnecessary. He had fulfilled his duty to the exact letter, just as it had been specified in the lengthy instructions from the Ministry of Marine. Besides, he jested, he still did not know whether they were formally at war with England. There was laughter, as he had intended there should be.

The Admiral and his staff observed the intensity of the darkness as the first round of flares were fired to larboard by the specified ships. Then, they returned below. Lunt followed them and again held up the lantern above the tactical board. D'Orvilliers took the first ship block and then proceeded to have it fall off and eventually jibe eastward towards land, then another and another, until he had selectively gone through the entire fleet, leaving only three of the ships in good condition, still firing flares. He hoped that the enemy, estimated to be five to seven miles distant of the rear van, would think the flares were alignment signals from flagships of the forward, middle, and rear vans. In French, the Admiral said, "Gentlemen, weather permitting and good dark cover, we do this at eleven this evening. Get some sleep, it will be a long night."

Lunt considered going to sleep for the few hours until eleven, but felt he could not. He wanted to see for himself the damage to the ship. Leaving the great cabin for the weather deck, he descended to the middle gun deck, and then to the lower. At that level, the rift on the starboard side was still present and he could see lantern light reflected on the open ocean. On the larboard tack, they were heeled over in the direction of the water. Lunt observed that several layers of tar hardened canvas were nailed tightly over the lower portion of the rift. The makeshift covering extended to the level below.

Lunt descended another level to the orlop deck and saw the level of the sea. The carpenters were busily nailing more layers of canvas over the gaping hole, which extended below the water line. Despite all of their efforts, water was still oozing visibly down into the hold. Lunt stood and peered down the stairwell, where lanterns were lit for some thirty men who stood waist deep in the cold Atlantic water pumping their hearts out.

"I hope that we will make it until eleven."

Lunt turned, it was the Admiral speaking to him in English. They both squatted together, peering into the cavity. The Admiral said something encouraging to the men below, there was a cheer and they pumped the more furiously to several chants.

"Sir, why did you choose to wait for eleven?"

249

'I have been on many English ships as a guest when we have been at peace. They always work on a watch system of eight bells. At eleven they will be starting the last hour of the night watch, and it should be the darkest then. In that hour, after a day of battle, they may be the least observant and perhaps we can slip away.'

The Admiral was silent for a time and then spoke again, pensively, deliberately, 'If I were a gambler, perhaps tomorrow I could be the one French Admiral in a millennium to sink an entire English fleet, or perhaps I could be the one remembered because he had lost an entire fleet and be vilified for centuries to come. I know that in the coming months, many at Versailles will accuse me of running away, because my own ship was sinking.'

He continued with a flow of talk from his heart. 'It is true I have concern for Bretagne, we started this voyage with a full compliment of eight hundred men, now we have far less than seven hundred, and half of them wounded. But I have no concern for my own life, it is mainly over. I am seventy years of age. But if this flagship sinks, so will the prestige of my Prince along with the life of everyone aboard. Even though I have carpenters above working on them in the darkness, the longboats have all been holed beyond repair. They would not last an hour in the open sea. Beyond this vessel, there are also the men of nearly thirty other vessels, some six thousand men. Many of our other ships are reported to be in a like condition. So too is the enemy. H.M.S. Victory sustained incredible damage, she also may not make the morning. These are the considerations which weigh on my mind.'

The Admiral then got to his feet and slowly walked away. Lunt wanted to express something to him, but was unable to find the right words.

An hour later, exhausted, Lunt went to the taffrail, curled himself into a ball and slept, until he heard the speaking trumpet quietly issuing orders to the ship astern. He heard the voices repeat again for another ship, and then another. When the trumpets again started to speak forward, they had confirmed that every ship of the line knew the signal. Every white stern light was doused, and then, a few minutes later, the three designated ships fired their rockets, three each, to windward. For a brief second each, they illuminated the cold surface of the water, and d'Orvilliers hoped the English would see sufficient telltale sail canvas reflected in that light to continue to believe that the French fleet continued along the same northerly course.

Within a moment, Lunt felt the great vessel fall off to starboard. He went to that rail and squinted to the south. Here and there, at what had to be some five miles distance, he saw the twinkle of faint lights aboard the English ships. They seemed to remain on course. Others joining him on the deck stared southward in total darkness, a match, a stray light, anything would give their ruse away. Men climbed aloft as best they could in the total darkness and set out course and lower course sails before the wind. Lunt was pleased that the vessel was no longer compelled to heel to starboard, and prayed that the rift was now above the water line.

The first half hour of flares would be the most telling. From the stern they could be observed shooting out to windward in three sets of three rockets each. The three French ships were now three to four miles distant, and the wind was freshening. Soon they would be ten and then twenty, and perhaps more miles distant before the dawn broke. Henry curled himself to sleep again and awoke by morning light.

He could see the British fleet far, far away. They would never stop them now. He saw the three French ships fire one more salvo each in the half light of dawn as if to say to the British, 'HA! HA! We deceived you.' Then they too tipped their sails eastward. From their more northerly position, and their greater seaworthiness, they would be in Brest before the remainder of the French fleet.

10
Return

$\mathcal{A}$ day and a half later, the tired, blown apart French fleet returned to Brest after only a brief three weeks at sea. Henry leaned over the larboard rail eagerly trying to ascertain whether or not the Ranger was still in port. When he finally located her, she seemed so tiny, bobbing there in the same anchorage. A small 18 gun corvette, compared to the 86 gun behemoth that he now rode into the French harbour, having just faced the mightiest navy in the world. Henry now saw through much wiser eyes how Admiral d'Orvilliers must have felt coming aboard the Ranger simply to congratulate her Captain for his victory and instead to have been dragged into the mire of ruined command relationships, an unhappy lady of the court, and over a hundred British prisoners that he had no legal right to detain. No wonder he had put the entire little flotilla under quarantine. Henry sighed inwardly.

The Bretagne did not drop anchor in her usual position. Instead she was towed by a small fleet of long boats in towards a sandy beach to a depth at which she could just barely drift at low tide. Then she was anchored securely, where if she sank, most of her hull would still remain above water. The process took nearly a day during which wounded men were ferried ashore to a special port hospital. Throughout the entire fleet, thousands of men needed medical attention. The Admiral sat in the great cabin of the listing Bretagne as each of his thirty-two ships' captains and four junior admirals came aboard to make debriefing statements, trying to arrive at an accurate assessment of the damage done to both the French and British fleets.

During most of this period of aftermath, Lunt had been doing a great deal of thinking regarding his disappointment at now not being able to return to America and see Sarah and his infant son. But another side of him was inwardly pleased to have returned to France where he believed he might be of greater use to the war effort through the associations he had made with the French. To go home to America and instead serve there, he would have to give up every contact he had acquired and start over and make new associations. Now that he was finally beginning to understand French, he believed he could accomplish more by working with the new allies. And there was the unfinished issue of the British spy at Passy.

As the procession of officers continued, an American Navy Lieutenant approached in a longboat and asked permission to come aboard in English. Lunt, quickly translated his request to one of the French adjutants, who were on perpetual duty outside the door that led to the Admiral's great cabin. Lunt waited at the top of the jacob's ladder to greet him.

It was Lieutenant Hall with whom he had served briefly during the Ranger voyage.

Hall first saluted the French officers who greeted his arrival and then said, "On behalf of Lieutenant Thomas Simpson of the Ranger, I present the compliments of the American Navy and wonder if there is any assistance at all we can render."

The French Lieutenant bowed politely and indicated that the Admiral was very busy, but, if the Lieutenant cared to wait, a brief meeting could be arranged. Lieutenant Hall half listened to the Frenchman's response, while the other half of his brain gaped upwards at the rigging of the Bretagne and at the immensity of the cannons on her deck. Then he acknowledged Lunt, who stood by quietly looking at him pensively. Hall came over immediately.

"Henry, you were aboard during this. They say you were eighty miles at sea. Yet, people from Brest said they could hear the battle clearly. At first they thought it was a coming thunder storm...say, this is an incredible ship." He was bouncing up and down on his toes as he talked excitedly, looking about.

"You said that Lieutenant Simpson sent his congratulations? Where is Captain Jones?" asked Lunt.

"Captain Jones relinquished command of the Ranger two weeks ago. He is at Passy with Franklin. I believe they promised him a larger ship to get him to drop the charges against Simpson. It seems likely that Lieutenant Simpson will soon get the formal command of the Ranger that he should have had originally in New Hampshire last summer. I'm sure that he'd be pleased to take you aboard..."

Hall ceased his bobbing up and down for a moment and lowered his voice, not looking at Lunt squarely, but away as if they shared a known confidence. He whispered, "Of course, you'll be next in command to me, but you'll get to go home with us. Under Simpson we're heading straight for Portsmouth. No death defying runs up the Irish sea. But you can be sure there will be prize money in it. Now that the British fleet has been cleared away, merchants should be easy pickings. Simpson says we'll be looking out for them. We've all felt a pinch in the old purse this past year under Jones. You'll come home rich with a Lieutenant's share if we take even one good sized merchant. I'll mention your transfer to the Admiral when I get in to see him."

He winked at Henry, then looked around to see if anyone else was listening. "Tell me about the battle while I wait to pay my compliments to the Admiral." He resumed his incessant bobbing again.

Henry said, "Lieutenant Hall, I can't right now, I have something to do right away, below. I'll return in a bit. In the meantime, take a look at the rift on the starboard side, go down a few levels. I think you'll find it educational."

Lieutenant Hall sauntered off, and Lunt went to the door of the great cabin where Captain Gautier, acting as an adjutant, stood greeting those who came in to see the Admiral.

Henry spoke to him in French, "Can I ask you a very special favor, Captain?"

The man raised an eyebrow without response. He was listening.

"Can I see the Admiral, for just three or four minutes before Lieutenant Hall does, please?"

The man pursed his lips, considering it, and then nodded as he looked across the deck at Lieutenant Hall, his mouth agape looking at the hole rent in the starboard freeboard.

Lunt hurried to his tiny quarters between two of the larboard guns on the third gun deck, near the stern of the vessel. He reached into one of his sea bags and took out the neatly tied bundle of letters he had first been given at Versailles. He untied the knot quickly and searched through the pile until he found Marie's envelope. He extracted the two smaller notes inside, read the French again and slid the one he wanted into his pocket. Lunt was nervous about what he was about to do, but Captain Jones had said that there sometimes comes an opportune moment when an officer has to make his own destiny. Lunt returned to the quarterdeck happy to see that Lt. Hall was still below deck surveying the damage.

Immediately upon seeing him, Captain Gautier gestured for Lunt to enter the Admiral's day cabin. As Lunt passed by him, the French Captain whispered to him discreetly in English, "You owe me."

Lunt smiled and nodded his agreement, "Oui."

"Yes, Lieutenant Lunt?" asked d'Orvilliers.

Lunt saluted and then stated, "Sir, I wish to stay under your command."

"You want to join the French Navy?"

"No, sir, I wish to stay under your command, at least temporarily." Before the Admiral could react, Lunt continued, "Sir, I believe you know Madame Chatelain, she is in the service of Minister Vergennes?"

"Yes, of course, she was a guest on this very vessel not two months ago," he cleared his throat, "when the Ranger arrived."

"Well, sir, she has given me this. I would like to request to remain in your service for a time sufficient enough to exercise it, and then, sir, to be transferred to Captain Jones' new command, whatever that will be."

Admiral d'Orvilliers opened the note in Marie's hand. Just a few seconds later, his eyebrows raised, he looked up very puzzled, and then read the last few sentences of the brief note.

"You want to be a spy?"

"No, sir, but I feel that I can best serve my country, and our mutual cause together, by attending this school. There are a great many things that we Americans are naive about. For example, you said you believe that there is a spy in our midst at Passy."

To the last phrase d'Orvilliers nodded his head and handed back the note to Lunt. "I sometimes forget that you came to me with the personal recommendation of my King. You are an unusual man, Lieutenant Lunt. I will speak to Lieutenant Hall now and decide after I speak with him."

Lunt saluted and started out the door, his tricorner hat tucked neatly under his left arm.

"Oh, Lieutenant Lunt." Lunt turned back towards the Admiral, "I was impressed by the way that you fielded such a large gun with only a few men. It gave us an opportunity to poke a few more holes into H.M.S. Victory."

"Sir, the gun was already loaded when I got to her."

"Yes, but my officers did observe you personally reload and fire the cannon several more times." There was a brief pause, "If I grant this request you will stop by at Passy first and send my compliments to Dr. Franklin and deliver a short memo about your mission for me? With all the other things on my platter, it could take a week or so before I get to it, that is, if Bretagne does not sink first."

"Yes, sir."

"You know, of course, that during our absence at sea, that the news of ratification of the King's treaty arrived here at Brest, aboard an American vessel called the Spy, a most appropriate name." Lunt smiled and the Admiral continued, "The acceptance message from Congress arrived on the tenth of July. On the fourteenth Louis declared war on England. On the twenty seventh of July, not knowing that any of this had transpired, we engaged the enemy. At least I will not be accused of starting a war, by engaging the enemy without orders."

'No, sir, an American would say that you are in the clear, sir.'

Both men smiled together.

'You will find out shortly what I have decided.'

On the way out Lunt passed Hall in the brevet corridor. He seemed surprised that Lunt had preceded him, but continued into the Admiral's great cabin without saying anything.

Hall emerged from the Admiral's office a few minutes later. 'I guess that you are needed to stay in the Admiral's service a bit longer.'

Lunt changed the subject, 'Was there anything they wanted you to do for them?'

'Well, the Admiral said he would appreciate any carpenters we had to spare.'

'And you are sending some over?

'Well, one, that's all we have.'

'Every little bit helps, Lieutenant Hall.' They shook hands and Lunt smiled as he watched Lt. Simpson's second in command descend the jacob's ladder down into his longboat.

*   *   *   *   *

'You say you've been in India. How long, dearie?'

'Eighteen years, until Walter got the shivers and died. I'm a widow now,' explained Sheila Armstrong, with her best mimic of a combination cockney accent with strong Indian influence.

'How'd ya har of this place?' said Martha Ray mimicking her accent.

'Me friends say it's always in the papers, the naughty ones.' There was a little giggle from Sheila, but not too prolonged, in fact just right. The men would like that. She put on a soulful look, the men would like to help her out of her knickers, thought Martha Ray as Sheila rambled on, 'I've missed a lot of life. I'd like to work where there's some fun, before I'm too old. I can laugh on cue and keep the gentlemen...' Martha Ray listened casting her eyes downwards at Sheila's deep decolletage, accentuated by a black widow's dress that fit snugly. The hair was a chestnut red, with a few grays showing here and there, and green eyes. The woman was a looker all right, and a bit older too. The Royal Navy bigwigs and their Tory pals would like that.

Madame Ray decided to state the situation as bluntly as she could. 'You know the men that come here are powerful. You don't say no to 'em. They are used to having their way with the women, if ya knows what I means. Mind you they treat you nice, they are gentlemen, but they must get their way in the end, that is simply how it is here. You have any children?'

Sheila shook her head, pretending she was sad, 'Can't have kids, never could.'

'Come inside a bit now. Do ya have a little proof of who you are, some papers from India and from your

261

voyage back?"

Sheila Armstrong nodded, but at that moment Martha Ray's attention was diverted by a large shiny black carriage coming up the narrow side street. The carriage pulled into the mews beside the gated mansion. Madame Ray descended the stairs as a large middle aged man in civilian attire got out of his carriage, and walked around the corner to the stone stairway.

"Why Admiral Howe, it has been such a long time. You have survived America?"

"Only because I knew that I would be coming back to visit Lord Sandwich's favorite domain, the other castle on the Thames. New York has nothing its equal." The Admiral, in civilian dress, bowed graciously and kissed her hand. "Has Lord Sandwich arrived as yet?"

"No, you wicked thing, you're too early," teased Martha Ray seductively.

Howe raised his eyebrows and slipped his arm around her waist, "Then I shall have you all to myself until Sandwich arrives." Then his eyes shifted up to the head of the stairs where they found the widow Armstrong. Like the withdrawal from Concord bridge, the Admiral's arm fell off Madame Ray's waist, "And who is this fair vision?"

Martha Ray took the Admiral by one hand and her new girl by the other and marched through the front door of the castle between both of them.

"It's going to be a real pleasure knowing that I'm the one who introduced both of you."

*   *   *   *   *

It was another Tuesday at Versailles. Vergennes greeted Franklin and Adams in his salon, 'Gentlemen, gentlemen, it is such a hot day, would you care for an ice? They are delicious.'

They were served a tall, rich, cold cream dessert which they ate while sitting in the extreme corner of the salon speaking in low voices. 'How, may I inquire, did the Charles de Weissenstein affair turn out?' asked Adams.

'Most intriguing, most intriguing. My agents went to Notre Dame at the appointed hour on the first day. There was a tall gentleman in his late fifties, perhaps early sixties, well dressed, but totally bald. He never came to the exact spot specified but never was out of sight of it either. He did not, thank goodness, wear a flower in his lapel. Such histrionics.'

Both ambassadors laughed, took a taste of their dessert, and listened intently.

'Well, we never contacted him. He waited around for a couple of hours. We simply followed him back to his hotel. We know his name and what he looks like. We will watch him now, always. We will let the situation develop, see who he associates with.'

'But, the principal reason I have asked you to sit down with me today is to tell you some very good news. You will recall that some time ago the Spanish court discovered that a Jesuit, who had served as King

263

Carlos' confessor was, in reality, a British spy and has been in their employ for the last half dozen years. As you can imagine, the Spanish King is furious and has just instructed Minister Floridablanca to arrange for the United States to receive a considerable donation, in gold. The Spanish Ambassador here wishes for all of the Ambassadors from America to come to a special dinner next week. He is indisposed with a brief illness but, as the Minister of a fellow Bourbon King, he has asked me in a brief note to tell you these things.' Vergennes handed an elaborately scrolled invitation to Franklin.

After a few minutes of jubilation the topic of conversation shifted as Vergennes asked, 'Now that Captain Jones has relinquished command of the Ranger, what will you do with him?'

'We don't know. We have promised him another ship, but we really do not have the resources.'

'These matters about money can be worked out now that we are truly allies, and by the way, thank you for coming to me about the Weissenstein affair. It has cemented our trust.' Both American ambassadors nodded.

'You know the English fear Jones greatly, above all other commanders. Even though the incident of landing in England by the Ranger was in reality a very small affair, they still fear him most.'

Franklin and Adams nodded.

Vergennes collected his thoughts, 'Have you ever had the feeling that you have a spy in your presence?'

"Captain Jones has identified one in Ambassador Lee's office. We have not taken action. The information was extracted at the point of a gun. Ambassador Lee feels it is therefore unreliable."

"Is that Mr. Sayre?"

The two Ambassadors looked at each other and then nodded in unison.

"Mr. Sayre is not a very good spy. I think we have known about him for a long time. No, I think there may be another. Do you remember the moment when the King was in your office and mentioned that d'Orvilliers would be sailing in a matter of days? Many of your staff were present, at least eight or ten people. And some of them might have told others what was said."

Vergennes continued, "Well, the British had a courier system in place. It was not four hours before that message was on its way to London via Dunkirk. Of course, we were not yet at war with them, and fortunately the British fleet was on patrol too far to the south to interfere with d'Orvilliers' departure."

"How did you come to know all this?" asked Adams.

"From Admiral d'Orvilliers, I believe his evidence is conclusive," replied Vergennes with a shrug. "But before you charge back to Passy and put your entire staff under house arrest, let me explore with you an idea I have. We are all in agreement that Captain Jones is much feared by the British. Their Foreign Office is constantly sending out inquiries wondering what enterprise he will be engaged in next. Suppose that you gentlemen now begin to plan somewhat openly one of Jones' future missions so that it may be overheard at your embassy. In other words, leave your spy in place, and use him to feed the British a few choice bits of erroneous information. Up to now they have had a very reliable spy feeding them valuable information, for the next few months they will not expect that suddenly the information they are receiving is a ruse.'

Vergennes continued, 'Suppose you drop hints about a coming raid on let's say Liverpool or Edinburgh to be led by Jones. Perhaps a few maps could be left out on the table with places identified, that sort of thing. The farther away from the Channel the planned enterprise, the better.'

Adams questioned, 'Wouldn't it be better that you make this diversion?'

'Ah, they expect it of us. We have been fighting the English off and on since 1066. They know our tricks and we theirs. But, I hope I do not hurt your feelings, gentlemen, with what I am about to say.'

There was a long pause as Vergennes searched for a delicate way to phrase his next sentence. 'The British view you Americans as being exceptionally naive, and on the world scale of things perhaps you are. Frankly, I find your honesty refreshing. In all the time I have known Dr. Franklin I have never found him in a lie.' A smile crossed Vergennes face, and he put out his finger in the direction of the other ambassador. "But you are a lawyer, Mr. Adams, and I have only known you a few months. You do not come to Versailles very often, I don't know about you."

Adams frowned a bit, but accepted the intended jest concerning his profession good naturedly. He had no choice.

Vergennes continued, "If you think about it. What would do the greatest harm to British capabilities to intercept our supply ships? British war ships are widely deployed already. The Royal navy has 150 or so ships of the line, and another 350 smaller vessels with which to accomplish this or that mission. If you are successful in deceiving them that an American expeditionary force under Jones is going to land somewhere on their island, then the ships that they will have to divert will thin out the numbers they can ultimately deploy directly against us in the channel. It will make them just that much more vulnerable everywhere. Already they have ordered Admiral Howe and many ships back from America."

Vergennes did not get much response from either ambassador. Adams in particular frowned, thinking privately that bringing more attention to Jones would reward his behavior and only increase the risk of everyone learning of the affair that was raging with Madame de Chaumont at Passy, right under the nose of her husband, their embassy's benefactor. If she knew about it, his Abigail would be furious. She was already raving about Dr. Franklin's affairs with Madame Brillon and now Madame Helvetius. Vergennes interrupted his thoughts, "Oh, some more good news. One good outcome of the Battle of Ushant and the clearing of much of the British fleet from our coast."

"Yes?" said Adams forcing himself to the present.

"Just a few days ago, a portion of d'Orvilliers fleet that was able to put to sea again, has seized 13 ships belonging to the British East India company as they were returning from India with goods of immense value. King George will be furious. That's right out of his personal treasury, you know."

Vergennes continued, "There are a few other items," he drew from his vest a small notebook, glanced at it and resumed speaking. "Have you ever been able to effectively get your pigeons to perform? To actually fly across the Channel?"

Franklin paused a moment before he replied. He was a bit disheartened that Madame Brillon must have recently told Vergennes about the pigeons that he kept at her chateau. Perhaps she was getting a small revenge for the attention he had been showing Madame Helvetius of late.

"We did have that capability last year. But now we do not know where the pigeons at Madame Brillon's would fly to if they were released. The man who had organized that portion of our operation has disappeared. We fear he is dead."

"Ah, your so called Spymaster?"

Franklin nodded, "So you have named him."

Vergennes was thoughtful, "The British mistakenly thought Lieutenant Lunt was your Spymaster a few months ago.' Franklin started to ask him something, but the Minister put up his hand, 'As you know the young man was aboard the flagship, Bretagne. Admiral d'Orvilliers was very impressed with him. He is still with us at Brest. He, however, has made an unusual request of us. He wishes for a time to attend a special school, for espionage, that we have here in France. One of my operatives has recommended he attend. We know Lieutenant Lunt prefers not to return to America aboard the Ranger, because Captain Jones is no longer in command. And regretfully, now it will be at least next spring before we have a fleet for Lunt to pilot into New England waters. With your permission, I would advise we let him attend this school for awhile. There will be no cost to your embassy.'

'We have no ship for him, until Captain Jones gets one. I don't see why not,' said Franklin, looking to Adams, who nodded. 'With all the espionage you have suggested is going on around us at Passy, this experience might be valuable to us. Where is this school?'

Vergennes spoke enthusiastically, putting down his goblet of ice, which he had let melt during their conversation. A servant instantly retrieved it from off their table. 'It is south, in a region called Foret d'Othe, perhaps one very long day's journey from Paris, a beautiful place. The man who teaches the school is a relic. He must be, let me see, oh, eighty years of age, but very fit. You would never know his age. I only know it myself because some thirty years ago

I also attended this school. The man is the grandson of a famous musketeer of the King. The dueling blood that flows in his veins comes from the days of the Sun King, and Cardinal Richelieu. In those days men fought to the death in the streets just to be first to kiss a woman's hand.'

Seeing that he was losing Adam's attention, Vergennes returned to the present, 'But enough of things gone by. If you ever get your pigeons to again fly across the channel, I have a growing need for receiving information from England swiftly. And if we could act rapidly on that information, well, let me just say it would be excellent for all of us.'

11
Spyschool

Lunt departed Passy by horseback at dawn and by mid morning the stench of Paris was left far behind, to the north. Lunt traveled in civilian clothing. His blond queue flopped over the back of the worn, hand sewn leather vest that Sarah had given him when he first departed for the war. He also wore a pair of brown breeches, white linen shirt, and a special sash for his sword and one pistol.

Lunt's hawk nose jutted out from under his brown tricorner hat with an embroidered black trim. He had a matching brown jacket to complete the suit, but, because of the oppressive heat, he had folded the jacket neatly into one of his saddle bags.

For the first time since beginning his service, Henry had acquired an outstandingly comfortable pair of leather boots whose high tops rose to just short of his knees. All of his clothing, save his sword and his leather vest, had come from the King's tailor, who was at first shocked that Henry had ordered the suit to be made so plain, but who eventually followed Lunt's directions to the letter after the second embroidered pattern had been rejected outright. Despite its lack of elaborate accouterments, the fit and material of the suit stood out in any company.

Dr. Franklin had risen exceptionally early on the morning of his departure to have breakfast with him, and had asked Lunt to first stop by the chateau of Madame Brillon to check if any pigeons had arrived. If so, he was to return with whatever message they carried. Otherwise, he should continue on his way south.

As Lunt mounted, Franklin came to the side of his horse and remarked, "You look especially dashing this morning, Henry. Be wary of all those Mademoiselles, remember Sarah." He winked with a broad smile.

Henry leaned over to whisper back good naturedly, "And Mr. Ambassador, you should be careful of too many other Madames, so that you will be able to venture to Madame Brillon's again!"

"*Touché*," laughed Franklin, waving goodbye.

Just after he had passed through a city called Montereau, Lunt waited for a rope ferry to cross the Seine. Several times during the day he had been stopped by soldiers or constables because of suspicion arising from his poor French, spoken with an American accent. One of several papers he carried was a passport signed by one of Vergennes secretaries complete with a royal stamp affixed. He was always treated cordially by those to whom he had to show these papers, and in one case was invited to share a lunch of bread and cheese with two of the King's soldiers, who guarded an intersection at which mail was stored for rerouting by coach. For nearly an hour, Lunt exchanged information about America and in turn was briefed about the famines which periodically ravished the French countryside. As a result, many young French people had left their family farms and had moved into Paris, and now were unhappy because there was no work, no way for them to earn money in the city. They did not wish to return to the countryside. America was very much on all their minds. According to the two soldiers, many, many Frenchmen, given the choice, would leave France immediately and go and fight for the Americans just for an opportunity to win for themselves the personal freedom that America represented.

One of the two solders was especially friendly and he pointed down the valley to a small farm house near the Seine where his family lived. The soldier said that he would welcome Lunt at any time to his home, and promised that there would be always a bed and a meal for him if he journeyed this way again. Lunt did not know it now, but many years later he would accept that invitation.

Lunt shook their hands and got on his horse. As he began to move along the road in a gentle lope, the two French solders shouted after him, *'Libertie! Libertie!"*

From these encounters, Lunt got the impression that many in the country would gladly free themselves of their King and pursue the course set by the Americans. For the next hour, Lunt wondered if a revolution would ever occur in France, and exactly what motivated Louis to help in an effort to have another King lose a large portion of his realm. There was a great irony there someplace or perhaps it was simply that the French court was still obsessed with getting revenge for losing Canada to England during the Seven Years War. Trusting Lunt's discretion, the two soldiers had offered the opinion that the French court was so isolated at Versailles that they had no idea of the true feelings of most the people of France towards their rule.

Soon Lunt's thoughts turned to the Chateau de Sens. With each passing hour he could see the mountains called the Foret d'Othe draw nearer. He passed hundreds of small farms, with low fences made of stone, obviously cleared from the land. Occasionally, there was a larger house that was framed by the smaller cottages adjacent. As the afternoon wore on, several times Lunt hurried his horse into an easy lope. He hoped to make the Chateau of the Count de Batz-Castelmore before dark, present his credentials and be admitted for the evening. He had no idea of what to expect within.

There was always the Chateau of Marie Chatelain which lay another fifteen or sixteen miles beyond Chateau de Sens, at a place called Dixmont which everyone had said was high in the mountains and very beautiful. Lunt preferred to press his horse in an effort to make the '*École des Espions*' that evening.

Just as the sun finally began to set, Lunt rode into the isolated forest trail to which he had been directed and arrived at a large wrought iron fence through which he could just view a germanic style building with sharply gabled roofs. At the gate, a guard challenged him, holding a crossbow threateningly in his hand. Lunt felt as if he had been transported back into the middle ages. Lunt replied in his crude French that he wanted to visit with the Count de Batz-Castelmore. The man let him pass through the gate into a dark forest road which was surrounded by a dense grove of trees.

Torches burned on both sides of a great stone arch which framed the courtyard immediately in front of the building. As Lunt rode under the archway, the full front face of Chateau de Sens came into view. There was a great door of immense, gnarled wood. To the left and right side were large protruding arched windows which gave the house the appearance of a large eyed monster with bulbous eyes and gabled ears. Twenty feet over the great arched door, there jutted out a parapet balcony. Above it, a flag pole angled outward towards the wall of forest trees which stood close in, surrounding the entire abode from only a cleared perimeter of fifty feet, and limiting the amount of natural light which penetrated the place. From the tip of the pole, Lunt could see by torchlight, that there hung a black flag on which a castle was depicted sitting on a field of crossed rapiers. The noise of forest creatures was everywhere.

As he glanced upwards towards the very top of the structure, it seemed to Lunt that the roof was flattened at certain points and that there might very well be a walkway and protecting rail surrounding the entire roof.

Lunt tied his horse to a rail and walked up the small pathway to the stairs that led to the massive door. He could see light peeking around the edges of the door frame. Just as Lunt reached out to lift a heavy iron knocker, the door suddenly creaked open. From within, Lunt found himself confronting a thin old man holding a rapier deftly. The point of the weapon was poised, threateningly, in the direction of Lunt's nose. At the other end of the rapier, the man smiled from ear to ear in appreciation of the startled expression on Lunt's face. Lunt considered stepping backwards to evade the range of the man's blade, but thought better of it. Instead, Lunt decided to state his purpose.

He spoke in English, 'I am here to see Count de Batz-Castelmore.'

The man replied in perfect English, 'I am he.' The blade of the rapier dropped a fraction of an inch.

'I have an introductory letter for you.' Lunt cautiously reached into the pocket of his vest and pulled out Marie's note. The man accepted the missive and deftly stepped backwards a few steps into the light of an enormous chateau room, at either end of which two hearths burned furiously. Halfway through, he looked up at Lunt, raised an eyebrow, and continued to read another moment. Off in the distance, somewhere in the house, Lunt believed that he could hear the sound of foils clashing, and then of a man screaming out as if on the attack.

'Can you speak any French?'

'A little, *un peu*,' replied Lunt trying to speak French as best he could for the remainder of the conversation.

'It is necessary for you to speak more than a little French to attend this school. There are certain subtleties you would surely miss. And these might later cost you your life. Do you realize what kind of subjects we teach here?'

Lunt struggled with his French, but managed to say, 'Yes, I believe that I have an idea. Of course, if I knew everything, I would not need to come to your school.'

'I like that answer,' said de Batz-Castelmore. 'How did you meet Madame Chatelain?'

'Aboard the Ranger, Captain John Paul Jones' ship.'

The old man raised an eyebrow, and seemed impressed. 'Of course, everyone in Europe has heard of the great Captain Jones. You were with him on his voyage into the Irish sea?'

'I am his lieutenant,' stated Lunt.

The eyes of the old man showed respect. 'I cannot take you in here now. You will have to find somewhere else to stay for a few days. Until, say next

Monday, four days from now. There are two rules, if you attend my school, Lieutenant Lunt.'

Lunt listened intently.

'First, you will never come to my school as yourself. You will adopt an identity which is not your own, and it will be that of a person from another country, which is not your own. There are several reasons for this, and as you attend my school, these will become apparent to you.'

Lunt started to speak, but the old man waved him off. 'The second rule...,' the Count de Batz-Castelmore lowered his rapier half a foot and flicked the edge of Lunt's vest, beneath which rested his pistol in sash, '...is that you will bring no firearms of any kind to my school. Spies do not use firearms...they use knives, poison, and strangulation, but never firearms. If you have to discharge a weapon, you have been caught. Your mission has failed and you know what happens to spies if they are caught, Lieutenant Lunt.'

Lunt started to ask another question, but the old man firmly motioned him backwards with the threat of his sword point, simply saying, 'Until next Monday, at dawn, your first mission will be to attempt to capture my flag from the parapet above this door,' he gestured upwards with the blade, '...before the sun rises. Stay unobserved and alive.' The dense wood door slammed shut with a firm hollowness.

Lunt stood alone in the darkness. The noise of the forest creatures was everywhere. He walked to his horse, took the reins, mounted, and returned under the archway towards the main gate. A little way along he glanced back at the jutting balcony, it seemed that it would be an easy drop from the roof. Surrounding him was the very forest he would have to penetrate in four nights time to make the balcony before dawn. He drew his horse to a stop, and looked into either side of the dark forest. The brush was thick. Anything moving through it would surely cause a commotion and subsequent detection.

At the gate, Lunt was slow to close it as he glanced left and right. The wrought iron fence went each way into the forest for some unseen distance. Lunt suddenly heard movement in the brush, someone was nearby. Lunt thought of the dark figure with the crossbow. He decided that this was not the time to probe further into the defenses of Chateau de Sens. He had four days, he would return in the daylight and survey the environs. In order to do that, he would have to stay close by. The chateau of Marie Chatelain in Dixmont, the French soldiers had said it was another four hours beyond Sens, on the other side of the mountains. That would be by daylight. Without sunlight it could take all night. Lunt elected to head into the village of Sens and look for a tavern that offered lodging. The experience would improve his French.

Inside, the Count de Batz-Castelmore returned to an upper floor to duel with the bald headed British

279

Major, who, according to his disguise, was posing as a shipping merchant from Brussels. The man was already good with the rapier and with the sabre, very good, very sure. The Count decided upon a distraction to win their final practice duel.

The Count crossed blades with the man and then circled slowly to his left. A few attacks and parries brought no decision. As the Count circled, the grip of his left hand took hold of the top of a chair and then he heaved it suddenly into the knees of the startled Major, who fell backwards momentarily. For just an instant, the Count had his opportunity. He lunged forward, the blue tip of his practice foil took the Belgian pretender under the arm for a crippling wound. The blue dye spot marked the place. How many more years would he still be able to out duel his students?

The Count de Batz-Castelmore turned and simply walked away. This was perhaps the last Englishman he might ever teach. He was a loyal Frenchman, in peace time, he would take their money. But in time of war he would not teach the enemies of France how to defeat his own county. Major Pitkan had started just before war had been declared, and so he had accepted him. In another six or seven years he would be approaching ninety, surely this would be the last of his wars to train the master spies of Europe.

It was deliberate that the young American Navy Lieutenant and the British Major could not be allowed to be enrolled at the same time. If they guessed each other's identity they might kill each other. The last time he had allowed that to happen was when a Silesian and an Austrian had discovered each other's identity during their nasty little war back in '58. It had been very bloody, very bloody. And he had lost both students. And, of course, he never got paid. Yes, the school of spies could take on some very real qualities.

It was time for his nightly cognac and then away to bed. He would get only a few hours sleep. There were traps to set before the students awoke in the morning.

*   *   *   *   *

Admiral Howe suddenly bolted up out of bed. Damn, he'd slept all night at Martha Ray's. He'd have to invent urgent Admiralty business to explain at home for his overnight absence. It had been a half dozen or so times over the past month that he had been intimate with this Sheila Armstrong. Each time he had lingered longer into the night. He looked across at her. She was extremely beautiful. The kind of woman that once you are seen with her, people think that you are something special. He needed that if he were going to succeed in becoming First Lord, someday after old Sandwich retired. She was a mature woman, far different from the mostly frivolous women that had resided at Martha Ray's in the past. She seemed to be loyal as well. Imagine her being pent up some twenty years in a remote corner of India with a husband who dutifully kept accounts for the East India Company. What a waste.

She stirred and then opened her eyes. "Morning, love."

He sat on the edge of the bed now half clothed, pensively looking across the room.

She sat up in bed and wiped her eyes. The sheet falling for just an instant to reveal her large breasts. She demurely pulled the sheet up again. "What troubles you, love?"

"Oh, nothing. Ah, well it's a little project I have been working on. Just Admiralty business, just an idea I had. A good one, but their Lordships haven't been very impressed. It's a system I've invented."

Sheila wisely did not press the inquiry then, but on another evening when the subject came up again, she enthusiastically jumped up and down on their bed. "Oh tell me, tell me. I can keep a little secret."

"Oh, well, I suppose it is not really a military secret because the Admiralty does not wish to adopt my code. So I'll tell you, if you don't consider it too boring."

"I love secrets," she giggled in her Cockney-Indian accent. "Show me."

"Suppose that you could issue two hundred and fifty-six separate and distinct commands to your ships by utilizing only two flags," Lord Howe was becoming very enthusiastic now as he went to the small writing desk at the corner of their room. "It's like this." Howe dipped his quill in the ink well and drew a series of lines, sixteen down and sixteen across. It made a grid of two hundred and fifty-six squares. Sheila Armstrong stood to his side looking over his shoulder staring at the paper.

"Suppose you had sixteen different flags. The first one is a yellow cross on a blue ground. Number two is blue and yellow squares on opposite quarters, three is a blue cross on yellow ground, and so forth."

Howe cleared his throat and continued, "Now, suppose that you put number one flag at the head of the very first column, number two at the head of the next column, and number three, the next." He drew little images at the top of the chart. "Now, suppose you use the same sequence going down the rows, one for the first row, two for the second row down, and so forth."

"Why do they have to be the same flags going across and going down?" asked Sheila Armstrong, conscious immediately that her question was too shrewd, and that she had neglected her accent.

Howe looked at her suspiciously for a long moment, but then shrugged it off. Continuing, he turned back to the table and pointed at the matrix. "They don't have to be. But it's far simpler if they are. You would have to show two flags anyway, why couldn't they be the same? Look, suppose you write 'follow me,' as the command in the box where the third column across, and the second row down intersect.' He minutely wrote an Fm in that square with his quill. 'Then from my flag ship I could post the blue cross on yellow, followed just beneath it by the blue and yellow squares on opposite quarters. On the other ship the flagman would read this as three across at the top and two down. He would call out this to the Captain below who would look at his identical grid to see what signal was written in that square of the matrix.'

Sheila mused a moment, in a deliberately accented speech, 'I still don't understand why this system is better than what you've got?' She helped him on with his coat, as he stood up.

'I can't talk about what we are using now, at least not exactly.'

Sheila nodded her understanding and pretended that she was only interested in hearing more if the Admiral wished to talk about it. She turned away to get on a robe.

'But...,' Howe paused a moment, 'now we use just a number system. A Royal Navy captain is currently limited by the smaller number of messages we can transmit using just flags which each represent different numbers. This new system would give him more box grids for messages. With a new system like this we can still retain all the standard Admiralty signals, and any van Admiral or even Captain of a flotilla can fill in any of the blank squares of the matrix with his own system of prearranged messages for special purposes. The system, if adopted, would give the Royal Navy tremendous signaling flexibility at sea.'

A few more weeks passed, and they were in a carriage together returning from a private theatre presentation for the Admiralty and a party afterwards. Lord Howe's family had gone to the country to see the autumn leaves change.

'How is your signal system coming on, dear?' inquired Sheila.

'The Admiralty has just about tabled it. Sandwich has shoved it aside, thinks it is too complicated,...that it might give the individual captains too much leeway at a time when the Admiralty needs more control of her fleets especially with England possibly facing invasion by the Frogs.'

Sheila mused, 'If the Admiralty were to have occasion to really notice your system, then it might be beneficial to your own advancement.'

Howe looked at his mistress and nodded.

The next morning as Lord Howe sat in a hot water tub on the third floor of Martha Ray's castle, there was a knock on the door.

'I've something to show you, dearie.' It was Sheila's voice.

'Come in.'

She was wearing a robe and from the cling of it, nothing else. Howe looked at her.

"What is it that a woman has two of, that men always notice? I believe that I have a way for your fellow officers to notice your two flagged system."

Howe continued to stare forward in puzzlement. He started to stammer because the direct discussion of sex always caused him to stammer, even at his age. He gave no certain reply and only waited in curiosity for whatever Sheila Armstrong was about to do.

She quickly opened half of her robe for him to see her nakedness. Over her right breast was pasted a petite rectangle bearing a blue cross on a yellow field. In a flash she closed the right side of her robe and opened the left, on the other breast was a flag with blue and yellow squares on opposite quarters.

"I think that perhaps Admiral Howe should give a signal party for his fellow Admiralty officers," Sheila suggested in her Cockney-Indian accent.

Howe just sat in the tub gaping, he was very aroused when she said, "Are you going to recognize your own signal, Admiral?"

She then giggled and turned right out the doorway and towards the bedroom they shared.

The Admiral rose from his hot tub in all the naked splendor of a very middle aged man who had not missed a meal in many a year. Aroused to the full extent that nature allowed, he followed her into the bedroom with great dispatch as the signal required.

*   *   *   *   *

Lunt arrived that September morning at the chateau of Marie Chatelain. It was pleasantly nestled on a south facing slope of the mountains the French called Foret d'Othe. It looked majestic sitting high up on the slope. The valley below was variegated with wheat fields, and at higher elevations many grape and apple vineyards. Henry stopped to purchase apples from one of the farmers. Upon ascertaining that he was an American, as all had before them, they immediately mentioned Dr. Franklin. Lunt was humbled at the fact that he could truly say that he knew the great man.

Riding up to the gate surrounding the Chateau, Henry was met by a gardener who was caring for the grounds. He asked in French if Madam Chatelain was about, although he already was certain from her letter that she was absent. The man thought a moment and told him to wait at the gate. Within five minutes he returned out the front door of the chateau with a well dressed, jovial man in dark breeches and a fringe of grey hair which surrounded the base of his bald head.

He greeted Lunt in French, 'So, you are the young American who Madame Chatelaine said I should welcome, should he come by. I am Jacques, the last name I have almost forgotten myself. I believe you know that Madame is away, perhaps for a very long time.'

Lunt smiled, 'Yes, I was just being polite by asking for her. I have a note.'

'Yes, I know that you have and I know that the note says for us to keep you happy and well fed, and to let you enjoy any facility of this house,' offered Jacques cheerfully.

'All of your things are in the saddlebags?' Jacques gestured for the gardener to take them.

Lunt nodded, and dismounted, handing Jacques the letter, which the latter slipped into his vest pocket without reading. 'Yes. Tomorrow, I must leave for the day. Does Madame have a horse I could borrow, one that is very fast? I am afraid mine is a very poky animal.'

'Madame has an Arabian, a mare. I'm sure that you will find it very swift.'

Together they walked up the steps to the chateau's entrance. Immediately upon entering the great drawing room, Lunt liked the feeling of elegant space within the chateau. Unlike the other houses of the French nobility that he had already visited, such as Madam Brillon's and that of the Duchese d'Anville, this one was furnished simply, using an absence of furniture to exhibit its wealth rather than the usual clutter caused by the possession of too many exquisite pieces. Even le Petit Hotel was over crowded.

Jacques showed him the house. Room after room on the first floor possessed enormously high beamed ceilings. All the floors of the chateau were of a gray slate, amazingly smooth, a tribute to the skill of some craftsman who had toiled laboriously to make them so.

"How old is this chateau?"

Jacques shrugged, "It is from before the time of the Sun King. Perhaps two hundred years. At the time, the family that built it was in disfavor of the King. This is where they lived for over a decade," reported Jacques.

"Do you know how Madame happened to come by this property?" Lunt asked, indulging himself in an uncharacteristic inquiry.

Jacques related that because Madame Chatelain was barren, and there was great pressure for her husband to have children to carry on the family name, he had no choice but to divorce her. The situation had involved a church arranged annulment in this very Catholic country. Her former husband had bought this home for her and his paternal family supported it for life, but the agreement was that Marie was not to spend more than an occasional visit to the French court to avoid embarrassment to the family. Jacques reported that Madame Chatelain was rarely at Dixmont and instead traveled a great deal. Often it was over a year between her comings and goings.

Lunt walked into another room and stopped to gape at a wall decorated with perhaps two or three hundred pistols.

"Madame is an excellent shot. Every time she is here, the mornings are very noisy. We store three barrels of dry powder in a room off the wine cellar."

Henry smiled, remembering the story that had already become a legend of her marksmanship across the length of the Stone Gallery at Versailles. "Where does she practice, show me."

Together they walked through a doorway into an open grassy garden on one side of the chateau. Several hundred yards off, one of the ridges of the nearby mountain ridge blocked them from having a horizon view.

Jacques explained, "You see the poles and the lines between them." He pointed off some fifty yards. "Madame stands some distance from the lines and I pull a target across her field of view. Would you like to try it?"

"Yes, very much, but a little later after I have changed clothes and bathed," said Lunt. "What is that?" he pointed to a net pulled tautly across some thirty feet of grass.

"Tennis, damn Henry the VIII's game," snipped Jacques. "But Madame is a good player. Do you know the game?"

Lunt shook his head.

"You hit a small leather ball over the net and you and your opponent try and keep it in the air. You use one of those paddles," Jacques pointed to one which lay on a window sill. "You are out of breath swiftly. Do you wish to try it too?"

Henry nodded, "Oui."

"I'll show you to the bedroom now, where you

will sleep tonight. It overlooks this view and the front of the house." Jacques pointed up to a set of shuttered windows on the high second floor.

After ascending a spiral staircase to the upper floor, Lunt was led toward the front of the chateau. Jacques opened the door for him to enter. Inside was an enormous four posted bed, whose base was set some three feet off the ground on a special platform. At the far end of the room facing the front of the chateau, was a huge tub which was built into the floor and stood in a location directly in front of the windows which opened onto a balcony.

"Outside," explained Jacques, "...is a pulley."

Lunt did not recognize the word '*poulie*' from the way that Jacques pronounced it and he went over to the window to look and then realized that Jacques was describing a system of getting the water for the bath up into the room. Jacques then pointed out to him that emptying was even easier. One just pulled the plug on the bottom of the tub, and the water drained down the outside of the building directly into a flower garden below. Lunt smiled and then turned to survey the room.

"This is Madame's bedroom, isn't it?"

"Ah, yes," said Jacques a little sheepishly.

"The room is very, very beautiful, but I think it would be best if I slept in another room," said Lunt.

"That is a problem, monsieur, for there are no other bedrooms."

"Surely you jest, this house must have ten or

twelve rooms. None of the others are bedrooms?"

"No, Lieutenant Lunt, Madame rarely has guests, and in eighteen years now, never another lady. When a gentleman visits he usually does not come to sleep in another room."

Lunt walked around the room once, his hand behind his back. He then looked up at Jacques, "I will be delighted to take a bath in this tub, it will certainly be the experience of a lifetime. But there was a sofa in the room downstairs with all the guns, I think it would be more fitting if I slept in that. I am a married man, Jacques, and, unlike Madame's other visitors, I feel that it would be preferable if you set up my bed down there."

Jacques raised an eyebrow, but said simply, "As you wish."

Henry spent the remainder of the day shooting pistols and trying his first game of tennis. In the warm evening he sat out under the stars alone with a bottle of wine that Jacques had selected for him from Madame's cellar. He thought about Sarah and then Marie. He fell asleep in the warm evening and awoke at first light of morning. Someone had thrown a large hand woven shawl over him. Save for a few mosquito bites, he had spent a comfortable evening.

In the morning Lunt quickly ate a breakfast of cheese and eggs and croissants. Then he took the fast mare and was gone to ride half the day to Sens where he circled the forest and the fence which surrounded the entire structure of the Chateau de

Sens. Henry's heart pounded as he tried to envision the spy games he would play in the school. Upon his return to the chateau of Marie Chatelain, he asked Jacques to bend the prongs of a pitchfork into a triple pronged grappling hook and attach a line to it. He also handed Jacques his pistol to be placed on Madame's wall as part of her collection. He announced that he would leave at noon the next day.

After a ride over the mountains of Foret d'Othe, Lunt arrived high above the dark forest surrounding the Chateau de Sens. Near twilight he watched to see if anyone entered or departed. Nothing was observed. The sun set to the west and then he went to work dressing for the evening's challenge. He took off his good clothing, excepting for his boots, and changed into some black breeches and a rough brown leather shirt he had secured from Jacques. Then, he put his sash and sword over these. Using water from his canteen, he sloshed a cupful onto the thick dark soil until he had produced a thick dark mud. By the fading light he applied that dark mixture to his face and hands. He took a knife blade from his saddlebags to crudely check his face and hands in the fading light. His only revealing feature in the darkness would be his blond hair and queue. He went to his bags again and found an old dark cloth he had used to wrap his lunch the day before. He pulled it like a kerchief over his head, in the fashion of a French peasant, and knotted it under his chin.

He then led his horse down the grade behind the chateau. Lunt presumed that he would be allowed to retrieve his horse and saddle bags after the entry game had been completed in a few hours time. If not, he would simply insist upon it.

In a grove of trees a few hundred yards from the dark forest surrounding the school of spies, Lunt secured his horse and took the only three tools he would use. The bent pitchfork and hemp line which now resembled a naval grappling hook, his sword, and a knife. He was determined to capture the flag before being detected.

The day before, Lunt had found a large tree whose branches hung over the wrought iron fence that circled the property. A meadow separated the grove of trees from the perimeter forest. He crouched and moved across the open field in increments of twenty steps at a time towards that tree. Crickets in the field chirped, but then fell silent each time he moved. During the periods of silence, he would crouch down, wait, and try to stay still until the noises resumed.

Suddenly, near the edge of the forest Lunt saw a rider. A man trotted with his horse along the line of the forest staying some twenty feet away from its perimeter. Lunt dropped to the ground and faced his head the other way so that he looked like a dark lump in the ground. The sound of hooves paused for a long moment. Lunt sensed that the man was not more than fifty feet away. Would they catch him so soon?

The horse resumed its stride again and after a full two minutes Lunt turned his face back towards the edge of the forest. In the distance he saw the tall rider continue his circle of the perimeter. Was that the Count, trying to find where his students had tied their horses, or was it someone else?

Lunt lay on the ground a full quarter hour and once even observed a fox that ambled slyly across the narrow meadow. When all animal sounds had resumed, Lunt again got into the low crouch position and bolted the remaining seventy feet into the dark edge of the forest. The giant Acacia was right where he had made note of it during his ride. Lunt twirled the triangular pronged pitchfork vigorously and flung it up and over the tall limb. Intuition told him that he had to get over the fence without touching it. He sensed that the fence was somehow fitted with a trip line that would bring the protectors of the flag in his direction.

The pitchfork hung up in the tree limb nicely. Lunt put his weight on the line to test it, and then, as any sailor would routinely climb a halyard aboard ship, Lunt raised himself hand over hand up some twenty five feet into the V of the tree trunk. Sitting on the trunk he coiled up the line and rested. The forest was too dark to see adequately. Lunt had hoped that he might be able to move inward towards the chateau a considerable distance by traversing from tree limb to tree limb above the forest canopy towards the back of the chateau. But now he could see that this was unrealistic, it was far too dark to work his way through the forest by traversing tree limbs.

Soon he would have to descend to the ground and make his way across the forest floor. The forest floor was particularly thick and any attempt to walk across it would lead to the sound of cracking twigs. Lunt regretted not having moccasins made at Marie's chateau. He remembered moving across the forest floor of Plumb Island as a child playing hide and seek in indian moccasins. They muffled most of the sound if one stepped cautiously.

Lunt thought for a moment and then decided to cut off part of his leather shirt, along the back, to make moccasins. The night was warm. He took off the shirt, and with his knife cut the back into two portions with long strips for ties. He took off his boots and wrapped his feet. He hoped he would be able to find his boots in the tree later. They were the most comfortable pair he had ever owned.

Lunt made his way as far as he could into the forest by moving across several adjacent tree trunks, until he could go no further. Unhitching the hemp line, he let the free end and the grappling hook end fall on either side of a convenient tree limb. Then holding onto both ends he descended, his rough leather shirt moccasins landed soundlessly on the forest floor.   For the next several hours Lunt crept cautiously in the direction he believed the chateau lay. From time to time he thought he heard movement in the forest somewhere, but always off in the distance.

Twice he came to a clearing, which he avoided. One of the clearings held several superficially constructed buildings and a rope ladder bridge leading to them from the forest. This must be one of the training sites, he concluded. He started away from it, when across the darkness of the forest, far to his right, he heard a blood curdling, high pitched scream. Everything living in the forest stopped making sounds. Lunt squatted frozen. After the last echoes of the sound faded, there was nothing more. Lunt had confirmation for the first time that he was not alone, that others lurked within the forest.

Lunt stayed in place for another quarter hour and then resumed his forward progress. It must now be within an hour of daylight. He had underestimated the time it would take him to cross the forest to get to the chateau. He was beginning to lose hope that his bearing into the forest had been correct. He might be off course and therefore not heading for the back of the Chateau de Sens at all. Then, suddenly through the trees he sensed, rather than saw, a towering dark shape. He moved slowly and cautiously forwards, trying to make as little sound as possible. Then he stepped beside the last tree at the edge of the wood. It was the rear of the chateau. He was there.

His plan all along had been to try and take the flag by scaling the building from the back and then traversing the roof, putting him in a position to dangle his grappling iron off the roof and snag the flag, and thus seize it without even setting a foot on the balcony below. Far ahead and off to his left, Lunt heard the sound of one man stomping through the trees. Then there was shouting, and the sounds of many twigs breaking as a group of people ran through the forest. Whatever was going on might distract those who might otherwise hear his activities. This was his opportunity. Lunt stepped out into the little clearing and twirled his grappling iron vigorously. Off to his left they were still running through the woods and there was loud shouting, in French, of several voices.

The fork head twirled in a circle at the end of the hemp line and then left Lunt's hand. The head of the distorted pitchfork soared up and over the parapet and onto the roof. Lunt heard it land. He tugged against the line, it moved a few feet and then hung up against something. He tugged again and brought his full weight onto the line. It held firmly.

Lunt began repelling himself up the side of the building. His moccasin feet padded silently against the rough hewed stone wall. Hand over hand, he ascended up the sheer face, evading the windows of both the first and second floors. The most difficult portion of the climb was the last five feet when he had to swing outward from the building to catch the top of the overhanging parapet. He worried that the bent pitchfork prong would not hold his weight, but he was committed now. It would be a fall of twenty feet if the prongs came unbent. He swung outward and, hanging by his left hand, he stretched his right hand up through the air and over the top of the parapet. The first time he was unable to hold on, but on the second attempt he succeeded in getting a hand hold. He pulled himself up over the edge and onto the roof.

Exhausted, he lay there a few moments and, then squatting, he coiled up his line. He looked up into the sky, it was brightening. In a few moments the sun would be up and he would lose the game. The roof top was not smooth, but instead heavily sloped with a kind of rough slate finish. His moccasin feet were soundless as he moved swiftly over it. There were two or three gables that he must move between. Lunt considered trying to get into the house through one of the windows, but then thought better of it. It would slow him down. It was now less than fifty feet to the front edge of the roof. From there he might be able to peer down onto the balcony and spot the castle flag below.

Lunt continued forward, when suddenly, a swift sliver reflecting morning light came rapidly out of the darkness, right at him.

*   *   *   *   *

Pitkan waited under a tall apple tree to the side of the road which led up from the base of Foret d'Othe. At the close of the day he observed small groups of servants leaving the chateau halfway up the slope. In another hour the egress had concluded. Pitkan waited several more hours and then mounted his horse and, under cover of the darkest of nights, he rode up the trail towards the Chatelain chateau.

At the gate, he decided to give no notice of his presence, and instead tied his horse to a tree alongside the high stone fence several hundred feet to the west of the gate. He stood up on the saddle of his horse, so that he was able to reach high enough to get a handhold on the top of the stone wall which surrounded the chateau's grounds. He pulled himself to the top of the wall and then dropped over onto the other side. Calmly he walked, not to the front entrance, but around the perimeter of the building. If she was there, he was certainly not going to announce his presence.

This was his own private operation. This time he did not have to follow the rules of Paul Wentworth and Lord Stormont. Imagine making him ride up to the American ambassador's residence, risk being shot by the American marines, only to throw a worthless rock and message through the window. If it had been up to him, he would have used a real grenade and have done with them all.

Now it was time for his revenge, and tonight the bitch would come to pay for what she had done to poor George Burden and all the others in Belfast, and no one would know who did it. He had learned her real name, Marie Chatelain. Her shot had brought her fame at Versailles, but had also unmasked her identity. He still felt the wound in his arm. Finding out where she lived had been simple once he knew who she was. Paul Wentworth had observed that French agents had recently begun to follow Pitkan everywhere that he went in Paris, and so with Wentworth's encouragement, Pitkan had gone to the Chateau de Sens to drop out of sight for a few weeks. Conveniently, the chateau of Marie Chatelain was just a few hours ride away. For weeks he had planned that he would kill her before returning to Paris. Tonight, he would not give her the opportunity to fire first, she would be dead instantly.

Halfway around the chateau, Pitkan found a door and tried it. It opened with barely a sound. He stepped into a large room, a small night lamp burned at the far end, he turned to look around and saw a wall of pistols. He'd had to leave his pistols behind while attending the school of spies, how convenient. He went to the wall and selected two of the largest caliber horse pistols he could find. A delicately carved powder horn lay on a small writing table beneath the pistols, it provided the powder. A search of the table's drawers revealed cubbies filled with balls of various caliber, another drawer contained wadding. He loaded both pistols, stuck one in his belt, and held the other in his right hand fully cocked.

He picked up the night lamp in his left hand and proceeded to explore the house. He looked into several first floor rooms off the corridor from the gun room and found no one. At the end of the corridor, he found the drawing room and then the winding staircase leading to the second floor and the presumably bedrooms where she must lie asleep. He started up, silently, but swiftly, taking two stairs at a time.

Halfway up he was challenged in French, 'Stop.'

Instinctively, Pitkan crouched low and pivoted on the stairs, aiming his pistol and firing without hesitation. The pistol roared and the man who had challenged him fell over making barely a sound. The echo of the blast reverberated throughout the chateau. The lamp Pitkan had held fell over the bannister and smashed onto the floor below. Burning oil spread out over the rug and some tapestry. She was alerted now. Pitkan could not take the time to stomp out the flames, he couldn't afford to give her more time to react.

Pitkan rushed upstairs and began darting low into each of the rooms, searching, then stopping, listening. Downstairs, he could hear the fire spreading. He did not care a damn for the property. He wanted her. He came to a bedroom lit by a solitary candle. It was the only bedroom he had found in the entire chateau. At first he was cautious entering, but then he saw that the bed was elaborately made up. It had not been slept in. It seemed that no one was here. He pushed papers around in one of the drawers of a desk, but found only letters of account concerning vineyards, nothing personal, nothing of military significance. He smelled smoke now, strongly.

Pitkan returned to the head of the stairs and looked over at the fire below. Flames were now climbing up wall tapestries towards the roof. Even the bannister of the staircase was burning. The level of smoke made breathing difficult. He covered his face and descended down the stairs hurriedly.

Where was the body of the man he had shot? He saw a trail of blood. The man had managed to drag himself out the front door. Outside, fifteen feet from the foot of the stairs of the chateau, he found the man, still crawling, still moving.

Pitkan turned the man over, "Where is Madame Chatelain?"

The man shook his head. Pitkan thought about the lessons he had learned at the school of spies. He should try first to give the man hope. "Tell me where she is and I will see that you will live, otherwise I will drag you back into the fire." Pitkan picked the man up by the arm pits and started to drag him back towards the building. The man screamed in terror, the gun shot wound in his chest bled profusely. The man started to lose consciousness. Stopping on the stairs, Pitkan hooked the trigger guard of the horse pistol under the nail of the man's middle finger and ripped it off. The man regained consciousness, screaming in agony.

"Tell me or we repeat that," threatened Pitkan.

He hooked the trigger guard behind the nail of another finger.

'She's in England, that's all I know, please,' the man wept convulsively in reaction to his own weakness and then lost consciousness again. Pitkan searched the man's vest and breeches. In one pocket he found a small note in French. He held it up to the firelight.

Jacques,

Please extend the full courtesies of my chateau and property to the bearer, Lieutenant Henry Lunt of the American Navy.

M. Chatelain

The man must have been telling the truth, she was not there, otherwise there would have been no need for a note. Lunt must have been there recently. He must learn where Lunt was now, and why he had been at the chateau.

Pitkan tried to shake the man, but found that he was dead. Pitkan stood up, angry at himself. He could have learned more if he had proceeded differently. Now a lot of villagers could be expected to rush up the hill, attracted by the fire and the gunshot. He would need to get away. He picked up the man, who was likely called Jacques, and dragged his body back

304

into the inferno by his boots. The fire might destroy evidence of the gunshot wound, but if it did not, he didn't care.

Pitkan hurried through the main gate and found his horse. Perhaps Lunt had visited for awhile, perhaps he was now somewhere on the road back to Paris. Where else could he be going? If Pitkan rode all night, and questioned others on the road, describing Lunt, he might just find him. But at least the bitch had been deprived of her lair. It was a token to appease his vengeance.

*   *   *   *   *

The shaft hit Lunt square in the stomach with considerable force, throwing him backwards. He lay on his back, struggling for breath, then he willed himself to sit up. There was a huge white spot on his dark leather shirt. He glanced beside him in the faint morning light and saw the feathered shape of a crossbow shaft lying a foot away.

Just as Lunt started to pick it up, a familiar voice spoke out of the darkness, in English, "How does it feel to be a dead man?" There was a faint chuckle. "You did very good, very well. What is your name?" said the Count, the twinge of a French accent revealed in his speech.

"I am Nathaniel Morris, a merchant sailor from

Halifax,' replied Lunt almost falling into the verbal trap.

'Well, Mr. Morris, you did very well.' The old musketeer stood over him, and then stooping, felt his foot, 'Ah, leather, very good idea. I did not hear you at all, only the sound of the pitchfork coming over the parapet. That was all. We wondered where you were, we never detected your entry point. You used the pitchfork to get over the fence without touching it?'

Lunt nodded, obviously disappointed.

'It may comfort you to know, Mr. Morris, that no one has ever captured the flag. You've come the closest in many, many a year. This is my way of showing all my new students that they need to pay attention to what I have to teach.'

The Count reached into his pocket and pulled out a hollow reed. He blew it with three shrill, piercing whistles, and then shouted out towards the forest in French, 'I have the last one, the game is over, cut that man down. Assemble in the great hall.'

His pride hurt, Lunt followed the venerable musketeer across the roof and then through an open window in a gable front, down an attic ladder, and finally down a sweeping central stairway from the second floor to the great hall.

As they descended, the Count de Batz-Castelmore spoke in a low voice, 'On the second floor you will be billeted with three other students. There are ten student bedrooms, so I take a maximum of forty students. With a current war raging between the

Austrians and the Prussians, and now the French and English, not to forget the American colonies, we have a full house. Only because three students left yesterday, do I have room for you and two others today."

They reached the lower floor, and the Count motioned for Lunt to precede him into a room. Inside there were thirty-nine others. One of the men lay in front of all the others on the floor, dressed brightly and tied up like a pig about to be skewered. His clothes, once beautiful, were now incredibly soiled. Another man, also tied up, was small and wore a dark moustache. His skin was naturally dark and his features were exotic. He was obviously from another part of the world. Lunt guessed one of the Arabian countries.

"Untie them, the game is over," the Count pointed at the captives, and several followed his bidding. He then gestured towards Lunt. "Gentlemen, may I introduce you to...Nathaniel Morris, a merchant sailor from Halifax, that's in Canada."

There was a chuckle.

"Mr. Morris made it to the roof. Observe leather tongs wrapped around the feet, and mud all over his face and hands for camouflage. And this, a pitchfork with which Mr. Morris successfully scaled both the perimeter fence and the back wall of this building. But you see he was not swift enough to dodge the shaft."

"I never saw it coming," said Lunt in French

pointing to the white powder on his vest and shirt front. There was laughter.

The Count held up his hand, "And now, I present Mr. Hauptmann, a banker from Zurich. You seem to have soiled your clothes."

"Well, the rope trap was not expected, but I am only a banker. I'm not used to hanging upside down in the woods like a stag about to be trussed up." There was laughter and several men around him good naturedly slapped his back.

The man had spoken in a Germanic accent. He could be either Prussian, or Austrian. If he was the former, he was nominally Lunt's enemy. There was a pact between Prussia and England, and just recently a German fleet had arrived at Gibraltar to shore up the English garrison there, should the Spanish enter the war on the French and American side. Lunt began to see the wisdom of every student here assuming both a false identity and a false country of origin.

"Our next new entrant is Monsieur Galien, a trader from Senegal. His French is not perfect."

The man raised his hand, pointed to his white powder wound and smiled good naturedly. Several in the audience clapped. The Count resumed, striding to the center of the great hall with a certain dash. His ancient wizened face lean and sunburnt, his slender form fitted with the cape and doublet of an earlier age. He held the crossbow in his left hand. Dangling from his sash the magnificent hilt and blade of his rapier glistened in the firelight. Henry looked around and could see the respectful glances of the students who had been there a long time. Everyone was attentive, glued to the coming words of the old master.

'Gentlemen, the business of being a spy is a serious one. In the coming weeks I shall teach you codes and cipher, how to use them and how to break them. I shall teach you how to use two, alas ancient, but deadly weapons that can kill silently at a distance, the bow and arrow, and my personal favorite, the crossbow.' He raised his hand to show the weapon he favored.

'I shall train you where to hit a man in personal hand to hand combat in order to kill him swiftly and without mercy. I shall teach you how to kill a man with a sword,' he drew his rapier, his blue eyes flashing about the room, enlivened, excited, 'not with the pretty motions of a fashionable duel, but with the deadly swiftness of a master spy, never giving your enemy a chance to succeed, never playing fair. And lastly I shall tell you how to kill yourself swiftly, and painlessly...'

'Yourself, why would you want to do that?' asked the banker from Zurich, his face distorted with anxiety as he asked.

The Count drew his blade and walked over to him, putting the point of his rapier against the man's chest, 'Because my rich banker friend, if your disguise is unmasked, suicide is often a far gentler reward for a spy than what the enemy has to offer. Have you read in the broadsides that the English had used a

Jesuit to spy for them, and that the man had served as confessor to King Carlos? Now what pleasantries, gentlemen, do you suppose the Spanish authorities hold for him? He is captured posing as a Jesuit, or perhaps in the beginning he was truly a Jesuit who sold out and...' The Count interrupted his own sentence with a derisive chuckle, 'Of course to be discovered in that predicament, he could not have been one of my students.'

There was laughter in the room when someone mimicked, 'Of course.'

The Count continued, '...oh, to be discovered in the country of the inquisition, where torture is a fine art. Would you not under that circumstance want to take your own life?'

Herr Hauptmann from Zurich nodded vigorously.

The Count de Batz-Castelmore continued, 'I shall train you to use poison and to detect when you have been poisoned. I will train you to wake every morning and so convince yourself of your assumed identity that you will not even recognize your own name when it is spoken in front of you. I read in the newspapers that the American privateer, Captain Jones, recently caught a man who was a spy on his ship, by sending him a message using his real name. The trick worked and the spy gave himself away. Captain Jones beat the man almost to the point of death, and then let him go. The man was so fortunate, the Captain must have been in good humor. For if I were Captain Jones, I would have killed him outright. For you see, you should expect no mercy if you are caught in our profession.

"One can also expect little glory, for you see, gentlemen, the successful spy is never caught. He or she goes about their business and no one knows what they have done. The generals and the admirals get their names recorded in the history books, the spy does not. When the war is over, very often the spy lingers in place, continuing to serve in a position of great responsibility for the country he has helped defeat. Remember, truly great spies are never discovered, but they do always lie lurking within the government of every county in the world and we may never, never learn of it. But spies, gentlemen, have conquered far more territory than any general in the history of the world. To take the enemy unexpected, is to defeat him with a minimum of force."

Lunt's eyes were riveted on the Count now. He wondered what stories he had in his brain, stories of his students' lives. Secrets he knew that could turn Europe inside out. Lunt had the feeling that this man never betrayed the trust of his students, which was why Marie had sent him here. He understood.

"The reward of a spy is then not the glory which comes after a battle, for the spy rarely gets that, the generals and the politicians claim glory." There was laughter.

"No, the reward of the spy is the quickening of the pulse during the act of deceit. The thrill of getting away with it. The pleasure comes in the rush of your blood when you take that chance and against all odds you succeed in stealing a secret. You want to jump for joy, but you simply cannot. Someone would spot your pleasure. You must hold the secrets within yourself. There can be no applause for spies.'

On the following two Monday mornings, Lunt would hear the speech again. He understood more each time as he progressed in his knowledge of the art of espionage and of the French language. By the second Monday, he had single handedly captured his own new student, garroting the man as he passed beneath an over hanging tree limb. The man fell to the ground under Lunt's weight, and then heard Lunt chuckle in his ear, 'Sorry, you are now dead, but nice attempt at the castle flag. I didn't succeed in getting it, so why should you?'

On the Wednesday after, in the middle of the night, someone came into his room and poked him awake. Lunt sat bolt upright.

'Mr. Morris,' said the Count. 'Someone is downstairs to see you.'

Lunt dressed quickly and descended the stairs, It was the American Marine Sergeant Hennessey from le Petit Hotel. He was in civilian clothes, they nodded and then went outside together.

The Sergeant whispered, 'Dr. Franklin needs you, sir, right away. Something has happened.'

12

Mission

Captain Jones was surrounded by a group of ladies, each eagerly seeking his attention, in the far corner of the main salon of Madame Brillon's chateau. Madame de Chaumont suddenly took his arm, her plunging decolletage almost eye level to the shorter Jones, who raised an eyebrow to indicate he was aware of her presence.

"Captain," she said aloud for the benefit of the other ladies within earshot, "You promised to show me how to tell by the night sky what the weather will be tomorrow."

Jones looked to the Madame and caught the intent which was as subtle as the tread of an elephant's foot. Smiling rakishly, his eyes darted around the room for Madame's powerful husband. Satisfied that the embassy's benefactor had departed, Jones and the Madame departed on foot for her astronomical instruction. Several courtesans, some of them old enough to have been the Captain's mother, sighed in disappointment as they saw the handsome American officer depart the gathering with Madame de Chaumont on his arm.

One matriarch whispered to another, "It's been brewing between them since they danced together during the Independence Day party." Many ears tuned in eagerly, hungry for gossip. "Well, she does have the largest bosom in Passy,...."

After a while the ladies finished their gossip with a salvo of giggles, and then broke up to scout out who else was available now that the most handsome man and the most powerful woman had departed.

Across the hall, Ambassador Adams watched the scene annoyed, and then whispered to Dr. Franklin, "I hope that my senses are deceiving me, and that we do not have a problem in the offing."

Franklin whispered back, "I'll have a word with our intrepid young Captain in the morning. It was an oversight for me not to have invited some more eligible mademoiselles. I'll manage better next event. There'll be lots of parties to attend with the Captain in the coming weeks, now that he has come to his senses and withdrawn all charges against Lieutenant Simpson."

"He does do exceptionally well representing our military," commented Adams. "Jones has the kind of flamboyance that fascinates the French. I see the respect in men's eyes when they see him in uniform." Adams ceased talking for a few moments and looked wistfully at the elegantly dressed party guests with whom he had never been at ease because of his deep rooted Puritanical upbringing. Soon all of this splendor would be just a memory. Again he tipped his head towards his co-ambassador, "Do you want me to make the announcement?"

"It would be best coming from you. I'll have Mister Hubbard translate it for you into French if you pause after every few sentences," advised Franklin. He motioned across the salon for Nathaniel Hubbard to come to the small rectangular musician's platform built into the salon's far corner.

A bell was rung and the hostess, Madame Brillon, made several frivolous preliminary statements. Just then, Henry Lunt, wearing his brown suit, entered through the main door of the salon, situated at the opposite end from the ongoing ceremonies. Unnoticed by most in attendance, he edged along the rear of the audience so that he could view the small dias, behind which the Stars and Stripes was mounted alongside the Fleur de Lis. Ambassador Adams was introduced and there was polite applause. Benjamin Franklin in his black Quaker suit with a small flourish of white lace at the sleeves stood out prominently amidst the peacock-like colors worn by most of the other guests.

There was a silence in the room, as Mr. Adams' shrill nasal accent sought to put emphasis on his words. As was their custom, most of the French pretended not to understand him.   "Ladies and Gentlemen, you will forgive me for still not being able to address you in your own language." He paused while Mr. Hubbard relayed the brief statement in French.

'I have so enjoyed the great hospitality of the French nation and the French people, and of course the exceptional hospitality of Madame Brillon and all of the charming people with whom she surrounds herself. My country could not have greater and truer friends.' There was a mild applause, and after his words were translated, considerably more.

'Just yesterday, the latest ship to arrive from America brought a letter from President Hancock that he has other work for me back in America. I regret to tell you that I will shortly have to leave France. But I know that our infant nation will continue to be well served by our new Ambassador Extraordinaire, Dr. Franklin, who will now serve as the sole official representative of the government of the United States to the court of Louis the XVI.'

Before there could be any translation, there was spontaneous cheering and applause amid the gathering, leaving poor Mr. Adams to wonder if the nobility attending Madame Brillon's salon were cheering for Dr. Franklin's new status or for his own departure. Everyone present rushed to surround Dr. Franklin, who blushed. Mr. Adams said a few more words, but even he appreciated that Franklin had their hearts.

Lunt watched Adams descend from the dias and then intercept a passing waiter to obtain a small piece of cream pie. He walked towards Lunt, his hand outstretched, a genuinely friendly smile on his face.

'Did you hear, the Adamses will be going home to Boston. I expect before Thanksgiving. Are you

316

going to come home too?"

"I don't know why Dr. Franklin summoned me here, Mr. Ambassador," said Lunt, wondering if perhaps he was now going to be asked to escort Mr. Adams home, and then to rejoin his family sooner than he believed possible. If so, why had they let him attend the school at Chateau de Sens the past several weeks? Lunt looked around for Captain Jones. He was nowhere to be seen. At that moment, someone hailed Ambassador Adams and he departed Lunt's side.

Feeling a tug on his sleeve, Henry looked down to his right. It was his friend, the Adams boy.

"I like you," said the boy. "I'm happy you're back."

Lunt stooped over. "Why I like you too, John Quincy." He patted the boy's tummy, and loosely brushed his finger nail over a portion of the boy's shirt which bore telltale marks of chocolate. "It looks to me as if you have been eating too many of Madame Brillon's desserts. Perhaps we'll run in the woods tomorrow and work some of that off of you."

Lunt pulled the boy closer to him and whispered, "Have you seen Captain Jones?"

"The Captain was here." The boy eagerly offered more, "Captain Jones told me all about the fight you had with the Drake at breakfast this morning. He's been staying with us at le Petit Hotel in your old room. He even gave me one of the Drake's signal flags to take back to America. I have it in my room." The boy said eagerly, "I'll show it to you."

Lunt put his hand on the boy's collar, restraining

him from running off in his eagerness to show Lunt his prize, perhaps forgetting that he was miles away from the grounds of Hotel de Valentinois. Looking at the boy, Lunt thought then of Sarah and the infant who bore his name, and whom he had never seen. A part of him would be happy if it was to be his destiny to take the same ship home with the Adamses. But another part of him wanted to remain and fulfill whatever mission that Captain Jones might have for him. He'd had the opportunity to sail home with the Ranger and had declined it. He wondered whether Mr. Adams would truly need him during the voyage to America. Perhaps the Ambassador was trying to bring him home as a personal favor to his father, Matthew Lunt.

'Father's angry at Captain Jones,' said John Quincy suddenly, '...but I like him. He's a brave and fearless fighter. He will beat the British again and again when they attack *Liv-a-paul*.' The boy stuttered through the last word, obviously unfamiliar with the city's name. At the same time he plunged his fist downward through the air as if to smash an invisible enemy.

'Where did you hear that?' asked Lunt, astounded that he should hear this from the lips of the boy.

'Why from the Captain himself, he told me a secret,' said John Quincy looking at Lunt's suddenly stern face. 'Is anything wrong?'

'No, it's nothing.' Lunt changed the subject and asked the boy if he had been playing any more chess. The boy said he had been mostly practicing with a bow and arrow. He wanted to show Lunt how well he could shoot his bow in the morning, early before his French tutor arrived. Lunt agreed, 'If Dr. Franklin has me stay on.'

Then Lunt led the boy over to a far wall, away from the other guests, and whispered to him. 'You know, if you should happen to overhear something that Captain Jones is about to do, it could be very dangerous if you repeat it. It could get Captain Jones hurt.'

The boy looked at him very maturely and then whispered back, 'I know that ...but, it's a game.' The boy suddenly bolted off, leaving Lunt perplexed.

Seeing that the rush around Franklin had subsided, Lunt moved within the Ambassador's field of vision. Franklin noticed him immediately and nodded subtly. Lunt went to a buffet table and took a small dessert while he waited. A few minutes later, he saw Franklin pull Mr. Adams into the center of a conversation in place of himself. He then walked towards the entrance door, beckoning Lunt to follow. At the door one of the servants offered Dr. Franklin his fur hat, but Lunt heard him decline in French, saying that he was only going out for a short walk and not leaving for the evening. Outside, the Ambassador, despite a limp, walked briskly around the eastern side of the chateau. Lunt followed him at a trot to catch up.

"You know Sean O'Mally very well, don't you?" It was a rhetorical question, but Lunt replied nonetheless. Lunt adjusted to Franklin's vigorous, but limping pace. Together, in the clear starlight, they walked several minutes across a small meadow in total silence as the sounds from Madame Brillon's chateau retreated behind them. They passed horse paddocks, and finally came to a small two story barn which appeared to have no windows. But Lunt could see light leaking through cracks in the wooden walls.

After fumbling for a key in the meager light, Franklin opened the door and urged Lunt to proceed ahead of him into a lantern lit room whose walls were lined with farm implements. The floor was padded with straw, but the smell inside was of something strange. Franklin took the already lit lantern off its bench perch and proceeded down a narrow corridor. The shadows cast in the room were intensely black and moved in a pattern outlining the Ambassador's form eerily against the narrow walls of the interior corridor.

The Doctor halted at a wooden ladder which led up through a square portal to the loft above. He turned momentarily to hand Lunt the lantern. Without speaking, he climbed upwards with some difficulty, into a dark upper loft. Lunt held the ladder and then followed. As he neared the top he heard strange cooing animal sounds, and then the flapping of wings as whatever was up in the loft was awakened by their nocturnal visitors.

As Lunt reached the top rung, Franklin's hand reached out to take the lantern. Lunt got to his feet on the second floor loft and looked about. He could see a long line of wooden cages stretching through both sides of the entire upper level of the loft. There were a great many pigeons inside some of the cages, flapping their wings restlessly and making frightened noises.

Franklin moved along one direction. Quickly examining tags on each cage, he finally said, "You can take this one, and the one beside it. That will give him thirty birds. Enough to start again. I'll help you, but you must lower the cages by rope yourself. I'm an old man with the gout. I can barely climb the ladder any more."

"Sir, I don't understand?" questioned Lunt.

"Yesterday morning, ...that pigeon," Franklin raised the lantern and pointed to a small white and creme colored bird, crouched in terror at the far end of an otherwise empty cage, "...flew into our coop. The bird was bewildered. As you can see, it is very old. There was a message on the bird's leg dated three days ago, in our code, everything correct." Lunt listened intently. "The writer claims to be our Spymaster. The message said simply that he was back, but not able to move about due to injury. He needed someone to bring him a supply of young birds because his are very old and may not remember their way home to Passy. The sender claims that he sings three evenings a week at a place called the Pirates Haven in the Hammersmith section of London, close to the river Thames.

"Lieutenant Lunt, I want you to leave for London immediately. At Dieppe on the Normandy coast is a small fishing sloop called Moonlight. It is piloted by a man who is, by day, a watchmaker. His name is Monsieur Trebon." Franklin looked over the top of his spectacles. "I suspect the man makes far more from smuggling than making watches. At any rate, I have arranged to have him take you from Dieppe tomorrow night to England. When you arrive in London, I want you to first verify that it is truly O'Mally, and send me a message forthwith by pigeon. I shall be personally elated to receive such good news. I can't tell you how much I have missed his help." Lunt understood and listened in silence.

"If it is he, then leave the crates of pigeons with him and help him re-establish the network of agents he had originally set up. Also, I want you to update Sean O'Mally on several new codes I have begun to use in the past half year and in return to bring back any new personal codes he is utilizing."

Franklin handed Lunt a rope to attach to the top of one of the pigeon cages, so that each could be lowered down through the ladder opening to the straw covered floor below.

"Finally, and most importantly, if you are satisfied that Sean O'Mally is physically and mentally capable of functioning as our Spymaster again, you will use your judgement to link O'Mally up with an extremely important spy which the French have put into a very sensitive position. You are personally to make that connection. Both spies know you, and trust you. This is not a mission on which we can send a stranger."

Lunt knitted his brow wondering who the other spy was, but before he could compose a question, the Ambassador motioned for him to take hold of two corners of the heavy wooden cage and carry it towards the opening in the floor.

Franklin continued, "To take greatest advantage of their new spy, the French need the speed that our over-water pigeon network offers. Eventually, I assume, they will breed their own birds from our stock, but for now, there are too few birds in existence which have been successfully bred to fly the channel. We alone have them, so two nations are relying on you to establish this network. You will do this for your country?"

"Yes sir, it is what I have been training for these past weeks," replied Lunt. There was a full five minutes of silence while they lowered the first cage and then Lunt descended the ladder to retrieve the rope in order to attach it to the second cage and repeat the process.

"Sir, are you going to tell me who this French spy is that I know, and how I am to establish contact with him?" questioned Lunt, suspecting it was someone he might have met aboard Admiral d'Orvilliers flagship.

Franklin cleared his throat. "I know that you are close to this person. But regardless of any personal feelings you might have, what she has managed to accomplish is of the most strategic importance to our cause. I must warn you that you must be scrupulously careful and prudent while you are in England. One chance slip of the tongue or careless misdeed could cost the lady her very life, and, I am certain, unthinkable torture. A lady named Sheila Armstrong has managed to become the mistress of Admiral Lord Howe, likely the heir apparent to eventually become First Lord of the Admiralty should the Tories remain in power.'

Lunt, still puzzled, made an observation, 'I thought, Sir, that Admiral Howe was in charge of the Royal Navy effort in America, and that he was headquartered in New York?' Lunt, searched his mind, trying to remember anyone by the name of Sheila Armstrong. He could not.

Franklin spoke urgently, 'When it became apparent that the French would join the American cause, and that strategic naval warfare would be involved, the Admiralty ordered Howe back from New York. It may hurt our pride a bit as Americans, Henry, but to the British way of thinking, Europe and contending with the French is now their major priority of this war. And ... Madame Marie Chatelain, in the disguise of a recently widowed wife of a civil servant from India, was at just the right place at the right time. Howe saw her the first free night he was in London. He was lonely after the sea voyage, and it all happened quickly. Vergennes is ecstatic.'

From the pit of his stomach, Lunt felt a deep sense of anger. He tried to suppress it. This was not

Franklin's doing, but that of the French. It was a superb 'placement' as the Count de Batz-Castelmore would have called it. But the thought of Marie bedding down again with another enemy officer, especially a middle aged Admiral, possessed Lunt with an anger he could not suppress from his face.

Franklin reacted, 'I dislike being the one to have to relate this to you. I knew that you would be distressed to learn of it, but remember that it was her choice to do this. Vergennes has reminded me that you are still on loan to the French service. He has specifically requested you, partly because you know Madame Chatelain and because he suspects you know the Spymaster, if you are not so yourself.'

Lunt was looking down, shaking his head. Franklin put up his finger. 'There is another reason. Apparently, two weeks ago Madame Chatelain attempted to explain a naval signal code to her first French contact. They did not get much time alone together. The system to be explained was complicated and the information arrived back muddled, unuseable. Vergennes feels that a certain bright young naval officer who has a comprehension of nautical matters would have a better intuitive understanding of such a code.'

Lunt ignored the compliment, snapping back, 'Then the French do not know that O'Mally is the Spymaster?'

Franklin continued to speak softly, despite Henry's angry tone, 'No, and I don't want them to. I do not appreciate the fact that Lord Stormont has been allowed back into this country. This only means that he will continue with his vile efforts to discredit me, more lies in the newspapers. So I think that we should not yet reveal O'Mally's identity to the French, until we are sure that it is actually him. From your description of his injuries, I do not see how O'Mally could have even traveled from Ireland to England. If we send someone other than you, and the person in England who sent us this message is not O'Mally at all, but instead a British spy, and if that British spy is not identified as such and then linked up with Sheila Armstrong the whole affair would be a calamity. You, Henry, know and have the trust of each of the contacts. In addition, you will likely be able to comprehend the naval signal code she is trying to communicate."

Franklin repeated himself, "So you are very likely the only one who can perform this mission, save perhaps Captain Jones, and I cannot risk sending him, although I have no doubt he would do it."

Lunt nodded, "I understand, sir."

They worked together silently for a few minutes to lower the second cage. "Sir, a question, when will Captain Jones make the strike on Liverpool?"

"Where did you hear that?" asked Franklin.

"From the boy, John Quincy. It is probably information he shouldn't have repeated to me. I thought it was a little odd to hear it from a boy, but if it is true, will Captain Jones finally get his Man of

War?"

Franklin smiled, "Our intrepid Captain is pursuing a ruse that Mr. Adams and I have perpetrated. Just yesterday, we set young John Quincy out with the task of casually telling members of the staff of le Petit Hotel that Captain Jones will lead a raid on Liverpool sometime this winter. It was his father's opinion that if we do have a spy at Passy, then the spy would not believe that either he or I would make such a careless divestiture of military information to anyone. Mr. Adams felt that we might instead induce young John Quincy to tell certain people this information more innocently. To the boy this is merely a game that his father has suggested. You see, Mr. Adams and I have decided to leave whatever British spy we may have at Passy in place, and to instead feed whomever it is with inaccurate information. That way we can divert a great amount of Royal Navy resources away from our primary area of concern, the coast of France."

Franklin shifted the weight off his bad leg and continued talking, "Eventually, if you succeed in establishing the link between O'Mally and Madame Chatelain, then we will begin to leak naval information to selected individuals at Passy and then wait to see if Madame Chatelain hears any of it surface again at Lord Sandwich's castle. Depending upon which story surfaces, then we will have our spy, but in the meantime we will utilize that unknown person to transmit inaccurate information which we want the Admiralty to believe. For now, the best way to accomplish this is to leak information about the Liverpool raid to everyone who resides in le Petit Hotel. If it surfaces through Madame Chatelain, then we will know beyond a doubt that the French are right, and that we have a spy residing right in our midst at le Petit Hotel.'

Henry listened intently to Franklin, 'In the meantime, if the Royal Navy believes that Liverpool will be raided this winter, then some of their remaining channel fleet may be diverted for duty in the Irish Sea, out of harm's way of intercepting our convoy of fifteen French merchantmen due to leave from Brest and Nantes within the month. Incidently, the Ranger shall be one of the convoy's escort vessels under Lieutenant Thomas Simpson.

'Just yesterday, Mr. Adams and I learned that General Washington is running frightfully low on saltpeter, for gunpowder. Since the beginning of this conflict, France has supplied ninety percent of this critical material to our forces. With the onset of the English blockade, very little successfully got through to America this past summer. It is crucial that this last possible convoy of the year reach America before a harsh winter sets in, otherwise, I do not believe the Continental Army has enough gunpowder to survive a major battle in the spring. That was the essence of one of President Hancock's messages.'

The lantern light flickered haltingly, and the atmosphere was becoming close. Franklin suggested, 'Let's descend. It is, pardon the pun, very foul up here.'

They descended the ladder, as Franklin continued talking, 'If we can divert five Men of War off patrol for three or four months, that is as effective as winning an actual sea battle.'

Thinking back to the lessons he learned at Ushant, Lunt agreed, 'Yes, sir, it is.'

Franklin observed, 'You have grown a great deal from the young lieutenant I found on my doorstep, what is it? Four months ago? So you see you will not miss any sea action by not being in the company of Captain Jones this winter, I promise you that, and if you still have a mind to, I promise that you will serve again with Captain Jones upon your return from this mission with O'Mally's pigeons.'

'Sir, I don't understand, why do I need to return with O'Mally's pigeons? I thought I was to take pigeons to him?' questioned Lunt.

'Communication would be best if it's rapid both ways. O'Mally used to have pigeons which we would arrange to send from here to London. If he has a new brood, we could use some of them. Tell me Henry, did you go first to le Petit Hotel before coming here?'

'Yes, sir.'

'You saw some of the staff?'

'Yes, several, it was they who told me you were here at Madame Brillon's.'

'Pity, I would have wished that I had been able to send you off without anyone knowing that you had been back through Passy.'

*   *   *   *   *

The mahogany carriage sluiced along through the puddle lakes that filled every street in Pimlico until it pulled into the mews adjacent to Lord Sandwich's retreat. There was a high hatted servant standing by the coach entrance. He held an awning extension out to protect the carriage occupants from the driving rain. After a little urging of the horses, the Royal Marine driver in the tar slicker maneuvered the carriage door just to the edge of the awning extension and descended rapidly from the drivers seat to open the door of the carriage, saluting perfunctorily as he did so.

'Very good, Sergeant Kerns, we'll see you in the morning, have a good evening,' said the First Lord of the Admiralty as he extricated his rotund body from the opening of the carriage. The sergeant held his salute and replied briefly as Lord Sandwich proceeded into the home of his mistress.

Just as he made the doorway, the new woman, Sheila, greeted him charmingly in her strange mixed Cockney, Indian accent, 'Good evening, your Lordship, welcome to Admiral Howe's Signal Party. You are the last of our guests to arrive.'

Sandwich cocked his head upwards in reaction to the peal of raucous laughter descending from the main living room salon upstairs. There was also music playing somewhere. The woman named Sheila handed him a large card, on the front was a formally printed Welcome. On the back was Howe's confounded signal matrix, the sixteen flags across the top and down the sides were different from those he had submitted to the Admiralty Board upon his return from America.

'Admiral, I believe you understand how the matrix works?'

Sandwich squinted at it, his middle aged eyes having trouble focusing on the actual words shown in the matrix boxes. But he was very aware of being in the semi-darkness with such a beautiful woman. He could smell her perfume.

She leaned towards him, her face very close to his, 'Remember, Admiral, you must be quick tonight to catch all the signals, and obey them to the letter or you could be court martialed before the evening is out.'

There was a very naughty, saucy tone to her voice, Sandwich did not care for her talking to him that way, but he found that he was becoming very aroused.

'Remember, Admiral,' she placed her fingers over his shoulder and stroked the hairs on the back of his neck. He tingled and his eyes became large.

'Tonight my right is on top, and my left along the side.' Sandwich looked at her blankly. As she talked she stepped back from him.

'You must be quick to catch the signal.' She dropped the shawl covering her bosom. She was naked excepting for two flags over her breasts. He just stared, part of him wanted to be angry, but he was very, very aroused. She covered herself up again.

Frustrated, he stammered a moment and then said, with his voice three octaves higher, "Can...can I see your signal again?"

Sweat dripping from his forehead, he tried earnestly to focus on the card. It was difficult. He heard them singing upstairs. He could smell her perfume. He tried to use the card, but couldn't see the board. She pushed the card aside, and welcomed him, her face now moving very close to his.

"The first signal was, Prepare to repel boarders." Her arms went around his neck and she leaned against his uniform, kissing him full on the mouth, deeply. He could feel the softness of her breasts against his chest, they felt cool through the cloth of his jacket.

Just as he was really starting to settle into her, she separated from him, wagging her finger. "I won't tell anyone you missed the first signal, Admiral, but mind you be quick to catch the other ladies' signals this evening, or you may find yourself in the same position as Viscount Keppel."

She wagged her index finger at him again and then slithered up the stairs in front of him. Her bottom moving from side to side, her thin waist outlined in the candlelight emanating from the room above. The First Lord of the Admiralty followed her up into Madame Ray's salon. It looked like it was going to be a party the Admiralty would never forget. A bit unorthodox, but Howe was certainly off towards making this a weekend to remember.

*   *   *   *   *

"Yes, Sir," said Paul Wentworth. "Our agent reports Jones is going to make a raid on England this winter. But he wants more money, before he will tell us where."

"The bastard, we ought to threaten to let Captain Jones know he's our spy. That will scare the britches off him."

"We can't do that, Mr. Ambassador. He is now the last spy we have. And believe me, he is terrified of Jones, because of what Jones did to Hezekiah Ford. That incident sparked his demands for more money. There is genuinely increased risk for him now."

Stormont asked, "What do you mean he is our last spy?"

Wentworth coolly continued to report facts, "A message arrived at Passy yesterday from the American Congress. Franklin is now to be called Ambassador Extraordinaire. As a consequence, Adams is shortly to return to America. Arthur Lee's status is indefinite, but he is no longer to be co-Ambassador. This means our two spies in his service have lost their value. Apparently the new French Ambassador to the American Congress dealt Lee out and insisted that Franklin be put in sole charge of the American delegation.'

'Incredible, that Quaker fop,' commented Stormont, 'but when our merchant revolt gets under way, that means we only need one target, Franklin. Are the broadsides ready to distribute, accusing the Americans of not paying their debts to other French merchants and accusing Franklin of absconding with their money? You have enough credible merchants to make the demonstrations believable?'

Wentworth nodded. 'We are organizing them right now.

'Another item,' Paul Wentworth continued, 'last night, we observed Henry Lunt, both at le Petit Hotel and later at Madame Brillon's. Franklin and he left the party for a long time together. One of our agents believes Lunt has just left on some mission for the Doctor.'

'Who is Lunt, do I know him?' asked Lord Stormont.

'He is one of Jones' Lieutenants, was involved in the H.M.S. Drake incident, and is possibly the American Spymaster, but our spy at Passy now doubts it. He is, however, the person who Major Pitkan almost killed at Versailles in that debacle several months back.'

'Oh, yes, the incident that came just in time for Louis to ask me to leave for England. I've had a hard enough time getting unofficial reinstatement. Don't let that sort of incident happen here again. Just watch him. Find out what he is up to.'

"We have reason to believe he is preparing to leave the country."

"You have a description of him?"

"Yes, he's tall, blond haired, in his late twenties. He is a bit balding, has a rugged face with a hawk nose."

"Good, we'll pass on that description to our port agents. Have them on the lookout for both Lunt and Mr. Adams. The latter should be easy to spot, he'll be traveling with his son, I suspect. Find out what ship Adams is on. It would be a coup if we can just happen to capture his ship while he is returning to America. That would be like money in the bank."

"What do you want me to do about the Captain Cook plan?"

"Have the sympathetic French newspapers run stories on the scientific, non military purposes of his voyage. How his discoveries in the Pacific and Far East could benefit all mankind. Have them explain how the good Captain is expected to return to the Atlantic ocean this fall and the concern that the English have that a French war ship might stumble upon and inadvertently sink the Endeavor, losing all of Captain Cook's scientific discoveries. I have an audience with the King in a week's time. I will ask him for amnesty for the Endeavor should a French war ship come upon her. I will mention that Captain Cook has been gone so long that he would have no knowledge that we are at war again. It will give Louis an opportunity to demonstrate his continuing sympathy for scientific endeavors, despite the war. It should soften him up a bit, especially if I can arrange the meeting without Vergennes being present."

"Shall we attempt to seize Lunt again?" asked Wentworth.

"Not on French soil!" said Stormont, "...just watch him."

"What if he leaves France?"

"Then he is fair game."

*   *   *   *   *

The Pirates Haven rocked with raucous laughter. The man in the overhead swing led them in a wild, difficult to pronounce, cockney sailors' rhyme,

> She be bett'r after a bob of the bott'l
> yo can wink her wrinkles way...
> yo can forgive her spread...
> all yo need is 'nother pint of ale
> drink, wink, drink...

In a corner, a man thumped on a drum and another played a fiddle. Below the man in the swing, two drunkards twirled arm in arm while others cheered them on, chanting and clapping. Outside, a set of stouts kept watch for the King's press gangs. One of them had a gigantic boatswain's whistle dangling from a cord about his neck. Each man had a brace of pistols in his belt and would use them, before letting patrons fall prey to the press gang's club. Seamen inside were glad to pay a bit more to enjoy their pints in peace rather than to awaken the following morning kidnapped for a decade or more of service on one of His Majesty's Ships.

Lunt walked up the street in the fog. He'd come into the tavern the previous night and had kept watch carefully over the crowd while a vulgar fat woman entertained, but to no avail. Several times that day he'd walked through the mews beside the castle and hoped he would catch a glance of the woman called Sheila. But he did not.

His passage had gone smoothly. At the recommendation of his pilot, Monsieur Trebon, he had hired his way aboard a fish wagon going from Hastings to London docklands with the morning's catch. He used as a cover that he was delivering two cases of fresh squab for some rich customers. He used nearly the identical cover that he had perfected at the school of spies. He was a down and out Halifax sailor, whom the fortunes of war had dispossessed. He was now back in the mother country trying to earn sufficient money to return home in style and buy another fishing boat. On the journey to London, Lunt had spent an hour describing the setting of nets to catch mackerel in Nova Scotia. The fish monger, Samuel Harrison, listened with interest, not knowing that he was hearing the New England technique instead.

Lunt now called himself Robert Shaw. He arranged to keep his two cages of squabs in his benefactor's fish warehouse near docklands. It was close to Captain Kidds' tavern, where the ironmaiden was still on display in which the bones of the New York pirate had rotted for all to see as a warning to pirates over sixty years before. The tavern owner inside claimed that the skull that hung above the fireplace inside was that of the much maligned pirate. At the end of their journey, Lunt had a flagon of beer with his benefactor and accepted a nights lodging beside his pigeons.

The next morning he smelled so bad that he changed to his better clothes while a washerwoman did his laundry in the Thames. He told the Harrisons he would return in a few days time. It took him most of the day to make his way across London to the Hammersmith neighborhood of the Pirates Haven. He carried a small pistol under his coat along with a large knife. He was a bit over dressed for the locale, but had no difficulty the first evening.

On the second evening, when Lunt came to the window, instantly he found O'Mally. The unruly red hair was dangling down over an outrageous Naval officer's uniform, bedecked with medals so large that they literally clanged together. The infectious smile was there, as the body rocked back and forth on a swing suspended from a ceiling rafter by three stout lines. But the left leg was noticeably absent. Lunt remembered the horror of the amputations aboard the Ranger. He remembered his last days with O'Mally, his back all twisted, somehow he was now straight, very rigid. Through the window Lunt made another observation, O'Mally looked ten or even fifteen years older. The once bright red hair was streaked here and there with grey. Lunt surveyed the room for a few minutes more, there was no one else inside he recognized save the same barmaids from the night before. He took a deep breath and entered.

Several people looked up as Lunt entered, but O'Mally happened to be looking elsewhere as he drank from a flagon of ale which someone had bought him. Then he began swinging higher and higher in his netted swing chair. Up and back, he was swinging a good distance through the air.

Just as Lunt was about to slip into a table before him, O'Mally's head turned back and their eyes met. His eyes focused on Lunt for just an moment and then his left eye winked. Lunt believed he saw a tear. He sat down and didn't look up until another song was begun.

'There's another song, we're forbidden to sing. Are any of ye the King's sailors or spies?' called out the singer.

'No, hell, no, we'd slice 'em in two,' shouted someone from the crowd.

'Tiss a tale 'bout a stout Scotsman who challenged the King, ye want to hear it?'

'Yeah, yeah!' cried the audience ready for a wee bit of rebellion in the form of a chorus of 'Did He Not?'

"Have ye heard of the pirate, John Paul Jones? took nine King's ships, did he not?

chorus

Have ye heard of the vagabond, John Paul Jones? Landed on our shores, did he not?

chorus

Have ye heard of the fighter, John Paul Jones? Bested the Drake, wrung her neck, did he not?

The crowd of mostly Tory hating Irish, Scot, and Welshmen sang along enthusiastically. Lunt saw immediately that O'Mally was in his element and that from the seeming attitudes of his audience he could surely draw men into the intrigues which he had so well propagated in the past. Lunt sang along with the tunes for another two hours more, until O'Mally announced his last song, and asked if some able bodied gentlemen would be willing to help push him to his quarters in his humble wheel chair so that he wouldn't have to sleep in the tavern. Lunt nodded and raised his hand.

O'Mally acknowledged the acceptance by pointing at him and saying, "I'll sing now a song to the stranger who helps me, 'tiss a song about a beautiful maiden. Someone the like of whom us poor slobs will never get to kiss. But the kind of woman who lies in the sweet memories at the very bottom of our glasses."

There was laughter and then quiet melancholy as the sweetest voice in all the British Isles began to sing the melody he'd sung at Henry's wedding in Newburyport only a little over three years before,

*"The pale moon was rising above the green
    mountains,
The sun was declining 'neath the blue sea.
When I strayed with my love near the pure crystal
    fountain,
that stands in the beautiful vale of Tralee.
She was lovely and fair as the rose of summer.
Yet t'was not her beauty alone that won me.
Oh no! T'was the truth in her eye ever dawning.
That made me love Sarah, the Rose of Tralee."*

*   *   *   *   *

When Monsieur Trebon rowed his tender into the small beach at Dieppe, a tall gaunt, military man stood nearby to where he tied up his tender. Several times

Trebon looked up, but the man just stood and studied him as he secured his things and then threw his bag of soiled clothing over his shoulder and started to walk away towards home. There was something frightening about the man's eyes and their intensity. The man did not look away when Trebon turned around twice on the beach to glance over his shoulder at him again. There was no pretense that he wasn't watching and now following Trebon.

Finally, as Trebon now increased his pace, trying to get home all the sooner, the man caught up to him and spoke to him in perfect French, "You carried a tall blond man with a hawk nose to England three days ago." It was a statement, not a question.

Trebon at first denied that he had ever been out of French waters. He had only gone to sea a few miles and had anchored off Quiberville, around the point the past three nights. Besides, he was a free man, he did not have to discuss anything with the stranger.

"You will never reach home this evening," warned the military looking man. "You will rot in the Bastille the rest of your life if you protect the enemies of France."

Trebon reflected for a moment. He looked up and down the beach. It was almost night fall, the beach was seemingly deserted. He just wanted to go home to his wife. He had not known the blond man's business. He'd had a hint that the man was from someplace far off, but he did not need the French military searching his boat. They would find the

342

English watches he had smuggled back, and put him in jail. Besides, he had promised the man only a ride. Nothing else.

The stranger interrupted his thoughts, "My patience is short. I will either take you away and your family will never see you again," the man pulled out a pair of hand cuffs, "...or you will tell me everything that you know."

Trebon was shaking. He was simply a watch-maker, the father of six children, he said truthfully. He did not mean to do anything wrong. It was simply cheaper to buy the watches in England, and to sell them here in France, than to make them himself.

The stranger did not seem to care about the watches. "Where did you take the man?" he asked, holding the set of hand cuffs up in front of Trebon's face.

"To Hastings."

"Where did the man go from there?"

Trebon shrugged, but the man seized his left arm and thrust it behind his back painfully. "You are lying to me," said the stranger. Trebon said that he told the truth. The stranger yanked him about so that he was face to face with Trebon. The stranger's cap had fallen off. The stranger was almost completely bald, only a wisp of hair about the base of his head. The stranger slapped him powerfully across the cheek twice, his face twinged with pain. His ears rang from the impact of the blows. Trebon repeated that he had taken the man to Hastings.

343

"Where did he go from there? For the last time," demanded the stranger.

"A fishmonger, named Harrison, he owns a warehouse in the docklands section on the Thames. Sometimes he comes all the way to Hastings in search of fish to buy at a lower price. He took the man and his pigeons to London."

"Pigeons?" said Pitkan.

"Yes, they were squabs for the gentry." Trebon tried make a joke to get the man to sympathize with him, "That is why I thought the fisherman would be a good companion for the man, both their cargo's stunk, the birds and the fish."

The bald headed man snapped the iron cuffs on Trebon, yanked him back towards his tender and compelled him to go back to sea again. Trebon never returned to his family again. His boat arrived in Hastings with only Major Pitkan aboard.

13

Friends

"There be four ye must contact for me as soon as possible, if 'yer here to help me rebuild the ring," said O'Mally, sitting up at the edge of his bed, and grimacing as Lunt fastened for him the stiff leather harness which supported his back. "Of several dozen or so contacts I used over the past couple of winters, these have been by far the most effective. Each of 'em works in different buildings within the government. Mostly, they do night work, which I likes best." O'Mally put up four fingers for Lunt to see. "Two be sweepers, including the widow lady, McCarty, who tidies up an entire building all by herself. Another is a guard, and the fourth is a cooper's apprentice near the docklands close to where yer pigeons are stowed. All of these people have collected reliable information for me. It is through one of the night sweepers at the Foreign Office building at Whitehall that I first learned that there was a British spy operating from Passy. The sweeper came on duty one evening and chanced to observe some correspondence from Lord Stormont referring to a spy in Doctor Franklin's office.

"All that was last winter. I've been out of this for

a half year, Henry. How many good supply ships have we lost because Dr. Franklin and Mr. Adams have failed to act on the information I sent with you to Passy last May? All Franklin needed to do was what Captain Jones did and to find a way to test each of his staff's loyalty. Or else just pitch the entire staff out on their rumps and get a new one. I suppose the good Doctor would never do that?"

Lunt confirmed that by shaking his head, "No, Dr. Franklin said to me just a few nights ago that he must have more solid evidence before he would be willing to accuse one of his own staff. But I feel that I must find out exactly what your agent saw, exactly in the most minute detail, then perhaps we can get to the heart of this. Now with Arthur Lee removed as co-Ambassador, the British agents who operated through his office and directed Hezekiah Ford will no longer be a threat."

"Ha," said O'Mally. "I favor Captain Jones' approach, meself. Beat the living hell out of 'em and find out everything right away. Make 'em pay the price for their treachery." O'Mally grimaced again in pain as Lunt tightened the final lacing of his back harness.

Lunt proceeded to pace the room, talking out loud, "I reason that the real question remaining is exactly what did your associate see? Did Lord Stormont's note refer to the American delegation in general, or did it specifically refer to a spy operating from Passy? Mr. Lee has never had his offices at Passy because he and Dr. Franklin have never been

346

comfortable working together. It is possible if your man meant the American delegation in general, then we may have gotten rid of all the bad apples already. On the other hand, if he specifically meant Passy, then we may still have at least one more spy left at the office of Ambassador Franklin. I told you earlier that Admiral d'Orvilliers is convinced that we do.'

'Truthfully I do not know,' said O'Mally. 'I got this information delivered by pigeon and in code, which sometimes distorts the meaning of an item, unless you take care to be very precise. I have not personally spoken to the man in over two years. Like the others, he has no knowledge that I am connected with the American espionage,' said O'Mally, stroking his chin.

'And he is one of the four men that you would have me contact on your behalf?' asked Lunt.

'Tiss, and his name be Campbell, a Scotsman with Jacobite sympathies. You'll recognize 'im when you meet 'im. He's the only one of your four that doesn't take money, has a sixth little finger on the left hand,' reported Sean O'Mally at the same time grasping for his crutch so that he could get off the bed.

'You are welcome to question him if you like. I'll write an introduction for you in code. Mind you, none of these people have received any communication from me in six or seven months. You could take the widow Meehan's one horse cart and travel to each address, and then fetch back the pigeons at the end of your journey. You could also start by taking a cage of pigeons from here at the outset, and trade 'em for one of those of Dr. Franklin that you stored at the fish mongers. T'will make it easier for you when you depart for France. The cart will only carry one cage at a time. If you help me up, we'll go across the attic loft to where the dear widow keeps her pets. We'll pick some choice ones for you to take back to Dr. Franklin.'

As he struggled to get erect, O'Mally noticed that Lunt remained in deep thought, his hawk nose remained silhouetted against the window. After a long moment of silence, O'Mally queried, 'What else is on yer mind, lad?'

'There is one other contact I must establish for you,' said Lunt. 'One that you are not yet aware of. The French have succeeded in putting a spy in the Castle, that's the whore house maintained by Lord Sandwich. Have you heard of it?'

'Oh, I know it well. It's been in the newspapers. Surfaces every couple of months when some of the not so loyal opposition bring it up in Parliament. Sandwich has had children by the madame. I recall the name Martha Ray, she is a singer of some regard. Surely the Frogs haven't gotten to her?'

Across the room Lunt was walking away, his eyes staring at the floor.

'One of the maids?' asked O'Mally raising his eyebrow wickedly.

Lunt turned to face him. 'I suppose, better than that, it's one of the women,' reported Lunt again staring down as he traced the gap between the worn oaken floor boards with the toe of his boot.

O'Mally suddenly raised himself gleefully up off the bed, and, using his one leg and his crutch, began performing an impromptu jig across the floor nearly falling over several times. He shouted something unintelligible in Gaelic as he twirled. Finally, he ceased movement, supporting himself on his crutch, still chuckling.

'How'd the frogs pull that off? I tried to penetrate it last year, but couldn't. That place is guarded to the hilt. They check everyone who comes in or out, day or night. Sweet Jesus, 'tis a Spymaster's nirvana.'

O'Mally raised his clasped hands towards the low ceiling, almost touching it. He resumed hopping wildly about. 'Tis a dream. A dream I say. Sweet Jesus, can ye imagine what those fat Admirals divulge when they're in their all together. What dreams they must have while they counts their sheep.'

O'Mally continued grinning from ear to ear, portions of his still bright red hair seemed to turn carrot red in the bright morning sun driving through the window. He clutched Lunt's hand vigorously. 'Just this wee bit of information has made my life, what havoc I can reap. Ah, many a night I've wished I was a leprechaun and could sneak into that gutter hole of the pompous Tory ....'

Lunt interrupted, looking up at O'Mally with sad eyes, 'The woman is Marie Chatelain.'

O'Mally's eyes suddenly widened, and with the flat of his hand he hit his forehead 'Ha! the whore has struck again. HA, HA," O'Mally cheered.

Lunt suddenly didn't like his friend. His fists were clenched. His demeanor became agitated. "That's enough," screamed Lunt over the din being made by O'Mally. "Don't talk about her that way. She is on our side. One of us."

O'Mally stopped his dance and stood a few feet from Lunt. He studied his friend carefully, and then reached out grabbing Lunt and pulled him by the collar of his coat, ripping it. Lunt tried to resist, but found himself toppling forward, off balance, as they both landed on the floor. He could smell O'Mally's whiskey breath. As they hit the ground, O'Mally scrambled on top of Lunt and sat on his chest, pinning his hands to the floor. Lunt tried to sit up, avoiding looking at him. He felt the blue eyes drilling into him. Lunt considered throwing his body off him, violently, but he did not want to hurt the one legged man. There was continued silence until he finally looked up into O'Mally eyes. His own eyes were full of tears.

"Has she her hooks into ye, lad? Com'on tell yer friend, Sean."

Lunt gave a gesture of surrender and then pushed O'Mally's hands away and his body weight off him, until they both sat together on the floor of the flat, with a horizontal rectangle of direct sunlight beaming onto the floor between them.

"Have ye slept with her, Henry?"

Lunt shook his head. He looked away towards his feet. "But she loves me, I know it in my heart," said

Lunt. He stammered, continuing, "She has done a g...great deal for me in France."

O'Mally whispered back coaxingly, reaching across the beam of sunlight to tap his friend on the arm. "What has she done, tell me what's happened from the time ye left me in Ireland."

For nearly an hour Lunt spoke with little interruption. They both sat ramrod straight on the floor facing one another as Lunt told of his stealing a fishing boat at Wexford, of his first meeting with Franklin and of his carrying the message from O'Mally that there were spies in the American delegation, of the assassination attempt at Versailles.

O'Mally interrupted at that point, "This Major Pitkan troubles me greatly. I remember his totally bald head, with a wisp of hair at the back. The man is the only one who could identify all of us from the Ranger incident. Remember that he had already uncovered Marie at the dinner at Carnarvon House in Belfast. He would have torn us limb from limb if it weren't for the grenades we had brought to threaten the entire dinner party with. Now he is driven by the fact that his best friend, Captain Burden was killed, not to forget his Sergeant Major who you skewered that night in Belfast."

Henry nodded remembering the fierce sword fight which had nearly cost him his life.

O'Mally repeated himself thoughtfully, "This is the only man who can identify all of us, you, me, and even Marie. If ever you have the opportunity to kill him Henry, you must, without mercy and swiftly. Remember he has tried to kill you at Versailles. You are the primary target of his rage. He now believes you are the Spymaster, so he has the approval of his government in his quest.

'Continue on with the rest.' Hanging onto Lunt, O'Mally pulled himself up off the floor and hobbled back to his bed. Once there he remembered something and tried to reach over towards the floor. Unable to extend his arm far enough, he looked pleadingly at Henry and pointed down towards the jug of poteen. 'Me leg's throbbing, Henry.'

Lunt handed him the whiskey, and continued telling the story of his recovery, of Marie's vigil at Versailles, of his near return home until interrupted by the battle of Ushant, then of his time at the school of spies, and of his time at Marie's chateau.

There was a bit of ridicule in O'Mally's voice, sharpened by his second gulp of whiskey. 'So the smell of her tempted ye,...and the presence of her bed made ye yearn for her body, eh,' observed O'Mally. 'Ye were thinking of what it would be like to romp with her in that big tub, eh! What about Sarah, Henry? Do ye know why I sang the Rose of Tralee last night when I saw you came in? It was for ye, Henry, for the moments we had. For the one true, incorruptible friend I ever had in this cruel world who risked his very own life to get me back home to me mother, not knowing I was going to drop all this espionage affair right into his lap and almost get him killed.'

O'Mally leaned forward shaking his long index finger at Lunt across the room. 'Get out of this, lad, get out of it, it's not for you.'

O'Mally stopped long enough to take another deliberately long swig of whiskey, 'You think that she loves you? HA! She wants you only because you're the only man she's never been able to have. That's the attraction, nothing more, lad. I agree, she's the most beautiful woman that I and most men have ever seen. Throughout her life she has had every man she has ever wanted, save you, Henry. Think back, Henry, do you remember Carnarvon House before dinner was out we had learned she had been sleeping with not only poor Captain Burden, but also Lieutenant Dobbs, and that shipbuilder, what was his name?'

'Wright,' remembered Lunt.

'And then aboard the Ranger, there was Captain Jones. Remember the Frenchie talk coming out of his cabin the night before the battle with the Drake.' Henry nodded, looking down as O'Mally recounted the truth, 'And now she is at Sandwich's castle. Who knows how many of them Admirals she has already topped off?'

Suddenly O'Mally had a thought. He was like a kid, trying to express it. He bounced on the bed, if he could have stood up he would have bounced all over the room again, 'I know why she wanted you to go to the school of spies, Henry. She wanted to corrupt you, to bring you down to her level, Henry. Because you were the only man she could not have.

Remember her husband divorced her, if they call it that in France,' O'Mally snapped his fingers.

'Annulment,' corrected Henry begrudgingly shaking his head to O'Mally's line of thought.

O'Mally persisted regardless, 'To continue, lad, her husband got an annulment because she was not able to bear him children, or so she says. Anyway, from that point on, all Madame Chatelain has been doing is getting even with men. And she has used them to get her excitement. That's all. She believes that every one of us is corruptible. Don't let her win, Henry. Go establish my contacts for me, ask yer questions of the sweeper, and then get the damn pigeons back to Passy to where Dr. Franklin can use them to send me messages,' said O'Mally.

'I don't agree with you, Sean, but I'll do your errands today and tomorrow. But when I return, I intend to wait outside Sandwich's castle until I see her, even if it takes a month or longer. Eventually she'll come out and I'll establish contact. That's the assignment I was sent to accomplish,' stated Lunt firmly as he started to get dressed to leave, pulling his long boots on.

'I can just as well do that job, boy, and more convincingly than ye. And I'll not be crying if I see an arm around her, fondling her like dirty old men do. I can sit outside, a poor wounded British sailor who has lost his leg at Ushant, now blackening boots for the gentry to earn his meager way.' Affected by drink, O'Mally had one hand on his chest, the other extended into the air as if he was performing on stage.

Then he changed his posture, 'Imagine what I can get out of them Admirals meself, in just the time it'll take to blacken their boots. Why Madame Chatelain can come over to me real regular, to have me take the scuffs off, nobody'll think she is interested in a one legged man. You couldn't stand the cross examination with that Yankee accent of yours. Leave this to a professional. Think about it, boy.' O'Mally took another belt of whiskey.

'If you call me boy one more time, I'll forget you have one leg,' threatened Lunt. 'What do you need for me to do? I need to leave now!'

'Let's go pet the birds,' said O'Mally gesturing for a hand to get up. Together Lunt and he ambled across the meager dormer room, and then opened what Lunt had previously thought was a closet door. It led down a narrow corridor, and eventually to a second door that opened to a long narrow closet shaped room containing a line of six pigeon coops. Under them, grain and water were stored. The smell was unpleasant.

O'Mally pointed to an empty cage, which Lunt picked up and placed on an adjacent table. 'Put any of these,' he pointed to the first two coops, 'into yer cage. Mind your hands, they'll peck at you if you don't pick them up just right.'

He watched Lunt's hands chase the birds around the cage and occasionally take a peck, until he had grasped one bird in particular. 'Here, let me have him a moment. It'll be White Wing, dark grey all over, but with one white wing, like the wing was mistakenly dipped in whitewash. He's my favorite.'

O'Mally cuddled the bird against his chest, and placed his cheek against its feathers. The bird seemed to relax in his company, as O'Mally continued speaking. 'As I said before, there are four people you will need to tell that the network has resumed. You can deliver all four messages, and then go to docklands, leave this load of pigeons there and exchange them for the homing pigeons you brought from Dr. Franklin. Make sure you take a little grain with you, the birds will do just fine for four or five days with little care so long as they're left plenty of food and water in the cage.'

O'Mally smiled conciliatorily, ''Tiss not even eight o'clock yet, you might even make it back tomorrow night to hear me sing again at the Pirates Haven, if yer quick. There's a lot of lads there that was with me in the Whiteboys movement a few years back. They dream constantly of America and of going there someday. They would love to hear ye speak of the place.'

Lunt was still angry and showed it in his tone, 'Why haven't you reestablished contact yourself with these four people? You've been here several weeks.'

'I repeat, cause they don't know who I am, and once they see me they can identify me. A couple of them know me as O'Mally who used to sing around Pimlico, but they do not know I'm the Spymaster. None of them do.'

Lunt let his friend know that he wasn't having the wool pulled over his eyes. 'So instead they will see me, will be able to identify me in the future, so I can't remain here in London. And when I return tomorrow you'll say that I'm too dangerous to have around and that I have to go back to France.'

'But you're not supposed to remain here indefinitely. I'm certain that Vergennes and Franklin did not intend for you to do so. You were designated only because Franklin knew you could identify that it was truly me on the other side of the first pigeon message in a half year. Vergennes agreed to use you because you know Madame Chatelain, but I am here and I know Marie as well by sight as you, and I know as much about nautical signals as yourself. So you are no longer needed. You are going to go back to Passy and find Captain Jones, and become Lieutenant Lunt again, and go back to Sarah at the end of this stinking war. Me, I'll likely get caught, but it's goin' to be a sweet ride 'fore I do.' He winked and took another jolt of his poteen, the whites of his eyes were red now. 'Leave me, Henry, we'll see you tomorrow night.'

Lunt started to warn Sean about his drinking so early, but as the man hobbled back to his room on one leg, his back twisted pathetically over the short crutch, Lunt realized the enormous pain he must be in. He decided to say nothing.

Later in Sean's room, Lunt was thoughtfully examining two pistols from his bag. They were too large to conceal under the old leather vest he had elected to wear. He could not wear a gentleman's suit and deliver pigeons in a one horse cart. O'Mally spoke up then, "Leave them here, Henry." O'Mally reached behind his bed board and retrieved an oval felt bag from which he extracted a very small pistol which he tossed in the air to Lunt. "Here, take this, it'll fit in your vest pocket."

"At the Count de Batz-Castelmore's school, they said if you have to use a pistol, you are not a spy."

And to that challenge O'Mally sat up, "And the next time you see that Frenchman, tell him that in Ireland, the wise men say that ...Them that can't, they teach, and them that can, they do. The hell with Monsieur le mooseketeer, take the damn pistol, Henry, it may save your life. We'll see you tomorrow."

Lunt took the four envelopes and a crude map he had been given and departed down the rear stairs of the building to the carriage house. With him, he carried a noisy, smelly cage of pigeons who cooed incessantly in the still early morning while he secured them rigidly onto a small place at the rear of the cart. O'Mally had said that the Widow Meehan and he had an understanding about the use of her swift little one horse cart. He did not have to wake the old lady to ask her permission. For the rest of the day, Lunt rode methodically across London from a dilapidated boarding house in Pimlico, to the back of a posh hotel in Mayfair, finally to an address in the old city, which belonged to the Scotsman, Campbell.

Tom McNamara

Henry knocked on the modest door off a mews. It was a tiny walkway, but the horse cart was so narrow, it maneuvered in there so that Henry was able to hold the reins of the horse, while he rapped on the man's door.

'Blast yer damn hand, I'll bit 'tit off at the wrist, if yer don't belay that rac..ket,' the burr of nearly unintelligible Scotch-English exploded out at him, as the occupant snapped open his door.

Henry simply gave the man an envelope. 'I'll wait here till you have a look,' said Lunt. 'But I need to speak to you. After you've read this. It's extremely important.'

Henry's strange nasal accent and serious demeanor startled the man. The man took the envelope gruffly and closed the door firmly in Lunt's face. Lunt stood in the narrow causeway for nearly twenty minutes, wondering if Mr. Campbell was ever going to open his door again. A few people wandered through the causeway, squeezing sideways between Henry and his horse and cart. The most embarrassing moment came when Campbell opened his door just as Lunt's horse was relieving himself.

Campbell wore spectacles now. 'Come in, but leave that foul nag away from my door.'

Henry was fearful that somebody would filch his valuable cargo, but he had no choice. He tethered his horse to a pole on the main street and entered Mr. Campbell's home. It was a modest place, over the hearth was a Scottish tartan and a coat of arms that Lunt did not recognize, but presumed was a Jacobean standard.

'You're a Yank, yerself?'

Henry nodded.

'I pray you'll do it, boys, for all of us. The poms need to be taught a lesson, they've been need'n one taught 'em for three hundred years.'

Henry put up his hand. 'Mr. Campbell, I've something very important to ask you.'

'Tit must be, fer you to risk a com'n here,' agreed Campbell.

'Last winter you reported that there was a British spy operating among the American delegation. Will you tell me the entire circumstances of how you came to that conclusion. Tell me everything you observed, please, but add nothing of your own. It is extremely important that I have as accurate a description as you can remember.'

Campbell paused deliberately and then started relating his story very precisely, 'I swept the second story of the Foreign office every evening with another man. There's a guard that's supposed to watch several of us all the time. Sometimes he does not. When that happens I sometimes sneak a peak at the papers on important people's desks. One of the offices I clean is that of Mr. William Eden, he is one of the Under Secretaries of the Foreign Office. On his desk one night, under his ink blotter was a diplomatic envelope. Seeing it, I first went to the door of Mr. Eden's office and looked out to see if the guard or the other sweeper were coming. They were not. I closed the door so that no one would see me.'

'Usually Mr. Eden is very careful. All his papers are locked away. I think that particular time the courier pack must have arrived late in the day, after Mr. Eden had departed. Whomever brought it in did not know what to do, so they just left it under his blotter. The rooms are supposed to be guarded so the messenger must have thought it would be all right.'

'Who was the diplomatic package from, wasn't it sealed?' asked Lunt.

Campbell held up his hand. 'That's when I decided to take the gamble that nearly cost me my job, pur..haps my life. It's the reason I don't clean the second floor offices any longer. There was a wax seal, but it had been nearly broken through from handling. It happens all the time. When I saw it was from Lord Stormont, the Ambassador to France, I decided it was important enough to risk opening. I thought I could look at it and then jam it under the blotter to make it look like the jamming had caused the seal to break.'

Lunt moved to the edge of his seat, impatient for Mr. Campbell to get to the heart of his story.

'But inside I found such a disappointment so as to have made the risk not worth the effort.'

'Yes?' said Lunt.

'The letters, everything was in French...and I don't speak French. I knew I had something very valuable, but I couldn't read it. Not a word. Remember I was in a great hurry. If I had been caught, it could have cost me my life.'

'I understand. Then how did you know about the spy in the American delegation?'

'There was one small note in English, it was attached to an old tobacco wrapper on which a series of letters and numbers had been hand written. The note said: *William - Here is the latest from our Doctor at Passy.* The note was signed 'S,' I presume for Stormont.'

'You're sure of the wording?'

Campbell repeated it, *William - Here is the latest from our Doctor at Passy.* The note was signed, 'S.' I went over it in my mind for days. You see, when I arrived at work the following evening we was all lined up, the night guards and the cleaners, and we was questioned for hours, one by one, by Mr. Eden, his'self. I told him that I did not even clean his office that night because it had looked clean. It was the truth, I had decided in advance to use that as my alibi, that I had not entered Mr. Eden's office at all. I had even left some trash in his basket instead of cleaning it out. Things were pretty tense for awhile, because after that I was watched. When I got home from work the following morning my entire apartment here had been searched. The following night I was questioned about that there Scottish tartan.' He pointed at the red cloth. 'I said truthfully that it was my family's and that it had no political significance. The next night I was reassigned to the first floor offices along with my cosweeper. It's there I have remained ever since, the bastards.'

Campbell continued, 'If'n you'd come here four months ago, I'd been afraid to talk to you. I can't risk any more involvement, but I hope you'll beat the crap out of 'em. A lot of us are praying for ye, including me poor father, hanged, he was, in '44, without a trial.'

'I'm truly sorry, Mr. Campbell,' said Lunt. 'I do appreciate your help. Tell me one thing though, when you sent your coded message to the Spymaster, why did you not mention the Doctor?'

'Because everyone knows that Doctor Franklin is at Passy. From the wording of the note - *Here is the latest from our Doctor at Passy* - I presumed that the message was about the activities of the famous Doctor Franklin. Could there be some other meaning?' inquired Campbell.

Lunt was non-committal and thought for several minutes in silence before he continued. 'Describe to me the tobacco paper on which the coded message was written, was there any writing, a shop name or anything.'

'Yer must understand I was very afr..raid, very rr..ushed, but I rr..remember that the paper was plain on the written side and had a red waxy sur..rface on the other. T'was the kind they stitch 'n fold over into thr..rees and then sew it up the side to make a tr..baccur pouch. The last third can be folded over the pouch to stop the tobacco from falling out. Ya sees 'em ever..rywhere.'

"And you don't remember any distinctive markings on the paper, other than it was red?"

"No, sir."

Lunt thanked Mr. Campbell and asked him to reconsider continuing to do work for the Americans. It was now late in the day, and Lunt found a room with a stable near the Thames docks. That night he tried to recall how many of the Passy staff smoked pipes. It was considerable. Before sleeping, he tore off and burned in a candle flame all but one corner portion of the London map O'Mally had hand drawn for him.

At first light, Lunt was astonished to see so many people hurrying this way and that. On every street corner, in any direction there were hundreds of busy people within his gaze. For breakfast Lunt purchased a pie which a street vendor brought to him, still steaming. A meat pie. He had heard that the English put meat in their pies. In Boston he had heard of it, but never tasted it, but in Newburyport he realized that the idea of putting anything but fruits or a few select vegetables like pumpkin or squash into a pie was all that the stern Yankee mentality could tolerate. He liked the warm pie better than any other food he had ever tasted, even the rich fare from the tables of Versailles.

As he ate, traveling along in his cart, Lunt wondered how much the average citizen on any London street really thought about the war and what it was doing to America. He didn't suppose they thought much about it at all. He had purchased a penny broadside, called the London Chronicle, from a street newsie of about eight. Stopped in the traffic, Lunt perused the paper and read to his dismay that the British Admiralty were court martialling the British Admiral Viscount Keppel because he had failed to defeat the French fleet at Ushant.

Lunt recalled the terrible exchange between the Bretagne and H.M.S. Victory and wondered how any man who had commanded such a valiant exchange on behalf of his own country could be caused to suffer the humiliation of a court martial proceeding. According to the broadside it was the Tory Van Admiral Hugh Pallisher who was acting as Admiral Keppel's primary accuser. Elsewhere in the paper there were accusations that the charge was being brought forth only because Viscount Keppel was a Whig. Lunt recalled that it was the British rear van, under Pallisher, which had been so far out of the British line that they had never engaged the French at all during the entire battle, and at one point had even sailed their ships away from the battle. Lunt was angry for the brave British Admiral Viscount Keppel and had a momentary impulse to turn his carriage towards Whitehall and set the record straight. Then he saw that on the fifth page of the broadside near the top, a letter was reproduced from the French Admiral d'Orvilliers. Lunt read it as if possessed, losing all consciousness of the city traffic surrounding him. The piece was entitled:

EXTRAORDINARY LETTER TO ADMIRAL
KEPPEL when he heard of the charges brought
against Admiral Keppel.

"I learnt with astonishment what has happened
to you. Our fates have been singular, and greatly
resembling each other. I have been dismissed
from the command of the French fleet, because
I did not take the English one; and you are to take
your trial for not taking two-thirds of the French
fleet. Like you, I had an Admiral under my
command, who did not comprehend my signals:
but for reasons which you may easily imagine,
I said nothing: he, however, has quitted the sea -
Your Admiral did not answer your signals; you
are silent, for reasons which I could never
comprehend: but he, instead of praising you,
attacks and accuses you of negligence and bad
conduct. This is my opinion, an ill timed pleasant-
ry; but I am persuaded, you will extricate yourself
with honour. I have the honour, with respect, etc.

D'Orvilliers

As Lunt drove on through the streets along the
Thames his thoughts were philosophical. This was
clearly a war driven by politicians. The average person
in London was simply going about their daily business,
there was nothing to distract him, to cause him to have

to rebuild his house because the British army had burned it or his sweetheart's home or had sunk his ship from which he had earned his livelihood from the sea. The people here were not even aware of the suffering in America, they might be paying an additional tax levy, but otherwise the incidents in America were as remote as the moon to the average citizen of London. Dr. Franklin was right, the way to fight this American war was not to make war directly on the British people, it was not their fault. It was the politicians, the damn King, Lord North and those people, and, out of necessity the Army and Navy which served the politicians' wishes.

If they should someday have to do battle with the British people, Lunt could see that this would be an enemy to be reckoned with. But for now, at least half of them were cheering for the Americans. It was best left that way. All of America could not even suppose to have as many people as Lunt saw in his travels that day in London. America could not possibly beat them all. Franklin was right, never get the British people angry, and America could win her freedom. Ultimately that would help the English people as well. Help them to shake off their own tyranny.

The fourth delivery, to a cooper named Somerset, was far to the east of the old city at a dock on the Thames. When Lunt found the man, he refused to take the envelope until his apprentice finished securing the last band over a small keg he had fashioned. Without giving Lunt a chance to leave, he hastily opened the envelope and seeing the complex alphabet code within, he looked up at Lunt, asking suspiciously, 'Is this from you?'

Lunt shook his head from side to side, and replied in his best attempt at a cockney accent which his nasal twanged Yankee upbringing could muster, 'They just pays me to deliver 'em,....don't know what's in 'em. Can't read.' The man obviously believed him and momentarily turned his attention to folding the envelope carefully into his apron pocket for examination later.

Lunt used the moment to turn on his heel and vanish before the man had an opportunity to ask him anything else.

Lunt liked the swift little one horse cart. Many times, because of its narrowness, Lunt was able to maneuver past larger carriages, stalled in a morass of city traffic. Lunt wove his way inland from the docks and took a road eastward which paralleled the Thames. He rode through vast neighborhoods of merchants and seamen who made their fortune from the sea. Guided by the remains of O'Mally's map, Lunt began to recognize buildings near the fish monger's shed. Finally, he arrived at the warehouse which unexpectedly reeked of the days catch, now turning sour in the mid day heat.

Lunt looked at the sky, there was at least five

hours of daylight left. With luck he just might make the evening festivities at the Pirates Haven, but before that he must decide if he would let O'Mally take over the initial contact with Marie. Perhaps his friend was right, his intense desire to establish contact was largely personal.

He walked into the storefront at the entrance to the shed. Good sized fish were still laid out on the counter, a mountain of flies buzzed noisily, too gorged to fly away unless they were truly threatened. Lunt was surprised that Mr. Harrison had left so many fish out on the counter to spoil, perhaps he was doing something in the back.

"Mr. Harrison," shouted Lunt, he waited a few moments but nobody came out from the back.

Lunt started to shout again "Mr. Ha......", when the man's wife thrust her face out from beneath the curtains. Naked fear showed in her eyes, nonetheless she waved him to go away. Lunt turned to look behind him, no one was there.

He walked forward a few steps until she shouted, "Run, he'll kill you too!"

Lunt turned on his heel, and started to run outside to his cart, when into view quickly stepped a squad of Grenadiers, the tall miter hats making each man seem a giant. Their muskets were at the ready, bayonets gleamed threateningly in the late afternoon sun. Lunt stopped and stared. Perhaps they thought he was just a smuggler. Resistance was obviously futile unless he could find a way past the Grenadiers.

He stood frozen, staring at the row of men only a few paces from him. On command their volley of fire could not miss. They would cut him down hopelessly. His mind reeled, trying to come up with a plausible explanation. He would admit to smuggling, try and bribe their officer into letting him go. Suddenly his plans for escape evaporated, and a tingle of raw fear rushed up his neck involuntarily as the sound of a familiar voice came from behind him.

"Well, what a catch this trip to the fish monger brings, Henry Lunt in England."

Lunt turned to see Major Pitkan, his bald visage supported by a high, black French collar. Beneath his dark cape was the prominent hilt of a sword, his right hand grasping it. His left hand now clutched the unfortunate Mrs. Harrison by the arm. She was crying. Two more grenadiers stood to either side of Pitkan. One was a sergeant, his horse pistol was cocked and pointed directly at Lunt's chest. Lunt had an impulse to reach for the tiny pistol in his vest pocket and hope he could get off a shot.

Just as he was about to make the attempt, his arms were seized from behind.

Major Pitkan walked forward until he was just inches from Lunt's face. "Well, well, the Spymaster."

"I am not the Spymaster. I am Lieutenant Henry Lunt of the American Colonial Navy."

"You are a spy. Remember this is not the first instance I have encountered you out of uniform. You are a spy, Henry Lunt. But your treacherous career

370

is at an end."

Pitkan looked to the sergeant on his left. "See to his cart, search it thoroughly. Strip him naked, search every inch of his clothing."

Humiliated, Lunt stood bare before his enemy and Mrs. Harrison, who despite her pathos, had the presence of mind to spare Lunt embarrassment and looked downward muttering about her husband, whom the Major had apparently killed. Two soldiers continued to hold Lunt's arms behind his back as he struggled from time to time to get away. Pitkan looked at Lunt's chest and drew out his sword. He placed the point directly over Lunt's heart, the flesh of his breast yielded. Pitkan traced the pink scars of his recent wound.

"I see that I did not miss at Versailles. It is unfortunate that I did not thrust just a little deeper." Pitkan pushed with the sharp tip until it pierced the scar of the old wound. Mrs. Harrison screamed. Lunt tried to fall back, but was held in place by the grenadiers.

"Now, tell me who is with you." Lunt felt a strong trickle of blood pour down his chest. Adrenalin pumped in his veins and he feigned a collapse, and then jerked to his right evading Pitkan's sword point and one of the grenadier's grasp for an instant. But the Major kicked him backwards so that he landed, his naked back on the dirt floor. Grenadiers seized each of his limbs, holding him down.

Pitkan came to his side looking down on him,

sneering. "I want to know who is with you. Is Captain Jones here in England?" he raged, "I demand you tell me. Speak up or I swear I'll make you an eunuch, right now." Pitkan whacked Lunt's privates with the side of his saber, cutting his scrotum. Lunt howled in pain, buckling up to the extent that his captors allowed. Pitkan walked around to Lunt's other side, his sword blade poised for another painful strike.

"Sir," the grenadier sergeant mercifully interrupted, "...there was a small pistol and a few shillings in his vest pocket, and a torn piece of paper with writing on it. In the wagon, under the canvas there were more pigeons."

"What does the writing say?" asked Pitkan.

There was hesitation on the part of the sergeant, "I'm sorry, sir, I can't read."

Pitkan diverted his attention from Lunt to examine the remaining portion of the map which was ripped off at the top and now held only the address of the fish monger and the tracings of a few nearby streets on it.

"Stand him up."

Lunt was jerked to his feet.

"Are you going to say anything?" screamed Pitkan. "What else was on this sheet of paper?" Pitkan held it threateningly in front of Lunt's face.

Lunt tried to put himself in the pain trance he had learned from the Count de Batz-Castelmore. He concentrated on everything else in his life except the immediate. Pitkan kicked him in the shin. Lunt willed himself not to feel it.

Pitkan walked around his prisoner thinking out loud. "Pigeons, you seem to like pigeons a great deal, Lieutenant Lunt. First the fishmonger tells me you are merely smuggling squab from France for the English gentry, then you show up here with more pigeons. What is afoot with pigeons?"

Lunt stood implacable. Saying nothing, concentrating on other, inconsequential events in his life.

Pitkan gripped his hair violently and jerked his head upwards so that Lunt's eyes were forced to look into his own. "I'm going to take you to someplace very dark, very slimy, and before morning you are going to tell me everything you know. You will beg me to die."

Lunt spit in his face and Pitkan punched him in the jaw with the hilt of his sword, knocking him unconscious for a few moments.

"Put his clothes back on. Take Mrs. Harrison too." She screamed in terror. "Sergeant leave about half of your men here in case anyone else shows up, if so, arrest them, and bring them to Traitors Gate."

"Yes, sir."

Lunt was placed in a military carriage. His hands were bound tightly behind his back. Mrs. Harrison was thrust up on horseback with one of the grenadiers.

"What do we do with his cart, sir?"

"Take it along." Pitkan entered the carriage and sat opposite Lunt. For the first few moments neither man said anything, until Pitkan, looking Lunt straight in the eye, started a conversation between the enemies. "You look so helpless all trussed up like a pig ready for the spit."

Lunt's mind raced trying to think of any way to get a meaningful strike at Pitkan. He could kick out with his boot but the odds were slim that he would get any satisfaction, and only another beating from Pitkan in the carriage. He glared silently forward.

Pitkan reached into his pocket and extracted the small pistol which Lunt had borrowed from O'Mally. For several minutes he examined it. Lunt looked out of the window. They were moving along the Thames docks back towards the center of London. Lunt's legs were unbound, if he could just evade Pitkan and get out of the carriage, he might have a chance of escape. Once he was secured in whatever dungeon Pitkan had in mind for him there would be no chance of escape. A bullet in the back of the head while he attempted escape might be more merciful. As the carriage turned he could see the shadows of the mounted grenadiers escorting the carriage. They were moving at a fairly rapid pace considering the congested streets of London. The horses' hooves pounded on cobblestones in a threatening rhythm.

Holding up the pistol Pitkan spoke again, "It's a coward's weapon, Lunt. I'm surprised at you. You should have stayed in uniform at sea, where you could have met an honorable death."

Lunt turned to face him, "It's no more cowardly

than attacking a man in the dark with four others. It's no more cowardly than hauling an innocent woman in for torture. The worst crime the Harrisons committed was acting as a storage place for squab. You didn't have to kill him. Let her go.'

'Well, well, how noble of you. At least you are talking. I'll let her go if you answer one question.'

'Ask it.'

Pitkan leaned forward. Lunt could see the veins in the side of his bald head swell. The man's breath was foul. Lunt noticed for the first time that Pitkan had a blood vessel broken in his left eye, leaving a portion of the white of his eye blood red at the corner.

'Are you the Spymaster?'

Lunt sat back thoughtfully. Should he admit it and take all attention off O'Mally and his efforts? Perhaps they would feel he was too important to murder if they believed he was the Spymaster. But the admission would certainly bring him endless hours of torture. He needed time to consider his response.

'That answer is worth your answer to another question,' said Lunt.

'You're not in much of a position to bargain, but there is no harm in the asking.'

Lunt was silent, wondering what he could ask that would unnerve Pitkan, make him reconsider his threat to kill him that evening. 'Name the spy in Dr. Franklin's delegation and I will answer your question.'

'Well, well, there is still a fox inside. Do you suppose that I would risk answering that question and have you pass it over ..."

Pitkan stopped in midsentence, suddenly there was a gleam of recognition on his face.

"They're carrier pigeons." He pointed his finger directly at Lunt. "That's it. That's why you took a cage of them away three days ago and are bringing one back today. But these are not the same ones you left the fish mongers with initially. You were exchanging them. The new ones must be...from..." Pitkan got up suddenly and leaned his head outside the carriage window, looking first at the mid afternoon sun and then he screamed at the driver, "Halt the carriage. Halt!"

Pitkan threw open the door, but before he disembarked, he glanced at Lunt, threateningly, "I've got you now, there'll be an even bigger gathering at the tower tonight."

Pitkan, ramrod straight, marched swiftly back behind his startled grenadiers, toward the small cart. He reached into the back and threw back the canvas exposing the cowering birds who made frantic cooing noises. He undid the latch and seized one of the birds so fiercely that it pecked at his hand. In retaliation, he squeezed the bird roughly, then threw it into the air and watched. The pigeon flew awkwardly, bobbing up and down and, only twenty feet from where it was launched, it landed momentarily. Pitkan stood, hands on hips, observing it.

For a few moments, the bird sought to recover from its rough handling by flapping its wings and straightening out its feathers with its beak. Then it rose up into the air, this time reaching an altitude of four or five stories in a slow circle. The bird then flew out over the Thames, circled even higher, then started to head in a definite westerly direction. Pitkan watched, his hand shading his eyes from the glare of the afternoon sun, until he could no sooner see the bird as it flew very close by the steeples at St. Paul's Cathedral and then disappeared out of sight.

Pitkan went to the cage again and selected a very distinctive bird with one white left wing in contrast to its grey body of feathers. This time he gripped the bird firmly, but gently, as he extracted it with both hands. After his extraction of White Wing, he had carelessly left the latch open and untended for just a moment. As Pitkan was busy releasing White Wing, an additional pigeon made its escape through the open portal. Seeing it fly off, Pitkan quickly placed his hand over the opening while still concentrating on watching White Wing. The escaped bird was now just behind the distinctive one. They flew in a formation one behind the other in the jerky erratic flight of pigeons. But their path was also directly towards St. Paul's. Pitkan looked down at the cage and counted the remaining pigeons. Seventeen birds left, enough that he could possibly go to a high place and observe the homing pigeons returning to their roost. Where would he go? Of course, St. Paul's Cathedral, the highest building in London, and in the very direction in which the birds were flying.

Pitkan barked orders, "You," pointing at a corporal on horseback. "Do you know where the building is that houses the Foreign Office at Whitehall?" The man nodded. "Go immediately to the second floor, the office of a man named William Eden, tell him I want a company of Royal Marines to St. Paul's immediately."

"Sir, I'm only a corporal. They won't let me in the door," said the Corporal, unsure that he could get access into an important building like that, let alone that anyone should listen to him.

Major Pitkan motioned for the Corporal to lower his head, and whispered in his ear, "Tell them Flagstone, have you got that? What's your name, Corporal?"

"Corporal Johnston, sir."

"Well, Corporal Johnston, you get me a company of Royal Marines to the foot of St. Paul's before sundown, and I'll make you a sergeant."

"Yes, sir," the man saluted, slapped his reins vigorously onto his horse's side, and was off with a gallop. Pitkan stared after him for only an instant, guessing that he had only three hours left until sunset. If he delayed the search until morning, he might miss capturing a den of spies. With three pigeons flying in now, they would certainly be alerted that something was awry. If he waited overnight, all might be lost. He had to continue the pursuit now.

Pitkan turned to his Sergeant, "Do you know the watchmaker at the top of High Street?"

"No, sir."

"Well, there is one there at the top of High Street!" He snarled. "Procure me the most powerful spyglass they have, and bring it to the west towers of St. Paul's immediately."

The man hesitated.

"What is it?"

"Well, beg your pardon, sir."

"Yes?" scoffed Pitkan.

"I don't have very much money, only a few farthings, sir."

Major Pitkan cursed under his breath, "An empire could be lost or won because he doesn't have a few quid, and doesn't have the initiative to commandeer a spyglass."

Pitkan reached into his cape, and extracted a cloth purse. Opening it, he dumped its contents into the Sergeant's outstretched hands. Two of the coins fell to the ground and the Sergeant wasted a precious few minutes descending from his horse to recover them.

Pitkan shook his head, walking hastily back to his carriage. He had split his original squad of twelve grenadiers and left half of them at the fish monger's to see if anyone else would show up. That was too many, and now he regretted it. If only he had known he had carrier pigeons before he departed. It was a half hour to go back now to get them. He couldn't spare one of his remaining four men. If Corporal Johnston made it back with a squad or two of Royal Marines or Grenadiers before dark, all would be fine. Meanwhile, he would continue to take the single cart with them to St. Paul's. It was fast. It could be useful to follow the pigeons' flight.

Seated inside the carriage was a sullen Lunt. Studying him a few moments, Pitkan began to speak, "You are, of course, aware that all the pigeons went the same direction. Now we are going to the steeples of St. Paul's to see where they fly to."

Lunt tried to show no reaction. For a few minutes there was silence between the enemies. Then Lunt spoke, "If you want to save time, I'll answer your question and tell you where the pigeons are flying to."

"How obliging of you. Any diversion to get me off course, so that we don't make your roost before nightfall. Give your friends a night to wonder why three pigeons have suddenly returned and to perhaps get away. Not in your life!"

*   *   *   *   *

The pigeon with the white left wing sensed he was near his home. He flew along over the great buildings, sometimes casting his eye below to sight familiar resting places. His instincts told him that he was flying ever nearer the food, warmth, water, and companionship of the coop. Inspired by this, he pumped his wings more vigorously until he saw the shed on the roof. One of the other birds was there ahead of him, standing outside on the window ledge

380

angrily walking back and forth, pecking at the one way door. It was closed. White Wing landed beside him and pecked intermittently for a short minute, then tried another entrance into another coop. But all the portals were shut. Where was the redheaded man who took care of them?

White Wing knew the man lived on the other side of the roof. The man had taken him over there, petting him many times in the past weeks. White Wing left the other two birds and walked along the very edge of the roof until he came to the sloping dormer window which faced out on the road on which the humans walked. There was warm afternoon sun there. The pigeon looked in and pecked at the glass. The man was lying across the bed, not moving, not seeing White Wing. The bird pecked again at the transparent barrier through which he could see inside but not enter. White Wing continued pecking, but the red headed man still did not stir. Frustrated, he returned to pace with the other birds at the portal of the coop. From inside, the three birds could hear their fellows of the brood calling out to them. The three pigeons wanted to get inside before dark, to eat and to snuggle with the others. If only the red headed human would wake up and hear them.

*   *   *   *   *

Corporal Johnston arrived with an aggressive gallop. Spying a gentleman walking along the sidewalk before Whitehall, he shouted out, "Sir, beg your pardon, is this the Foreign Office?"

The man was a trifle affronted at being singled out from the crowd, but nevertheless nodded in the affirmative. Johnston instantly dismounted, but there was no place to hitch his horse. Along the road there were mostly carriages in the street, no obvious place to hitch a horse in front of the building. He couldn't just leave the horse there. He spotted the post of an oil lamp halfway across the lawn between the flower beds. There was no place else near the building. He reluctantly led the horse up onto the sidewalk, tipping his hat to several shocked passersby and then proceeded to lead the animal up onto the lawn. Until he heard the scream of a bull of a voice, "Halt."

Corporal Johnston tried to explain to the screaming Sergeant Major that he was carrying out the orders of his Major and that the matter was urgent. But the Sergeant Major was unrelenting. He insisted that Johnston take the beast off his guard station and put it in the stables ten blocks down, like every other soldier. Otherwise the Sergeant Major would haul him away to the gaol that very moment. At one point, Johnston even tried bribery, as he offered another passing soldier money to lead his horse away, but the Sergeant Major insisted that he must secure the animal, personally.

In frustration Johnston played his last card.

Tom McNamara

'Flagstone!' he whispered, looking around to be sure that only the Sergeant Major heard the word.

'Are you daft, man? Flagstone, hell. I'll have you thrown in gaol if you don't get that horse off the parade at Whitehall this very instant. Horses are not to be hitched here, period. That is the rule.' The tall Sergeant Major pointed firmly down the walkway towards the end of the long row of white buildings that extended for many blocks.

As the Corporal rode off, for several moments the Sergeant Major shook his head for the benefit of the small collection of pedestrians who had observed the disturbance. 'Younger generation, don't know the proper thing to do. Can't have them galloping all over Whitehall, can we? Leaving horse dung all over the walkways.'

*   *   *   *   *

O'Mally finally heard the incessant pecking. He tried to jerk his left leg and felt the surge of pain through the still alive nerves that tried to bring his missing leg into action. He grimaced. His head throbbed from too much drinking that had been the inevitable aftermath of his argument with Lunt. The damn rapping, what was it? He looked towards the window. It was a pigeon. He sat up, his hideously misshapen back ached in its leather harness. Nonetheless, he saw that it was the white winged one he had selected just yesterday morning for Lunt. Back so soon?

O'Mally reached for his crutch and seizing it, he hobbled, his back arched over the short staff. He passed through the two doors which led through to the pigeon coop walkway. Leaning through the first coop, he slid open the portal latch to bring in a shaft of light. Momentarily thereafter, one bird, then another, as he waited patiently several minutes later, White Wing, himself, entered. O'Mally soothed the birds and gave them fresh water, and grain. He picked up White Wing, who protested until O'Mally held it close to his cheek, soothing it. There was no message on its leg, nor on any of them. These were the very birds that had been put into the cage taken by Lunt yesterday morning. Birds that had somehow been unexpectedly released. Had Lunt had an accident and turned his carriage over or was it a fast signal from him that something was wrong? Whatever it meant, O'Mally couldn't ignore the potential threat.

O'Mally hobbled down the flight of stairs to the quarters of the Widow Meehan. He knocked and then turned the knob to enter. She was asleep in her bed. He woke her.

'Emma, dear, remember that I once told you that there might come a time to leave here on the quick?'

She nodded, frightened, pulling her bed sheet up to her mouth.

O'Mally continued, 'It might be a false alarm. It

384

might not. Some of the pigeons have come back too soon. And I must be cautious for your sake. Don't worry about yer things, take what you can carry. I have plenty of money to start over. You must get now some of the Whiteboys, understand, from the Pirates Haven.˙

She nodded.

˙Michael Fagan, and Cormack, and others if you can find 'em.˙

She nodded and hugged him, terrified, almost toppling the twisted, one legged man to the floor.

˙Ah, we've had a sweet ride, haven't we, dear? I told you not long ago that nothing is forever. Tell Fagan and Cormack to look to the roof. I'll be there and if they see in me eyes that it's all right, then to come in and to bring the carriage from the Pirates Haven. Tell them to take warm clothes, we may be riding tonight.˙

After another hug, the Spymaster pulled himself away. He had work to do. To put a collection of his almanacs all into a special satchel along with the vial of oil to burn its contents if he were going to be caught. He would also want to take the cage of pigeons that Lunt had just brought in from Franklin. He pulled himself painfully back up the stairs using the rail which Cormack had hammered into the wall a few weeks back. He reached his roof top home and dragged himself over his crutch a foot at a time until he returned to his bed.

Then O'Mally dropped on his knee with a grimace and searched under the bed for the rope beneath.

He laboriously braced his one foot against the bed post and heaved with great effort four or five times until he had succeeded in hauling out the heavy flat chest from beneath his bed. His trembling hand worked open the lid. Inside there were five muskets, and an assortment of nearly twenty small arms including pistols and swords, along with enough ball and powder to make them fire all day. His favorite, though, was the ship's swivel gun. He checked it first. With it he could clear the stairwell at least once before they got him.

After a half hour, he heaved himself out onto the dormer sill on the opposite end of the roof from the pigeon coop and took a swig of poteen. He rested up there, three stories above the street, unobserved by passersby, as he surveyed the sky and the activity in the streets below him. A few miles in the distance he could see the handsome silhouette of the twin west towers of St. Paul's.

*   *   *   *   *

After making his apologies to the vicar on duty, Pitkan pushed Lunt ahead of him up the spiral staircase leading to the very top of the southwest tower. Pitkan cursed again at his stupidity in attempting to locate the pigeon roost with too few soldiers under his direct command. Having come from France, he carried no identification with him and when he had tried to forcibly recruit two uniformed soldiers he saw in the street, they had walked off hurriedly, ignoring him. There was so little time now. But if the home of the pigeons was nearby, and if the Sergeant returned in time with the spyglass, there was a chance. Otherwise the effort was doomed.

Pitkan roughly prodded Lunt up the winding stone stairs, forearms and hands securely trussed up behind his back. Two of the Grenadiers followed them, muskets and fixed bayonets at the ready. He had left the two other men below watching the carriages and Mrs. Harrison. Pitkan tried to decide if he should go with the soldiers if they did locate the pigeon roost. He might risk losing Lunt, the only prize he had so far. No, he must rely on the Sergeant and the Corporal to accomplish their tasks. If the Corporal did deliver his thirty men, everything would be all right. But he also couldn't afford to wait until morning, it would be just too likely that the American spies would flee. The sooner he tried the birds the better. He did not have to use all of them now, if it became obvious that the birds still had a long way to fly.

About mid way up the spiral staircase, Lunt became purposefully slow, and Pitkan kicked him in the small of the back and the two grenadiers then dragged Lunt up the remainder of the stairs.

Both of the twin west towers of St. Paul's in that year contained hugh bells which pealed in unison every hour and could be heard throughout the city. People below opened and closed shops by their sound and otherwise organized their day. They were supposed to toll again in twenty minutes, and the vicar had warned Pitkan that it could drive them all deaf to be in the same room while one of the bells tolled.

The four men reached the top of the stone stairs out of breath. A choirboy behind them panted, trying to carry the cage of pigeons. Pitkan looked out each of the stone framed windows until he located the westerly direction. Below, he could see the Thames to the south, and Whitehall to the southwest. From down the stairwell, Pitkan heard the Sergeant calling up that he had the spyglass and was coming. One of the grenadiers repeated the message.

The Bell Tower was thirty feet square, with an enormously high ceiling from which hung the bell, some dozen feet in diameter. Around the cavity for the bell was a stone walkway some five feet across. In each of the four primary compass directions the portals of the bell spire opened into an arched window designed by Christopher Wren a half century before. A few minutes later, the Sergeant reached them, out of breath from the rigorous climb upstairs. He placed the spyglass in the Major's hand.

"Cost a few quid, sir. But it's the very best they had."

Major Pitkan looked at it, and then pointed at Lunt. "Keep him on the ground, he might try and jump. If he even attempts to get up, see to it that your men run a bayonet through his leg so he never walks again."

'Yes, sir.'

'How is your eyesight, Sergeant?'

'Bit misty, sir, but Parker here has the eyes of a hawk.'

'Parker, take the spyglass, level it to the west and follow the line of birds, I'll release one every two minutes or so. Mind you follow the birds' flight until you've got sight of a particular building. Understand? Once you see the pigeons land don't lose sight of the building, understand?'

The man nodded.

Before Pitkan released the first pigeon, he leaned out of the open stone portal to look down over a hundred feet below to the street and then towards Whitehall. He could see the houses of Parliament by the Thames, and Whitehall, itself. He could even see hundreds of bureaucrats streaming out of buildings at the end of their day, but he did not see a company of Royal Marines or any other soldiers coming towards St. Paul's on the run. He cursed under his breath and signalled for the Sergeant to release a second pigeon.

'Can you still see the first pigeon?' asked Pitkan, now having lost it amidst the background of buildings.

'I can, sir. It's still flying west. Once in a while wavering a bit but still going in the same direction,' reported Parker.

'If it lands, mark the building, Parker, and mark it well. We'll have to be able to identify it later from the ground.'

*   *   *   *   *

Out of breath and ragged from blocks of running, Corporal Johnston staggered up the steps of the Foreign Office against the crush of bureaucrats streaming like ants out of their buildings. All were trying to get into their carriages or to walk briskly enough to get well along their way home before nightfall. Johnston stopped one person and asked him the location of William Eden's office.

"Why he would have gone home now," responded one well dressed bureaucrat, refusing to be halted in his progress towards his waiting carriage.

"He'd be off now," said another, but advising the now panicky Corporal that the office was on the second floor up the stairs to the left.

Johnston made it to the top of the stairs and down a long corridor where he was stopped by two Royal Marines stationed in front of the Office, whose sign proclaimed:

Under Secretary of Foreign Office, Continental Affairs.

"I must pass. I must see Mr. Eden. It is urgent," pleaded the Corporal, his face dripping with sweat.

"Not without an appointment," replied one marine, his musket lowered threateningly. "Look at your uniform, you're a disgrace, man. A disgrace. Where's your hat? Begone now, before we turn you in to the Provost Marshall."

Discouraged and dejected, the Corporal turned on his heel and started back down the stairs. Just then he had an inspiration, he turned suddenly and cupped his hands to his mouth bellowing at the top of his lungs, "Flagstone! Flagstone! Flagstone!"

He heard his words echo down the long corridor and waited for a long moment before he continued slowly down the stairs. He had failed. He would not make sergeant that evening, perhaps never.

He had just reached the bottom of the stairs when he was hailed from the top. "Are you the man who shouted, just now?"

"I am, sir, I am looking for Mr. William Eden. I have urgent information for him."

"I am he, wait there!" said Eden.

"Thank God, sir, thank God." The Corporal clutched onto the railing. He was afraid his knees would not support him any longer. The middle aged man descended the stairs quickly to find out why this unknown Corporal had shouted a hitherto secret password openly within the marble halls of the Foreign Office.

*   *   *   *   *

O'Mally saw huge Brian Cormack in the street below and waved him up into the building. It was a moment later, glancing up, that he saw the first pigeon. It was about a hundred feet out, flying in a characteristic zigzag fashion, but surely heading directly for his roof, from the east. O'Mally squinted out over the haze of buildings, and spied what seemed to be another bird a quarter mile behind the first, coming from the same direction.

Cormack reached the top of the stairs behind him and entered his room. "What's up, Sean?" he called to his compatriot.

"Trouble, lad. We haven't a moment to dally. We must be gone from here. Do you have the carriage?"

"Michael's bringing it. Be right around in an instant."

"How's your eyes, sharp as ever?"

Cormack nodded.

"Give a look at that bird."

"What bird?" said Cormack leaning out of the window. The first one had landed and so O'Mally pointed at it just as it pushed through the hole to come into its coop, but then he pointed to the one flying towards them.

"Can you see where they're all coming from? How many can you count?"

Cormack gazed a long moment. "Three or four are in the air. Ah, there's a new one. They might have come from near the twin spires there at St Paul's."

392

"Tiss not good," said O'Mally, perched on the sill, thinking aloud. He rose from off the sill and began to give orders, now leaning on his crutch, "Brian, haul down that there pigeon cage and then the weapons. Put them both inside the carriage, then return for me. I'll tidy up here." O'Mally sat a moment thinking half aloud, "Smart, very smart. But it'd be at least a half hour before they could locate this building on the ground even with the fastest horses. We'll be a good distance from St. Paul's, and by the time our pursuers find this building, it will be in flames."

Cormack returned for the armory case, and tugged it noisily down the two flights of stairs. O'Mally said he'd follow directly. He held a lit oil lamp in his hand. He paused, ready to hurl it and then make his agonizing descent of the stairs. Then, he considered the pigeons, they were all homed for this building. They would be of no further use to their cause, but he could not let the poor things die. He put the oil lantern down and hobbled painfully along the corridor and opened the door to the long attic room containing the coops. Inside, he extended his crutch through each cage so that he swung open the door leading to the outside. The smoke would drive them away. After a few days, they'd find another home. Dr. Franklin's pigeons were coming with him, that was all he would need to carry on his work.

O'Mally hobbled back along the corridor and through the doors to the home he had known for the past few weeks. A shame, but he must move on.

He picked up the oil lamp and hurled it across the room. The glass shattered on the wall above his bed, the flames took hold quickly. O'Mally turned to hobble down the stairs, carrying a satchel in his hand. He could hear the carriage arrive in the street below. They would get away. It would be dark in a short time and London was a big city.

14
Ambush

Pitkan had waited as long as he could for Corporal Johnston and the reinforcements. Parker must have time before dark to locate the building he had spotted from the tower. Once they had identified it from the ground and surrounded it, then Pitkan could send for reinforcements before storming in. Pitkan ordered Parker into the same small, two wheeled cart that had been driven by Lunt earlier in the day. He would lead, while Pitkan, the sergeant and most of the remaining grenadiers took either the carriage or followed on horseback. Lunt was to be kept in the carriage under guard. Pitkan elected to ride up with the carriage driver so that he could see ahead. One grenadier was left behind at St. Paul's, to guard Mrs. Harrison, and to direct Corporal Johnston should he arrive with soldiers shortly after Pitkan departed.

The search convoy started out with a thunder of hooves, intimidating everyone off the road before them by brandishing their weapons. For the first mile they progressed rapidly and then became slowed by end of day traffic. Parker and his one horse cart got a few blocks ahead of the carriage, but was still visible.

*   *   *   *   *

O'Mally looked up at the building. Smoke was now pouring out of his bedroom window. So were the pigeons, fleeing their coop hurriedly, driven out by the thick black smoke. In a few moments someone from the street would notice the smoke and sound an alarm. He doubted if it would be in time to save the building.

'Once we are a few streets away, anyone coming our direction will not know what they are looking for. We will blend right in with the other carriages. So let's get a look at what's coming after us,' ordered O'Mally.

'Only if you'll stay inside the coach, Sean. That red hair is always remembered. And you'll have to keep them damn birds quiet,' demanded Cormack.

'Tis a bargain. Head east now, straight away, 'fore they start noticing the fire and people begin a com'n this way.'

The small carriage rolled out of the carriage house at the fastest speed her driver could manage. Inside the coach, O'Mally threw a canvas over the pigeons and then opened the latch to check the small armory which had been previously stored under the bed in his room. He began checking the pistols, their flint and prime.

When they had proceeded a few streets he called out, 'Michael, something for you.' O'Mally winced as he had to contort his back to lean his arm out of the

396

window to pass two pistols out to Fagan's outstretched hand. Then he stuffed his two favorite pistols down into his belt and hooked his right leg under him so as to better see out the carriage window. He sat on the right side so that he could observe the traffic that would pass, coming from the other direction.

A quarter hour passed and then, just as the sun was going down below the buildings, Fagan leaned over to shout into the coach window at O'Mally. 'There's a little cart coming like hell's on fire, with one grenadier driving it. It looks like the Widow Meehan's punt.' Just as O'Mally looked up, the little wagon passed him, flying along perilously close to the line of buildings, as pedestrians scurried out of its way. O'Mally leaned his head out of the window to see if the cart carried pigeons, but the small trunk area was covered by a canvas.

'I can't believe they sent only one man after us. Must be more a com'n, lads. Hang tough. Stay on course, bear to the left and be ready to take a side street if necessary,' Sean shouted, still leaning out of the carriage window.

Another city block passed and Cormack called down, 'Drop ye down, Sean. There's more grenadiers and a carriage a com'n.'

In the distance they heard, 'Out of the way, out of the way, for the King's business.' Two mounted grenadiers yelled at people, animals, and carriages alike who were blocking the streets. They brandished their weapons threateningly, obviously trying to clear the way for a larger vehicle, still a block behind.

O'Mally looked to his left and spied a residential parade which forked off from the main street. He leaned out the window and taking his crutch thumped Cormack's shoulder. "Turn in there and rest a wee bit. We'll just see what passes us."

Their carriage turned into the smaller street and stopped at the corner. A vehicle behind them objected to their stopping at the intersection.

O'Mally leaned out of the window again. "T'will be a minute, whilst we pick up his Lordship," shouted O'Mally, "...if ye mind yer manners. Otherwise the lot of us t'will all go into yonder tavern for a pint and you'll have to wait it out. And that will surely take an hour or more. We have a terrible thirst."

The driver of the open wagon behind them cursed and then was silent, obviously outnumbered, and out weighed by Cormack, who had stood up waving with his fist, displaying his enormous size.

The black military carriage progressed down the street through the path opened by the grenadiers. It took about five minutes for them to make their way opposite O'Mally's coach on the broad street. They seemed to have no great band of redcoats coming behind them. On the open escort seat of the carriage, O'Mally spotted Pitkan's bald head, his visage accentuated by the dark black French cape he wore.

At that same instant Pitkan spied O'Mally peering out from the window of his coach. He shouted orders ahead to the two grenadiers on horse. The sergeant, driving, also responded to his command and began to steer the black coach across the thoroughfare towards the smaller coach. O'Mally quickly pulled both horse pistols from his belt and thrust them out of the window of his carriage. There was a double spark of flint on steel, a swift hiss of fine powder, and then the twin roar and flame of .54 calibre balls erupting from his pistols.

The sergeant beside Pitkan fell dead off the driver's seat. The two lead grenadiers' horses reared in the ensuing confusion as their riders sought to alter their direction. Women in the street screamed in terror and pedestrians fell to the ground everywhere, trying to huddle behind anything that could afford protection.

'Jesus, Mary, and Joseph, why did you do that?,' cursed Cormack trying to get his horses under control. Seated in the companion seat, Fagan had brought both pistols to the ready. Inside the coach, the pigeons squawked frantically in the darkness under their cover, most of their bowels emptying in fright. O'Mally had two fresh pistols in hand and took careful aim at the mounted grenadiers, one brandishing a raised sabre, another close behind, wielding his musket.

Pitkan descended to look into the military coach from the far side, away from the attackers. To the lone guard with Lunt, he shouted, 'If I do not come back, kill him. He is an enemy of the King.'

Terror stricken, the guard thrust out his pistol in the direction of Lunt to show that he would do as the Major ordered. The pistol in his hand shook violently. Lunt looked away and squeezed deeper into the corner of the coach. Somewhere in the street outside a grenadier discharged a musket and a man emitted a blood curdling scream. The soldier looked away from Lunt an instant, half standing up, leaning on the door of the carriage trying to peer out of the window to see what had happened. Lunt had his only opportunity then. He used the back wall of the carriage as a brace and lashed out with his foot knocking the man into the door on the far side of the coach. The guard dropped his pistol.

Somewhere, just outside, a small pistol discharged towards the attacking coach. Lunt, with a vigorous effort, kicked again at the guard as the man tried to recover his pistol. A third thrust succeeded in popping the door so that the man fell out onto the street yelling for help. Lunt pushed violently with his back against the opposite door and fell out the other direction, landing on his shoulder and head.

The grenadier on horseback, who had discharged his musket, now proceeded towards O'Mally's coach, trying to stop it. Its driver had slumped over, the other man was struggling to recover the reins which had fallen between the horses. From out of the window, O'Mally took deliberate aim with a fresh horse pistol and fired again. His ball took the charging grenadier in the sternum and pitched him violently back out of the saddle.

Hands and forearms tied behind his back, Lunt struggled to his feet in the semi-darkness of the shopping street. Some shops had already placed candles or oil lamps in their windows. The flashes of gunfire amidst the shop lights were bewildering. Not realizing he had been a prisoner, people screamed at Lunt to get down. Another musket exploded from up the street, the small one horse wagon driven by Parker had returned. Lunt stumbled forward, disorientated, until someone knocked him down, trying to protect him from being hit. He shook them off by rolling on the ground. Shifting to the left and right vigorously, he then struggled to get to his feet again. He had to get away, but where? Just then, he saw the flash and roar of pistol fire coming again from the smaller coach that had ambushed them. He saw a charging grenadier fall victim to that fire.

Lunt began to run, hands tied behind his back. Somewhere behind him he heard pounding feet running in pursuit. The blade of a sword caught on his queue as it just missed severing the back of his neck. Lunt pumped his legs to run faster. Just a few feet ahead he saw the carriage door swing open and he lengthened his stride. He saw O'Mally's face. He held a pistol in his left hand. It was pointed right at Lunt's face.

'Down!' O'Mally screamed.

Pitkan had lost a stride to draw back his sabre a second time, but now the sword in his hand stood poised high, ready to sever Lunt's head from his body. Lunt suddenly fell to the ground in front of him. Now, pointed directly into Pitkan's face, was a large calibre horse pistol. Pitkan was not five feet distant, it was the end of his life. He knew it. He did the only thing a soldier could do, Major Pitkan continued to charge. He got another step before the muzzle exploded out at him. The ball struck his chin with such force that it entirely blew his head off his shoulders in an instant. The head tumbled violently across the street before coming to rest many feet away.

Lunt's ears roared from the explosion just above his head. Through the din he heard an Irish brogue calling out anxiously, "Ye have to get up under your own power. Hurry, lad. I have only one leg. Hurry. 'Tiss all over. But we must get away from here, now!" urged O'Mally.

Lunt struggled against his bonds to get his aching shoulder into the ground so that he could get a knee under his body. He felt a hand tugging on his collar. He turned his head up. O'Mally had dropped his smoking pistol to help him. Lunt got to his knees and then lunged into the carriage. For just an instant, he had to crawl over the headless trunk of Pitkan laying at the foot of the carriage. The hand still clutched a sabre.

*　　*　　*　　*　　*

A few weeks later, Franklin, Adams, Jones and Henry Lunt sat in Franklin's office at Passy. Their mood

402

was black.

'I don't care for this at all. I am most uncomfortable. We have no conclusive proof that the man is a British spy. Aren't we fighting for the right of men to have a fair trial? Isn't that what this revolution is all about? The man has worked for me since my days as colonial agent in London. He owns extensive property in New Hampshire. The man has a lot to lose if he were proved a spy.'

'Only if we win, but if the British win and he is their spy, he could wind up owning the entire state,' observed Jones with Scottish sharpness. 'Taking sides is a gamble, which ever..r way you decide to play it. We all have made our choices regarding these matters, pur..rhaps he has made up his mind differently than we.'

'This must not be turned into an inquisition, Captain Jones,' stressed Adams.

'That is purr..cisely why I think that I should be allowed to conduct this inquiry alone, Mr. Ambassadors. I promise you both that I will not harm a hair on his head, but I will find out whether or not he is a spy. I surely pr..romise you that.'

'No, Captain,' Franklin held up his hand, 'I cannot do that. He is a long time friend, I cannot permit you to offer the threat of a similar punishment as you exacted on the unfortunate Mr. Hezekiah Ford. We are still reeling from the broadsides' coverage of that transgression. If he is guilty, and admits it here I will be surprised. He is a very thoughtful man and will

403

likely make you prove your case. But in letting you make the accusation in my presence, I know that I am forever losing the love of a valued compatriot. If he admits to this guilt, I shall simply ask him to leave Passy this evening. There shall be no physical violence, is that clear, Captain Jones?"

"Even if the inferr...mation that he gave to the Br..ritish resulted in the loss of dozens of ships carrying valuable supplies to America? Even if he was responsible for stopping all of ye..rr letters of 1777 from getting to the Continental Congress? Even if he is responsible for the curr..rrent merchant riots against you in Nantes, and Brest, trying to break up our saltpeter shipments to General Washington? Even if," Jones pointed towards Lunt, "...he was responsible for the near assassination of my Lieutenant."

"Even if those accusations are completely valid," said Franklin firmly. "But do not sell Mr. Adams and me short, Captain. You may have correctly found out that Arthur Lee's staff was riddled with British spies by terrorizing Mr. Ford, but lest you forget, it was through working with our allies that the new French ambassador got rid of them all in one sweep by simply telling Mr. Hancock and the Continental Congress that they only wanted to deal with myself as sole ambassador. I might add that this was with the acquiescence of Mr. Adams, who had been sent here primarily to find out why they had received no messages from me in over a year. Mr. Adams has always been desirous of returning to America as soon as he had completed

404

his mission here."

Adams nodded in the affirmative, his hands folded across his stomach as Franklin continued, "You see there are many ways to skin a cat, Captain Jones. Since we have become aware that there may still be leaks from this embassy, we have begun speaking, as you are aware, of invasions which you might lead against Liverpool, or Edinburgh. French intelligence has subsequently reported to us that many British Men of War have been shifted to patrol duty in both the Irish and North seas where they now cannot possibly interfere with our Atlantic shipping routes. Perhaps, if you are correct in the accusations you are going to make today, then you may succeed in closing our leak. Then the rumors will cease and soon we will have to contend with the entire British fleet again. Have you thought of that, Captain Jones?

"Yes, sir, I have. But I am a fighting man. I feel that 'tis best to destroy one's enemies forthwith, not to play at games with them."

Franklin turned towards Lunt, who had been sitting in a distant corner of the room, listening intently. "Henry, I think we are ready to proceed. Would you escort him up to my office."

As Lunt departed, his own stomach churning, he heard Captain Jones continue, "Remember..r, Mr. Ambassadors, you have agreed to let me give the appearance that we know more than we do while I make this accusation...."

Dr. Edward Bancroft sat at his desk at the rear of the great salon, busily writing the draft of an acceptance letter for Franklin to speak at the French Academy of Science the following February. He would soon have a draft ready and show it to Mr. Hubbard, whose classic French was the purest of the entire staff. His difficulty was, as always, in attempting to delve into the mind of Franklin and to make it seem as if the great man himself had composed the letter. To turn this trick he needed to put some touch of the philosophy of Franklin into this particular letter. A little indecisive, he took a file from a nearby cabinet and browsed through a packet of similar acceptance letters he had helped to draft before.

Bancroft glanced up, Lunt was coming towards him, ah, perhaps he was finally going to make an arrangement to play chess with him that afternoon. He had missed their games of last summer. But Lunt seemed to have been avoiding contact with him since his sudden return to Passy several days ago. It was unlike Lunt, the man's feelings were often readable. Where had he been anyway? Haven't seen him since the salon party at Madame Brillon's, and that was very brief. Here he comes.

"Dr. Bancroft, Dr. Franklin wishes to speak to you in his office."

There was no friendliness in his voice, and Henry did not look him in the eye. What was wrong? Mr. Adams must surely be upstairs too, he was not at his desk at the opposite side of the salon. He had seen

Captain Jones strutting around in his uniform a few hours ago and had assumed that he had left, or was he still here? Most of the other staff had already left for the day.

"Does he want to see my drafts of his letters?" Bancroft asked Lunt. "I have one more to complete, I can bring the rest, however."

"No, that's not it. Just bring yourself. He has something to discuss with you."

Lunt's voice was very stern. Bancroft looked about, no one else was in the salon. The others had slipped out without saying goodbye to him, including Hubbard and Hanson, the assistants he worked with most closely. As he got up, Bancroft noticed that Lunt wore his sword. Ambassador Franklin did not permit weapons in his house. What was this?

Bancroft, trembling a bit, got up. Surely it's nothing to worry about. He was imagining things. He walked over to the flight of stairs along whose walls he had tread many times. He scarcely saw the tall stately murals as he placed foot after foot proceeding deliberately up the stairs. He did not feel well, perhaps an early winter cold coming on, that was all. He reached in his pocket to find his pipe, it was there. He would have to ask Dr. Franklin if he could smoke. Lunt followed him up the stairs. Once he turned to say something light, but Lunt's stern visage silenced his effort. What was wrong?

Bancroft put his hand on the door knob leading into Franklin's office, inside he found the office somewhat rearranged. There was a chair in the center of the room. Captain Jones gestured towards it. Bancroft looked towards Franklin, but his face was implacable. Adams sat beside him, looking down. Oh, my God, they've found out, his inner voice warned. He felt his heart pounding. His breath became insufficient. He deliberately breathed deeply as he took the chair. Stay calm, he thought, you have covered every possible situation they might have discovered.

Franklin spoke first, 'Edward, Captain Jones and some others have identified some distressing things about you. I want you to answer all of the Captain's questions truthfully so that we can get to the conclusion of this with the least amount of distress to everybody.'

Jones, his face resolute, walked between Franklin and him. As Bancroft waited, he observed that the Captain was deliberately taking his time to heighten the tension. Unlike the loud voice he anticipated, Jones spoke in a low volume, but very precise, and without a hint of his usual Scottish brogue, 'Dr. Bancroft, you are a British spy...'

The abruptness of the accusation startled him. They must surely have gotten irrefutable evidence for Franklin to have allowed this. Was Jones going to be allowed to beat him, right here in the Ambassador's office as he had Mr. Ford?

'...you have been seen meeting with known British agents, and we have intercepted your messages to the British government. Dr. Franklin, in his mercy, wants this unpleasant matter put aside quickly. On the table to your right is a quill and paper. We wish you to simply write out a confession now, then you will be permitted to collect your things and leave this office and Passy without physical harm to your person. This is in deference to the good Doctor's religious beliefs, not mine, I assure you. Take up the paper now and let's get this unpleasant matter over with.'

Captain Jones pointed at the paper. Bancroft glanced at the table. How could he be sure that Captain Jones had caught him? The offer was generous, usually spies are shot. This was too quick. Should he risk irritating Jones? Damn, he had covered every possible move. There was never any physical information, everything he removed from Passy was always in his head. He did not write anything down until he was near the hollow tree at Tuilleries gardens. How had they possibly seen him, the tree was in the middle of a woods, how the hell did they find it? Had the Foreign Office dispatches been compromised again? They had said that the new system was foolproof. Could he trust them? Had they been careless again?

'Come on, man, quit stalling. Write out the bloody confession and be out of our sight!'

This was too quick. Jones was trying to rush him. Call the man's bluff. Stall! Think! Use your intelligence. Admit nothing. Buy time! Stall! There may be a way out of this. Hold on, get Franklin's sympathy.

"Captain Jones, your accusation leaves me shaking to the core. I need water, please."

Bancroft put his hand to his throat, while Franklin asked Lt. Lunt to bring him water. As he was handed the glass, he looked into Lunt's eyes. "Henry, do you believe I'm a spy as well?"

Lunt eyes avoided him, but he muttered, "Answer Captain Jones' questions."

Questions? There were no questions. He saw a line of defense, ask questions yourself, make Jones prove it. See what they had, perhaps the precautions he had taken would cover anything. If they had physical evidence, it must be from the British. Start easy. He sipped the water thinking, 'Here goes.'

"Your accusation is so astounding, Captain Jones, I cannot even fathom why or how you came to this conclusion. Please, cite me one piece of evidence which you have so that I may defend myself."

Jones was pacing back and forth like a caged lion. He looked at Bancroft like he was going to pounce. His voice grew louder, angrier now, "You have been observed every Wednesday evening at Tuilleries Gardens in the company of known British agents. That is, of course, the day after Dr. Franklin meets with the King. The very time each week when your letters for him are filled with the very latest information."

Why, he's bluffing, thought Bancroft. I have deliberately never talked to anyone at Tuilleries Gardens. I simply drop the message in a hollow tree under the pretense that I am going into the wood to have privacy with which to relieve myself. Did they perhaps seize one of the couriers who picked up my message last week? It's been five days since the last drop. Surely Paul Wentworth would have sent me word by now, so I could have escaped. No, it cannot be.

'Surely, you can be more specific than that, Captain Jones.'

Wait, half a year ago, Lord Stormont warned me that a diplomatic pouch which contained one of my coded messages might have been opened in England, either by accident or deliberately, but nothing had been taken out.   Just to be sure, Bancroft had immediately changed stores where he purchased his tobacco, so that he no longer carried the same tobacco wrappers.   Were the Americans that slow?   He remembered the incident, for weeks and weeks last winter he had carried a pistol in his pocket, in case it should come up, but it never had. That was back in the days before Mr. Adams arrived and before there were marine guards at the door of the embassy. In those days everything was looser here, and he could have walked out with anything, but he had always been very careful, even back then.

'You have been seen there in the company of John Thornton, who was formerly Ambassador Lee's secretary. We know he is secretly a major in the British army,' said Jones coldly.

'You have seen me, yourself, talking with this man? Why, I only know him casually. To the best of my knowledge I have never had anything but the most casual conversation with the man, and never to my recollection at the Garden. You know, 'Hello,' 'Good Evening,' the tipping of the hat, that sort of thing.'

That was the truth. It was always better to lie with the truth when one could. He was beginning to settle down, to compose himself. Why not throw in a convincer, 'Have you ever thought, Captain Jones, that perhaps this alleged British spy was simply following me, just as you obviously have had someone engaged in following me these past weeks. Note I say alleged, for I trust, Captain Jones, that you have better evidence against this man, Thornton, than you have against me.'

The chess player in Bancroft was utilizing his full faculties now. He looked around the room. Perhaps he should try and see if any of this did stem from that incident of last winter. He deliberately craned his neck past Jones, as if he didn't count, to look at Franklin.

'Dr. Franklin, I must confess that this little meeting has turned my insides into gelatin, and the gelatin is quivering. I pray, sir, may I be allowed to smoke my pipe?'

Bancroft, striving to look as innocent as possible, started to fish into his pocket for his pipe. Every eye in the room was on him.

Franklin did not speak. Jones did, somewhat sarcastically, 'By all means, Dr. Bancroft, have a smoke.'

The invitation was telling. Bancroft looked up as he deliberately lengthened the time it would take to extract his tobacco pouch. He fiddled with his pipe clearing it with a small metal ramrod. He got up and knocked the contents into a tin. He looked up, still every eye was upon him. He put his left hand into his right vest pocket, extracted the pouch, deliberately covering it with his hand. Finally, when it was in front of him, he let the pouch fall open. It had green wax paper on the outside, and on the inside as well. Bancroft looked at Jones, who turned away obviously disappointed. If that was their best evidence, from an intercepted message of almost a half year ago, then this would be over soon.

But Jones started speaking again, "Approximately two weeks ago you were seen entering the French shipping offices of Monsieur Daniaud. You were in there for several hours. I point out to you that this firm is a rival of the firm of our host here at Passy, Leray de Chaumont. It is also the firm which French authorities have identified as being responsible for inciting the current riots against Dr. Franklin, and against the continuance of shipping more saltpeter and other supplies to America." Jones put out his hand in an accusatory manner. "There can be no good reason why you should meet there with our enemies. None."

Bancroft puffed on his pipe while he thought. He had not wanted to meet in person with Lord Stormont's people, but they had insisted. After the battle of Ushant, they needed the name of every ship scheduled to carry saltpeter to America in the coming

413

months, its current port, its scheduled departure date, its destination and receiving agent in America. Information far too complex and detailed for coded messages, but he had foreseen to cover his visit there with a deception. Instinctively, he had sensed that he had been followed.

'Henry, could you please go down to my desk? In the upper left drawer, the flat one, there are some sheets of blue foolscap. Could you bring them up for me? This will explain my visit.'

While everyone waited for Lunt to return, Bancroft began speaking again, 'Captain Jones, if you are going to truly lead an expedition to Liverpool, as hints have been dropped over the past many few weeks,' glances were exchanged around the room, '...then, I presumed that you would need a ship.'

Lunt returned into the room carrying the papers. He had not examined them, but listened as Bancroft continued speaking, 'I knew that you had, very likely, the eager assistance of Madame de Chaumont,' he cleared his throat to leave the point discreetly unsaid, 'to search the Leray's dominions for a promising ship or fleet of ships. But I also know that after the tremendous wreckage of French war ships at Ushant that you have very little likelihood of having the French just give you a man of war this winter. There is a long line of French naval officers, of far greater rank and influence than yourself, who are also now in need of a ship. I thought that perhaps the firm of Monsieur Daniaud might have a listing of available larger sized

414

foreign merchant vessels which perhaps could be converted into a warship."

Bancroft puffed a few times on his pipe thought-fully, "On the foolscap, you will see, I have made a listing of those merchant vessels which they knew were available for sale at neutral ports. On the sheets of paper are listed ships currently available in places like Rome, Tunis, Copenhagen, and Texel in the Lowlands, perhaps the nearest port. I believe there are two possibilities there."

Jones held out his hand, and Bancroft handed him the handwritten listing. Jones looked at each page for some long moments while Bancroft continued to blow smoke from his pipe.

"I did not show this listing to you earlier, Captain Jones, because I have sent inquiries of availability to each ship owner. I have not yet received any replies."

He had not done that, but if this deception worked, he would do it immediately to cover himself. The important point was to get out of the hot seat now. He looked up and saw Franklin shake his head at Adams. He might have won. He took every measure to appear conciliatory towards the accusation.

Jones leaned over him, "This is a Dutch East India merchant, you say?"

Bancroft tried to appear as helpful as possible, "Yes, she is about 1,000 tonnes in her present configuration. I thought you could put over 40 guns on her at two levels. She reportedly has a stout lower deck, just the sort that could be converted to a second tier of guns.'

After a few minutes of discussion about Bancroft's list, Franklin got up and went over to Bancroft, extending his hand. 'Edward, I am thoroughly embarrassed. Please accept my apology for letting this go on. There was a great deal of circumstantial evidence pointing at you. We had no choice but to let Captain Jones try and scare a confession out of you.'

Bancroft kept his conciliatory posture by remarking light heartedly, 'I tell you, if I had been your spy, I would have died of fright right there in that chair, you wouldn't have had to shoot me.'

Everyone laughed.

*   *   *   *   *

As October progressed it became colder along the Thames. It was a bright, crisp morning when Martha Ray walked out of the door of the castle with her leading temptress. Part of her resented the way that Madame Armstrong had begun to lead many of the activities at the castle. But Martha's position with Lord Sandwich was secure, and Sheila Armstrong definitely commanded the affections of Admiral Lord Howe, who, now that his signal code had found favor, might well become the next First Lord of the Admiralty. Sheila Armstrong was becoming a powerful person to stay on the good side of, in case of a change in regime at the Admiralty.

The two nodded and smiled at the guards as they passed out through the gate and continued along towards the park for their stroll. Midway up the street they could see that a beggar was sitting along the road, with a box in front of him.

"Blacken yer boots so fine, Madames," said the voice. The man was dressed in a navy boatswain's jacket, but it was torn and tattered.

Martha Ray looked away from the sight of the one legged man with the hunched back. She disliked having to look at misshapen people of any kind. "The marines are supposed to keep this block free of riffraff," she said deliberately aloud for the benefit of the beggar. "I'll see that they clear that one out upon my return."

The man began singing a tune aloud:

"Have ye ever been to Carnarvon house,
where Henry cuts the meat so fine?
Have ye ever been to Carnarvon house,
where t'ings are not what they seem..."

Madame Armstrong tripped during the second stanza, and managed to get a look backwards at the figure as they rounded the corner. For weeks she'd carried, hidden in the lining of her parasol, a copy of the newly issued Signals by Night of the Royal Navy, another signal innovation of Lord Howe. She had been waiting, frustrated, unsure why a liaison had not contacted her as yet. This had to be it. Only a few persons could know of Carnarvon House, from which she and Lunt had escaped in Belfast during the Ranger Incident.

Her heart raced as Madame Ray asked her, 'Carnarvon House...what is that old beggar singing about? Never heard of it, but it sounds like a delightfully wicked place.'

'Let's ask him about it when we return, if he's still there. I've never heard of the spot either. Maybe it's someplace we should go. Besides we could get our shoes blackened, mine are a bit scruffy,' suggested Madame Armstrong.

They both giggled like the wicked girls they were as they paraded, their bustles swaying in rhythm along the street together. Every block, men's heads turned to watch after them.

*   *   *   *   *

Mid October changed to early November and the Atlantic breeze blew stout in the late afternoon as a swift French schooner beat past Point St. Mathieu and then continued out into the North Atlantic. The ship carried on her deck only two sixteen pound cannon and no cargo in her hold to weigh her down. Her only extravagance was additional sails. Her lines were swift, and she could outrun and sail closer to windward than most vessels on the oceans of 1778. The foremast was just the right height and raked back towards the stern as with most schooners of the time. Her main was similarly raked back and all running rigging, from main to foremast to bowsprit, was in the normal proportion. Her one peculiarity, however, was the extraordinary height of her main mast, extending upwards to nearly twice its normal height. The extension flexed forward and aft with the movement of the ship.

'Will she hold, Lieutenant Lunt?'

'She should, Captain. Mr. Gunnison and I have hoisted the signal triangle aloft several times and it has held firmly. After this night's work we can cut it free. It's just a long piece of timber.'

'You've sailed with me long enough to know I'll tolerate no waste of stout lumbu..rr on any ship I command,' replied Captain Jones. 'You'll send the signal now for Captain Simpson to weigh anchor with the Ranger and to get his convoy under way, and then you'll come below yourself, after you've confirmed his return signal.'

'You've heard that, Mister Madden, send our signal to the Ranger,' relayed Lunt across the deck.

'Aye, aye, sir.'

419

Jones continued, "You'll now douse every light on this deck, nothing is to show. There's open ocean before us on this course. Maintain it."

"Very good, sir," replied Lunt.

A quarter hour later, Lunt knocked and then entered the modest day cabin where Captain Jones was bent over his charts. Lunt took a standing position across the chart table.

"Sir, the French station has signaled back that H.M.S. Robust and Fox are on patrol due west about twenty miles. Several English privateers are patrolling to their north. The French have indicated that they will send L'Orient and two other frigates out behind our convoy in case the deception fails. These will provide cover for the convoy to retreat back to Brest if it is detected."

"And with that would go all hope that General Washington will get saltpeter to make gunpowder this winter. We can't have that, can we? We must get Simpson through. Let's go over his planned course again."

On the chart, Jones drew a course past the head, Point St. Mathieu and then southward a good fifteen miles and then west again. Jones spoke then, "Tiss known that at least two British second raters are outside Nantes as well. The convoy will need to thread the needle by beating in the general direction as near west of south west as possible until dawn. If this blow persists they will be a hundred miles out into the Atlantic by then. Mercifully, the cloud cover is dark."

Lunt nodded.

"Henry, you still propose using H.M.S. Victory as the signaling ship?"

"Yes, sir, the Spymaster has reported that H.M.S. Victory has been repaired and will soon set to sea again. I feel that if the British patrol believes this signal to be from the flagship, sir, they'll be hard pressed to disobey it. Also, any of the British privateers from Jersey will likewise be obliged to follow. Because of the shortage of British ships, they have just been allowed to share in Royal Navy signals. They would not dare to disobey a signal from the Royal Navy flagship this soon."

Lunt cleared his throat. "We have the primary signals already on the cross trees of the main. Two men aloft should be able to raise them up the extended main mast, after they are lighted. Provided the sea is not too violent, we should be able to keep them aloft at one hundred and fifty feet all night. All the oil levels have been rechecked."

"The backups have been checked as well?" inquired Jones, his hands clasped characteristically behind his back.

"Yes, sir. They are secured at the base of the mast, all in proper configuration. They need only be hauled up."

"And the signal will read..."

"After the exchange of recognition signals, it shall read; *Form behind H.M.S. Victory.*"

Jones repeated their plan, "So we leave the signal

aloft for 2 to 3 hours and then douse it and try to evade them by beating on an opposite tact in the darkness the remainder of the night. You'll keep up a tactical board below here, as you described aboard the Bretagne.'

'Aye, aye, sir.'

'Good on ye, Henry.'

At four bells Jonathan Harken reported spotting two large ships signaling each other to the southwest, from five to ten miles distance.

Jones confided to Lunt, 'I believe that we should be windward of them a bit more before we raise any signal. If we're downwind they'll catch us surely. Steer west by nor'west or as close to that position as the wind will tolerate.'

'Have you ascertained their course, Mr. Harken?' asked the Captain.

'It appears to be a casual reach to the south, Sir. One ship did appear to be five miles more southerly than the other. But I have lost sight of her now.'

'Change to a starboard tact, Mr. Madden. That should compensate for their progress south. We'll hold our signal until we're a wee bit westward of the line they sail, say a quarter hour's more time,' commanded Jones.

'Aye, aye, sir.'

Lunt went into the cabin to correct the tactical board and then joined all, save the helmsmen, on the larboard rail. The dozen or so men of Jones' signal ship watched for signs of the British Men of War, but their lights were becoming fainter and fainter. The enemy ships were moving south at a good clip. To the east, the American crew could see some lights from along the French coast. Somewhere now, hugging that coast, also on a parallel southerly course was a convoy of eleven merchant ships carrying saltpeter, led by the Ranger. Soon the convoy would all turn westward according to plan, but there was now a good chance that, ten to twenty miles onto that new course, they could be intercepted by British Men of War criss-crossing their path.

"Damn, they'll intercept the convoy," cursed Jones. "Simpson will swear to his dying day that I deliberately set him up to get even."

"Mr. Madden, fall off."

After a few minutes, it was apparent that the schooner on a reach could not hope to catch up with the British Men of War with their vast square yards of sail and much longer water lines. Only in a direction towards the wind could they keep pace with or ahead of a British Man of War.

"Can't see any lights at all now, sir," reported one of the crew. "They're too far to the south.

"Sir, I have a suggestion, though it may be an uncomfortable one," said Lunt.

"Go ahead, Lieutenant Lunt."

"Since we believe they would not be able to see our signal lights, they might be able to hear our guns and catch sight of a fire?"

"How, Lieutenant Lunt? Would you have us burn our own ship?"

"No, sir, but we could burn our longboat. Pile canvas on top of it. Oil it up and lower her away whilst we not lose time on this course. We could tow her, sir, while we continue south. We could pitch a lantern into her and blow off our sixteen pounders as rapidly as we can. There's nothing else out here. They must surely see us even if their lead vessel is fifteen miles distant."

"Make it so, Lieutenant Lunt."

A quarter hour passed as the schooner continued southward in a vain pursuit of the two British Men of War. Into the long boat, the small crew piled every spare stick of flammable furniture and extra rigging which they could detach that would not directly affect the sailing of their vessel. When they had the longboat ready on the davits, the sailing master gave the command to ease off sharply on the schooner's fore and main sails.

As the schooner's speed momentarily dropped to nothing, officers and men together bent their backs to lower the large longboat into the open sea.

Captain Jones handed the horn lantern to Lunt. "Your suggestion, Lieutenant Lunt, we'll hold her close, but mind our own freeboard."

Lunt walked along the larboard rail until he was directly above the longboat only fifteen feet below. With a double handed grip he hurled the lantern down atop the oil sodden canvas and wood. For a moment it seemed that the fire would not catch and that someone would have to do it over. But then it became obvious that the lantern chimney had cracked and the prospect of so much fuel was too tempting for the flickering flame. Soon the conflagration ignited.

'Harden up on the sails, Mr. Madden, and let's let out a good quantity of line so that we can sail free from that mess. Lieutenant Lunt, get the guns started. We'll continue a southerly course, Mr. Harken.'

For a quarter of an hour the towed, fire ship decoy burned vigorously and the two 16 pounders boomed as often as they could be reloaded, their resonance enlivened by double loads of powder. After a third of an hour, the flames began to abate, and the longboat began to list badly. A hand let her painter go. All the while, the 16 pounders continued their vigorous fire, and the schooner's deck reeked of cordite.

'Sir, there be a signal light advancing towards us. Eight to ten miles distant.'

The crew cheered, and clapped their hands together.

'Mr. Madden, come about, close beat to nor'west, if you please.'

All hands participated in the maneuver.

'Tiss time for Victory's signal,' ordered Jones.

'Aye, sir.'

Harken reported, 'They've signaled they are H.M.S. Fox, Sir.'

'Hoist the signal triangle aloft now, Lieutenant.'

After the task was accomplished, Lunt went to his Captain's side. The two men studied the signal lights, until they were satisfied that it gave the proper perspective to the enemy. Then, from the taffrail they looked astern and observed the bow signal of at least one Man of War.

'Hopefully, he'll relay the signal.'

Jones turned on his heel and shouted towards the bow. 'Set all the sail you can, Mr. Madden.

Jones waited for the characteristic, 'Aye, aye, Sir,' to indicate the command had been heard and the order was being carried out.

For an hour Lunt and Jones watched the bow lights of at least one enemy vessel, following them some ten or more miles distant.

'So you will be unlikely to want to risk another trip back to England in the near future, Henry?'

'No, sir, I would prefer to stay at sea.'

'How is your Spanish, Henry?'

'There is none, sir,' said Lunt, then excitedly he pointed, 'Look, sir, another light to leeward. It must be the second man of war.'

Jones repeated the information so that all of the crew could hear. Men on the deck congratulated each other. Every crew member knew that if they could lure the British ships in their direction for an hour or more, then the saltpeter convoy would slip past them far to the south. And then in another hour or more's time they would simply douse their signal light and

426

make their escape onto another course under cover of darkness.

"Sir, why did you ask if I spoke Spanish?" asked Lunt later.

"I think it's time for this Captain to get a new ship, Henry. I'm told the Dutch want to stay neutral so they won't sell ships to the English, the French, or the Americans. But why wouldn't they sell one to a Spaniard?"

"So I conclude we are off to Texel in the Low-lands," said Lunt.

"Aye, Henry, our next adventure will begin in Holland, with the canals and the beautiful blond women who will do anything to please a sailor's heart. I've told ye that I wish one day not to have to run from those British Men of War, but instead to command a ship large enough to stand and fight. Aye, and perhaps one day soon this Captain will get his wish."

The reader's attention is called to the Author's Historic Notes beginning on the following page, and then to the series of children's books by my son, George, "America's Youngest Author."   T.M.

Author's Historical Notes

Although this work is fiction, Henry Lunt was a real person who served as John Paul Jones' next in command on either four or five ships. My stories of Henry Lunt are based upon Lunt family legends passed on to me by his descendent, George P. Lunt, who was my stepfather and a renowned scientist in his own right. In his capacity as Jones' Lieutenant, Henry Lunt would have known and been known by Benjamin Franklin, John Adams, John Quincy Adams and the other members of the ambassadorial staff at Passy, including Dr. Edward Bancroft.

Dr. Edward Bancroft was very likely the greatest spy who ever eluded detection by the American Government. We only know of his conspiracy because, in the mid 1800s, the British Foreign Office made public his many messages. This was some eighty years after the actual events. It is very likely that the information Dr. Bancroft provided to the British was responsible for the sinking or capture of over thirty French and American supply ships leaving from French ports to America during 1777 and 1778. As Franklin's personal secretary, he also was very likely responsible for the blockage of all of Franklin's letters to Congress during 1777. At least one early 19th century biography reports that Captain Jones directly accused Bancroft of being a British spy in late 1778, the period of this book. Interestingly, this biography was published before the British made their revelation. As this is a work of fiction, I invented the scene in Franklin's office in the last chapter to show how he might have evaded Jones' accusations. In fact, Bancroft was such a polished spy that by 1779 Captain Jones, in several letters, mentions how helpful Dr. Bancroft has been. He must have been truly a master spy to have successfully deceived the likes of Franklin, Adams, Jones, etc. and to have never been caught. My compliments to the British Foreign Office.

One cannot research John Paul Jones in 1778 and 1779 without drawing parallels between him and General George Patton. Both of their respective opponents, the Royal Navy and the Nazis, shifted great military forces at just the suspicion that either figure would lead a campaign against them. Both Jones and Patton got into hot water with their superiors after having personally beaten men. In Jones' case the traitor, Ford. And in Patton's, an alleged coward. Both returned however, to vanquish greater foes and to achieve immortality in American History.

As I was conducting newspaper research of the period at the British Newspaper Library, I discovered an authentic act of forgotten chivalry. Reproduced on page 366, verbatim, is the French Admiral d'Orvilliers' open letter which he apparently paid to have published in the London Chronicle on December 10, 1778. In it he was attempting to clear his honorable opponent at Ushant, Admiral Keppel, of the court martial charge of malfeasance. A charge which, earlier in the century, had cost at least one British Admiral his life. I have compassion for Keppel who suffered a humiliating castigation by the Tories, but who was ultimately acquitted, as was d'Orvilliers by his French peers. Incidentally, a group of stalwart English citizens went on a rampage the night of Keppel's acquittal and burned down Lord North's residence and threatened Lord Sandwich's as well. Good on them!

My rendition of the first battle of Ushant was largely based on the various testimonies given at the court martial of Admiral Keppel. The methodology of the French escape the evening after the battle was my own. The second Fourth of July party did occur at Passy and was a stunning success, and the British attempt shortly thereafter to bribe both Franklin and Adams was turned over to the French authorities. John Paul Jones did have a torrid affair with Madam de Chaumont, and Benjamin Franklin, in his mid seventies, was in close company with the two ladies mentioned in my novel.

As for the grandson of the Count de Batz-Castelmore, I used him as my own voice to express some thoughts about espionage. It might interest readers to know that the original Count was the swashbuckling gentleman whom many French historians have credited as having served as a real life model for Dumas' immortal character, d'Artagnan of the Three Musketeers. I do not know if the real gentleman had a grandson, or if that grandson ever ran a school of spies, but my work is fiction and this author just couldn't resist the temptation.

The "castle" of Lord Sandwich actually existed. Based upon the accounts of the English newspapers, I could have made this an X rated book had I wanted, but that's not my style. The place was the scandal of its time and subject of much commentary by Tory opponents. The actual madame was named Martha Ray, not to be confused with the 20th century American movie actress and comedienne of a very similar name. The latter did the very patriotic, but politically unpopular thing, and came over to entertain our GI's in Vietnam in 1977. This Lt. McNamara had the great privilege of meeting and sharing some conversation with her in Nha Trang after she entertained our men in a rather low budget, but terrifically enthusiastic U.S.O. show. To a great American, Martha Raye, my appreciation.

Was there really an American Spymaster in Europe pitted against Paul Wentworth and William Eden? Including the arson of John the Painter, the incidents are too frequent, our intelligence too specific, and Franklin, a great man, but as former CIA Director Allen Dulles has put it, "he was naive in his attitudes." There may not have been an American Spymaster, but this author believes there was.. . so to Sean O'Mally, or whatever your real name was, thank you.

In Appreciation

Although this work is fiction, not a biography, a considerable amount of background research was accomplished with the help of the following organizations. The author wishes to express his appreciation to:

The National Maritime Museum
Greenwich, England
The British Library-Newspaper Library
London, England
The United States Naval Academy
Annapolis, Maryland
The Navy Historical Center
Washington, D.C.
Society of the Friends of Versailles
Paris, France
The Portsmouth Historical Society
and The John Paul Jones House
Portsmouth, New Hampshire

About the Author

Born in 1944, Tom McNamara was raised in the Boston area where as a boy he received first hand exposure to the historic surroundings from which the American Revolution evolved. He attended the oldest public high school in the United States, Boston English, and by 1966 had received a degree in chemistry from Boston University. After military service, he received an M.B.A. from Northeastern University.

Upon graduation from college, Tom joined the United States Army and after completing Officer Candidate School, served in Vietnam as an ordnance officer. After Vietnam, the army assigned him as a project officer with the Army Missile Command, where he worked on assignments at both Redstone Arsenal and Cape Kennedy.

For most of his professional career, Tom has been involved in corporate market research and new product planning. He has conducted international business research for many of the world's largest corporations. Over the course of his business career Tom has also been a frequent speaker at conventions and conferences, and has contributed articles to various industrial and trade magazines.

In 1974, Tom received considerable nationwide publicity as the recipient of both a Presidential and Chicago Police Department commendation for capturing a mugger in downtown Chicago.

In 1977, Tom married his wife, Ellen, and in 1983 they moved to San Diego. They have one child, George. Both George and Ellen are also published authors. In 1990, Tom co-authored his first book, *America's Changing Workforce - About You, Your Job, and Your Changing Work Environment*, which received nationwide attention and made Tom one of the nation's most sought after TV and Radio talk show guests.

In addition to a love of tennis and baseball, Tom is an avid amateur sailboat racing skipper and was appointed an "On Water Advisor" for the past three America's Cup® races held in his home San Diego waters. In continuing the Henry Lunt series, Tom is fulfilling a lifelong dream of bringing the adventure and romance of America's early sailing history to the attention of the world.

"America's Cup" is a registered trademark of America's Cup Properties, Inc.

- Stories For Our Younger Readers by -
GEORGE McNAMARA
"America's Youngest Author" ™

GEORGE And The PITCHING MACHINE

5 year old George has started his first year in Little League Baseball. George relates how his team mates learn to work together and play the game. The manager tells the youngsters they will be batting against a pitching machine the next game, which makes George very worried. You'll enjoy this story about a child dealing with the unknown and learning what happens when he goes to bat against the Pitching Machine. **PHOTO of TONY GWYNN, four time National League Batting Champion on back cover. Full color illustrations.**

GEORGE And The TRICKY FISH

George loves to go sailing with his family. While on vacation on their boat off Catalina Island, George asks his father to teach him how to catch the fish who are swimming all around the boat. George discovers fishing is not as easy as it looks. A fun story of how George tries to catch a very tricky fish.

GEORGE And The SAILBOAT RACE

George and Dad enter a sailboat race series with George as the skipper and Dad as crew. You'll cheer as 5 year old Captain George runs the helm of a 34 foot sailboat in San Diego Harbor, with the other boat skippers & crews cheering him on.

About The Author:

George learned the art of storytelling from his parents who are both published authors. He began working on computers at age one, and starting dictating complete stories to his father by age three. George wrote the story of "George And The Pitching Machine" when he was 5 years old, and "George And The Tricky Fish" at age 6. George loves baseball, sailing, soccer, swimming, fishing, reading & writing adventure stories, castles and valiant knights, pirates, and meeting new friends.

GEORGE AND THE PITCHING MACHINE

GEORGE McNAMARA
AMERICA'S YOUNGEST AUTHOR

Mystery/Thrillers by LIZZ RAINES

WIDOWMAKER

YOU CAN NEVER BE TOO RICH OR TOO THIN AND BLACK IS DEFINITELY 'IN.' Murdered husbands are turning up all over the luxurious coastal village of LaJolla, California in this fast paced mystery thriller by LIZZ RAINES. World renown as the playground of the rich and famous, LaJolla is also the hunting ground of financial scam artists and other criminals who lure victims through their gullibility and greed. Beautiful Jackie Jenner, daughter of the president of a powerful multi-national corporation, finds herself in a web of deceit, betrayal, and death when she returns to LaJolla for her father's second marriage.

One by one, the partners of FCDC are disappearing or dying. Will Jackie's father be next?
Can she stop WIDOWMAKER?
...or will she become the next victim!

LOST LUGGAGE

New mother can't wait to have infant son meet his father, who is overseas on six month tour of duty on submarine. Their wonderful family holiday turns to terror when mother and baby son board the plane for the international flight home .... but only mother arrives at their destination.

ROADS KILLS

You scream, we scream, we all scream for... Serial child killer turned cross country RVer.

"MYSTERIES...aerobic exercises for the mind."
Lizz Raines, author

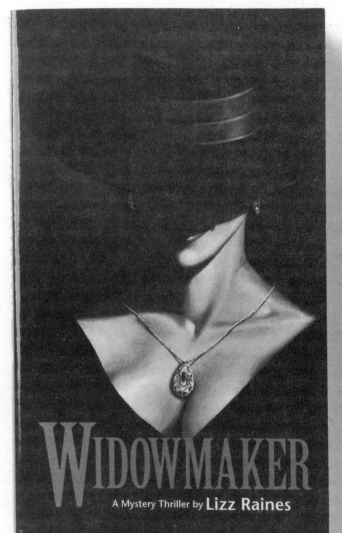

WIDOWMAKER

A Mystery Thriller by **Lizz Raines**

GREAT ADVENTURES
by TOM McNAMARA

HENRY LUNT & THE RANGER

Rescued from a Welsh prison by Captain John Paul Jones, young Colonial Navy Lieutenant Henry Lunt is sent into Belfast harbor with the mission to discover what secret weapon is being tested aboard a British man of war, the Drake. Lunt's efforts uncover a web of concealed espionage and lead to one of the most thrilling pursuits of modern literature. Ultimately, Lunt's mission leads to the stirring 1778 engagement between the American corvette, Ranger and H.M.S. Drake.

HENRY LUNT & THE SPYMASTER

Colonial Navy Lieutenant Henry Lunt carries a grim message to Ambassador Benjamin Franklin: That there is a British spy operating from within the offices of the American delegation to France. Meanwhile, the British Foreign office is convinced that Lunt is the mysterious American Spymaster because of his connection with the Ranger incident. This initiates a fearsome sword fight at the French palace of Versailles, followed by sea battles, double crosses, and a deadly exchange of fire right under the very shadow of London's St. Paul's cathedral.

HENRY LUNT AT FLAMBOROUGH HEAD - ('95)

Amidst an atmosphere of political intrigue and espionage, Captain John Paul Jones finally obtains command of a small flotilla of men of war. Henry Lunt becomes one of the Lieutenants aboard the Bonhomme Richard. Their perilous voyage around the British Isles ultimately climaxes in the greatest individual square rigger engagement in American History.

SKULL & CROSS BONES (Coming in '96)

"Tom McNamara is the Tom Clancy of a bygone era."
- Jack Baldwin, WMVU (NH)

"If you enjoyed C.S. Forester's Horatio Hornblower series you'll love HENRY LUNT & THE RANGER"

- H_2O Magazine

"In addition to a great adventure story, I really liked Tom's writing style, it was reminiscent of Rudyard Kipling's 'Captains Courageous'."

-Mike Brady, Copley Cable TV (Los Angeles)

ORDERING NUVENTURES TITLES

NUVENTURES titles are available at fine bookstores nationwide. If your local bookstore cannot obtain a NUVENTURES title for you, then you may order direct from us. Send a check to: NUVENTURES Publishing, P.O. Box 2489, LaJolla, California 92038-2489 U.S.A. Please allow 4-6 weeks for processing and shipping.

TOM McNAMARA Titles:	Price
HENRY LUNT & THE RANGER	$18.95 or $5.95 soft
HENRY LUNT & THE SPYMASTER	$10.95
HENRY LUNT At FLAMBOROUGH HEAD	$10.95
SKULL & CROSS BONES	$10.95

LIZZ RAINES Titles:	Price
WIDOWMAKER	$5.95
LOST LUGGAGE	$5.95
ROAD KILLS	$5.95

George, America's Youngest Author	Price
GEORGE And The PITCHING MACHINE	$4.99
* TONY GWYNN Photo on back cover!	
GEORGE And The TRICKY FISH	$4.99
GEORGE And The SAILBOAT RACE	$4.99

ADD California or other Applicable State Tax.
   Plus   ADD Shipping & Handling
        $3.00 for single book or T-shirt orders,
        plus $1.50 for each additional item ordered.

Remember to clearly PRINT your mailing address and zip code. All direct orders are AUTOGRAPHED.